ABRAHAM DANIEL HAJJAR

BALANCE
OF THE
ANCIENTS

ISBN for Print: 979-8-9897737-0-1

*To my daughter, Gabriela, the light of my life, and
my wife, Pia, my best friend and partner in life*

BALANCE OF THE ANCIENTS

AZRA
USALL
DJUNALL
OLD ELGATEN
LAZZOS
KETIDA
SHEKAT
GOLD MINES
CERZAI
RUROM
NAV
PEAKING HIGHLANDS
SALT MINES
FRAYJEN PATH
BLOODERED HILLS
TOBACCO FARM LANDS
MOJ
RICE FIELDS
IRON MINES
BOGRAH
GOBRI
SILKROAD
CAPITALS
LAKES
RIVERS
CASTLES
FORESTS

One

The snow sat silent and smooth atop the mountain's face, high above the clouds and higher still above the silent woods that blanketed its feet. A shrine cut into its side between the sharp cliffs, long forgotten to those who traversed and dwelled in the realms below. Deep in its cold walls lodged a tired few who were spoken of only in whispers of myth. They troubled not with words except in times devoted to prayer, meditation, and observance of the realm.

A mage stood dressed in a thick black cloak and dark fur hat, the same color as his long, aged beard. He exited the dimly lit cave through its tilted-triangle entrance, his worn, mountain-ready-leather boots crunching the frost beneath them with each step. He paused at the barrier to breathe in the frozen air. As he did every last day of the fortnight, late in the afternoon before the sun set, the cloaked man perched over the snowy cliff in full view of the pathway that led up to the shrine, peering carefully into the flurries that obscured it. He watched patiently for an expected visitor carrying supplies and word from the realms below.

The mage looked down almost as soon as he observed the first show of movement from the corner of his eye. Expecting his visitor to have arrived, he turned instead to face a gust of wind carrying thick red flakes of ash accompanied by an odious smell akin to that of rotting flesh.

His muscles tensed and with great haste, he arose from his perch and rushed up a side pathway to the left of the entrance which only went in one direction —up the mountain. The path had not been trodden in many years and proved difficult to overcome with every ascending step as the snow grew ever deeper and gusting winds ever faster and more violent. The late afternoon sky slowly sank to a deep blue color as he rushed to climb before it began to darken further into a low, flat black hue pierced by the light of the stars. The mage persisted through the pain that grew in his legs and arms. Each step proved steeper than the last. He felt the frost clinging to his beard which he quickly brushed away with the cusp of his elbow, all the time focused forward.

Just as the pain reached an unbearable level that brought him to his knees, the mage made out makings of an iron metal structure in the near distance. The top was covered in several meters of snow which fell around the base. He shot up with renewed energy and rushed to retrieve a shovel fastened to the structure. He cleared the snow away from the top and then around the base to uncover its full form, a wide cone, at least two men lengths in diameter emerged. He then unfastened the leather tarp wrapped around the stone poles to its side to reveal firewood ready for kindling.

He grabbed a small clay flask and sparking stones and proceeded to drench the wood with the fire oil inside. He welcomed the smell of the oil. *Click, click.* The mage attempted to ignite, with the wind blowing harder and the temperature dropping even further. *Click, click,* his frozen hands struggling to clench.

Click, click. It worked. The wood lit slowly at first as if on the brink of being extinguished by the elements before bursting suddenly into a great yellow flame. The mage fell back and stared into its glow.

Afterwards, he stood and monitored the dark horizon, waiting as the wind blew in all directions around him. *This tower had never been needed before,* he thought. After some time, the mage finally saw another fire post lit high above at the peak of the Ancient Heights. Without any lingering or time to ponder, the mage mechanically shoveled snow on the fire to put it out. He quickly re-assembled the leather tarp and put everything back the way he had found it earlier.

The journey back took much less time than expected despite the darkness. Upon nearing the cave entrance, he saw one of the men of his order from within the cave beside his expected visitor. He held onto a leash strapped to a mule that carried leather bags of grain and food to sustain them for the next two weeks.

The mage broke his long-standing silence in a calm and focused tone, his voice coarse and broken from disuse.

"I lit the tower, and the Ancient Heights received the call," he said.

"That can only mean one thing," the other mage began.

"Yes, it has begun."

Two

"Ozy. Can you fetch me fresh linens?" Vira requested as a man exited her room. The man kept his eyes fixed on the floor, descending the crooked and worn-out stairs.

Ozwald sat aside a wide, heavy table in the common hall, his back arched over a small book opened at its middle. The walls that encased him had a red carpet that hung on it. Its once vibrant color had somewhat faded, and the edges of the rug were frayed and gray. Despite its condition, it still held a sense of grandeur, a memory of the elegance it once possessed. The loose strings only added to its character, telling a story of its long history and adding depth to its simple yet striking appearance. Scattered candles set up around the room emanated a warm glow over the room. A tall boy with a patched beard half grown in and loose, messy hair, Ozwald replied hesitantly, "Right away, ma'am."

He rose from his chair and made his way to the cabinet

behind him as the wooden floor beneath the carpets creaked with every step. Linens in hand, he walked slowly to the entryway, avoiding those bends in the wooden panels he knew to create that sound he found much too unpleasant. In fact, Ozwald hated the sound of the beams groaning almost as much as he did those cries of pleasure, which rang through the halls and competed with one another for volume through the night. The corridors of the brothel smelt thick with perfumes from the city of Shekat in the distant east and the kindling of incense from the wood that encircled the Haefe.

Just before reaching the door, Vira swung out from within, gleaming with sweat. She held on tightly to the frame with one arm while the other hung loosely beside her, "How long does it,"

"Here you go," he stuttered before raising his hand to cover his face and eyes. She reciprocated with a smile.

"Such a gentleman. Why don't you come inside? I should be done for the night. Come on. Don't be shy like your usual self," she had a way of leaving him speechless. He hesitated and smiled uneasily for a moment before she grabbed him by his hand and guided him inside to sit on the stool opposite the bed.

"Hope you don't mind waiting while I dry off, Madame Lissany and her strict rules," she continued.

"I don't mind, I uh—I'm used to seeing you like," Ozwald started before cutting himself off.

"What is that I hear? Enjoy watching me?" Vira was strong in her words and quick to use them carelessly. She spoke without thinking, without looking back. She felt his unease, though, and offered an abrupt, gentle smile, something rather unusual for her. Ozwald caught her eyes and then looked the other way quickly as his face reddened.

"Thank you. You are, always kind to me, Vira," he stuttered, still staring away and avoiding eye contact.

"It's my pleasure, love."

Ozwald heard two doors opening shyly from outside. It must be getting late. He glanced into the hallway catching sight of exiting customers hurrying through. Ozwald turned back to Vira. "Don't worry about them, Ozy. All who seek pleasure here, men and woman—they're all alike. They never dare to look after they've finished. It's like the feeling of shame overcomes them the moment they got what they wanted."

Vira observed his face carefully. Although she did not quite understand Ozwald and what so evidently plagued his mind, he intrigued her. Most men she encountered only looked at her, or rather, pieces of her. Here Ozwald sat within an arm's reach, avoiding her gaze altogether. Still, for a reason she had yet to discover, Vira felt seen sitting next to him.

"Sometimes I feel I might rather die than live out my days in this place. This town, this house of pleasure," she continued.

"You're exaggerating, Vira."

"Don't you think they're sort of the same?"

"How do you mean?"

"I mean shame and death. Isn't shame a sort of death?"

Ozwald looked up to face her. "Yeah, I suppose it is."

Breaking the silence that followed, Vira stood and removed the course, dampened towels and laid them carefully atop a velvet cushion before making her way to the dresser. Ozwald looked away.

"It's time for me to get back home."

"Never seen a woman get dressed?" She mused.

"I have a long day tomorrow," Ozwald hesitated.

"That Merrick still giving you a tough time, I see," she continued looking lazily through her cheap garments for the right nightgown.

"My work there warrants my little freedoms elsewhere. You know this. Really, I must get going,"

Ozwald shot back as he stood and took a deep breath. Vira glanced over to him, maintaining that haunting grin she so effortlessly wore on her face as she slipped into her gown.

Ozwald had not always seen eye to eye with his father. Those early, damp mornings in the mud and those many hours of plowing, seeding, weeding, seething, they fell on him hard and heavy. Even when he was young, he often lurked off into the woods, wandering through the thickets and following the shallow streams, much to his father's distaste. He had known, perhaps for some time, that he would taste more of life's flavors. Still, the mud kept him grounded, and the fields gave him respite. For whatever it meant, this truth lingered there, too, in those moments when his eyes would peer off over the hills and away from the Haefe. He never ventured that far, save for once or twice in his younger years. For now, the brothel was his adventure, albeit a dishonorable and unexciting one.

"At least keep me company for a bit, then. We never get much time to talk these days between the customers and that incessant reading habit of yours," Vira exclaimed. "What is it that you're reading about now anyways? Something that might get you into some trouble, I hope," she joked.

Silence overcame the two as Ozwald contemplated how he might respond.

"If I could read, Ozwald Stonne, mark my words, I swear by all the Ancients, I wouldn't be here," Ozwald paused for a short while. "And if you're still here with all of that, then you're just a boy who reads at a brothel. Nothing more," Vira chastised. Sensing his unease, she cushioned her words with a smile. Her warm yet distant smile had a way of rectifying her abrasive words by means he could not quite explain.

She walked back to her bed. "So, are you going to tell me what the book is about?"

"Farming," she sensed his growing tiredness of the conversation and stared more attentively now.

"Anything interesting?" She gulped. Ozwald sighed.

"Nothing I don't know already," he exhaled, "I have to go."

She rushed towards him and wrapped her hands around him for a tight hug. She pulled him down and gave him a kiss on his cheek.

"I'll see you tomorrow, though, won't I?" She asked, her eyes glistening.

"Where else would I be?" He exhaled before forcing a grin.

Ozwald said his final goodbyes for the night and left Vira's room. He walked to his desk and packed his things into a small leather traveling bag his mother had crafted for him many years ago. He paused for a final check with a deep breath and then descended to the lobby via the old and narrow stairwell across the lounge area. The stairways carried aging oil paintings of a time that once was, when Azra and Eurst were one, Eursazure. Ozwald, not too particular about paintings' artistic importance, barely noticed them.

The smell of smoke and brandy flooded downstairs. Madame Lissany. He peered out through the corner of his eye to find her chatting intimately with a man. She rarely served anyone, and from that, Ozwald collected that this customer, though the shadows obscured his aged features, was of some special value.

Madame Lissany's eyes rolled in pleasure as the man sprayed a barrage of kisses across her neck and cheeks. His hand, all the while, roamed gently under her dress and inconspicuously up and down her inner thighs.

Madame Lissany was a direct and commanding figure, her chin always held high. Her eyes had a piercing gaze, seeming only half open as if she was above the petty worries and concerns of those around her. She always exuded an air of knowledge and unwavering conviction. On this night, she wore her traditional black collar necklace tight around her neck and her famous tight lingerie top.

Ozwald looked away.

He arched his back subconsciously and crept towards the brothel's red wooden door. He reached for its knob and squinted, pulling it open slowly.

Creek. He froze in his position, eyes closed, waiting for the inevitable. *Silence.*

"Ozy baby, why the secrecy? A cultivated person like yourself should always address those they find in a room. Where are the manners that I taught you oh so well?" Lissany hummed. "Here," she whispered to the guest while pointing her finger beneath her ear. Goosebumps shot up the back of Ozwald's neck. He paused and then turned to her. Her eyes were still shut while the man continued his throws of pleasure undisturbed, Ozwald heard.

An awkward silence prevailed before Ozwald cleared his throat, all the while his hand still held to the doorknob.

"...err... I did not want to disturb you, Madame. I know how important that is to you," he murmured, lowering his gaze. She responded without taking time to think and barely affording him the time to finish.

"I've made it clear to always check with me before leaving, have I not?" She muttered before pausing to release another rehearsed moan. Ozwald remained looking away.

"Our guest of honor here, Sir Johnson, rather enjoys this public setting. He would never have minded you speaking with me," she concluded.

Ozwald cleared his throat again. "Err... yes Madame Lissany. I'll," he started to blurt out before she cut him off again.

"See you tomorrow, love, and try to come in a bit earlier."

Ozwald glanced up at her quickly as she opened her eyes toward him and winked. He glanced at the black-cloaked man's pointed nose and thin mustache.

"Rest well. You never know what tomorrow holds for you," Sir Johnson commented eerily from behind his cloak.

Three

"Girl, tighten the laces here — and here. My daughter will not leave this room in a loosely fastened dress," Adra barked. She stood in a long, rigidly cut, velvet dark green dress with a gold scarf folded strictly over her shoulders. She had a lean and tall figure with a nose that rose in height with every passing spring. She picked a golden hair net from a box on a nearby table and forced it into the girl's hand.

"Girl, my daughter's hair is to be tied back with this. How often must it be repeated until it is imprinted in your little head?" she hissed while fidgeting with her fingers. The girl's hands trembled as she fixed the hair net to the young lady's head.

"Finally. Move, girl. Now, what do you think, Aelav?" the woman retorted as she stared into a rusted mirror, waiting for confirmation from her daughter, who sat in front of her. *Always seeking perfection.*

"Mother, what exactly is wrong with loose hair?" Aelav bleated. Her mother stood behind her, tightening her grip as she cupped Aelav's shoulders.

"An appearance akin to a whore, is not an appearance to muster trust, confidence, and support. Every lord of every realm of Azra is out there. Perfection is your priority, young lady. And you, girl, you can leave now. No point standing there useless any longer," Adra's response landed sharply as she pinched Aelav's shoulders.

The girl's name is Cara, which you might know should you spend even a bit of time getting to know anyone other than lords, mother, Aelav thought. The servant exited with her head bowed and her lips pressed in fear.

"Everyone has consented. That is the hardest part. You said that yourself before. There is nothing that can change. Anyways, let the envious be haunted by their own concerns. I did not write the rules that only two should be chosen in a year for this council," Aelav grunted, ducking her shoulder away from her mother's piercing fingers.

She carefully gauged her beauty in the mirror, staring intensely into her own eyes. "What I want, Mother, is that after all this, grandfather not offer my hand wastefully like all the other useless girls of this realm that marry those crazy and uncivilized eastern lords."

Adra breathed deeply before opening her mouth. "Quiet, Aelav. You are to do as you are told. That's how it has always been. I'm sure your grandfather already has a perfect alliance. But nothing is official until after the ceremony. Consensus has been withdrawn before, and my daughter will not become a laughingstock in this court of conspirators and snakes. This is the game. Keep your calm and wait. No time to act recklessly," she spoke, her voice shrewd and fed up with her daughter's continuous complaints.

Aelav stood and swiftly faced her mother, momentarily holding her gaze before returning to the mirror.

"Do you know, at least, did you hear anything?" Aelav asked with a slight tremble in her voice. She saw her mother look away at the question.

Ehem. "Ten mar' minutes m'Lady Aelav and m'Lady Adra," intruded a helpless-looking mage through the circle entryway. His ragged grey cloak dragged in a revolting musk through the chamber. Aelav's heart started to race at the interjection. Lady Adra spun her head and glared directly at the mage, her piercing gaze delivering a message without words.

"I will be outside, waiting, once you are ready," trembled the mage, bowing his head and disappearing silently.

"No alliance is declared until a fortnight after the ceremony. You won't see your grandfather after the ceremony, so speak, before he leaves. Maybe he'll give you an idea. Also, keep cautious about what you say to the guests. They are not your friends," Adra whispered softly, a rare warmth in her voice.

Aelav remained silent, stood up, and further inspected the fine details of her garb and jewelry through the reflection. Her eyes wandered, glossed, and disconnected. Her heart paced faster with every glance. She saw her mother fidget again through the corner of her eye, this time with a box on a nearby table.

"Stand where you are," Lady Adra said. She unbuckled Aelav's pearl necklace and looked briefly at the mountain lion pendant it carried as she held it in her hand. She replaced it with a golden one, from which a large phoenix medallion hung heavy. Aelav smelt her mother's sharp scent as her hands passed over her face to adjust the ornate piece of metalwork.

"Now we are done. No one can question your allegiance. The symbol of a balance everlasting." Lady Adra said, a devious grin appearing on her face for a moment. *Always the one for appearances.*

"Why must you fix everything? As if anyone will ever notice. The mountain lion is our house emblem. The phoenix…" Aelav began.

"…is the emblem of Valya, a symbol of continuity and sustainable balance, your home and where your father is warden, in the north at Ol'den," a deep voice intruded from the vaulted hallway to the room's entrance.

"Where have you been, Berdol? One might have thought you wished no part in your daughter's preparations for the council. What have you been up to?" Adra sneered at her husband through the mirror, her eyes pinched and tired. Aelav froze and stared at her father broodingly.

"What do you think? Every house complaining about the others and every lord demanding their offspring pass through the council at once. No one wants to follow the bloody rules anymore. Why were they written in the first place? The realm of Bograh was not designed to accommodate the six children of house Mason all at once. Nowhere was! And Queen Petra and those seven squealing pigs in Cerzai, will never marry them off all at once. They act as though the red blight halts for them to discern upon which damned alliance they think their offspring deserve," Lord Berdol fumed, his words struggling to catch up with his frustration.

"Well, Berdol, have you then something new to share? Or would you prefer rummaging about what has already been decided? I told you inviting these people will do nothing but disturb you. Who does their presence serve? I trust them like I trust a net to hold water. So long as their keep stands decorated and adorned, they will pay no mind to the quicksand that sinks beneath its foundations. Pageantry," Lady Adra remarked with a curled lip.

"In any case, my work here is done. I will await you in the great hall," she rearranged her dress to straighten it and turned towards the exit. With a clear path ahead, she walked out of the room with her nose held high.

"Your mother, she won't let you forget anything. Are we finished, Aelav? They are waiting for us to walk you in," Berdol, gritted his teeth. *Father always finds a way to avoid answering the questions that matter most. I've grown tired of it. I need to know.* Aelav thought.

"Father, what is to become of me?" Aelav asked firmly, her eyes squinting at her father, pacing in short steps through the mirror. His face sank at her question, stroking his eyebrow before raising his eyes to meet hers. But no words came out.

"Father, is everything all right?" Aelav asked, focused ever more carefully on his mannerisms, attempting desperately to decipher his reaction. She turned in her chair to face him.

"Aelav, a decision, better yet, an idea," he hesitated. "Actually, a suggestion is in the making, but we'll talk about it after the ceremony. Remember, though, that in the end, you still have a say but be careful. Such a conversation should not be handled loosely. It should require great care and discretion…and as I said before, if there's anything you feel you must say to your grandfather, now is the time. Make sure to see him before he rushes out afterward," Berdol said.

Aelav's heart started to race again. *Sometimes no answer is better than half answers.* Aelav opened her mouth to speak but was cut off before she could make a sound.

"Let us make haste, dear. The court is waiting for us," he rushed. Aelav's eyes hung on her father wanly, succumbing to a truth she did not yet know. *More waiting, more secrecy.* Without a word she advanced to the door with her head down. She felt her father stand beside her, and, with a soft voice, he muttered "Here we go."

As they exited together, Aelav's hands began to shiver gently. *This hallway seems longer than when I came in. I need to be done with this formality.* At the last turn of the corridor, a black shadow became visible.

"Let's see what your Mother wants," Berdol said before pausing abruptly.

"Queen Rose, I did not expect you here," he continued as he bowed his head slightly.

"You know more than I do; the rules give precedence to one of my male grandchildren, Jerome and Jassonte, over your girl," she said as she glared at Aelav. "Our consent rested on the guarantee that one of them would be on the council this year as well. And I've come to learn that no longer holds. I'm sorry, but I will not let this fiasco proceed. Just because she is the emperor's granddaughter does not mean that she deserves favoritism," her eyes fixated on Aelav. Berdol hesitated, attempting to draft a careful response in his head.

"Well, my," Berdol began before being interrupted.

"My queen, you are justified in your grievances and so should your objection with our dear Lady Aelav. However, every case that the council considers is carefully studied. That we can agree on. You are part of the deciding council yourself, are you not?" The voice asked rhetorically, meeting silence as expected. Aelav focused her ear on the source of the sound, attempting to decipher the owner.

"Now, may I ask, did you find a place for Jerome and Jassonte in any realm? Per our rules, a suitable alliance is to be found among the ruling families of the realms. Not outside of the ruling families. Otherwise, we won't survive another generation with all this offspring and no deaths," The voice demanded as a man appeared at the other end of the corridor. *Rorik, perfect timing.*

"...*ahh...*" Queen Rose attempted to respond before Rorik cut her off.

"You have not, if I may answer on your behalf. That was clear before tonight's ceremony, your grace. If you had accepted one of your grandchildren to move from Bograh to Valya, tonight's ceremony would have been quite different indeed. For any other case, if anyone is thinking of objecting as well, no suitable places were found either. It has been our agreement since the chasm to preserve the balance. Excess and carelessness are what got us here in the first place. How are we to preserve that agreement if we retract on our decisions as the sun rises and falls? We have a serious problem in Azra and Eurst, for that matter, threatening our very life, and all you care about is who is ascended or not? We discussed this already. Let us make haste and get this ceremony over with your grace. The red blight is not waning," Rorik asserted. Queen Rose paused and stared at Lord Rorik.

"Very well Lord Rorik. We shall see what happens," Queen Rose uttered, her face stern as she turned and rushed out of the hall without taking care of who stood in her way. *Can she stop the ceremony?* With the queen gone, both men stared at each other while Aelav shifted her focus between either.

"Tomorrow morning, we either wake up comfortably and get on with our lives until this blight kills us. Or armed men would be knocking at our gates," Lord Rorik whispered, scratching his beard.

"Aelav, let's make haste and get through this. And don't forget to catch your grandfather right afterward." Berdol prayed with glaring eyes. He pulled her hand gently as they made their way out of the corridor, with Lord Rorik walking in front of them to lead the way. *Nothing can change now.*

~

Aelav stood next to her father, who wore a grey-colored cloak as per ascension ceremony tradition over his slightly oily, long, and tied back hair, at the entrance of the underground Fallgarde's Grand Temple. All the while, a group of mages hymned from inside. Their song echoed through the corridor and filled the space around her, reminding her of the times she would linger in the Grand Temple of Ol'den as a young girl. Despite all the occasions for which she had made the journey to Fallgarde with her parents, she had never descended to this ancient chamber.

The hall laid past a small, simple wooden door, one unassuming for a space such as this, one shrouded in such legend and lore. They waited at the entrance for a few minutes until the voices subsided. Standing at the entrance,

Aelav felt a light draft of air, carrying with it the faint stench of mold mixed with the musk of incense and perfumes. She peered inside and was at first taken aback by the massive size of the interior. The walls were constructed from carefully laid large stones which curved into one large dome in the center, adjoined by two smaller ones on either side. The path ahead was lined with spice pits, which burned bright green and purple, dousing the hall with their color.

Aelav turned her gaze forward, landing her eyes, for the first time, on the mythical Promise Well. It stood atop a not-so-glamorous centered and elevated platform at the end of the aisle. The attention shifted to the crowd, at least a hundred people. She could not recognize anyone, given their heads were all turned forward and covered in dark grey hoods. They stood on either side of the hall, split evenly.

Berdol tugged gently on her hand to suggest they begin their procession. She looked up at him, anticipating guidance and warmth, only to be met with the sight of his rather sullen and dreadful-looking gaze as he stared flatly into the distance of the hall. As she turned away, she noticed, from the corner of her eye, worn out engravings in the arced slab of wood above the door.

Two halves to one whole, two brothers torn asunder. A left hand and a right hand, though by one body separate, doth ebb and flow as they wander. Unto a great prince they shall emerge, though long after he departs should they meet, one's blood will soak the other's cloak at the toes of destiny's feet.

"Father, what does it mean?" Aelav whispered, rereading it a few times to herself.

"Not now," Berdol grunted, jolting from his deep

trance. Aelav pulled on her father's hands, as a few faces turned around at the sound of his voice.

"Not too loud, father," Aelav snapped, and like dominos, all those turned their gaze towards the back to face Aelav and her father.

"We ask you, oh mighty ancients, to bless our daughter, Aelav, daughter of Lord Berdol and Lady Adra of house Toren, wardens of Ol'den of the realm of Valya. Give her the might and the wisdom to serve the dominion of Valya and all of Azra," shaman Solomon prayed from the opposite corner of the hall in a frail voice just audible by Aelav all the way at the back. A frail and old figure which she had known since childhood, shaman Solomon leaned over a small wooden table with forward arching shoulders and a grim look. He wore a red cloak with sleeves pulled up and led the proceedings in an unenthusiastic mood.

Berdol stepped forward, and then Aelav. With every pass of every guest, her heart raced faster. *No turning back.*

Berdol nudged Aelav, lifting her out of her dreading thoughts and back to her duty. She proceeded to nod at each guest as previously instructed upon eye contact. Many familiar faces and others oblivious to her. Some sneered at her, others glowered, and few smiled for her, save her grandparents, who stood at the end beside the well.

Berdol released Aelav to proceed freely towards the steps of the platform, and in front of the crowd, as he receded to join Lady Adra.

"Gathered we are for the Ceremony of Ael... Aelav Toren. As handed down by the Ancients all those years ago, we embrace rules and rituals. Without them, we would succumb to our old ways that led to the chasm between

Azra and Eurst." The Shaman proclaimed lethargically, Aelav all the while standing in her place. "With these rules, lies responsibility on those who uphold them. All here have consented. House Toren of the realm of Adrovia, house Lygem of the realm of Valya, house Haelin of the realm of Usall, house Walda of the realm of Lazzos, house Mason of the realm of Bograh, house Haemel of the realm of Cerzai and house Shobo of the realm of Shekat," shaman Solomon orated before pausing. Aelav fidgeted in her place and attempted to glance to either side of the hall for any signs of objection. The silence continued for a while with audible whispers heard to either side of Aelav as she clenched her fists. With every passing second, she could feel a larger throb of her heart in her neck as if her heart grew, until the Shaman murmured.

"As the red blight ever so vociferously knocks on our door, Aelav shall help light the path to overcome it. No challenge is ever so great that Azra, united, cannot overcome. Lady Aelav, do you accept to safeguard the realm of men of Azra and serve it as it sees fit, wherever your alliance shall lie?" The severity of her throbbing heart not subsiding.

Without a word, Aelav took a deep breath and walked to the Promise Well inside the circle carved platform. "Bring in the sacrifice. Aelav. Please stand there," shaman Solomon instructed his open hand raised to the bewilderment of Aelav.

Out of nowhere, a new mage dressed in the same ragged grey cloaks appeared from behind the Shaman dragging a small goat that had remained silent throughout the ceremony and oblivious to the hall's attendees. The new mage approached the Promise Well while Aelav waited for her cue to proceed.

Without any warning, he dragged the goat, proclaiming in a loud voice, "we offer this as atonement to our straying from the way. We offer this in sacrifice to redeem us from the chasm! As you proclaimed that one's blood will soak the other's cloak at the toes of destiny's feet. We ask in all your glory to bless Aelav Toren so that her alliance, with whoever it may shall fall with, result in the wisdom this realm needs until her dying breath."

Without warning or hesitation, the new mage pulled out a dagger and approached the small goat, standing still in its position, oblivious, as was Aelav, to coming events.

Slash.

The new mage slit its throat with one motion of his frail hand. It fell to the marble alter floor, head hanging weakly backward from its back-neck skin. It began to kick and hiss through its now exposed windpipe.

A streak of red blood splattered on Aelav's face and dress, releasing a quick and concealed screech. Her hands began to shiver gently. The platform they stood on slanted inwards and down, with blood collecting at the center and away from her feet, she noticed. The new mage retrieved an old iron looking cup with subtle flower engravings long faded away nearby the Promise Well and filled it from the flowing water. He then lifted the little goat's still kicking carcass and positioned it right over the cup's head to collect a small portion of the blood still oozing out of it.

The crowd remained silent as if used to such brutal occurrences. She hesitated for her next move for a moment until the new mage handed her the cup and whispered, "Drink this." Aelav paused for a moment, her eyebrows raised. Aware of the staring around her, she wasted no more time reconsidering and gulped one sip from the cup, holding her breath to avoid the taste.

She found the slight blood and water taste revolting, hiding her repulsed face momentarily behind the cusp of her now blood-stained elbow. After a short recovery, Aelav regained composure and faced the Shaman.

"I swear that I will do justice for the sake of men, for the sake of Azra I proclaim, no matter the alliance I am chosen for," Aelav stuttered while gasping from the blood-filled water taste. Recollecting her composure, she faced the Shaman and then the crowd with the cup still in hand and her lips drabbed in red.

By the grace of the Ancients
She has proclaimed
Azra she
Serves you for eternity

Aelav, heard an ascending commotion. The audience spoke in low voices among each other. She could not make anything out. Unannounced, the new mage approached her from her side, "Congratulations, my Lady, may your future be filled with courage and success. My name is Jeb by the way," he congratulated.

"...err...thanks," she stuttered.

He removed the cup from her hands with no word and handed her a dry rag. She stared at her hands and her dress, observing the mess. The blood, by then, had almost dried and would prove hard to rub off without water, she knew. As if reading her mind, Jeb, the new mage, held a large jug of water above her hands, waiting for her to initiate the spilling motion.

Aelav quickly washed her hands and soaked the rag as well to scrub her hands and face. "Thanks, Jeb," she muttered, casting a hesitant smile, which he reciprocated. Just as he had appeared, he quickly vacated the area as if he had never existed.

Hands cleaned, Aelav looked to the guests and prepared to handle incoming congratulations. Guests, though, stood in small groups speaking among one another and scattered across the hall, their appearances analogous to conspiring circles searching for means to nullify her ceremony. She looked for her grandfather and saw him rushing from the end of the hall. She clenched her teeth at the sight and began to walk quickly with the sound of whispers and murmurs increasing from each part of the hall.

"Do not mind them Lady Aelav," Lord Rorik's voice shot out from her side as she raced away from the alter. She paused and turned quickly, "Uncle Rorik. Thanks again for what you said, but I have to run to my grandfather if you don't mind," she exclaimed. Lord Rorik did not talk further and only smiled courteously while she continued forward.

Aelav saw her grandfather walking swiftly without stopping to chat with anyone, in deep conversation with her father.

"Grandfather," she called while both men continued to walk. She quickened her pace and was on the verge of a run to reach her grandfather. Once in clear hearing distance, she cleared her throat and cried out to make sure he heard.

"Grandfather! You honor me with your presence," she quickly stuttered. Her grandfather and father paused in their place, turning abruptly to face her. Aelav halted as well, nearly ramming into them.

"Congratulations Aelav, hope the sacrifice did not disturb you too much. It is tradition to keep the ascender oblivious to the act. Gives a rather genuine introduction to the world we uphold. Don't you think Berdoly?" Emperor Conrad smirked, nudging his son's side. He reciprocated a hesitant smile. "Ok, not the best joke. I personally apologize for that, dear, on behalf of Azra," he finished before taking on a suddenly serious look in preparation for the conversation. "Grandfather, can we have a word," Aelav said, mustering strength from within.

"At the end of this night, you will know the details. Nothing official, though, until after a fortnight. No matter the task, you will be supported. Remember, we have much to do to protect Azra from its enemies that would rather see us hang than talk with us," he cautioned.

"But what do you mean by task, and what support will I need?" Aelav badgered, not breaking eye contact with her grandfather.

"Watch your tone with the emperor," Berdol interjected immediately.

"Calm down. Family does not quarrel. She is rightly concerned about her future. Nothing wrong with that, Berdol," Emperor Conrad heaved, waving his hands as if about to reveal a secret. Her grandfather squinted his eyes slightly and pondered his next words carefully.

"Very well, no point in delaying. Your assignment will be two-fold," her grandfather asserted before pausing while staring at Berdol. Meanwhile, Aelav forgot about the guests in the hall and their judgmental gazes in her general direction. None of that mattered now, she knew.

"Until your alliance is completed, you will be assigned

here with Rorik in Fallgarde, supporting the realm's financier. Your father and I agreed that it is the right start for an intellect as yourself," he started.

"And who is my alliance with?" she questioned immediately.

"I warned you Aelav," Berdol interjected again.

"It's fine. It's fine. She is a Toren, after all. But I'm afraid that will have to wait till later," he grunted.

"Why?" Aelav shot back. Berdol gritted his teeth while Emperor Conrad clasped his shoulder gently to calm him down.

"Because it is a challenging alliance. We will meet soon and talk about it, that I can promise. Today though, let's all make haste. You need to get to your feast. I heard that your mother has prepared something quite exquisite. Sadly though, I won't be attending. I must get back to the capital on some urgent matters. And remember, you are the guest of honor, Aelav, even though the rest in this hall may not care," he instructed.

Her grandfather and father both turned and made a hasty exit from the hall with only a simple smile to her. She remained to observe them leave, all the while feeling a small sense of defeat despite learning where she would be.

Reluctantly following her grandfather's suggestion, Aelav made her way out of the hall, which cued the others to do the same. The group of mages continued chanting in the background at a low volume, a tradition, until all vacated the hall.

Four

Ozwald took one step into the spring night. The cool breeze caressed his face. Down the cobbled path, a small crowd huddled into Wyder's Tavern, spilling into the alleyway. Their shadows danced on the street, colored dimly by the warm candlelight that lit the tavern's interior. Their voices and laughter echoed softly down and around the town's narrow thoroughfares. Such was the typical scene in the Haefe this time of year when the sun cut through the frost and the first flowers bloomed in the fields.

All the Haefe's many farms circled and branched out from the town's center. Ozwald turned and headed opposite the revelry and back towards his home. The moon shone uncharacteristically bright on this evening, illuminating the pastures and fields as he passed them. The town's temple sat on a hill overlooking the clusters of houses below. As he approached it along the path, the sound of the priests' rituals grew louder, a bit late for a ceremony.

He approached the temple's heavy doors just as their song reached its crescendo. Then, as if all at once, silence. The temple itself stood higher than any building in the Haefe. Its carefully stacked white stones met at its top to form three domes. Atop them, Ozwald could see the three white marble statues of seated Ancients erected, each with a long, ornamented beard and each peering in a different direction. From the outside, Ozwald peeked through the doors, which had been slightly left ajar. Inside, he could make out the procession of mages as they circled slowly around the temple's central feature: the well of whispers. He transfixed to the scene. The longer he lingered, the more he felt frozen. As the chanting grew louder and louder, Ozwald felt the hair on his neck rise.

"Prayer and meditation do the body good, Ozwald," a voice spoke. Ozwald jolted back, nearly falling. He twisted his neck around to see who had spoken. His glance was met by the cracked smile of an old, dirty man fitted in worn-out linens.

"You seem to know my name while I know not yours."

"My name, my name is long forgotten, I suppose. I am a servant to those who need to be served, to those who write the will of time. A servant need not have a name, don't you think? What should be in a name anyways, if not the very thing that sets us apart? No, I no longer carry the burden of a name," the man said, making no eye contact when he spoke. He looked excitedly in any number of directions and played with his fingers violently.

"You seem to enjoy riddles as much as you enjoy creeping in the dark," Ozwald cried back.

"The question is not how I know your name. The question is how many more will know it soon enough," the man continued to babble with an uneasy smile. Ozwald's face remained tense as he looked around for anyone else who might have accompanied the unwelcomed stranger.

"I have no time for your riddles and games, sir. Please speak plainly," Ozwald trembled.

"I shouldn't be here. No, no, I shouldn't be here. They said not yet. But I saw you. I saw you from afar, and I knew it. I knew that the time had come. But is it now, or is it soon. Oh dear, oh no, it's not time just yet. We will speak soon, that I know of," his smile sank, and his eyes fell back in fear. "There's much to carry on with, too much. Not enough. And time, it's not the time just yet. But," he paused suddenly and stopped his fidgeting. Ozwald, too stood frozen, his breathing growing deeper and faster. Then, quickly as he had appeared, the man sprinted off into the dark of the wood, the crackling of leaves growing faint as he vanished in the night.

"But maybe it is time. Soon we will know," the man's voice faintly floated.

Five

than's heart beat steadily as he reached for his quiver, his movements slow and measured. He kept his gaze fixed on a large deer grazing un-assumedly in the clearing ahead, its amber coat glistening in that early morning sun that filtered through the tangled leaves and bushes that concealed him. The dew on the grass and foliage sparkled like virescent gems, bold but still. A symphony of birds chirped and sang from their lofty perches in the canopy.

Ethan was a young man with a mere eighteen years under his belt. He was the son of the Emperor Rhyker of house Raynel. Emperor of Eurst and all its three realms. He stood tall, his lean build a testament to the many days he spent training with his bow away from the palace grounds. His eyes were blue like the eggs of a robin, and they gleamed with a focus capable of shutting the whole world out. His hair, thin and light like the ivory beaches of the south, was tucked behind his ears, revealing on one side of his face a scar that marred his otherwise unblemished profile. Despite the rough, jagged line it etched above his cheek, he wore the disfigurement gracefully. It reminded him of the quick cruelty of his elder brother, Soren. The morning was his respite, and the thicket his sanctuary. As the gentle dawn mist dissipated, he found the space to breathe.

As he notched his arrow delicately, he took a deep breath and relinquished a slow, steady exhale. Time seemed to stand still as he drew back the bowstring and, in one fluid motion, released the nock from between his thin fingers. As it hissed through the air, an unfortunate ground bird took flight to meet its course, falling with a loud thud back down to the forest floor. Startled by the sudden commotion, the doe bounded away in a few gentle leaps, vanishing back into the woods.

Ethan pressed his lips. He had mastered the bow and arrow under Master Boshol, who saw to it. He always bragged that he had trained him at the palace and in the wilderness, the best place that a man should learn from. "Nothing teaches a man more than real life. Nesting in this palace will keep you fragile." He engrained it in his head. Ethan had been on his hunting trip an hour before the sun rose. Standing deep in the forest, he gazed toward his family's palace in Horos. Sagging tree leaves cluttered his view as he stepped in its direction. Never had he ventured off for more than an hour's journey on his hunting trips. He preferred to spend more of his time out hunting than just walking. Today, however, much had been on his mind. He had lost track of time and ventured past the Nomad Hills to the south, the supposed first settlements of Eurstians more than three thousand years ago. With each step, time became insignificant as his mind wandered off in its own direction, and his body walked on its own.

~

Ethan snuck into Horos palace's downstairs kitchens. His family, house Raynel, had resided in it for generations long forgotten. In the western part of Horos, the palace reigned supreme, nestled within its towering stone walls and overlooking the bustling city below. Its grandeur was unmatched, standing out distinctly from the rest of the city's structures. While Horos's other buildings boasted intricate designs and flourishes, the palace's foundation was hewn from large, pale stones, giving it an air of majesty and timelessness. As one approached the palace, the scale of the walls was daunting, looming high overhead like a protective sentinel. The architecture was intricate, with carved details adorning every inch of its facade. The palace was a true work of art, a testament to the power and wealth of its inhabitants. To any traveler passing through Horos, the palace was an impressive sight, drawing the eye with its stark contrast to the rest of the city's smaller and more artistically designed buildings. It was a place of wonder, where legends were born, and stories were told for generations.

The kitchens, built on its western side, had a small door making it easier to sneak in unseen. It featured wooden counters etched with marks from years of chopping meat with the kitchen's large knives. Pans hung on hooks, with black specks visible on their lids. Wooden cabinets were mounted on the walls and beneath the counters while a raw meat smell permeated the air.

He handed the cook his kill. "For supper this evening,"

he exhaled. "If anyone asks, just say that one of the other cooks caught it."

"Very well, sir. But we are expecting a guest. From out of town, sir," the cook uttered, his face and voice pale and mechanical.

"More guests. Always busy with other people," Ethan exhaled. "Do you know who?" He questioned.

"No. Sir. I only know that it is one person from Sydol," the cook uttered. Ethan nodded as the cook gave the ground bird to one of his staff with instructions. The last time he brought in a bird, his siblings mocked him for a week, making it a point his father joined in on the frivolities. This had never phased him, however. Master Boshol had trained his muscles, skills, and mental toughness. "A true warrior leverages mockery and doubt to his advantage. You must train your mind," he repeated continuously.

Ethan went to the palace's vestibule with his head bowed and thoughts still swirling. The rich taste of the space was immediately apparent, with its shimmering greenstone floors glinting underfoot. The walls, crafted from meticulously stacked megalithic beige stones, enclosed the cool, still air within, creating an atmosphere of regal tranquility. At the end of the vestibule, a grand spiral staircase awaited Ethan. He took a deep breath, centering himself, and looked up at the winding ascent before him.

"Sneaking in through the kitchens again?" A voice sneered from inside the empty throne room. The young prince held his ascent, standing at the entrance door, marveling at its lavishness. Every time his eyes set sight on it, he could not help but feel a sense of reverence for the grandeur of the space. The throne room's walls were decorated with richly carved wooden planks that depicted the history of Eurst, the kingdom his family had ruled in absolute for the last five hundred years. The carvings were so intricate that he could make out each detail of the scenes, from the battles fought to the alliances made. He could not help but be drawn to a wall section depicting a mighty ship sailing across rough waves, its sails billowing in the wind. To his left, the wall was lined with tall windows that shed natural light into the room, illuminating every detail of the room and its furniture. The windows looked out onto the palace gardens, which he had explored many times since childhood. The floor of the room matched the vestibule outside, with smooth greenstone that gleamed in the sunlight. His father's throne sat on the opposite end of the room, made of the same pale stone as the palace's outer walls. The throne was lavishly decorated, with gilded edges and intricate carvings showcasing the monarchy's grandiosity. The prince felt a sense of awe as he gazed upon it. To each side of the hall, basic wooden benches had been set up for those who attended his father's court. On the throne, he saw his sister Elysia sitting sideways, a book in her hand as she eyed Ethan's every move. He sighed as he walked towards her down the aisle.

"You wait on me now from your mighty throne, Elysia? Have you got nothing better to do?" Ethan said.

Elysia was a head shorter than Ethan, and her hair was just as blonde. It unfurled into long, well-kept locks that framed her young but tired face. Her eyes were green the way the sea was green after a storm, and they changed their tone with her mood. She had a large presence but a small heart, one that had been eroded away by her seemingly constant displeasure with the circumstances afforded to her. A peculiar combination of comfort and entrapment had left her frustrated, disagreeable, and blunt.

"Still opposing every one of Mother's requests. What is it now? She said you wasted six perfect matches, a threat to the family's political future," Ethan said, his face stern as he continued walking. "I hear someone is coming today. Think it's another failed match?" He added as she exhaled and adjusted her boots on the throne. "She won't like that," he pointed as Elysia did not react.

"Mother and her concerns. It wouldn't be so hard if the men were worth it. I thought that council would bring forward reasonable alliances, not useless ones," Elysia exhaled while Ethan shifted in his place.

"Have you seen Father?" he asked, his voice serious, and taking a seat in front of her.

"He still hasn't told you what alliance will befall you," Elysia mocked. "You'll know soon and have a part with us for Eurst. I mean, I'm sure the role of master of shit collection won't go away," she scorned, menacing laughter breaking out intensely.

Ethan rolled his eyes. "Everything is a joke to you. Once you get what you want, nothing else matters," Ethan exhaled. "Have you seen Soren at least then?"

"Why. I care dearly for you, little brother," she spoke directly, Ethan glaring at her while she remained silent and stared back until she eventually shrugged. "He's probably entertaining his usual guests in his chambers," Ethan smiled.

"Was it so hard?" He waved his hands and rolled his eyes. Not looking back, Ethan rushed out of the throne room. Making his way up to the family's private living quarters on the third floor.

He enjoyed climbing the palace's grand staircase, surveying its impeccably preserved stone engravings every time. They told the stories of battles and triumphs now long gone and half shrouded in legend. He would pause, marveling at the intricate scenes that unfolded before him. He found these works of art to be the most breathtaking in the castle and, indeed, all of Eurst. What caught his attention was the story of the chasm, when the Ancients split Eursazure into two and demanded payment for redemption.

He knocked on Soren's door as the sound of women's pleasure spilled out from beneath the cracks in the frame. He pushed the door open enough to slip his head in without a second knock. He saw his brother sitting naked in bed with two women.

Standing just a short measure taller than Ethan, Soren was a slim, wiry man. He had a pronounced forehead, a sharp nose characteristic of the dynastic line he sprang from, and cheekbones that protruded from his face like small plums. He was handsome, though in an unsettling manner. Soren was a large personality with an even larger voice to match. His laugh haunted Ethan, scraping against his ears like a blunt knife, distressing but never deep enough to make its incision. His temper was known to all who staffed and maintained the tall halls of the palace grounds. The servants tread carefully in his presence.

"Don't you know how to knock, little brother?" Soren calmly mocked. "Can't you see that I have company? But hey, since you're here, what do you think? This is Kayla, and this is Quayle. They're sisters," he smiled, pointing to the both of them. Ethan shifted uneasily, remaining silent.

"Come on, what do you think?" He heckled.

"Brother, haven't I taught you that it's rude to let your mouth open in such an offensive manner?" Soren laughed menacingly as the women on either side grinned compatibly in a rather condescending manner. Ethan, his face now flushed red, nodded in placating submission.

"There you go. Wasn't so hard after all. They are beautiful indeed. Now, which one do you want to come pay you a visit? I'm sure you'll have a bit of fun. I'm your brother, needn't I look out for you?" he beamed. Ethan cleared his throat.

"Soren, that's enough. Can we please have a word outside?"

"Why can't we speak here?" Soren refuted, both ladies groaning.

"You know me, brother. I'm scared to speak in front of an audience. Isn't that what you told father?" Ethan smirked.

Soren pressed his lips. "All right, I'll be up in a bit. You go ahead."

Ethan grinned as he left his brother and the women and walked up to his room. Once there, he freshened his hands and face in the washing basin and prepared for the day ahead. He was due for lessons with Master Shehwen, the imperial master of scrolls, followed by his much-preferred archery and combat trainings with Master Boshol.

Master Shehwen was a foreboding figure, tall and lean. He carried the weight of a thousand tomes of wisdom on his mind, and it often left him impatient and abrasive. His skin was the color of fertile soil, and the silver hairs on his face folded together beautifully to form a long, distinguished beard that met at its end in a single point. His calloused hands scaped crudely against the pages of his books as he parsed through them. In every encounter, the master made it a point to open conversation on a topic of his choosing. Most assumed him oblivious to the interests and attentions of others. Ethan, however, knew this to be a false assessment. Master Shehwen, if anything, was overly observant of others' thoughts. He just did not care.

As much as Ethan respected the strong-handed guidance and instruction of Master Shehwen, his untampered passion for study, and the way his silken garments fell elegantly over his shoulders, he enjoyed his time with Boshol more. The two stood in stark contrast beside one another. Master Boshol was a small but strong man. He was equal parts light-footed and heavy in his stance, perfectly agile yet impossible to bring down. He spoke little, but his wrinkled face said volumes about what he knew. His wisdom was derived less from faded ink and leather-bound chronicles and more from an astute appreciation of the physical world he moved through. He knew the trees and how they swayed, how flocks of birds moved in perfect harmony, how the tides on the shore ebbed and flowed by the weight of the moon, the corrective force of the winds on an arrow's fletching, and perhaps most of all, Master Boshol knew a man's thoughts from the way his feet met with the earth beneath them. He did not smile often, but when he did, his face beamed with the soft warmth of a summer morning.

After a few moments, his brother stepped in barefoot with no knock, wearing pants and an unbuttoned white shirt, his bare chest visible for all to see.

"So, what is it? Let's hear it," he shot, his arms folded. Ethan turned, taking a deep breath. "You and Elysia already went through the council right after your eighteenth birthday. It has been almost a month for me, and I know nothing. No council date has been set. It's as if I'm going to be sidelined. As if he wants me to live out my life out of his sight and away from Eurst," he blurted as Soren stared at him with crossed eyebrows.

"All that matters to me is this family. And that we secure the continuity of this dynasty. That's what you should worry about instead of always worrying about yourself. No wonder you barely have any friends," Soren hissed. His face was visibly upset as Ethan gritted his teeth.

"You speak as if I have disobeyed this family," Ethan growled.

"Your every existence disobeys the family," Soren added, a condescending grin appearing on his face.

"It's as if all our time together as children means nothing. I've always covered up for you when you asked. This is how you repay me. You've completely changed these last few weeks. And for the worst," Ethan barked. Soren did not blink, seriousness covering his face.

"What do you want me to do?" Soren exhaled, looking away from Ethan.

"He tells you everything. Speak with him. He's never given me a straight answer," Ethan shot back, fuming and holding his head, thinking for a moment.

"Tonight, we have a guest. Another one of Father's attempts to betroth Elysia. As if she hasn't given us enough trouble with that unfiltered mouth of hers. I'll ask him then when I see him," Soren relented while Ethan remained silent. His face showed an insistent expression, urging him to do it earlier.

Soren nodded, his face still stern, and approached his brother. He clasped his shoulder and walked him to the window overlooking the back courtyard. A large group of armed men dueled with wooden sticks in the distance. He could see Master Boshol standing by supervising training.

"You see those men over there," Soren pointed. "Our Father is busy keeping them vigilant. Without those men and others like them, we'd be in complete anarchy. I'll speak with Father tonight as mentioned," Soren stressed, conviction sharp in his voice.

Tension built up in the air, and Ethan stared out the window.

"Lighten up. Tonight will be fun. We're about to witness another disappointment for the parents. Father is riding hard on tonight's new prospect," Soren said, cutting through the tension, his voice mischievous.

"We'll see about that," Ethan began as he stepped back.

Soren bowed his head. "Come ready and hungry. I heard bird is on the menu," he mocked, casting a furtive glance.

Before Ethan could respond, Soren dashed out, closing the door quickly behind him. Ethan followed after a short stutter. However, Soren had already reached the stairs and was too far away for Ethan to call him back. He rolled his eyes and got back inside as he thought deeply about his father's plan for his future.

~

The Raynel family gathered in the grand dining hall, opposite the throne room, for the evening meal. The thick walls were adorned with ornate tapestries that hung from the high ceilings. On one side, a parade of pointed windows opened to the courtyard below, providing guests with an unmatched view of the carefully planned gardens that filled the spaces between the thin footpaths. Fig trees, exotic flowers, and tall grasses all weaved together in a deliberate orchestra of fertility. Thin streams and small ponds cut through them. From the perch of the great dining hall, under the gentle light of the garden torches, one could almost make out the silhouettes of the fish that circled within. Emperor Rhyker always made it a point to pause at the glass windows when touring guests and dignitaries.

Rhyker and his wife, Empress Myrae, dressed impeccably at all hours of the day. The Empress was a slender woman with thick, black hair that she wore in a heavy braid down her back. She was never seen without her many jewels and adornments, and she was slow and regal in her stride. Her face was strong, evenly tempered, and noble. The wrinkles around her features revealed a peculiar quality about her. The Empress spoke with her eyes more so than with her tongue, and the top half of her face had aged at twice the rate of the skin around her lips.

The Emperor stood tall in defiance of his age. However, the effort he asserted in this vain was apparent to anyone who stood before him. He was tired and stubborn. None of this negated the stately presence he carried on his broad shoulders. His large nose and long forehead were dignified, though aged, and his head was shaped perfectly for the heavy crown that sat atop it. The throne held more authority over their minds than they over their subjects.

The Emperor and Empress sat at the head of the table, while the guest of honor, Sir Dirk, son of Lord Madoc of house Hyshmi from the south of Eurst, sat beside Elysia, directly opposite the two princes.

"How has your father been?" Rhyker asked as the servants began to bring in the many colorful dishes. Dirk, caught in a light conversation with Elysia, stuttered before clearing his throat to answer.

"Ahh. I could never mince words with you, your majesty. He's quite bored. He's quite round at his belly and hasn't found a reason to remove it yet," Dirk subtly mused, visibly satisfied with the sound of his voice. Rhyker joined with his subtle laugh.

"Not much action when everything runs to plan. Am I right?" Rhyker grinned.

"Murder and unrest are not meant to be fun either," Ethan interjected, glaring at his father, who smiled back as the guests at the table went still. Tension built up in the air.

"My son here, the idealist, does not yet grasp the full weight of responsibility individuals of our stature bear," Rhyker stressed, staring directly at Ethan. "He believes still that peace paves the way for progress, when in fact, peace is rather merely a pause in the never-ending battle for truth, the battle for justice." Ethan lowered his head and the Empress Myrae shifted uneasily as her other two children looked away. Ethan's face reddened as he gauged the others' disinterest in intruding on the conversation.

"Well, at least we can drink more ale and wine in peacetime," Dirk chuckled as the others joined in the laughter, shattering the tension in the air. Smiling with the rest, Ethan gave an uneasy glance to his father, catching his disapproval. Dirk was a barrel-chested man with a booming voice that echoed through the hall when he spoke. His hair was unkept and greasy, and he tied it up haphazardly in a thin ponytail. He was many years the senior of Elysia, whom he leaned ever closer toward as he brazenly attempted to win her favor. Ethan's father invited him on the request of Lord Madoc of house Hyshmi to build a relationship with the Raynels among all his other brothers. Emperor Rhyker considered it another opportunity to match Elysia. Despite the age gap, Sir Dirk presented a better match than wealthy merchants.

The night continued uneventfully, save for Elysia's overly confident drinking. Ethan saw her genuinely enjoying conversation with a suitor for the first time. He saw it in her eyes and the eyes of the rest. Nothing would be the same. He had felt it all along but did not want to believe it. Now, it had become as obvious as night and day.

"Dirk, tomorrow I'm taking you around. I'm sure Madoc would like you to meet as many people in my council as possible while you're here," Rhyker boasted. Ethan fumed inside. His father had openly welcomed a stranger, for all he knew, to his household and had immediately decided to treat him as his own. Dirk, speaking quietly with Elysia, quickly glanced at Rhyker, half smiling as Ethan peered at his reactions.

"That would be perfect. Thank you, your majesty," he said. Rhyker smiled.

"Dinner was marvelous. Myrae, Dirk, and I are moving to the study for a smoke. We have a few private matters to discuss," Rhyker smiled as Myrae nodded. "Soren, come with us as well." Rhyker grinned, avoiding eye contact with Ethan.

"Elysia, why don't you come with me and leave them

alone. I want to speak with you," Myrae beamed. She left the dining hall, giving a cold glance to Ethan, who remained seated alone.

Ethan glanced around to the empty hall as servants began to clean up. Clattering glass plates and silver cutlery replaced the murmuring of evening conversation. Suddenly, his face lit up. He got up and ran to the central hall. He paid little attention to his path and almost crashed into one of the servants carrying a tower of plates. He reached the bottom of the stairs, pausing and looking up. After a quick run, he made his way up to the first floor barely panting.

He heard his mother and sister chatting on the first floor in one of the lounge rooms. He slowed down in front of the half-open door while avoiding being seen.

"That Dirk has built a liking for you. I can see it in his eyes. He is a suitable match and he's different than the others," Ethan heard Myrae beam before Elysia intruded.

"Yes," Myrae sighed. "Maybe we'll talk later. He's not going anywhere," Elysia said, an excited tone clearly audible in her voice.

Ethan, refusing to linger any longer, kept moving. He glanced down the stone-laid corridor, counting doors. The galleries on the first floor were long and straight, and portraits of Ethan's ancestors hung scattered across the wall.

He took a brief walk and halted before a door, clenching his fists. He held his breath, pressed his hands against it, and upon entering, found only a luggage case. At the sight of Dirk's belongings, he felt a prickling sensation down his back. Mindful of his actions, Ethan whispered to himself, aware that if he left evidence, his father would eventually discover it. Quietly, he shut the door and tip-toed to the other end of the room, near the fireplace.

Hearing faint footsteps from outside, Ethan froze midway through his walking. With his heart racing and pounding in his throat, he quickly looked back at the door. Its silhouette of light visible. After a short moment, he looked back to the fireplace in the dark room. The floor had been covered end-to-end with a thick red carpet. A wide bed with a wooden cage stood on one end, with a small chair and desk setup on the other. A half-opened notepad, feather, and ink rested on it.

Ethan fought the urge to go through it, eventually making it to the fireplace. Holding onto the vent latch, Ethan held his breath and opened it slowly, releasing black dust into the room. He quickly dusted as much of it as possible back into the fireplace, feeling a draft of airflow through it. With the opening visible, Ethan brought his ear closer to it.

"Sydol is ready," Dirk uttered. His voice moved around the room.

"That only leaves Mallyn in the Fraeland up North," Rhyker said with a short pause. "What do you think?" He badgered. A silence followed by a stuttering voice.

"If you thought less with your dick and more like your brother, you'd have half a functioning brain to say anything meaningful," Rhyker snapped, uneasy tension hanging in the air.

After a short while, Ethan heard Dirk speak. "And what of him? Is there something I should know?" Another pause lingered over the conversation as Ethan frantically pressed his ear to the opening.

"What had always been," Ethan heard his father speak just as his voice disappeared.

Sweat fell down his forehead as he continued to listen for voices. Nothing. After a short while, he heard a commotion behind the room's door. He held his breath. He thought it must be one of the servants in the corridor outside. Ethan turned back to the opening and tried to catch any other words. Nothing again.

"Dirk, why don't we head inside?" Ethan heard a voice speak from outside of the room. He flinched back immediately, dusting whatever black dust he could into the fireplace and closing the vent in a frenzy. His heart raced, rushing to the door and slowly pressing on it. It cracked open, and he saw Rhyker and Dirk standing at the beginning of the corridor.

"I need to pass by my room for a moment," Dirk said as he began to walk toward Ethan. Before he could think of a plan and move, Rhyker called back to him and insisted that he join immediately. Ethan saw Dirk nod his head and turn back as the door opened with Elysia standing at the entrance. Ethan's nerves relaxed.

"Hope we aren't intruding," Rhyker stated as he nudged Dirk in.

"We've been waiting," Elysia said as she let the rest enter. After the door closed behind them, the corridor went back to silence. His opportunity finally arrived, and Ethan did not waste time. He pressed the door open and began to walk towards the stairs. His back arched forward as he tip-toed. Ethan passed the first-floor lounge door and began to ascend the stairs as his breathing returned to normal.

"Where were you?" a voice spat immediately.

Ethan froze in his place, holding his breath. He quickly glanced back. "Were you eavesdropping again?" Soren growled. Ethan did not speak.

"Things spoken in private are meant to remain in private. Otherwise, everyone would know everything and complete anarchy. Don't you agree?" Soren snarled.

"All you do is hide things from me and expect me to be ok with it. It's obvious that Father doesn't want me anywhere useful. I'm not sure what privacy matters at this instant," Ethan shot back. Soren glared at him, his eyes wide open.

"You are something. Never backing down from an argument," Soren smirked. "Anyways, what do I care? It's not like something new was discussed," he added. Ethan's eyes lit up.

"What isn't new?" Ethan questioned, raising his eyebrows. Ethan paused before breaking out in a condescending laugh.

"You are sneaky little brother. If I told you, then it wouldn't be private anymore. Right?" Soren sneered as he patted Ethan on the back. He nodded to the first-floor lounge. "You know you're always invited," Soren winked.

Ethan nodded and exhaled, shrugging off his brother before continuing up the stairs while he heard Soren open the door with a creak.

"Oh, and brother," Soren called from behind. Ethan glanced backward. "Good luck," he smirked eerily before closing the door behind him.

Six

Ozwald exhaled and wiped the sweat from his forehead as the noon sun clamored down on him. He had put the cows out earlier in the day to graze but now had to bring them back in as a heavy rainstorm was coming. His uncle Merrick had a knack for reading the clouds, although he never understood his thought process. The cows gave him a hard time as he struggled to bring them back in. He stared at them, just waiting for them to move. His verbal commands felt futile. "Let's get in. Come on!" He instructed. He hated this part of the day, hated waiting idly. No matter how much he tried, they would not move faster. One more task, and he would be free for the day.

Since childhood, Ozwald and his brother Marcus had been competitive. They would compete in everything, no matter how pointless or how dangerous. They once competed on who could last the longest on the barn roof in the middle of a cold winter storm night. Although they could not stop grinning afterward, they both caught colds for a week afterward. Today was no different. Marcus sneaked up behind Ozwald, nearly startling him off his feet.

"Never could beat me with your tasks! Eyy!" He gleamed from behind as Ozwald held the gate signaling the cows in vain. Not too happy with his gloating, Ozwald did not look back.

"Don't have an answer for your brother?" Marcus continued. He walked ahead of Ozwald and stared directly into his eyes. "If I were you, I'd do the same. Find a place for myself and hide away forever from the shame. Maybe you'll find some mud to hide in when this storm comes in if it ever does," he mused. Marcus, who was barely a year older than Ozwald, radiated confidence with his beaming smile. Despite the rough scruff on his face, his well-groomed beard gave off an air of assuredness that everything would always work out. He sported a thick white shirt that had turned a mottled grey and yellow from years of wear, yet he wore it with effortless ease, regardless of the weather or time of year. Leaving the shirt unbuttoned at the collar and rolling up his sleeves, he exuded an approachable, relaxed demeanor that was ready to work. To complete his friendly appearance, he donned a brown vest that complemented his ready-to-action visage.

Marcus immediately jumped onto the wooden rails of the barn fence and stared at the cows as he began to shout at them. Not like Ozwald, though, but with a personal touch. As if he personally knew each beast.

"Come on Svenna, you can do it," he encouraged the animals in front of him. And just like that, the final two stubborn cows began to move to the sound of his voice.

To the cows, Marcus spoke their language, and they could easily relate to him and understand his commands. Ozwald remained silent as he eyed his brother.

"Svenna! You know you want to," Marcus continued, his voice warm and forthcoming to the beasts as they both picked up speed and rushed in. Ozwald exhaled secretly as he quickly closed the long barn fence gate.

"See, it wasn't so hard. What can I say? I'm better at everything. The trick to it, is to know their names," Marcus smirked.

Ozwald remained silent, looking at the cows. They existed within the fenced area behind the barn peacefully as if they had been there all day.

"Remember that. You can tell your lady friends at that brothel that your brother Marcus is. Well, you can just say my name. That'll be enough. They'll know," he joked. Ozwald broke out laughing with Marcus following suite.

"Are you always going to make me look bad. Show off," Ozwald beamed.

"I'm not even trying brother at this point," Marcus said his face lit.

"Still got the pigs to tend to, care to join?" Ozwald said, tapping his brother on the chest.

"You'll probably need my help on that I suppose,"

Ozwald rolled his eyes as Marcus followed with a small prance in his stride. The day's tasks had ended for him and whatever followed, he would consider pleasure.

At first, the pigs had been situated on the outskirts of the forest, nestled beneath the comforting shade of tall oak trees. However, a few months back, Ozwald found a dead piglet. He observed it for a while and saw that foxes had been jumping over the fence. His father blamed their death on the harsh winter weather. However, Ozwald knew otherwise. Without any approval he erected a new and high fence around the back portion of the barn for the pigs to stay in below tree shade. And Marcus, who believed in his brother, helped as well with no questions asked.

"Is he still mad about earlier?" Ozwald sighed. Their father wanted to take them to Wyder's tavern for beer and ale in the evening for Ozwald's name day. However, Ozwald refused as he had to be at the brothel. Their father did not take the news so easily.

"Honestly, I'd be a bit careful about what I say if I were you. He was pouting and talking to himself the entire morning in the field," Marcus said. He reached the wooden fence of the pig's den underneath the trees and rested his hands gently. He began to make sounds to attract the animals towards him as Ozwald fetched two buckets.

"I love him. But we're growing up. We should be allowed to start making our own decisions. It's not like I'm leaving and never coming back," Ozwald mocked as he brought the buckets to a nearby storage tank and began to fill them up. The tanks had been connected to a nearby water stream that originated directly from the Ancient Heights up north near Fallgarde. The water was always ice cold and Merrick had constructed the tanks out of oak wood and applied mortar within it to hold the water.

"You know, I can see you leaving here. For sure. I mean, I can imagine that the shame of always coming second to me will grow to an inconceivable and unacceptable level very soon," Marcus joked while Ozwald filled the two buckets to the rim and carried them over to the pigs' drinking tanks.

The animals cluttered around the tank, anxious to get every drop that they can. Ozwald watched the pigs drink for a while and saw the tank to be broken at its side.

"These beasts are relentless. I need to fix that," he said, pointing to a broken plank in the tank's side. Marcus nudged him playfully. "Pig Lord. We better be getting back." They walked back to the farmhouse, walking along the outer part of the livestock fences.

"Don't worry, I'll get that fixed for you," Marcus said as he looked up to the sky, assessing the sun's position. The conversation quickly shifted back to the topic of his father's insistence on the evening's outing. Marcus, determined to hear a confirmation, demanded again that he make it. "Is there no way?" He continued to probe.

Ozwald remained silent, keeping a watchful eye on Marcus throughout. He saw no need to alter his routine for this occasion, as there would undoubtedly be many more like it. The tavern was hardly necessary for ale and beer, as Ozwald's mother, Ivy, was skilled in brewing her own delicious batches. His father, on the other hand, was hard to convince otherwise when his mind was set on something.

Suddenly Marcus jumped in front of him, pressing his hand to his chest.

"Just some advice from your brother. Just be careful what you say. You know how much he cares. We all do," Marcus consoled. Ozwald looked away before nodding.

"Lunch is ready," Ivy called from a distance. Both boys stopped and stared at each other with menacing gazes.

"Are you sure?" Marcus taunted, his eyebrows angled, the tension between both brothers at a pinnacle.

Without another waiting instant, Ozwald and Ethan

bolted ahead, each one in their own direction. He knew the drill, and more importantly, he knew his brother. He ran around the cow fence using his hands to swing himself ahead as much as he could. He had a great head start, he knew.

He glanced back, eagerly searching for his brother. He knew not to stop. He would not make the same mistake twice. Marcus always had a knack for using unorthodox and risky routes, and Ozwald did not want to stand by and see him do that and regret it. He made it to the straight dirt path directly leading to the farmhouse, glancing around erratically but still not able to see Marcus.

Suddenly a loud breaking sound from the other side of the barn house. His vision was glued to the source of the sound as he caught sight of his brother landing on a wooden wagon ahead of him.

"Cheater!" Ozwald shrieked, his voice flustered while he began to run even faster.

They ended side-by-side with no clear victor yet. Ozwald pushed as much as he could, knowing that he could beat his brother in a straight sprint. He had done it before and every time they trained together, Ozwald would always finish first. His breath quickened, trying to take longer strides with every step, hoping to cover the remaining short distance quicker. Marcus though, began to pull ahead. Ozwald saw it and pushed even more, trying to make up for the gap. He knew it would be close, too close for him to be satisfied. Only a handful of steps till the kitchen entrance, he needed to think fast. With one final attempt, he decided to pull off a trick he had not tried before. Just at the end, Ozwald jumped and slid on the ground with one foot ahead as he passed their imaginary line to the kitchen first.

Ozwald immediately jumped for his victory once he came to a stop. Marcus on the other hand remained standing and swung in through the ajar kitchen door right behind him.

"I win," he declared calmly, just as he caught Ozwald's glistening eyes.

"No! You didn't. You're not taking this from me, you cheating bastard," Ozwald bleated out, panting. Marcus stood over him while pressing his finger on his chest.

"Oh yeah, and how is it that I was inside first?" Marcus smirked as both looked inside the kitchen.

"That's enough! Get up, boys. The both of you. Wash up outside before coming in," Ivy commanded from the kitchen doorway, her face not willing to accommodate their foolishness. Marcus helped up a reluctant Ozwald as he dusted off his clothes before heading to the washing basin nearby. Cleaned up, they rushed in for lunch, which had always been Ozwald's first real meal for the day.

He reveled in it as it marked the start of his real day outside of the farm. After lunch, he would spend a few hours sparring with his brother outside. They always used wooden sticks and then followed that with whatever physical dares they would challenge each other with. Afterward Ozwald would read for some time, which Ivy always helped and guided him on. And just when dusk began, he would freshen up and head off to the brothel for work.

His father had always been against work at the brothel when he joined three years back. However, Ozwald did it anyways. Lissany, a family friend, opened up her doors for him with wide arms when she found out that he was looking for extra work away from the farm. The brothel, although imprisoning in and of itself, gave him freedom from the fate of farming his father planned for him.

"Now sit," Ivy sneered, glaring at both of them while standing over a boiling pot of pottage. She cooked over a separate fire oven which Ozwald, Marcus and Merrick built the prior summer for her inside the kitchen.

"Are we all ready?" Merrick asked as he rushed into the kitchen carrying a few pieces of carrots and cabbage from the field. "Ivy. Why don't you put these over the fire too, wouldn't take long to cook," he asked, his eyes wide open as he handed them to her. Merrick, their father, loved freshly cooked vegetables, especially those that became ripe early.

All three waited for Ivy to bring the hot bowls of pottage in silence. None liked to speak on empty stomachs. No one started while they all waited for her to sit down with her bowl.

"Well, why don't we eat," she commented softly, casting an uneasy glance at Merrick as he began to eat, followed by the rest. They had not eaten much in the morning and therefore, they dived into their bowls of pottage while their slurping mouths and the clacking wooden cutlery prevailed.

"How is the corn harvest?" Ivy asked, no one willing to speak while engulfed in their bowl.

"Well, it's not ready yet. Still needs a few more months. The rains later today should help though," Merrick said, not interested in speaking more until he finished. "Young corn cobs should stick to their roots," he added mockingly, casting a smirk at Ozwald, who caught the hint.

"Father, I know what you're insinuating. I know what you're doing. I just politely asked that we do tonight another night," Ozwald snapped as Ivy and Marcus put their wooden spoons down and switched their vision between the two.

Merrick refrained from responding quickly, taking deep breaths and rubbing his eyes. Ozwald knew he did that to control his temper, otherwise he would fire up, which he had a history of doing. Despite Merrick's pure intentions, he always wanted to have a say in Ozwald's life in some shape or form.

"I thought about it. I understand. You have commitments. Why don't we avoid being stubborn," Merrick began as the rest held their breath.

"What about we go earlier? That way, we just may beat the storm. Afterwards, you can go to that damn brothel of yours," Merrick suggested curling his lip. Ozwald looked up as the others waited for him to speak in anticipation.

"Sure," he exhaled as Merrick clapped his hands, a wide smile planted across his face while the rest joined in the laughter of joy as well.

"Then be ready in, say, three hours?" Merrick asked the group as they quickly nodded while all breathing easier after reaching, a solution to Merrick's stubbornness.

~

"Conwell, you ass!" Cried Sir Jonas from a table in Wyder's tavern. Ozwald heard from across the room.

The tavern, dimly lit, consisted of scattered worn-out wooden tables and was packed with customers drinking and talking as day turned into night. A visible layer of pipe smoke lingered above the crowd. The owner, Wyder, had wide hands and a thick mustache. He stood behind the tavern's bar serving customers with a smile.

Ozwald stood at the bar waiting with Marcus for the

food and beer to come out. They both saw the entire array of tables, already filled up, while the sun had not set yet. Some tables laughed while others murmured among each other, Ozwald saw.

Both boys chuckled as they made up stories of each of the groups they saw across the tavern. The sky outside had already turned a dim grey, the clouds visibly heavy with water and it was a matter of time until the heavens opened up on the Haefe.

"What do you think they're whispering about Ozy?" Marcus laughed, both catching sight of two men and a woman whispering among each other. Marcus smiled and deep in thought.

"You see those two. The woman and the man?" Ozwald asked as Marcus nodded. "Well, they're planning to build a house and they need that guy to do it for them," Ozwald blurted laughing while Marcus was not amused.

"You really are boring, you know that," Marcus snapped before patting his brother's chest. "I have a proper one," Marcus started. "That man and woman are lovers and the woman. Well, she's married. They're asking that man to kill him for them so that they could live with each other," Marcus mused as Ozwald broke a smile. "You always see the good and never want to see the bad in anyone. Better be careful with that," Marcus added.

"Whatever brother except those are Mr. and Mrs. Mreisse and they are asking that man to build a house for them. This town isn't that big you know. And I'm not going to insinuate infidelity for them. They've always been kind to us," Ozwald grinned as both boys broke out into laughter.

"I sure miss her apple juice. Another three months I'd

say, then we'll pay her a visit," Ozwald added.

They both leaned over the bar waiting for the food to come in. Two farmers, Barver and Lorno, stood next to Ozwald deep in conversation. Ozwald winked and flicked his head to Marcus towards the two huddled up farmers.

"No more water coming to my farm. The streams are drying up. Lost half the farm already," Barver wailed to the other in a hushed voice.

"This Jonas bastard thinks that he can drink and feast instead of doing something. I don't know how long I can last," Lorno concurred.

"There will be unrest soon, surely," Barver cautioned.

"Aye, what are you staring at boy?" He jolted while eyeing Ozwald.

"I. I wasn't. Sorry Sir," Ozwald stuttered before Marcus nudged him to keep quiet.

"Ahem. My brother, Sir, was merely admiring the wall behind you," Marcus interjected hesitantly.

"Is that your protection boy?" Lorno mocked before Ozwald saw his father from the corner of his eye.

"Hello gentlemen, Barver, Lorno, hope the crops are doing well. Ah the food is here. Let's go boys, off to our table. Good evening gentlemen," Merrick uttered with a nod to each of them.

He handed Wyder a Lirkin coin who waved back with a smile. Ozwald and Marcus picked up their plates quickly, while avoiding eye contact and headed off to their table, while Merrick continued to stare at Barver and Lorno before he followed his boys.

"Don't bring your negativity to my boys. Otherwise, you know what'll happen," Ozwald heard Merrick hiss to both men.

Seven

"Shhhh," Lissany hissed, her finger covering her mouth. A group of six men sat drinking and smoking and laughing vociferously amongst each other in the brothel lounge. She stood midway on the stairs overlooking them, her eyes squinting fiercely. Ozwald stood behind her. He had left his family at Wyder's tavern after spending a great part of the evening in their company. Although Merrick was unhappy at his departure, he hugged his son before Ozwald took off.

Lissany turned, and as if reading his mind, spoke pointedly, "These drunkards have paid to stay the entire night. You may have to stay until the morning. No questions about that you hear. This is purely my decision. Now, go downstairs and stay with them until they all come up here," her gaze fixated on the men below, taking a long inhale of her pipe. "Who would've thought? Rumors of a drought circulating, and all these men want to do is fuck," she mocked.

Rumors of a drought had in fact been slowly growing around the Haefe, Ozwald knew. He did not though believe that such an event could ever happen in his hometown. He had been so nestled up on his farm that change seemed hard to come by no matter how much he tried to bring it about.

"But I have an early morning tomorrow," Ozwald hesitated.

"Our deal has always been that your work here and at the farm never overlap. I don't see how that is the case," she said, cutting him out while he simply nodded after a short moment.

"Good," she said, catching his nod from the corner of her eye. Ozwald had never slept at the brothel and had no intention of doing so this evening. Even at its busiest at the height of summer, he had never been asked to stay.

"What would you have of me?" he relented.

"Whatever it takes. You know the drill, chat, and drink with them, just so long as they keep their voices down and don't get out of control," she instructed with an insidious wink. Ozwald nodded again mechanically. He walked down the stairs with a quickly crafted smile, a talent Lissany engrained in him in the three years he had labored at the brothel.

"Gentlemen, mind if I join?" he enquired, gritting his teeth. Silence fell over the crowd as twelve piercing eyes chiseling through Ozwald's face.

"Well, my boy, that depends. Would you pour a drink with us first?" One of them interrogated sharply, malice clear in his voice while the rest remained still in anticipation, their eyes soaking up every moment.

"Yes, of course," Ozwald jolted back, breaking the tension. Suddenly, all six men broke out in laughter and stood up in quick unison with a loud "Hurray!"

The man nearest Ozwald had wide, course hands and a carefully shaved head, save for a thin strip in the middle. He handed Ozwald a wooden cup from a nearby table and filled it to the brim with wine, spilling a few drops in the motion.

"My apologies," he grinned. His unsettling smile revealed two missing teeth from his cracked mouth. Ozwald, not much of a wine drinker, smiled. He knew he could not drink much without drifting to sleep.

The guest shoved the cup into Ozwald's hand who immediately peered down into its dark pool while the rest raised their cups together. They waited for Ozwald to reciprocate who hesitated for a moment as he raised his cup as well.

"To the friends we have, and to the friends we make along the way! Cheers to our newfound friend, the young," one of the men saluted, staring at Ozwald attentively.

"Ozwald, my name is Ozwald," he exhaled.

"Cheers to our newfound friend, Ozwald!" the same man continued, followed by a loud, collective "Here! Here! Cheers Ozwald!"

"My apologies, my good patrons, but could everyone please not be loud with their revelry? We have some guests upstairs, and we don't want to bother them," Ozwald stuttered.

They said nothing. They quickly sat back upon their stools and chairs before one of them motioned for Ozwald to sit on the chair centered in the heart of their party. For a moment, it seemed as though they might not speak another word more for the duration of the long night as they began smiling and nodding at one another as they sipped from their cups in silence.

This precarious silence carried on for a few more moments before one burst suddenly into laughter, almost spitting out his wine. Ozwald devised another method to quickly quiet them down, and he blurted out the first thing that came to his mind.

"And you, my friends, what are your names?" Ozwald enquired, sipping his wine and speaking with a low voice to set the required volume.

"Well, my name is Harold, this is Grant that's Garry over there, Patrick, Murray and that lad over there. Well. We call him Rainbow on account that he fucked eight women in eight dress colors at the same time," Harold said, seriousness clear in his voice.

"Nice to meet you. Harold, Grant, Garry, Patrick, Murray and Rainbow. What brings you to the Haefe?" Ozwald repeated, sipping his wine slowly.

The six men just looked at each other before breaking out in mocking laughter. Ozwald knew there was something he did not understand, and before he tried to quiet them down, Harold raised his hand for them to go silent. Instantaneously, they ceased their bellowing laughs, becoming severe so quickly that it alarmed Ozwald.

"Well, young Ozwald, in our previous lives, each of us was something. I was a baker, if you'd believe it, like my father and his father before him. Patrick and Murray practiced the same trade. Grant and Garry... they were blacksmiths. Rainbow here, well, he's never been anything, really. He's more like a bird that jumps from branch to branch. We're lucky to have him, though, if I'm to speak plainly," Harold orated as if he had introduced them in the same way before.

Ozwald, finding the testimony interesting, shifted in his seat before probing further. "Your previous life, what exactly did you," he began, his voice direct, however unable to overcome the strength of Harold's voice cutting him out.

"I'm just getting there, actually, if you'd allow me to finish," Harold grunted, an aggressive grin stuck to his face. "We work together now doing two things rather than one, actually," he added as the rest of the lot shared his aggressive grin and patiently waited for him to finish. "We are traders of certain sort by day. And, debt collectors, as is needed. Depending on who's asking, of course," he concluded without blinking.

"For Lirkin? I never knew that was a job. I'd assume that trade rather arduous," Ozwald said, his face curious, waiting for one of the men to clarify. Harold grinned and looked around at his friends, who held their laughs half in their guts and half in their reddened faces. Ozwald did not understand the group's reaction.

"Well, my dear Ozwald, for anything, actually," Harrold clarified, looking up suddenly at the ceiling as crackling wood sounds emanated from above. The muffled echo of approaching voices followed before a group of seven men made their way down the stairs and out into the night.

Ozwald, feeling slightly relieved, hoped they might remain silent until called upon. He knew that the women would be getting ready now and that it would be but a matter of minutes before he would be finished from this lot. He was wrong.

"Come on Harold, ask our dear Ozwald about the

boat," Patrick insisted eagerly.

"Yes, ask him the boat question. Let's gather a real measure of the man," Murray said, chiming in. The rest of the men joined the request. This time though, Harrold silenced them with the raise of his hand.

"Lads, alright. I'll ask him," Harold relented.

Ozwald sat attentively, placing his cup of wine on the nearby table. "My friend, suppose you're on a boat —an assumption, of course, nothing to do with reality," Harrold began as he took a deep sip. The rest of his gang glared up at him, their eyes wide and restless.

"You're the captain of this vessel. You're in the middle of a great storm, and the ship has begun to capsize. You know for good fact that you could save the boat by one of two means — either by jumping overboard, or by throwing someone else overboard otherwise, the vessel would be too heavy to sail on. However, because we are now good friends, my good self, and your good self, I'll offer you a third, albeit riskier, choice. You attempt to fix the boat with no guarantee that you could fix it in time to spare it from the depths. What do you do, Ozwald?" Harrold investigated every corner of his face as though prying open his thoughts, crossing his arms in anticipation.

Ozwald contemplated for a short while before he broke out into a hesitating laugh. "You can't be serious. That's not a normal choice."

"That's the question," Murray shot back, the rest remained focused on his face and its features, while Ozwald gulped glancing around as he contemplated his answer seriously.

"Well, I don't know. It doesn't seem fair, though for

me to have that choice. I mean, I would never ask anyone to throw themselves overboard and risk their life for the rest. I don't know if I would jump overboard. I still want to live. I think myself rather unselfish but there is so much of life I've yet to see. I...I... I would probably try to repair it," he said, losing his breath at the last few words.

Harrold's flat expression broke into a grin as Rainbow handed him a six-faced die. He held it up between his fingers for Ozwald to see.

"Well, my friend, you've reached a dangerous point that no one likes to reach. You've eliminated the two choices that would've given you a definite result. Instead of pursuing the path that saves everyone's life save for one soul, you've put everyone's life at risk," Harrold continued. Ozwald, now entranced by the unusual posturing of the men, leaned in closer. "Sacrifice the few to save the many," Harrold added.

"This die here, it represents your chances of living. How many numbers do you say we let him pick, lads?" Harrold asked, his voice already predicting the fate that awaits as a result of Ozwald's decision.

"The same as the others, one number!" Rainbow said above the murmuring of the rest. The pack went silent as they waited for Harrold's decision.

"For our good friend here, well, we'll give him another chance, so that's two numbers to pick out of the six," Harrold said, looking at Ozwald to obtain his approval who nodded in return. Without any more words, Harrold shook the die in his hand, the tension in the air mounting in accordance with the ascent of the men's deep humming.

"So what's it going to be? Two numbers from the six," Harold asked, a mischievous grin now planted on his face and clearly enjoying the moment.

Ozwald thought about it for just a moment.

"Two. And. Three," Ozwald blurted out closing his eyes.

"The numbers have been chosen and we're ready. My friends, follow the die closely," Harrold instructed. With one quick flick of his hand, he threw the die on the wooden floor as it clicked and rolled across it. Instead of stopping on the floor in front of everyone, it continued underneath the bench that Rainbow, Patrick and Murray sat upon and out of sight.

"Where is it?" cried Rainbow getting quickly and looking for it between everyone else's legs.

The rest leapt up and proceeded to do the same, scouring the floor, as they struggled to find it. Ozwald though remained seated with his hands folded neatly in his lap, disinterested to join the search, and contemplating the question again. Would he leave everything to chance? Never once had death stared him in the eyes. Should he jump overboard or ask another to sacrifice their life for the rest? Never had he been placed in front of such a decision and it was not any clearer what he would choose in the future, no matter how much he thought about it.

However, he knew that life rarely presents such straightforward questions. Even a boy from the Haefe knew this.

"I found it!" cried Rainbow with his head ducked deep under the furniture. He pulled the die from below and held it in his hand in front of the others to see as the commotion of the search finally ceased.

"Ahem. Gentlemen, your pleasures await. You may

make your way up now," Lissany announced from upstairs. The six men looked at each other smiling, losing interest in their recent conversation. Rainbow did not even mention the number out loud, leaving it on the end of the table for all to see as they passed by on their way up for their night of pleasure. All of them grinned and mumbled among each other after catching sight of the number, casting awkward glances back at Ozwald, who shifted anxiously.

After a short while, no one remained save for Ozwald, who stared coldly across the table at the die. Half of him wanted to get up, while the other half kept him anchored to his seat.

"Let's have it then," he said to himself, getting up and rushing to the die for a clear view.

His heart skipped a beat. *Six.*

He had killed them all. He failed everyone because he could not sacrifice to save the rest. Ozwald looked around at the state of the lounge and quickly cleaned up. He asserted the cups and put away the wine before locking up and heading upstairs to see Lissany. He needed to leave. There was no good reason to linger around longer, he knew.

"Ozy! Everything clean downstairs and locked up?" She inquired, holding her pipe in one hand and observing the alignment of her nails on the other. She sat in his chair at his usual desk post, her feet resting upon it lazily.

"Yes," he said gently. She began to massage her forehead and puff more smoke towards the low ceiling.

"Good. I've decided you'll rest here for the night. I need you," she instructed before pointing towards the floor mat on the opposite end of the lounge.

"Lissany, I have an early day at the farm tomorrow,

father needs me. There's heavy rain outside, and there will be a lot of things to attend to, you know how it is," Ozwald started with his head bowed down — a common reflex for him when he requested something from the Madam, against her usual orders.

"You're staying Ozwald Stonne. I won't hear it. Those are my orders for tonight. Your father will understand!" She said, her voice sharp, direct, and not accommodating to any sort of response he may have. Taking a few more puffs and glancing around the room, she turned around and made her way to her own chambers. Closing the door behind her with an unusually loud slam.

Eight

A week had passed since Dirk's visit to Horos. He originally planned for a two-day visit, but then extended it indefinitely. His exact mission was never made clear to Ethan, although he could sense a shift in the momentum of the palace. More visitors and more armed men showed up. Something was in the air.

Under house Raynel, no all-out war had taken place since the Dark Night more than five hundred years ago, which eliminated claims to the emperorship from house Barekian and house Nethen. Ethan had been refuted each time he attempted to enquire about the purpose of the current mobilizations, and his father had become ever more inaccessible than usual. Soren disappeared entirely. Elysia told him that Soren was with his father and Dirk the entire time, but Ethan saw Dirk multiple times throughout the castle talking with his sister.

To clear his mind, Ethan finally agreed to go out with

his friend Lokren for a night of frivolity in Horos. Lokren was a slender young man, only two years Ethan's senior. He had a protruding chin and thick eyebrows. He was the tallest in his family and always bent forward to speak, which arched his posture with time. That was always the first thing anyone noticed about him.

"You need your own breathing space to get away from all of this," Lokren told Ethan, eventually convincing him. His security detail obligated that he never be left alone. Therefore, once out of the castle, Ethan was followed by two armed men inconspicuously and from afar.

Nestled among towering trees, Horos was a city built in a hilly region, where the ancient Aelgan trees, also known as "origin trees," stood tall and untouched. These sacred trees, gifted to men by the Ancients upon their arrival two millennia ago, were scattered throughout the city, providing shade and comfort through all seasons. The city's houses, constructed from wood, had been efficiently designed to fit the needs of all Eurstians who chose to reside there. They were built on the hills within the city walls, located on the eastern coast of Eurst.

Horos, like the rest of Eurst, was renowned for its calm towns and villages. Eurstians believed that life was more fulfilling when taken slowly. This was reflected in the city's daily routine, where all shops closed, and trading areas were vacated just before dusk to prepare and refresh for the next day.

Ethan and Lokren walked along a dirt and cobblestone road between houses, down from the northern part of the city. The houses were built with at least two or three floors, their rooftops shaped like cones and painted green to match the Aelgan tree cover above. The air in Horos was always fresh and moist, making every breath a refreshing and invigorating experience.

"Father told me that he heard nothing, and he would know. His spice routes spread all across Eurst, not to mention the secret one with Shekat. He told me though that this type of thing happens every now and then. He called it 'scheduled training' — to make sure everyone was always ready. But honestly, he never made it clear for who or what purpose," Lokren explained. "Anyways, there's no one and no reason to fight in Eurst. So, you're not really missing out on anything," Lokren said as the boys strolled through the city's vacant streets.

"No one wants to talk. It's as if the secret would be revealed to everyone if I were to find out," Ethan snapped, frustration clear on his face. Lokren cupped Ethan's shoulders, toiling to cover a deep laugh from within.

"Put it this way, less knowledge, less responsibility. Why work or worry about anything when we have everything we could ever want at our fingertips," Lokren said as a mischievous smile appeared on his face, one that Ethan knew too well.

Ethan broke free of his embrace. "I'd rather die than be useless. I will be more than just the son of the emperor," Ethan snarled, beginning to fume. Lokren, anticipating his refute, embraced him before he could object.

"Apologies if I bothered you. I was just trying to reason why somebody would go out to make wine, when they have a supply of bottles to last a lifetime. But you don't have to agree with that, you've never liked to cut corners," Lokren soothed.

"This way, come on," Lokren instructed, immediately changing the subject. "Otherwise, we're going to be late for Iza's gathering," he added, walking ahead of Ethan to avoid debating with him.

Ethan had heard him say this before but could never agree. A chilly breeze caught up with him while Lokren continued ahead, carrying with it a subtle stench of death, a smell that had become more and more common over the past few weeks.

"Do you smell that?" Ethan asked from behind.

"Of course, it comes and goes. Everyone knows that, and it's mainly in the north," Lokren said from ahead, articulating the words clearly while avoiding raising his voice. Ethan capitalized on Lokren's pause and rushed to him.

"What else have you heard?" Ethan asked his face lit up with curiosity.

"Well, father's trade routes have been affected. More convoys than usual have been raided so father doubled the armed men on each trip. It's costing more but at least it keeps the Lirkins flowing," Lokren explained.

"Does he know who's raiding? It can't be the Fakhrils Otherwise, we'd have war," Ethan badgered.

"Just a bunch of independent bandits. He caught one of them. Just farmers looking for food— the idiots. Father killed the woman thief himself. One slit to the neck, the usual. What he did find out though, was the source of the smell. I can't believe you haven't told me yet. I've asked you a ton of times, and you've never budged."

"What do you mean? I don't know. I don't lie."

"Well, one of the trading parties up to Haelar, on the northern shores of the Fraeland, made its monthly trip and, they found the town abandoned and the crops withered. Whoever did not leave, lied dead, burnt to a crisp — pure terror," Lokren said as his eyes wandered off into his imagination.

Ethan looked into his troubled face. A great part of him did not believe his friend's anecdote and he studied the details of his expression. Such an event would have surely washed across every corner, and yet it had not.

"You don't believe me. That's fine," Lokren began.

"It's not that I don't believe you... it's just...that's a rumor from Haelar which has no place here in Horos," Ethan interjected.

"Think of it. Doesn't your father and his court use rumors to sway opinion, for or against someone or something," Lokren shot back as his eyes fixated on Ethan, who nodded in agreement. "Well, they're hiding this. From the looks of it, they're hiding it from you as well," he added before he glanced to the two-armed men behind them and then to the path ahead of him. "Let's go. We've wasted enough time," he urged, grabbing on Ethan's arm, and pulling him ahead without letting him speak further.

Lokren led them through a side road beneath an arched wooden ceiling. Ethan glanced around quickly in an anxious assessment of the path.

"I don't think you've ever been here," Lokren said, seeming to read Ethan's mind. "All the beggars of Eurst pass by here at some point."

"Master Ethan, we can go around," one of the armed men quickly urged from behind.

Lokren interjected, "That won't be necessary. There's not a beggar in Eurst we can't handle." Ethan's men stood waiting for confirmation, and he gave them an earnest nod. Lokren saw it and pushed ahead through the covered alley while Ethan and his guards followed.

The path lied in the narrow space between huddled houses and stray branches sprouted out from its top, as if an extension of the massive Aelgan trees nearby. It smelt damp and moldy and only one lit torch hung at the end of the path, rationing the light inside.

"We definitely took the wrong turn," Ethan said, already panting lightly from keeping up.

"Sometimes, you have to take a wrong turn to get to the right place," Lokren said, smiling back at Ethan from ahead, oblivious to the volume of his voice, which rang on the walls as he picked up the pace.

The pathway turned into a tunnel eventually, becoming tighter and narrower as the echo of their movement and voice disappeared. Dark openings in the wall became apparent, leading to places Ethan did not know.

"I wouldn't venture inside of any of those gaps unless you want to get your hands dirty," Lokren added, after catching sight of Ethan lingering for a moment.

"We're almost out," he added.

Ethan saw the lit exit at the end of the dark tunnel and pushed ahead.

"Watch your head, aye?" Lokren warned, tapping the wooden beam above the exit with a loud bang. "See, our destination is there — would have taken another fifteen minutes if we didn't take this route," Lokren said, pointing ahead to an estate at the top of the hill.

"It would have taken us less time on horseback, Master Ethan," one of the armed men complained from behind.

Suddenly, shouting and crying rose from a corner near the exit of the tunnel. Ethan saw two men exchange punches and he turned to Lokren, who began cheering them on, his eyes glowing with excitement as he watched. Both men were dressed in ragged, dirty clothing. The first man was heavy, with deep wrinkles lining his thick neck and bulging lips. The second was short with exaggeratedly long fingers, and his cheeks sunk deep into his face as though being pulled from inside his mouth.

Ethan began to fume, clearly disturbed by the scene.

"Will you look at that? I bet you that the chubby bastard will beat him up. No doubt," Lokren commented, assessing each fighter's skills as they raged on, unaware of the boys' presence.

"Stop it!" Ethan commanded.

"No, no. Keep them," Lokren dripped with excitement, urging the two to continue their brawl.

Ethan, forfeiting his words, caught the chubby man by the arm, pushing him to the floor.

"No bastard is going to stand in my way," he barked on his back, spitting dirt and wiping blood from his forehead.

"That's no way to address prince Ethan," one of the guards growled. The fighter shuffled and repositioned into a kneeling position as though bowing, though a scornful grin crossed his face. Ethan folded his hands while the shorter man stared on petrified.

"How humble of you to visit us in our dwellings. This man you see over there has robbed me of my bread. And I would like it back," he explained, his voice dripping with venom.

"He's lying! This man has been stealing my food this

entire month. I've been hiding in different places just to run away. He's a thief!" The shorter man exploded in outrage as the guards rushed to hold him back. The heavy man kept his gaze lowered and avoided eye contact with the prince.

The short man, frightened, managed to break free of the guards. But the guards were bigger, taller, and stronger, and his victory was short lived.

"He's trying to kill me!" he trembled, his entire body shaking in fear. "I just wanted to sleep for the night over there. I meant no harm," he stuttered, pointing with his hand while panting rapidly.

"Silence! We can solve this," Ethan snapped.

"This scum is a liar," the other man shot back, jumping up and attacking once more. Both fell to the ground and wrestled one another viscously.

"We can find beds for all of you," Ethan stuttered, failing to calm the situation.

Both of the guards, ignoring Ethan's demands, encouraged them to fight even harder, clapping and whistling as if they had placed competing bets.

"Punch him in the face!" one of them shouted.

"The chubby one. See? Takes plenty of fights to get good at picking winners," Lokren commented as he joined in on the excitement. The heavier man managed to pin down and serve several blows to his foe.

Ethan could not stand watching. He pushed Lokren and his men aside and then pulled the larger man back and off of the other, who now lay motionless on the ground. A puddle of blood began to roll out from beneath his battered head, to the snickering of the rest who continued in their revelry.

Ethan patted the smaller man's face and shook his chest. Nothing. He was no more. Both guards picked up the victor and held him by his neck in front of Ethan.

"My prince, what shall we do with him?" one of them asked. The combatant showed no remorse in his demeanor, angering Ethan all the more and a rage built up within him as his thoughts raced.

"He's to be trialed," Ethan snapped, frantically shifting his eyes.

"I don't think that's necessary. We know how this is going to end. No need to delay it," Lokren stated with clear conviction. He approached the man, who now stood with Ethan with his hands bound behind him, and quickly pulled out a dagger before thrusting it into him just below the chin.

The man squirmed, unable to speak. He shook for a short moment before falling still and stiff. The guards quickly threw his body to the side of the road and dusted off their hands.

"That should solve it, Prince Ethan," one of the armed men said, adjusting his weapon and armor.

"We have a gathering to get to," Lokren inserted quickly, his tone not reflecting the scene which had just unfolded. Ethan's eyes were pale, as though the life had been drained from them.

"How could you? That man should have been trialed," Ethan snapped, halting Lokren as he began to move ahead.

"He was always going to die. We just saved everyone involved a bit of time. You saw it. I saw it. Justice served. No one will care how. No one will mourn his loss."

"He's right, Master Ethan," one of the guards jumped in, patting Ethan on the back. "We need to keep moving.

It's not safe to stay in this place."

~

"You should've seen this man," Lokren beamed, holding Ethan and Iza by their shoulders as he intruded on their conversation. "I'm sure he's never shown you that side of him," he continued, taking a gulp of wine. Iza blushed as she pushed back her hair. She had a lean figure with a long neck and long fingers. Ethan, uneasy, broke away from Lokren's embrace.

Iza's family estate was carved out in a tall hill in the center of Horos. Windows and doors had been carefully placed into the hillside to provide the necessary light and access to the outside. To an observer, the house was not clearly visible unless the lights were on.

Iza had organized her gathering in an underground hall illuminated by the vibrant glow of hundreds of candles precariously placed on the room's many chandeliers. They emanated a strong yellow light that fell on the entire crowd as they drank and conversed deep into the night. At least fifty people had gathered, and Ethan recognized only a number of faces. All the guests, however, were the offspring of wealthy officials and the merchant class of Horos. Ethan lost interest in mingling with them following the events earlier in the day.

Ethan had recently built a liking for Iza, though. He knew she was different. Her warm smile and welcoming eyes protruded kindness and understanding, the kind he rarely saw in his usual circles. She had to be different.

"Were they scary, big, and armed?" Iza asked, her eyes glistening at Ethan, who did not enjoy the question.

"A bit of a moral debate transpired. I won't lie," Lokren intruded, eager to share the story's details from his point of view.

"You can't tell me that his life meant anything to you. Father always said, and he's right, that everyone has a role, and the purpose of men like him is to serve *us*. I see no reason to debate the fates of such men," Iza commented.

"Exactly what I said. Prince Ethan here needs to see the grey when he makes emperor," Lokren said, speaking in a matter-of-fact tone.

"And when will that be?" Iza asked, clearly excited. Ethan was caught off guard by such a direct question and took a moment to respond.

"You don't care that someone just died for no reason?" he asked as Iza's smile disappeared.

"Honestly, no. Why should I and why should you?" she uttered with assuredness. Ethan had no answer. "All I want now is to have fun, not worry about others. Are you with me?" she said as she held out her hand, Ethan staring at it as a mixture of excitement, disgust, and empathy overcame him.

Nine

"Row men! Row!" A man cried with the full strength of his chest as the sea's salty water splashed into Ozwald's eyes. He held a massive wooden oar in his fists. His hands looked larger — more powerful, and they ached in the knuckles as though he had been rowing for a whole week. He sat on the side of a large vessel struggling through every breaking wave as it traversed a harrowing storm. He saw waves peaking at heights three times that of his humble home in the Haefe. All around him, men worked tirelessly against the rage of the winds and water. Ozwald rowed in unison with them as though his muscles knew every movement. And, like the rest of the crew, he wore a thick leather vest over his shoulders, delicately embroidered with the sigil of a single sword. The wooden hull crashed again and again into the waves.

"Row men! Row!" The same voice cried out again.

Suddenly, lightning struck across the dark clouds of

the night. His heart raced at the sight of another incoming wall of water.

"Row men! Row! We need to get to the top!" The man cried once more, this time the wind muffling his strong voice.

The ship sailed up as everyone, including Ozwald, continued to row with all their might. The wooden frame creaked as the gusts tightened and rolled in faster. Ozwald continued to row even as the boat almost tipped back in its ascent.

"Row men! Row!" The captain repeated.

One of the sailors from the other side fell from his post down back into the dark depths below, disappearing in an instant.

"Man overboard!" A voice behind him shouted.

"Keep rowing men, or it'll be us as well!" the captain screamed.

Scanning the vessel through flashes of light for the voice, his eyes found a frail old man with long grey hair and a golden crown fixed tightly upon his head. He wore heavy armor over his whole body, plated with silver and ornamented with gold patterning. He made no apparent move as he belted his commands and appeared as if he himself was a part of the ship, conjoined by years of arduous seafaring.

"We're almost there, men! Row!" He continued.

Ozwald held his breath as the ship stalled in its place just at the top of the wave. It made it. However, Ozwald was oblivious to what would happen next. After a mere second or two, the bow began to tip forward, picking up speed as the vessel coursed down the slope.

"Brace yourselves!"

Thud. Splash.

Ozwald tucked his head away as the ship crashed back into the sea.

"What did I tell you, men," the captain shrieked, his voice clearly audible over the calm waters ahead. Ozwald relaxed for a moment and took a deep breath, turning his head to speak with the man behind him.

"Where are we?"

The man did not answer nor look up. Instead, he continued to row in unison with the others.

"Sir, where are we?" Ozwald asked again, this time shouting. No response.

He tapped the back of the man in front of him, but he did not move either. Ozwald stood up, widened his stance as the ship swayed, and made his way forward to the captain, the sea spraying water across his face. He brushed away the water from his chin and brow and squeezed his hair back. No one noticed him or looked at him. As he approached the bow of the ship, though, his heart raced more while he struggled to stand his ground with each sudden rock and tilt of the ship.

Once at the bow of the ship, Ozwald extended his hand to touch the old man's shoulders. However, before he could reach him, the captain turned around and fixated his menacing gaze on Ozwald, who immediately flinched backward.

"This ship isn't going to move itself. Pick up your oar and row! Row!" The old man growled. "Row! Row!" He continued to shout, pushing Ozwald backward with the palm of his hand with great power, forcing him to fall backward.

Ozwald, however, felt time slow down, suddenly

finding himself frozen in midair and horizontal. He looked around and saw that the world around him froze as well. Droplets of water hung in the air between himself and everything else. He glanced toward the frail old man who stood stuck in time, his piercing gaze still fixated on Ozwald.

Then, without signal or warning, the world quickly picked up in pace.

Thud. A sharp pain shot up from his lower back to his head as he collapsed into the deck. He closed his eyes in pain and grabbed the back of his head, appeasing it from the impact.

"Get up! Get up!" The old man shouted over the sound of crashing waves.

"Get up! Get up!" A softer voice shouted as sea water splashed into Ozwald's face while he rubbed his eyes to clear them, but to no avail.

Ten

"Ozwald, get up!" A familiar voice cried out.

He opened his eyes and stared directly into Vira's. He started to touch each part of his body and face before asking, in a pale voice.

"Where am I?" Vira held a finger to his lips before letting him speak more, her eyes fraught with worry.

"Ozy, it's me, Vira. Calm down. You've been screaming for the past half hour. I tried to wake you up earlier, but you just wouldn't. It must've been a very bad dream," she asserted, a comforting smile crossing her face.

Ozwald sat up, trying to recollect his thoughts before closing his eyes and dropping back into his makeshift bed on the brothel couch upstairs. He exhaled deeply.

"I must've scared all those men away," he confessed, rubbing his eyes and embarrassed at his behavior.

"You didn't. They left really early, even before the sun rose."

"What do you mean already left? What time is it?"

"Ozy, it's almost noon," she said.

"What?" he gulped. "I need to be back on the farm! I'm late!"

"We tried to wake you, but you just wouldn't. It was like you were in a trance," she sighed, her voice and face unusually depressed.

"What's wrong? You never look this way," Ozwald asked, his eyes filling with anxiety.

"Then I have to get going. I never sleep this late. My father will be furious," he explained, getting up quickly and looking for his things quickly forgetting Vira's mood.

"Wait Ozy, there's something else you need to know," Vira said hurriedly, her head still hanging. "The boy from the Chaden farm just came in. He says…" she gulped. "…He says there was a fire at your farm," Vira gasped, covering her mouth while Ozwald did not know how to react.

"I'm sorry Ozy," she sobbed, planting her head in her hands. She knelt near Ozwald's couch before pitching her head between Ozwald's chin and chest. Ozwald shrugged her away and got up with a jolt.

"Ozy, I'll come with you," she offered, tears falling down her face. He did not want to reply. He only shook his head while he quickly found his shoes and ran for the stairs. Each of the ladies stood at their doors, glazing at his state while Vira silently sobbed.

The stairs creaked loudly as he ran down. Lissany stood at the window downstairs, gazing outside into the wilderness with her hands folded. She glanced at Ozwald once he came in sight.

"Don't talk to me!" he uttered, his hand raised in the

air. She looked back through the window while he walked past her and out into the spring afternoon.

"I'm sorry, Ozy," a voice said from behind him. He froze in his place. "Be careful," she continued. Ozwald turned around immediately to face her.

"I told you that I did not want to stay! Look what's happened!" Ozwald cried as tears fell from his eyes. He wiped them with the back of his hand, turned, and took off in a sprint, adamant to reach back home immediately.

Eleven

Knock, Knock

"Good morning, Master Ethan," Eidlor announced, opening the door without the proper permission. Eidlor always moved with a subtle limp. He never talked about it, but Ethan knew that he had a wooden leg. The original was amputated after suffering a serious injury in his previous line of work as one of the emperor's emissaries.

"Eidlor, where are your manners? It's like order is no longer a necessity," Ethan badgered, peering out of his window, which overlooked the castle's courtyard, his back facing the door. Ethan could not sleep through the night and had been up since arriving back from Iza's gathering.

Pressed for time, Eidlor cleared his throat.

"Apologies, Master Ethan. However, your father requires your immediate audience. I wouldn't have barged in otherwise," he exhaled, his head bowed to Ethan, who nodded in acceptance.

"You go ahead. I'll follow."

Eidlor cast a curious gaze at Ethan. "Is there anything on your mind, Master Ethan?" Eidlor coughed. Ethan glanced toward Eidlor, his bulging eyes catching Eidlor's calm demeanor.

"Nothing new, Eidlor," he grunted before turning his attention back to the window.

"Ahh. That. Master Ethan, I've been with this household since long before when you were born. I can confidently say that we are what we decide to be and not what others decide or say we should be. Have I mistaken you for a man that understands that?" His conviction and wisdom clear in his words. "I'll be gone now," Eidlor declared as he closed the door behind him.

Ethan walked to his dresser and put on a shirt and vest, taking his time in the process. Once done, Ethan left his room and made his way down to his father's office on the ground floor. He remained deep in thought as he passed by the many servants and officials busy with their work at the palace. Arriving at the door, he took a deep breath, knocked lightly, and waited for a response.

"Come in."

The emperor's office was not as luxurious as the rest of the castle. It was plain and aged. Shelves were crafted from marble slabs, and he sat at a large desk covered in intricate engravings, upon which laid a few rolled up scrolls which would occupy his father's attention for the morning. The only magnificent part of the office was the view it had of the blooming gardens below. He had hung daggers on his wall, handed down across many generations. They were the only daggers, Ethan knew, to be made from Krutium steel, a rare ore last mined in Usall in the old mines of Helgaten.

Ethan quickly caught site of his father's guests, his eyes racing between them, attempting to absorb as much as they could. Dirk and Soren sat on opposite ends of the desk while his father, Emperor Rhyker, sat with his hands folded, leaning forward.

"Sit," his father instructed, pointing to the chair next to Dirk. Ethan gazed at him for a brief moment before following the instructions.

"Do you know why you're here?" Rhyker asked, his composure serious. Dirk and Soren made no show of emotion and their eyes stayed fixated on Rhyker. Ethan shook his head. "I would've expected you to have had a faint idea at least. The simple truth is that we're sailing to Azra," he growled, pointing to the front courtyard. "Finally, I might add, and we need your help."

"Eurstians don't sail to Azra, save for the occasional trade mission. But we don't mix with them easily," Ethan snapped, failing to understand the depth of the conversation.

"You see those daggers up there? Those are your legacy. Those are our legacies. If it weren't for the risk they took, the walk into the unknown, Eurst would not be the great beacon of light it is today," Rhyker sneered, pulling out his already-filled pipe. "If it weren't for that dark night, then those blood sucking Barekians and Nethens would have dried up this land already. Each one of those daggers secured our future, the future of Eurst," he continued.

Ethan was silent, unaware of what to say, his father continuing to take deep puffs from his pipe. Before Ethan could do anything, though, Rhyker leaned back, visibly relaxed at the revelation.

"The reason you are here is because you are key to all of this," he began, standing up and scanning the gardens through his window. "I think that apologies are in order. You've been left in the dark for good reason," Ryker continued in a warmer tone, a surprising shift from his stern demeanor. It was short lived, though. Rhyker quickly turned, facing his two sons and Dirk with a face that wore the weight of all his years in power. Ethan understood well that he had no choice, regardless of what his father was asking, but it would bring him closer to being put forward on the council. The council was his key to more responsibility in Eurst, and although his father's assignment could prove difficult to follow, he felt the respect he longed for in closer reach.

"What would you have me do?" Ethan asked. His father did not respond immediately, instead pausing to listen to the sound of the burning tobacco. "What are you hiding?"

"You will not be put forward on the council," Rhyker began.

"When then? Next year?" Ethan badgered. Just then, Soren cleared his throat, preparing to halt Ethan's onslaught of questions.

"You will never be put on the council," Soren replied, his voice bleak and cold. Rhyker held up his hand for him to stop speaking.

"You are to be betrothed to Princess Aelav of house Toren," he said. "Those are the terms of the agreement."

His father's words sunk heavy, the revelation stabbing deep like daggers. Ethan had felt that his family had lost interest in him, but he had never imagined that it would be this way.

"So, my place in Eurst is no more?"

"We leave in a week's time," Dirk interjected.

"We?"

"My men and I will accompany you to Baykela Bay in Uhaela. Your father and the family will follow after two months," he said sharply.

"The Fraeland has been overcome by a massive drought. There's no telling when it will move south. We need this," Soren added.

Just before Ethan could say anything, a knock on the door rang loudly, diverting everyone's attention.

"Who is it?" Rhyker growled. Without a word from the other end, the door swung open, and Eidlor appeared quickly.

"Your Highness, my sincere apologies. The battalion you asked for — it has arrived. General Shamol is waiting in the other room," Eidlor declared.

"I'll be with him shortly.".

"Very well." Eidlor bowed his head and walked out, closing the door softly behind him.

Dirk began to speak. "We'll be there with you at all times through the first phase — until the wedding, that is. We'll keep you company. You may think this is pointless, but it's for the good of Eurst, and you are key to our mission's success. It'll be an honor to sail with you," he added with conviction.

"You will see this through. Enough talk. You'll prepare yourself at once. Liaise with Dirk at all times," Rhyker added, tapping his finger on the table to attract everyone's focus.

"You're abandoning me," Ethan snapped.

"You are departing to live in Azra to save Eurst. The

ends justify the means," Rhyker scolded, standing up abruptly. "I have matters to attend to with Soren and Dirk. We will speak again later."

Ethan, knowing that there was no changing his father's decision, rushed outside of the office, slamming the door behind him. A dark rage pulsed through his body as he stood with his back against the now-closed door.

No one had been waiting in the hall save for General Shamol, who stood immediately at his sight. "My prince," he saluted.

"I bid you good fortune on your mission."

"My life is forfeited," Ethan whispered to himself, walking away with his head down.

Twelve

"You speak as though you're just discovering this. Look at those men over there. Do you know their story?" Master Shehwen probed, leaning on the railing of his balcony at the top of the Southern tower of Horos's palace. Master Shehwen, the palace's longest living scholar, had a plump belly and round features, the smell of tobacco always lingering on his tongue. His white beard was always covered with yellow stains from his constant, heavy smoking.

Ethan nodded and looked over the southern neighborhoods of Horos. It was late afternoon, and a cool, salty breeze blew up from the east. He saw people rushing around the town streets as they returned to their homes for the evening. He saw the city gates beginning to close while guards raised the drawbridges and closed the city's large wooden doors. To the east, he saw ships already at dock and a scattering of fishing boats making their way back to shore. He leaned with half his weight on the balcony rails, staring intently at the men Master Shehwen had pointed to.

"The forgotten Azrians, of course. But that's just a myth. This is just who these people are, what they've always been. The chasm was more than two thousand years ago," Ethan said.

"To you, that's what they are. You were born, and they had always existed," Shehwen began. "To them as well. They were born to their Azrian families and have accepted this fact."

"What fact would that be?" Ethan asked, shifting in his place.

"The fact that no matter what they do, they will always be who they are, devoid of liberties that many people of Eurst take for granted. They can never get out of their confinements. They can never run away or complain. They can never marry out of their community or aspire to anything more than the areas designated to them by your father. Not to mention, Azra has forgotten about them," Shehwen added. "A small and tight space north of the city. That is their destiny. Is that fair?"

"No," Ethan glanced at Shehwen uneasily.

"Of course not, but then again, you've never complained on their behalf. If you go to them, you'd see them living in overcrowded, dirty streets. There's a sense of hopelessness that hangs in the air always. And they've come to accept it. However, on the bright side, they have food and the right to live. Your father sees to it that they are aided in this regard — as did your ancestors. You don't complain because they have accepted what they are. They don't complain because, at the brink of doom, the emperor and his ancestors have provided them with that hand of life, and they accept it and do as he wills. The terms and things that people accept under torment are always minimal and basic," Shehwen continued. He looked up at Ethan, waiting for him to react and say something, but he did not. His mind instead lingered, attempting to imagine the lives of the lost Azrians.

Ethan exhaled, moved inside, and passed through the long and soft white drapes. The rich aroma of aged leather and musty paper greeted him. He sat at his seat and massaged his head. Master Shehwen entered shortly after. The shelves that lined the walls were overflowing with books, their spines creased and worn from years of handling. Papers stuck out haphazardly as if they had been tossed about by a sudden gust of wind. An ancient rug, its edges frayed and thread bare, covered the entire floor, with its intricate patterns hinting at a history of long use. The wooden furniture also showed signs of wear and tear, with countless scratches etched into its surfaces, giving it a sense of warmth and character. The smell of tobacco, a reminder of hours spent lost in thought, hung heavy in the air and clung to everything. Shehwen's desk was a chaotic jumble of scrolls and torn parchment, their scribbles and notes a reflection of his cluttered but brilliant mind.

"I'm leaving in two days. Azra bound. This may be our last meeting," Ethan sighed, taking a sip of Shehwen's famous berry juice as the Master took his seat at the desk.

"In Eurst, just like the forgotten Azrians, it is near impossible to move far from where you're born. If your father's a farmer, you're most likely to be one. If your father is a merchant, the same. Also, if a servant is lucky enough to bear a child, that child would become a servant too. You get the picture," Master Shehwen explained. "There was a poor man that I heard of from Lazzos. He grew up in the small city of Ketida. We've spoken about him before, if you remember when we spoke about the wealthy families of Azra," Shehwen continued. "He was the bastard son of one of the maids of house Walda, specifically, Queen Bethany's personal chamber servant. His mother smuggled him out of the realm of Ketida to Bograh. He had a rough upbringing, growing up without a mother. He spent his early days as a beggar, eating whenever he found food and sleeping in any shelter he could find. Survival was his aspiration. That's what life meant to him," Shehwen uttered, taking a brief pause and shifting in his chair.

"Where are you getting to, Master?" Ethan demanded.

"In Bograh, it took him a good twelve years to discover that he looked at life the wrong way. He had been used to survival when what he really wanted was life. He was fortunate enough to make friends with Jasonte, who was Lady Mia's son of house Mason. Jasonte built a friendship with him and took him in. One thing led to another, and that bastard became the owner of the largest tobacco plantation in all of Azra," Shehwen said, pausing to let his words sink in.

"All of my tobacco is from there. The best there is, if you ask me," he grinned, picking up a handful of tobacco from a nearby table for Ethan to see.

"Although, it's not all that legally sourced," he whispered, his grin mischievous.

"So, he capitalized on an opportunity. Okay. The point that you're forgetting is that I don't care about Azra. Why should I? What good has come from them? A bunch of liars and thieves," Ethan interjected. "They don't deserve our attention."

"If there is anything I've taught you, humility goes a long way. Watch your tongue, be careful who your friends are, and never forget what we have discussed here," Master Shehwen instructed slowly and solemnly. Ethan knew the end of their conversation was imminent.

"I have work to attend to, Prince Ethan, and I am sure you do as well. This is the end of our journey, although I sense we just may meet again. I hope. I bid you farewell and success in your journey, my prince. May your trip be filled with success and prosperity. Goodbye," he stood up and gave Ethan a rushed hug. Master Shehwen was not one for dramatics or goodbyes. Ethan enjoyed fooling around with him from time to time, especially as it would easily flutter him. This time, however, Master Shehwen was visibly emotional at the embrace, avoiding eye contact until they reached the door.

Staring into Ethan's eyes for one last time, he spoke slowly and clearly, "I see a great future in you, Prince Ethan. I'm sure of it," Ethan grinned as he reminisced at the door before taking off back to his chambers.

Thirteen

Aelav peeked outside her chamber doors and saw only darkness. Burning torches could be seen at either end of the stone corridor. She held her breath as she listened intently to the silence outside for any movement. She exhaled and tightened her black hood, slipping smoothly through the door. She tiptoed on the cold stone floor, continuously looking over her shoulder. The corridor had no windows, with closed doors lined up on each side. The ceiling had been built low and made of wood for the living quarters of Fallgarde castle.

It had been two weeks since her council ceremony. Her grandfather, the emperor, had ordered that she stay in Fallgarde until further instructions. He had promised to meet her. However, it had not happened yet, until she was asked for a late-night meeting. She had been given specific instructions to follow, which she did to the last detail.

She reached the end of the corridor at the lit torch,

taking off her boots before descending the wide wooden stairs. The stone walls were not properly visible and had nothing memorable on display. At the bottom of the stairs, the unlit back courtyard became visible to her. She scanned the open area, a cool breeze grazing her face while her heart raced. High walls circled the courtyard, and Aelav monitored them for movement, seeing no one on top. "Just as he said," she whispered to herself.

The back courtyard loomed before her, an expanse of green grass surrounded by dark, stone-tiled walkways. The half-moon lit sky cast an eerie glow upon the scene, illuminating the hedges that towered above her like a labyrinth. Her heart raced as she hesitated, searching for a way forward. She knew the risk she was taking, but the urgency of her meeting for orders from her grandfather pushed her forward. Suddenly, her face lit up with determination, and she crouched low, rushing across the courtyard's outer edge, jumping from shadow to shadow. Every step felt like a gamble as if she was playing a deadly game of chance. She could not shake the feeling of being watched; every sound made her jump. Aelav scanned the top of the parapet for any sign of movement, her heart pounding in her chest. The tension was almost unbearable, every second feeling like an eternity. And then, she saw it, a lone lit window, standing out from the rest. She froze, waiting for a sign, a clue, anything. But there was only silence and no movement. The weight of uncertainty bore down on her, making her feel as though she was standing on the edge of a precipice.

She looked towards the end of the courtyard, and without another moment of hesitation, she moved ahead swiftly. She continued ahead until she saw a small roof to the side of the wall, just as her instructions had mentioned, and took a seat on one of the nearby benches. She did not know what to expect and for the next almost hour, she waited. After no one showed up, she began to make her way back, frustrated at the failure.

"Why the hurry?" A voice suddenly broke the silence. Aelav froze and turned toward the source of the voice. Behind the benches, she saw an open door in the wall behind, with a subtle beam of light now visible. She would have never seen it if she had never looked at it closely. Aelav hesitated for a moment before making her way inside, closing the door behind her while the smell of old mold filled her nostrils. She walked down a narrow spiral wooden staircase, holding on tightly to the railings. Her feet made a scratching sound with every step as her eyes frantically searched the area. At the bottom of the stairs, lit torches hung across the long stone corridor in front of her. Suddenly, she caught sight of a moving shadow flickering at the end of it. Determined, she moved ahead, her head down.

She took a deep breath and ran across the dirt-covered floor.

"No need to rush. We have time, my lady," the same voice spoke quietly. Aelav stopped in her walk.

"Are you going to keep playing games, or are you going to show yourself," she badgered, resting her hands on her hips and looking around condescendingly. "I don't play games," she added, fuming.

"You are indeed the granddaughter of Azra's emperor," the voice said maliciously just as a shadow of a man appeared from ahead of her at the end of the corridor. The man slowly approached as Aelav waited impatiently.

"When will I see the emperor? Grandfather said that I would see him soon after the ceremony, and it has been more than two weeks," she growled, the man now standing in front of her. His head and beard were shaved, save for a small patch of hair on his chin. Shorter than Aelav, his body was frail but durable and able to take a beating if necessary. The man chose not to answer, glaring at Aelav while his teeth flashed in the yellow torchlight.

"Are you going to at least give me your name?"

"Kodren, my lady."

"And what is your message? You obviously have one."

"I'm here to tell you that your grandfather will not be visiting here for a while. He's asked me to relay his commands to you. He assures you that your father agrees as well as he always does with everything that I'm about to say. He told me personally."

"Come on, say what you have to say. I'm used to receiving secondary information," she sighed.

"You are to marry the coming prince Ethan of Eurst," Kodren uttered and paused to let the idea sink in.

Aelav's eyes stopped blinking as she gasped to speak. Before she could say anything properly, Kodren cut her off.

"Before you object, just like your father said, you would hear me till the end. This marriage is to be short-lived," he spoke slowly, staring straight into her eyes while handing her four small vials. She took them and looked at their contents. "This mission is critical to Azra and your grandfather only trusts you with it," Kodren added.

"He made me wait a week for this?" She growled, eyeing Kodren's pale and cold face. He looked like a man of only business, not interested in the pleasures of life. "Why is it critical?" She questioned, curiosity building up on her face.

"You'll understand soon enough." He paused, looking down the corridor behind Aelav. "Arrangements have been made for you to be in Fallgarde for the next week before traveling to Hardn. He'll be docking at Hardn. After you meet him, you'll do the business either right before or right after the wedding," he ordered, Aelav still not believing his instructions. "Complete discretion," he added.

"I'm just to accept," she finally fumed.

"You are to do as you are told. Your choice does not exist," he snapped, his voice ringing on the walls of the corridor. "Your grandfather knows what you want, and this is how you get it. Your allegiance must lie completely with him," Kodren continued.

"What if I refuse?" she said, frustration washed across her face. "What if this is not what I want?"

"You can try to refuse," he spoke eerily, his voice filled with an eagerness for blood. Aelav began to pace in front of the man, flustered at the request.

She finally stood in her place and looked at Kodren.

"You gave me all instructions before I even accepted. You honestly thought that I wouldn't refuse," she questioned, Kodren visibly unhappy with the continuous questions.

"I don't have any more time. I will reach out to you shortly after the prince has sailed into Hardn. In the meantime, you will be working with a man called Sir Walrick. He will approach you tomorrow. You are to do as he commands. Are we clear?" Kodren instructed. Without waiting for a response, he took off up the stairs towards the courtyard, not even taking the time to bid her farewell. Aelav, still lost in her thoughts, shook her head and followed up the stairs.

"Wait. Kodren. What am I to do with Walrick?" She asked, rushing behind him as fast as she could. Kodren quickly exited the top door to the courtyard, while she followed and exited the door after him in a short while.

Outside in the open again, the cool night breeze hit her perspiring face. She could smell the same moisture filled air. However, this time a stench of dead corpses could be smelt as well. She rubbed her nose, expecting it to disappear, but it would not.

Fourteen

When Ozwald was but a boy of eight, he and his brother would often journey down past the last post marker of the farm to the brook. In the spring, the water broke free of its binds and flowed effortlessly over the rocks while wood fish feasted on the water bugs that gathered in the muck along the stream's edges. One afternoon, Ozwald went alone. As he lay in the moss, he thought to himself that he should like to return to this place after some years, when he had grown old and had seen all of Azra. By then, he knew that he would have made a name for himself, taken a bride, borne many children, and grown tired of people and their incessant bantering. And of the many sounds that rose from the town. He would rest there again in the woods of the Haefe, and it would be just as it was at that moment.

"No!" Ozwald said to himself as he saw smoke rising in the distance. He saw it as he ran along the leading road to his family's farm. At this moment, it was as though no other farm existed except theirs. After running for ten minutes, his lungs began to burn, but he did not care. All he wanted was to reach his farm as fast as possible. He needed to make sure his father, his mother, and his brother were all safe and unharmed. Nothing else could occupy his mind. Nothing else mattered.

The road to their house passed over a hill. He knew that at the top, he would be able to see everything. At the peak, he slowed down and stopped, scanning the house and farm from afar. His heart sank.

Since he had first seen the smoke, he had dreaded what he might find. He felt it. And now he could see it. Everything had been burnt down. The house had been earthed, and barely any remnants remained standing. The entire corn fields had been burnt while the livestock was piled up to the side, slaughtered, and stacked carelessly. The stench of burnt wood and crop was undistinguishable in the air. Without another instant to lose, he took off, eager to get down there as fast as possible.

Suddenly, he saw horsemen ride out of the trees from behind the barn. He ducked for cover at the edge of the nearby forest, counting five riders. He peaked down at them, but they were too far away for him to recognize any face. They lined up facing the burning house standing firm and unwavering in their positions.

Ozwald waited a short while longer before deciding it was safe to continue without being seen, taking cover behind trees as necessary. All the while he kept glancing towards the horsemen, who remained facing the opposite direction. His eyes, wide open, continued to scan the farm and house in detail as he got closer. He yearned for one glimpse of life — of anyone.

Ozwald reached the bottom of the hill directly before his now burned down house. Everything he saw had been burned and turned black. Nothing had been left with life in it. All his memories — gone in an instant, as if they were meaningless and of no value.

Ozwald gritted his teeth and wiped away teardrops. He quickly searched for anything he could use nearby him. He picked up a few rocks and a branch he knew to be useful, holding them in his hands while adjusting his standing position. He eyed the nearest horsemen and lodged his hand on the tree, preparing to leap forward in attack.

Suddenly a clicking sound emanated from ahead of him as if calling a cow or a dog to move. Ozwald froze, searching for the source of the sound, scanning the field. The five horsemen remained undisturbed, as did the rest of the now-empty field in front of him.

"Stop playing games and get out," a voice spoke, calmly and from behind Ozwald, who flinched, his eyes eagerly searching for the source. Nothing. He found a small patch of wild grass and crouched behind it, half expecting the statement not meant for him.

"Such a beautiful metaphor of life on display, I say," the voice continued. Ozwald peeked around, still unable to catch clear sight of the man with the voice.

"When the unseen cannot notice the seen. I'm over here Ozwald Stonne. Turn around," said the voice, a chill shooting up Ozwald's spine. His eyes forgot to blink, scanning the condensed array of trees behind him for any sign of movement.

"I'm here," the voice whispered directly in Ozwald's ear, blowing gently on it. He flinched to his side, catching sight of a man crouched next to him wearing a metallic mask with horns, which covered his entire face save for his green eyes, mouth, and chin. The man's eerie smirk and hypnotic eyes sent shrills down his spine.

"Come on. We've much to discuss and much to do," the man urged, signaling with his hand for Ozwald to follow. Ozwald followed orders, letting go of the rocks and branches, while his eyes fixated on the masked man and his captivating demeanor and voice.

The man led them out of the trees and into the open space that was once crop near to the farmhouse. Roughly the same height as Ozwald, he wore a red cape attached to a metallic armor plate without any sleeves to cover his muscular arms. The armor clinked as he walked, and the smell of burnt wood increased with every step Ozwald took towards his house. His memories had all burned up in flames in an instant. This man, however, absorbed his entire attention.

"I've been searching for you my entire life. Who would have thought that I would find you here of all places?" The masked man said, a certain amount of warmth emanating from his voice while staring ahead.

Just as they made it into the open space, all five horsemen rushed to encircle them as if forming a ring of protection. The hoofs of horses rushed and clattered in the air before coming to an abrupt stop once in position. The man signaled with both his hands to get the horsemen into position while he twirled in his place, observing their progress. The man began to sound off a menacing laugh, one that Ozwald had not heard before, a laugh that could suck the life out of anything. The laugh eventually absorbed Ozwald, it was contagious, and just as a grin reciprocated on his face, Ozwald covered his mouth with his hands, shaking his head from shame. This man had been fooling him, he knew.

"Where is my family?!" Ozwald spat out. The man did not respond, his back turned to him. Not willing to wait for an answer or be ignored, Ozwald saw an opening, and as his heart pounded and without any second thought, he ran the short distance between him and the masked man. "Ahh," Ozwald cried out, all his lungs contributing to the war cry while he raised his hands, ready to fight.

Just before he reached the masked man, as if timed precisely, the man turned and smacked him in his torso with the back of his hand. Ozwald fell back while flying backward, crashing into the ground holding his gut and screaming in pain.

"You disappoint me," the man uttered, his frown now visible through his mask. "I'm not your enemy — I'm your liberator. Don't shit on the helping hand. That's my advice to you, boy," he added, his voice dripping with anger for the first time.

"Where is my family?!" Ozwald demanded again, picking himself off the ground and dusting off black dust from his pants.

"My boy, they are all in good hands. I told you, I'm not your enemy."

"You're not my friend!" Ozwald spat back, ridiculing him and cutting him off. The contempt in his voice matched the disgust etched on his face. The man initially remained silent, his eyes and mouth protruding warmth and affection towards Ozwald.

"Very well," the man sighed as he raised his hand and bowed his head. "But let me say this first. This world is evil. This world is dangerous. I'm here to save you from all of that. I want you to join me in this cause. Will you do that? Will you join me and my men?" he asked, his warm smile still visible.

"Join you in what?"

"Join me in stopping deceit, greed, injustice, and every other form of evil that comes to my mind. Azra is drenched in it, and it is up to myself and my men, and hopefully yourself, to bring back the truth and goodness into this world," the masked man blurted out, his eyes sinister and his grin deceiving as he spoke eloquently, precisely and shrewdly.

"Truth? What truth? I already have my truth. You burned down my farm, and for all I know it, you killed my family. That is the truth I believe in. I see that truth."

The man raised his hand as he chuckled and coughed at the same time. "Ozwald, your truth, the truth that you so tightly hold onto, has been a lie, a lie since you were born. I'm here to see that you know that. I'm here to show you truth so that you may believe me," the man said. "In fact, I've come a long way to show you this truth," the man continued. He spoke with words Ozwald did not believe, however, his demeanor portrayed otherwise. A certain part of Ozwald could not but help believe and trust him. But what lie did he speak of?

"I have no time for this. Show me my family, now!" Ozwald demanded. His authoritative voice reverberated throughout the nearby forest, scaring away a small flock of birds nestled in its trees. The man, lost for words, shook his head.

"Very well. You will understand soon, I am sure," he sighed.

Ozwald heard movement from behind the trees on the other end of the farm. He glanced towards it and saw another horseman riding out. This time though, the horseman pulled onto a long rope, but Ozwald could not see the other end yet.

"Remember, Ozwald, If the truth hurts, then you know it's real," the man spoke calmly behind him. Ozwald did not turn nor attempt to respond as his vision remained fixated on the incoming horseman. Ozwald persisted in his gaze, finally spotting what he had been waiting for, filling him with joy. He could not hold himself anymore.

"They're alive!" Ozwald shouted, beginning to break free of the masked man and five horsemen. Quickly though, the horsemen repositioned and blocked his passage, holding up their long swords in his face.

His father was the first saw to hear him behind the wall of horsemen. "Ozy!" he shouted, his voice filled with pain, as the rest noticed too. They began to run together. Ozwald could see through the small gaps in front of him.

They did not make it too far, though before the horseman cracked a whip and pulled them back. Marcus faired his chance and tried to pull as much as he could to topple the rider before he was whipped as well. They all fell to the ground on top of each other, the horsemen around Ozwald breaking out into a mocking laughter at the sight.

"I'm sorry, Ozwald, but I don't think you'll care for them after you hear the real story."

"What story?" Ozwald badgered, the man clasping his shoulders from behind, which he quickly shrugged off. "Let me go! Let us go free, now," Ozwald shouted, tears falling from his eyes.

"Father, mother, Marcus, Are you alright?" Ozwald called at the top of his lungs from his position. He could see that save for their dirtied and charred clothes, they had been unscathed. "What story does he speak of?" Ozwald questioned, his voice ringing across the open field, as they wept as well.

"You see, I told you that this world is full of hatred, greed, and liars. The very fact that you call them *your family* and *father* and *mother,* disgusts me. This is not your real family. They've lied to you. You can see it in their demeanor," the man said. Ozwald studied the masked man's body and facial features, searching for the truth.

"What do you mean?" Ozwald barked, his tears not relenting, sensing an unwanted truth rushing his way coupled with rage that quickly built up inside.

"Why don't they tell you themselves?" the man postured calmly as he nodded towards them. Ozwald looked to them, speechless.

"Father?"

"It was never meant to be this way. I don't care what he says, you will always be our boy, since the day we hid you hear in the Haefe," his father began, Ozwald did not hear the rest as it became just a blur. Questions of himself and identity, for the first time rushed to his mind. "We love you," he suddenly heard Merrick end, staring deeply into Ozwald's eyes. "We always will."

Ozwald remained distant, his father's words taking

time to sink in. He could no longer feel time, nor could he hear anything.

"Ozwald," a low and familiar voice suddenly whispered, but he did not flinch this time, there was nothing to worry about anymore, he knew. "Ozwald!" The voice shouted now as he woke up from his daze.

"You see? Liars. What did I tell you?" the masked man spat as he clasped his shoulders. "Now you're wondering where this leaves us. How do we go from here you may ask?" he continued. Ozwald glared at his family with a mix of sorrow and fury.

"I take your silence as a yes. Well, join me — join us in this sacred mission. We will see to it that everyone answers to their injustice. Waiting for the Lords and Kings of Azra to carry out justice has proved just as futile as it has counterproductive. They are all a bunch of greedy thieves themselves. They, too will be dealt with. In good time," the masked man said.

Ozwald's thoughts were in a world of their own debating what parents meant. But he stopped himself abruptly, his parents, his real parents did not matter as much as the parents that brought him up did. He loved Merrick, Ivy and Marcus, and he could not lose them, not now and not like this.

Suddenly, with a new sense of purpose rushing through him, Ozwald shrugged off the man abruptly, looking directly at him. "You speak of justice and your sacred mission as if only you are upholding that. Was it justice when you burnt down this home?" Ozwald spat, pointing to the farmhouse. "These people have done nothing but love and care for me. What wrong have they done? We don't even know how they were to gain possession of me, all those years ago. Hasn't their sacrifice atoned for this lie?" he continued. He looked at his family again, pausing. "These are my parents. That's my brother, blood or no blood," Ozwald flared as he pointed in their direction. "Let them go now. Leave us be and be gone from here, now!" Ozwald stuttered as his finger shook.

No one moved and Ozwald could only hear the wind. Suddenly, all the horsemen broke out into a condescending laughter, as if they spoke with each other secretly.

"See, Sir. He's a *fix-the-boat-kind-of-guy* — never thinks about a small sacrifice for the lot," one of them said.

"Rainbow, is that you?" Ozwald said, looking closer towards the familiar voice that he heard.

"In the flesh, Sir Ozwald Stonne. Chance didn't fair so well with you yesterday now, did it? And, you had two chances! Here, you can still change your mind if you so chose, I think," Rainbow chimed in, still caught in the mocking laughter of the others until the leader of the group raised his fist for silence.

"Release us all now and leave us be!" Ozwald shouted again, this time his voice more confident.

The masked man's smirk disappeared as he exhaled and closed his eyes. "So be it."

Ozwald glanced to the horseman holding his family behind. They looked up to him and began to shout.

"No!" they cried in unison as the horse stood up on its back heels. Ozwald glared upon them in disbelief as the horse came down and knocked them over with one swift kick, his mother screaming at the top of her lungs. The horseman dismounted and Ozwald quickly rushed to their aid before being held up by the others in the party. Then, he saw the horseman unsheathe his sword and approach his fallen family on the ground.

Without any remorse or hesitation, he slitted his father's throat with one slash. Merrick fell to the ground holding his neck as blood squirted out. His mother screamed as well at the sight of his father and while attempting to break free of the horsemen. Marcus got up and used a rock in his hand to punch the horseman, who easily defended himself. These were well trained men, Ozwald saw.

"Let me go!" Ozwald cried, pushing away from the assailants. He managed to break free and ran to his family, hoping that he could aid them somehow. "Father!" he called out as Merrick raised his frail hand while lying on the floor, blood still gushing out from his neck and his mother's voice ringing throughout the air.

Ozwald needed vengeance, his blood boiled and his eyes flared as he caught sight of the horseman that slit his father's throat.

"You! Come here," he pointed, a lust for blood clear in his demeanor. However, just before he could attack, another horseman came around and rammed the hilt of his sword directly into Ozwald's face, almost dropping him subconscious, falling to the ground.

All he could remember was the sound his mother's screaming fading away. His vision quickly followed as he fell deeper into unconsciousness.

Fifteen

*S*mack.

"Ozwald Stonne. Welcome to Vareston's Keep."

The voice left a soft ring in the air. Ozwald's senses gradually returned as he began to move his limbs. He felt the waves of pain surge, well through his limbs. His hands and feet, he felt, had been tied with a thick rope, his eyes blindfolded.

"Where am I?" Ozwald demanded, mustering as much of his voice as he could while attempting to break free from his ties. The smell of mold hung thick in the air. His nose grazed the cold stone floor as small bits of sand stuck to its tip. When he ceased his writing, the silence of the space fell on him heavy.

After a short while, Ozwald heard the murmur of two men behind him, to which he rolled over, with difficulty, to face. "Fidgeting won't do you any good," a voice commented before Ozwald relented, exhaling as he lie on his back.

"At least remove my blinds," Ozwald spoke slowly from between his parched lips.

"Even if we removed it. You still wouldn't see the truth," the voice sneered. Ozwald moved his head and held for a moment as if scanning through his blinds.

"Hasn't enough been taken of me? I am already dead," Ozwald said, exhaustion clear in his voice as he heard a sinister laugh.

"A man who is willing to give up life is a man that deserves to live, wouldn't you say?"

"I'm in no mood for wisdom," Ozwald fretted.

"Boy, you take me for an assassin. I am quite the opposite. In fact, I have a proposition I'd like for you to consider. That is, in essence, why you are here. We're talking about life and freedom — of light, not the shadows by which you appear so vexed."

"I'm thirsty," Ozwald announced, relaxing his body, and surrendering his futile attempts to resist his binds. His captors took a moment to meet his request, until he heard steps rushing nearby as the door to the cell clicked open.

"Sir Ozwald, please accept my apologies for the delay." The entrant rested his foot gently on Ozwald's arm, his scent of damp sweat and pungent onion assaulting Ozwald's senses. Though the man stood straight and still, Ozwald could feel his heavy breathing all the way down to the floor, the odor of stale beer lingering heavy on his breath. Suddenly, a wooden bucket swung back and forth on a creaking metal hook.

Ozwald felt a wooden cup touch his parched lips. He began to drink as fast as he could. It tasted bitter, and it tasted wrong. After a few gulps, he spat it out with a cough.

"That's not water!"

"Took you more than half that cup to realize. Fascinating what the mind believes in its desperation. In sheer thirst, you assumed vinegar to be water," the man mocked.

"Your wisdom I see is not to trust anyone," Ozwald mumbled still spitting vinegar out of his mouth.

"Very well," the man sighed. "You'll get your water."

The wooden bucket creaked again on its metal hook. Ozwald flinched to his side, half anticipating another wooden cup filled with vinegar. However, he found himself gasping for breath just as a rush of liquid struck his face. This time though, it was not vinegar. He could taste it, and it was cold. He suddenly turned, without a second thought, and rushed to drink as much as he could off the uneven floor.

Ozwald drank until he could no longer feel the dust on the tip of his tongue. Over the sound of his desperate slurping, a slow clap began behind him as if commending him for his accomplishment.

"Where are your manners Vyshan? Why don't you help him to the chair over there."

Suddenly, Ozwald felt hands lift him up roughly, gripping him by his shoulders and shirt. Despite his attempts to stand, his efforts proved futile until the bounds that tied his feet were cut free with one swift slash of a dagger by another set of hands. After standing on his own, Ozwald was pushed into a chair.

"We're not animals, Vyshan," the voice hissed, the chair bouncing irritatingly on two of its legs as Vyshan, he could smell, violently tied his hands and feet to the chair. He turned his head away throughout, gasping for air.

"Will you look at that? Softest skin I've ever seen. A work of art, honestly," the voice spoke softly while caressing Ozwald's neck, a subtle smirk emanating from Vyshan, he could tell. Ozwald moved his face to the other side, tucking his cheek away, all the while unable to see anything through his blindfold.

"Never laugh at a guest!" The voice barked, smacking Vyshan across the face, Ozwald could hear. "You can agree or disagree, but a guest deserves the utmost respect," the voice added.

Suddenly, a hand caught the back of Ozwald's head, untying his blindfold. He blinked his eyes rapidly, trying to catch a glimpse of the figures that stood before him as his eyes took time to get used to the light. One man was of average height, while the other was tall and bulky, and Ozwald knew Vyshan to be the latter from his wide hands. Vyshan towered over everyone in the room. His massive figure commanded attention. His forehead was creased with thick, weathered skin that spoke of a lifetime of battles and challenges. His square jaw, cleanly shaved, was supported by two imposing chins, and his flat nose gave him a stern, almost inhuman look as his breathing could be easily heard. Vyshan's sleeveless vest hugged his chiseled muscles, revealing the raw strength that lay hidden below.

Ozwald found himself in a windowless room, its only light coming from a few flickering candles that were hung haphazardly on the opposite wall, casting eerie shadows on the damp, musty air. The ceiling was made of long wooden logs, their surfaces dotted with wet, moldy spikes that protruded menacingly into the room. The walls were made of rough, uneven stones, held together by crumbling, uneven mortar that had been chipped away by the ravages of time. From the corner of his eye, Ozwald caught sight of a small, thick wooden door that was slightly ajar, revealing a corridor, lit by a slightly brighter light. Ozwald knew that the room had served as a dismal dwelling for countless prisoners who had endured unbearable hardships and suffering within its walls.

"Welcome to our humble keep," the voice suddenly spoke as Ozwald caught sight of a pair of green eyes. He knew these eyes very well and would never forget them until his last breath. This man exuded an air of dangerous intelligence. He stood with one hand nonchalantly anchored to his hip, staring aggressively in Ozwald's direction. His long, straight hair was carefully tied back in a perfect knot, shining in the meager light in the room. His nose was pointed and tilted downwards while his piercing eyes glinted with a fierce determination, leaving Ozwald uneasy. This man was warm and personable, but there was a dangerous edge to him that Ozwald could not quite put his finger on. He wore a long, plain coat that hung perfectly straight, without a single crease to mar its surface, and a white shirt beneath that contrasted starkly with the dark fabric, his sleeves expertly rolled up. Ozwald knew that this man was not to be trifled with.

"Who are you?" Ozwald demanded, violently wrestling to move in his chair, his ties making it difficult to get up. "I would've at least expected more of a man after witnessing this entire show of strength," he continued, halting his attempt to break free, frustrated with his situation.

"Sir Kraegan is my name," the man said, his face neutral, despite the insult, as he stared deep into Ozwald's eyes, making him feel uneasy.

"Why am I here?" Ozwald demanded, this time his voice low and looking away. He saw Kraegan's shadow in the flickering candlelight, standing next to him. He felt his smirk without seeing it but chose to look away.

"Will you look at that, Vyshan? You take care of someone, and all they want to do is shit over you and your generosity," Kraegan began, visibly impatient, as if he would snap any instant like a viper catching its prey. Ozwald opened his mouth, ready to speak, before Kraegan placed a finger on his lips to stop him.

"I lead the discussion," he said, pulling up another chair, facing Ozwald directly, and exhaling as he adjusted his seat. "You upset me. My patience, regrettably, has grown rather short these years," Kraegan continued. "I'm afraid, Vyshan is going to have to engrain it in your head." Vyshan came back into sight, towering over Ozwald and flexing his arm muscles. Without any warning, he saw from the small corner of his eye, Vyshan's swinging arm moving with great speed just as he punched him center in the stomach. Ozwald gasped for air as pain shot up his stomach while groaning in pain.

"Are we clear, Ozwald? Rules are essential, I'm afraid," Kraegan said, pulling out a pipe from his pocket and lighting it from a nearby candle with a wooden flick, filling the room with thick smoke. Ozwald blinked a few times to clear his vision as Kraegan sat back on his chair.

"Eighteen years we've been looking for you," Kraegan said, his voice sharp. He continued smoking his pipe silently, with decreasing intervals between each puff. "You know how many babies were born that year?" Kraegan fumed.

"You know how many we had to track down."

"A lot," Vyshan said, standing behind Kraegan. Just as Ozwald's gaze shifted to him, Kraegan swung his hand and slapped him across his chest, with visible force. Vyshan squirmed for a moment without flinching.

"Apologies for his intrusion. That is not a representation of our manners here," Kraegan exhaled. "As you heard. A lot of babies," he stressed. "And we've monitored them all. You, my dear Ozwald, are the one, though. I'm sure of it," Kraegan continued.

"What's so special about me?" Ozwald heaved. A small smirk appeared across Kraegan's face as he continued to puff more intensely.

"You wield power more than you can imagine."

"If I had any type of power, I'd break free and see to it that you and that Vyshan over there don't leave this room alive. If I had power, none of this would have happened." Kraegan raised his hand, his smirk still visible.

"Not that power, but power to save our lands. To save Eurst and Azra from eternal damnation," Kraegan began. "There are those that, if they knew about your existence and what you represent, would kill you without hesitation. I. We. We are here to save you," he added, truthfulness clear in his voice.

For a moment, only Kraegan's smoking made any sound before Ozwald spoke. "You lot are mad. Death does not seem so bad at this point," he mocked, spitting in Kraegan's face.

"Why do you make this so difficult?" Kraegan exhaled, sounding a clicking sound with his mouth, Ozwald could see. Without hesitation or any warning, Vyshan punched Ozwald in the stomach followed by a hard slap across his face. Ozwald spat blood after the impact, his body unaccustomed to abuse.

"There's a story I'd like you to hear," Kraegan beamed, shifting in his chair, his voice audibly excited. "There was this young little boy about half your age whose parents were farmers. He wasn't on good terms with them as he wanted to play while they needed him to start helping on the farm," Kraegan began.

"He knew that the day would come when he would have to play less and work more. One day, he and his younger brothers and sisters were playing in the field. Sadly, he fell and broke his leg," Kraegan paused and took a deep inhale of his pipe, smiling.

"The child, naturally petrified, screamed and cried. *Please help me. What do I do*? He shouted. The natural course of action would have been to call for his parents to take care of him. His brothers and sisters said that rightly so. But what did he tell them you think? *I can't go to them, this will be the end of my time of playing once they find out. I don't want to work* the boy cried. His siblings were lost for words. No matter how much they tried, he continued to refuse their advice. He eventually disturbed them to the point that they left him there to make his own way back to the farmhouse. He convinced them that he would hide out until his foot was better. A crazy idea, to be honest," Kraegan paused, looking at Ozwald while smoking his pipe.

"Do you know what happened to that little boy when they came back with their father just half an hour later to help him home?" Kraegan continued with an inhale of his pipe. He nodded to Ozwald and waited for him to respond.

"Found him in the same place where they had left

him?" Ozwald muttered, rolling his eyes.

"Dead! A bunch of bandits passed by, raped him and then stabbed him in the heart. He was found naked, and all bloodied up," Kraegan uttered, the room eerily silent save for his puffing. "He should have accepted help," Kraegan added before relaxing back in his chair.

"Poor boy. What does this have to do with me?" Ozwald hissed, looking away from Kraegan. Kraegan dusted off fallen ashes on his cloak instead of answering. "And why do you care about saving *Eurst* and *Azra*?" Ozwald mocked.

"Life. A free life is always important to fight for. Troubles only make it more worth it. *The end will always define the means*," Kraegan hissed as Vyshan pounded his chest. "And you, my Ozwald, will help ensure that it continues. How it should continue. I am here to save you to save us," Kraegan exhaled.

"What if I said no?" Ozwald spat. "I'd rather you killed me and got over with it."

"Boy! If only you understood the truth I speak, then we would have already done all the saving and spared everyone's time," Kraegan immediately shot back as tension built up in the room.

He began to clean his pipe before refilling it with tobacco from a small leather pouch he had produced. Ozwald's eyesight followed his every action while he breathed through his mucous and blood-filled nose. Vyshan lit a wooden flick for him this time and stood over as Kraegan lit up his pipe.

"You can refuse all you want. Soon you will understand. Don't fight it," Kraegan exhaled as he got up and walked to the door. "We will do this the easy way and the hard way. We'll be visiting Aurom soon. You'll see what you'll be saving. That's the easy way. You are dear to me, and you deserve the truth. But compassion also requires a bit of toughness. That is where the hard way comes in. Vyshan will show you that. Am I right?" Kraegan spoke before he quickly slipped out and closed the door behind him. Just before the door clicked to a close, Ozwald heard the same snapping sounds emanate from outside the room.

Shrills raced down his spine at that sound as Ozwald quickly caught sight of Vyshan's eyes. Vyshan locked the door from the inside and then turned back to Ozwald, his lustful grin clearly visible across his face as he cracked his knuckles and neck.

Ozwald exhaled. He did not care at this point what would transpire. The weight of the loss of his family overcame his anger and will to fight. He wanted to get out of the keep and away. But he knew that would not happen and, therefore, death would be his only freedom and his quickest freedom from his captivity. He faced Vyshan with a wide chest, not thinking of what would result nor the pain that would transpire.

"I'm going to enjoy this," Vyshan muttered as he walked towards Ozwald and ripped off his shirt. Ozwald's skin came in direct contact with the damp chilly air as Vyshan grazed his chest with the back of his warm and rough hand as Ozwald immediately flinched away.

"Get your hands off of me," Ozwald hissed, trying to topple the chair back towards the ground and away from Vyshan's reach.

Vyshan immediately caught hold of the chair while picking up an object from the nearby corner. Ozwald tried to catch a glimpse; however, he failed as Vyshan came into view and began to caress Ozwald's chest, hiding that object behind his back. Without any prior notice, Vyshan took a few steps back and cocked his hand high, holding a flexible whip in his hand. He whipped Ozwald across his bare chest three times as he groaned in pain while red marks quickly turned into blood.

Ozwald's heart was heavy with grief, and his mind was consumed by the memories when his world shattered into a million pieces. The pain of losing his beloved parents was still fresh and raw, gnawing at his every thought. As Vyshan's whip struck his chest, he could feel the sting of the leather cutting through his flesh. It was as if the physical pain reflected the agony he felt inside.

Despite the excruciating pain, Ozwald did not plead for mercy. He knew that it was pointless and that he had already lost everything that mattered to him. Instead, he allowed himself to surrender to the brutal punishment, accepting his fate with a strange sense of resignation. In a way, the pain provided a temporary respite from the crushing sadness that had already consumed him.

At that moment, Ozwald realized that he was ready to face death. If it meant reuniting with his parents and escaping the unbearable pain of his current existence, then so be it. He had nothing left to live for, and the thought of an end to his suffering was almost a relief. He was at peace with the idea of his mortality, and even welcomed it as a long-awaited release from his earthly torment.

Ozwald's head eventually started to bobble on his chest as he began to lose consciousness. He felt Vyshan catch hold of his head, barely seeing him through the slit of his eyes.

Vyshan breathed heavily down on Ozwald's neck, his sweat dripping on his face and bare chest. Suddenly, Vyshan struck him across his face with the back of his hand with such force that he slammed into the ground backward while the chair was still tied to him.

Vyshan quickly dropped to the ground and began to untie him before putting out all the candles save for one short one. Making his way out of the room with no attempt to check Ozwald's vitals.

"Enjoy that light for a bit while you can. You won't see much of it for at least a fortnight, maybe even more," he sneered as the door slammed shut behind him.

Ozwald saw blood make its way along the grooves of the uneven and interlinked stones as green moss mixed with white and then mixed with red blood. His thoughts started to race as everything went black, and he dozed off.

Sixteen

Ozwald was suffering from excruciating pain as he sat huddled in the corner of the dark, damp dungeons of Vareston Keep. His wounds were a constant reminder of the passing of time, at least three weeks by his estimations since he had been first imprisoned. The pain that throbbed relentlessly in his chest was so intense that it made it difficult for him to move or even breathe without feeling immense agony. In an attempt to stem the bleeding, he resorted to using his shirt to tighten different portions of his chest, applying pressure to the areas where he felt the wounds deepest.

The physical pain, however, paled in comparison to the shadows that danced in his mind. Ozwald had been broken, consumed by grief and regret. He tried to occupy himself by reminiscing about the dreams he had shared with his brother of a life of adventure and joy. However, memories of his family brought pain and sorrow more than they did anything else. He blamed himself for their untimely deaths, convinced by his own remorse that he had been the cause of their demise. The burden of guilt and loss weighed heavily on him, nearly draining him of all his remaining hope and will to live.

Desperate for release from the agony of his own existence, Ozwald silently longed for death to claim him. Nothing else made sense to him. To die, though, he knew he would need to entice Vyshan, Kraegan, or someone else to do so. He could not bear to take his own life. He had not been raised like that.

In a futile attempt to attract attention, Ozwald started to bang on the thick door with all his strength, calling out for help, but no one came. The silence of his captors was deafening, making him feel invisible and insignificant. Eventually, he gave up, resigning himself to his fate as he sat motionless in his corner, devoid of thought or feeling.

Ozwald began to speak with the door as if it were a real person intending to inflict pain on him. He cursed it and even spat at it in disgust as retribution for what it had done to him. The only solace he found in his dreary existence were the soft indistinguishable footsteps and meager food rations that periodically slipped through the small opening at the bottom of that door. It was the only thing that kept him alive, barely sustaining him until his next meal.

~

Ozwald flinched at the sound of footsteps coming down the corridor outside. They were different, heavier than what he had become accustomed to. He stood up and dashed to the door, pressing his back to the wall beside it. The pain no longer mattered to him as his senses became clouded with the possibility of something new, something different. His heart raced faster with every approaching footstep.

The sound abruptly ceased in front of the door, and Ozwald peered down to study the shadows flickering in the thick steam of light from outside. A shrill noise of fiddling metal keys tore through the silence, slicing the air like a knife. Ozwald's heart leaped with hope as he awaited the creak of the door. His plan was to pounce on whoever entered and fight until he could no more until his body could not keep itself going. Nothing else mattered to him now, he had no reason to escape from the keep. His hands quivered with anticipation as he pressed them against the cold, unforgiving wall, waiting for his moment of reckoning. He waited for the door to open as his heart throbbed in his neck.

Suddenly, a small latch at the bottom of the door unfastened, a sound he knew well from the sliding of the many metallic trays that delivered his sustenance. Then, it closed again almost as abruptly as it had opened. A sense of betrayal overcame him as he gently kicked the tray to gauge the amount of food he'd been brought.

Ozwald spat on the door and cursed it under his breath as he picked up the tray and took it back to his corner. He devoured it in an instant, leaving not a crumb, for it was not much anyways.

"I'm sorry," he whispered repeatedly to himself, hoping the mantra would somehow help atone for his guilt. He repeated the words with his head resting in between his knees, rocking back and forth.

A while later, he finally lifted his head, this time at the sound of new footsteps approaching from outside. He knew it was unusual and did not want to get his hopes up, but he was not going to waste his chance. He quickly stood up and once more, pressed his back against the wall next to the door, waiting. As Ozwald strained his ears, the footsteps grew louder, each one falling like a hammer on his already frayed nerves. These were different, he could tell. Lighter, more hesitant. Whoever was approaching was not like the others. The sound of each step seemed to echo through the room, reverberating off the walls like a warning.

He held his breath, the anticipation building as the footsteps grew closer and closer. Shadows flickered across the visible door silhouette, teasing him Ozwald's heart pounded in his chest, each beat ascending like a drumroll heralding the arrival of his visitor.

Suddenly, the door creaked open, flooding the room with a blinding light. Ozwald squinted, shielding his eyes as he waited for the figure to step through the threshold, but there was no warning, no creaking floorboards or rustling armor, just a sharp intake of breath as the door swung open, revealing the slim silhouette of a stranger entering from the other side.

"Where are you, bastard?" The figure whispered. Ozwald recognized the voice. He remained pressed to the wall, his hands still shading his eyes. "Come on, Ozy!" The voice whispered again.

"Marcus?" Ozwald stuttered. "How did..."

"Let's go. We need to leave. We have maybe minutes before they realize I've escaped!" Marcus explained frantically, finding his brother in the darkness. Ozwald remained motionless, though, before Marcus caught him and dragged him away by his arm.

"Can you hold your own?" Marcus asked, tapping Ozwald on his cheeks. Ozwald jolted and nodded back his answer. "That's good for me. Let's go," he continued as he led the way out of the room.

Just as Ozwald passed by the door, he paused to take it in one last time. He could see its brown color properly from the outside. Without hesitation, he spat at the door, cursing its existence with a subtle whisper only he could hear. He pointed his finger at it as Marcus shot a quizzical look back at him.

"She cheated me," Ozwald muttered as both brothers rushed down the long, eerie corridor.

Seventeen

Marcus and Ozwald, shaking from adrenaline, scampered out of the depths of Vareston Keep's dungeons and scurried upwards in search of an exit. Every flicker of a shadow and creak of a door set them on edge, and they treaded lightly, eyes and ears peeled for any sign of danger. They advanced cautiously, peering around every corner, scanning every shadow, and ensuring the coast was clear before moving forward. Their adrenaline-fueled bodies propelled them up three levels with lightning speed to finally reach the ground floor.

"Stay quiet!" Marcus whispered. Huddled together in a dark corner of the open courtyard, the two boys strained their eyes to assess the vast area before them. It was unlike anything they had ever seen, larger and wider than any part of the modest dwellings of the Haefe. Despite the darkness, torches had been hung on every column, casting a flickering light that illuminated every detail, and the open space had been surrounded by two more towering floors above. Ozwald gasped for breath at the sheer grandiosity of the structure. Each level above seemed like an entire town unto itself.

Still, the scale and majesty of the keep were a stark reminder of the danger that lurked within its walls. Despite the light that bathed the courtyard, the surrounding darkness seemed to press in on them, filling the air with an almost tangible sense of fear and apprehension. Both boys huddled closer together, seeking comfort in each other's presence; they knew that they would soon face danger.

"We're going to have to fight an entire realm to get out of here," Ozwald whispered, Marcus pressing on his hand to stop him from speaking more. They hid behind a stack of beer barrels and wheat and barley sacks, Ozwald could tell while scanning the area ahead of them.

"This is a lot of grain for a small estate," Ozwald whispered as he patted one of them, releasing a small wind of dust.

"There's more downstairs," Marcus whispered back, still peering carefully across the courtyard.

"Where do you think we are?" Ozwald continued before Marcus pressed his fingers to his lips.

Ozwald getting the hint, went silent before scanning the area. However, no one was in sight. He wanted to move and would have, but Marcus held him back in diligent protest.

"I can't see anything from here," Ozwald sighed as he looked over toward his brother.

"I can. How about you let me think for a moment, and we'll get out of here?" Marcus sneered.

"Fine, you decide," Ozwald relented.

Ozwald squinted his eyes at the sight of two men at

the top of the roof standing guard. He pressed Marcus to look, who quickly jerked his head up toward the watchmen.

"Wherever we go, they can hit us with those damn arrows," Marcus cursed, returning to his original observation areas. "We'll deal with them when we have to. Otherwise, we're never getting out of here," he added, exhaling.

Ozwald, unperturbed, followed the guard's movements until they disappeared past the boys' line of sight. Merrick had always taught them to be weary of mercenaries, especially when they passed by the Haefe; those who fight without cause are the most heartless in their violence, the least compassionate in their justice. Private mercenaries, he said, create turmoil at the beckon of the highest bidder. They know no master but the most sinister of masters: gold.

Suddenly, Marcus nudged Ozwald forward as both boys moved across the courtyard and ducked under cover of another large stack of barrels. The lid of one of them had been slightly open, and Ozwald peeked inside. His eyes lingered on the mysterious substance in his hand, his curiosity evident in his expression as he held his hand out to show Marcus.

"It's not food," he said as Ozwald dusted the substance back inside.

From their new position, Ozwald's face washed with anxiety. The main gate to the courtyard towered before them, a massive structure of black iron bars. Jagged spikes protruded from each bar, a menacing deterrent to anyone foolish enough to approach without permission. The gate rose two stories high, stretching all the way to the roof. Its grandiose size only added to its overwhelmingly foreboding nature. Ozwald's heart leaped at the sight of it, but Marcus pointed him to look toward the much smaller gate embedded in the wall beside the main entrance.

"That's our destination," Marcus said, excitement and hopefulness clear in his voice. Ozwald submitted himself to the lead of his brother for the escape.

After a short while, Marcus nudged as both boys began to run along the edge of the courtyard toward the main gate. They stopped at the side door, their backs against the wall as Marcus peered inside. No one and nothing could still be seen save for the flickering shadows from the torches. A cool breeze gusted through as both took a deep breath. Marcus began to sniff excessively, curiosity filling Ozwald's face.

"Can you smell that?"

"Smell what?"

"It's like rotting flesh," Marcus whispered, Ozwald picking up hints of the scent as well. He grimaced while nodding in agreement, worry evident on his face. However, he knew it was not the time or place to linger on a hunch.

"What's taking so long?" Ozwald asked, attempting to peek through the side door and changing the subject.

"I'll handle this. You keep a lookout for anyone coming in," Marcus commanded, pressing on Ozwald's chest.

Suddenly, both boys flinched at the loud tolling of a bell, its urgency clear as it rattled Ozwald's head and body. The sound caused his heart to race while his brother began shaking, pressing Ozwald even firmer against the wall.

The humid air was thick, with the sound of shuffling feet echoing through corridors above and below. Ozwald's eyes remained fixed ahead, unblinking and anxious, as he kept watch for the first sign of men that may locate them. Even Marcus, who began to fidget nervously with the lock on the gate behind them, could not help but glance over his shoulder in fear at the sound of approaching men.

Ozwald desperately wanted to warn his brother about the imminent danger that lurked ahead, but he was at a loss for words. What more could he say that had not already become painfully obvious to them both? The mounting tension made it clear that it was only a matter of time before the keep's inhabitants would mount their attack, and the risk of being caught — or worse, killed was a constant threat that loomed over the moment. Every second felt like an eternity as they waited for Marcus to open the lock, the sounds of their impending doom growing louder with each passing second.

"Almost done," Marcus whispered as he attempted to push the side door open.

"Whenever you're ready," Ozwald gulped as his focus erratically jumped from the courtyard to his brother, who still carefully fiddled with the door. The loud tolling bell continued.

"There!" A voice signaled from the tower opposite the boys. Ozwald caught sight of the man and turned back quickly.

"Marcus!" He began, looking around frantically.

"Where are you?" he cried, nervously surveying his surroundings.

"I'm over here," Marcus said, appearing from the shadows holding a small metal rod.

"Where were you?" Ozwald snapped.

"Not now," Marcus whispered. Ozwald held his breath, catching sight of men ascending.

"Maybe we look for another way," Ozwald stuttered,

impatient.

"No! Just a bit more," Marcus shot back, fiddling with the rod in his hand. His complete attention focused on it, while Ozwald alone watched the men filling the open-air courtyard with unrelenting nervousness.

"A bit more? We don't have a bit more!" Ozwald sneered back. Hissing through the air, an arrow struck the wooden pile in between their heads. Marcus did not flinch, even as wooden shrapnel flew out from the point of impact.

"Just a little bit more. An arrow doesn't change anything," Marcus exhaled as two more arrows struck the ground near their feet.

"There are hundreds more coming," Ozwald stuttered, the commotion beginning to build up in the courtyard. Ozwald counted at least four men, hearing much more coming. One of them carried a wooden horn strapped over his shoulder while all had drawn their weapons, standing ready to fight.

"Just a little bit longer," Marcus repeated, licking his lips and jabbing the rod with as much strength as he could muster into the lock.

Suddenly, both boys heard the sound of a deep horn wailing from behind them. Ozwald covered his ears while the sound of more scrambling men redirected his attention toward the courtyard. One by one, they stood near to each other, forming a wall to enclose the boys.

"All that noise from that small fucking thing," Marcus jabbed, turning back to focus on the lock.

Bowmen stood ready to fire from all the turrets above while those that flooded the courtyard drew their swords. Ozwald gulped, avoiding any rash movement.

Just when the last of his hope had nearly drained from him, Ozwald heard a gentle click. He turned around quickly, catching sight of the door swinging open before Marcus pulled at the back of his dirty, bloodied shirt to follow him. They ran down a short path with a ceiling low enough to force them to bow their heads. On the other end, Ozwald saw another black metal barred door and a torch hung beside it. Much to his relief, keys hung nearby on the wall and Marcus rushed to grab them.

"Only two keys," Marcus exhaled, beginning to try the first one when an arrow grazed Ozwald's shoulder and flew through the bars of the gate ahead. Ozwald immediately pressed down on his shoulder before checking to make sure it had not torn too deep into him. Glancing back to his brother, Ozwald tore another piece of his shirt and wrapped it as best he could around the wound. Marcus not breaking his calm, poured his focus back onto the door.

The guardsmen began to swarm in, one by one, the tunnel becoming ever more crowded. The leader of the assault shouted for the boys to stop, his sword held high and his voice bellowing through the narrow hall. Neither of the brothers complied while Marcus continued onto the second key while Ozwald guarded the rear as best he could.

Ozwald heard the sharp cling of metal on stone, glancing back to see his brother squirming on the floor. "Fuck," he shrieked, grabbing the torch to better illuminate the ground below.

"Lads! On your knees!" The armed man spat, beginning to push forward with the rest of the guards. They had less than a few seconds, Ozwald knew.

As the guardsman came within swinging range of

Ozwald, he caught hold of the stone wall and pivoted to kick with all his might. The guard blocked with his shield and kicked with his foot, catching Ozwald in the stomach, and pushing him back a few paces in quick retreat. Seeing another opening, he kicked the soldier dead center in his shield with enough force to topple him backward, forcing him back onto the men behind him. Creating a bit of an opening, he glanced back only to hear the ring of the metal key in the lock. Fearing it might not work in time, his heart skipped a beat. Instead, he felt his brother's hand pulling him through the night's cool breeze while quickly closing the door behind them.

"Let's go, shall we?" Marcus smirked, and both boys began to run. Men began to shout from the top of the walls as the main gate creaked slowly open. He pulled Marcus to the side just as arrows landed near their feet. The keep had been built within a forest on top of a small hill, and the boys continued to run down that hill without looking back. Marcus led the way into the forest as fast as they could, barely paying attention to the ground.

Ozwald could not link the landscape with any place he knew. The ground was soft, and with every step, they left deep prints in the moist mixture of soil, dead leaves, and fallen trunk wood.

"They'll see our footprints," Ozwald signaled.

"If we spend time covering them, they'll find us anyways," Marcus shrugged, shaking his head while pulling them ahead.

The more they continued forward, the less the forest appeared to change. Everything looked the same, while even the owls hooted at the same monotonous rhythm.

Eventually, they heard a gentle sound of rushing water near them while a colder and mistier breeze struck their faces.

"I think there's a river over there," Ozwald panted, prompting Marcus to redirect their run.

"I hear it, too," Marcus muttered. He stood calm and steadily as though their flight from the keep had not tired him at all. Ozwald, on the other hand, bent and rested on his knees while Marcus looked for a trail.

"Where do you think we are?" Ozwald enquired, looking around quickly. The forest was bathed in darkness, with only a few beams of moonlight managing to break through the leafy canopy above.

"We must be somewhere near the frosty hills. There's no other place with a running river nearby in Valya. That's if we're still in Valya," Marcus said, blinking quickly as he assessed possible paths out of the thicket.

"I think we're safe," Ozwald exhaled, still leaning on his knees.

"Safe from them, yes — from me, no," Marcus growled, staring at Ozwald with his menacing eyes.

Without prior notice, Marcus rammed Ozwald with all his might, bringing him to the ground while attempting to strangle him. Ozwald blocked his grip just as Marcus laid a barrage of punches on him. With no clear end to their squabble, both boys began to roll down the hill. Ozwald felt his brother breathing down his neck, hearing a rush of birds awaking from their slumbers in the trees above.

"They're going to know our location," Ozwald struggled to squeal, both boys continuing to roll down the hill.

"The only reason I helped you out is so that I can kill

you myself," Marcus bellowed out at the top of his lungs.

Before any one of the boys could gain a defining advantage, Ozwald felt himself flying freely. He glanced back and saw that they had fallen off a short cliff. As quickly as they had flung themselves into the air, they both slammed back into the ground and continued to roll as the sound of running water grew to a powerful rumble. Both boys shrieked in pain, turning their attention away from the fight while letting go of one another. Ozwald glanced to his brother and saw him grabbing his foot in pain.

He quickly rushed to his brother, "Let me help you," he hesitated, standing over him.

"You can't help. You'll just get me killed like. Just like you did my parents. You're just pain," Marcus spat, continuing to punch the ground in his pain.

"At least let me wrap it so that we can get out of here. There's water below, and once we're there, I can wash it and then try to straighten it for you," Ozwald sighed, searching for a way to hold his brother up.

"Leave," Marcus barked, turning away from Ozwald and beginning to slide himself in the direction of the water. Ozwald slumped his shoulders, his thoughts clouding up as he felt the exhaustion he had thus far staved off begin to set in. Trying to be of help, he looked around for something that he could use to remedy the injury. A small jolt of energy surged inside of him after spotting a sturdy branch on the forest floor. Ozwald, unwilling to leave despite his brother's insistence, sat next to Marcus as he tore up another piece of what remained of his shirt and worked to tie his foot, using the sturdy branch to straighten Marcus's leg.

"Did you know before?" Ozwald finally asked.

"They told me just a few days before what had happened," Marcus exhaled.

"I didn't mean for this…"

"Well, it happened. They should have never taken you in. I've heard of these stories before, and they never end well. They brought this doom on us," Marcus snapped, breaking away Ozwald's hands, trying to wrap his foot around the branch on his own.

Marcus held his breath as he tested the tightness of the branch around his foot. Satisfied, he looked back to Ozwald.

"Look," Marcus began before he paused for a moment.

Before he could finish, they both jumped at the sound of something approaching, turning their heads toward the noise. A snapping noise, he knew too well. Ozwald's heart began to pound with what energy it had left.

"Ozwald, how good to see you. But you've escaped. How disappointing," Kraegan grumbled, his face appearing from the shadows. "You see now how cruel the world is? Cruelty that will never go away. Don't you agree? And you, Marcus, I see that you need help. How about we let our dear Vyshan over here help you back to the Keep? He won't be cruel, I promise. He'll take care of you immediately, that I can guarantee," Kraegan continued as Vyshan emerged beside him, smirking, and cracking his neck.

Ozwald searched quickly around him for anything to use in the ensuing fight he knew was imminent, spurring Kraegan to sigh.

"I am here to protect you. Out there is death. That's all the world would want to bring you if others knew who you were and what you are capable of," Kraegan exhaled.

Ozwald picked up his brother from the ground while

Marcus held on tightly, without objection and clenching his teeth. Ozwald turned around sharply behind him and toward the river below. "That's high," he whispered to Marcus. "We'll take the side path over there. I can carry you," Marcus nodded calmly.

"On my signal then," Marcus whispered.

They glanced back as both Kraegan and Vyshan slowly approached.

"Marcus, did Ozwald get a chance to tell you about the story of the little boy, by any chance?" Kraegan smirked before Marcus broke out in a menacing laugh of his own, a laugh Ozwald had never heard from him before.

"So, you fancy little boys as well? Didn't think that as your taste," Marcus spat.

"Frankly, there are many things you don't know about me, boy. But I confess that I do enjoy an occasional dab in something new — from time to time, of course," Kraegan smiled, looking to Vyshan and raising his fist for them both to hold their positions.

Snap. Snap. Kraegan suddenly sounded with his mouth. Vyshan immediately charged toward Ozwald and Marcus, his eyes bulging and his course, bare hands spread open wide.

"Now!" Marcus shouted, and just then, Ozwald began to run, only making it a few steps before Marcus pushed against him and threw the both of them from the adjacent ledge into the dark depths below. Ozwald's heart raced at the sensation of falling before plunging suddenly into the cold water of the river.

Eighteen

Ethan grasped tightly to a wet rope in the center of the ship as it sailed through turbulent waves. He had never sailed this deep nor imagined he would ever sail in such weather. The waves looked more grand than any painting he'd ever seen in the palace. It was still early afternoon, and the dark sky showed signs of settling. Dirk commanded him to remain crouched down throughout the storm to avoid falling overboard. His men rowed with long oars in synchrony with Dirk's ordering. "Just keep that fancy sword of yours safe," Dirk told him at the beginning of the voyage.

Ethan glanced at Dirk as he stood at the stern of the ship, holding tightly to its wooden frame. He shouted through the splashing seawater and gusts of wind, to synchronize the rowing. He kept their spirits up high through the entire storm, chanting and signaling with his hands.

"Row men! Row!" Dirk cried out.

Ethan had been sailing with Dirk and his men for the past five days, but they had yet to see land. As per the crew's navigator's initial estimates, they should have already arrived.

Ethan spent most of his time getting to know Dirk, initially underestimating the extent of his beliefs.

"Remember this," Dirk eyed Ethan. "If you give an Azrian just a bit of room, they'll end up stabbing you in the back when you least expected it. Each of the seven realms is worse than the other — bastards."

"Once we're in Hardn, you'll meet your bride, and your father and his court will follow two months later. That will make it official. Once you're married, we will have made our alliance. That's when the hard work begins," he added as he stared out to the sea and the horizon, taking a deep breath.

"What hard work? You'll be back in Eurst by then. It'll just be me living my life alone with my bride," Ethan shot back.

"We must maintain the routes. Otherwise, there's no purpose to all of this. And you won't be alone. I promise," Dirk stuttered as he slapped Ethan on the back and returned to his men, leaving him on his own at the stern of the ship. He heard Dirk laughing with his men at the center of the ship as they threw back glances.

Standing alone at the back of the ship felt no different than the few days leading up to his departure. No one had been available to bid him farewell. His father only shared instructions through Dirk. Ethan even searched for them in the castle, but to no avail. They had vanished, he concluded, and he did not know to where.

"Stop rowing, men!" Dirk cried from the bow of the ship. "Ethan, get below deck. Hurry!" Ethan gazed upwards and his eyes fixated on a towering wave that loomed twice as high as the castle towers of Horos. The round, menacing shape of the wave drew the water from beneath the ship, lowering it towards the sea floor. On either side, all Ethan could see was the wave advancing with relentless confidence. At its crest, white foam churned and frothed in fierce competition. Fear consumed him and hesitating before sprinting towards the bow of the ship, towards Dirk.

"It is not safe here. Get below deck now!" He shouted, pushing Ethan flat on his back. He saw Dirk laughing maniacally with the raging storm in the background. Ethan got up and caught hold of a large beam between him and Dirk.

"I'll be crushed down there. You don't care about my life," Ethan barked. The men on either side remained arched forward and still while Dirk ducked back behind the railings. Ethan heard him laugh ferociously, his apparent willingness to die clear on his face.

Suddenly, the ship began to tilt backward as it ascended the wave, moving up quickly.

"Keep her straight, Captain," Dirk shouted. Ethan glanced back. The captain was nowhere to be seen, and the wheel moved freely. Ethan caught hold of a nearby beam and began to make his way toward the wheel of the ship, his heart racing with every movement. The ship bounced on its ascent and began to slow down. They still had half the wave to ascend, and fear washed across Ethan's face.

The men on both sides of the boat began chanting in unison.

"Eurst's strongest! Eurst's guardians!"

"Maniacs!" Ethan said to himself, disgust overcoming

him as he continued his push towards the ship's wheel, which was now almost within reaching distance. He stuck out his hand as the wind gusted faster. The sound of the raging waves increased as more seawater splashed on his face. He spit water from his mouth, coughing violently. Just as he grabbed the wheel, he heard a large cracking sound from across the ship. The ship came to an immediate halt.

Just then, Ethan saw the bow of the ship break off and fall backward on its own. He watched as a spectator while his part of the ship continued to move forward until it came to a stop and began to fall backward. "This is the end," Ethan said to himself, closing his eyes, feeling nothing as he and the ship fell backward in freefall.

~

"Ethan!" shouted a voice from a distance. His heart began to race. Ethan lay on a sandy beach, the sun shining in his eyes as he spat dark sand from his mouth. The sea breeze blew across his face, filled with a cool, salty aroma. Seagulls mewed high in the sky and across the shore over of the sound of gushing waves. Ethan saw the wheel of the ship hanging in the air nearby, and two dead rowers hung on the boat from their feet, a sullen sight to gaze upon. Although pain ached throughout his entire body, he could flex every limb.

"Ethan!" The voice shouted again as he clenched his fists at the sound. He looked across the small hill he lay on but saw no movement.

"Ethan!" The voice shouted once more. He gritted his teeth this time, peering up the hill and searching for movement.. He exhaled, remaining flat on his back and closing his eyes.

"Dirk," Ethan whispered to himself. He knew he had to get moving.

Suddenly, he jolted up, running with purpose up the nearby hill towards the cluster of trees. He kept looking frantically toward the direction of the voice, searching for any movement but finding none. He underestimated his pain, and it became harder to run with every new step. The slope became steeper as the ground became drier. Dark brown sand began to change to black soil, blacker than he had ever seen in Eurst.

He finally reached the cluster of trees at the top of the hill, which turned out to be the edge of a large forest. He found a small crevice and jumped in, all the while hunting in every direction for the person who'd called his name. Nothing moved, and Ethan's hands began to shiver. After a short while, a figure appeared far away on the other end of the beach.

"We saw you from afar. Come out," the man commanded. Ethan tracked him as he continued to walk towards the ship wreckage, stopping to inspect the dead bodies before staring off at the horizon. With his back turned, Ethan got up and began to run into the forest without looking back, directing himself towards the more condensed areas. The soil became darker and the tree trunks thicker the more he ran.

Ethan suddenly stopped in his tracks. His senses were assaulted by a foul, familiar odor that made his stomach churn. He smelt a rotten stench in the air, more poignant this time than what he had smelt in Eurst. For the first time, though, he caught sight of the source of the foul odor, small patches of dead, blackened trees mixed with red dust scattered across the otherwise green landscape.

He heard someone speak suddenly from behind him, "So much red dust." He flinched, his breath short, searching frantically for the source of the voice until he made eye contact with a familiar face.

"We've been searching for you for the past two days. You must be exhausted," the man sneered, his voice full of malice. "My prince, is everything alright? You don't look too well. Let me help you down," the man continued.

"Risst, that's your name, right? I'm going to say this calmly and only once," Ethan said. Risst grinned back, visibly ready to attack.

"Whatever it is my prince, I hope it involves returning to Sir Dirk. He wouldn't be too happy. And plus, we're already late to Hardn," Risst explained, tilting his head back.

Ethan's heart throbbed through his neck as he pulled out his sword and swung it in Risst's direction, who unsheathed his sword just in time to block the attack.

"It is unwise to fight me, my Prince. My job is to help you. You think that I could be knocked down with the feeblest of swings?" Risst spat in Ethan's direction. He quickly swung his sword and managed to punch Ethan in the chest. He fell to the ground, fumbling the blade to his side. Risst smirked as he stared down at Ethan who tried to reach for his sword. Risst, seeing his movement, stepped on his hand. Ethan cried out in pain as Risst stepped and pushed down on his wrist. He towered over Ethan, his sword extended out, and dug in the ground next to Ethan's neck, who froze and stared up into Risst's eyes.

"My prince, you can't overpower me. Your actions are futile. I'm going to take you back to Dirk, and then we're going to find our way to Valya," Risst sneered.

"You're forgetting one thing, though," Ethan began, a smile forming across his face.

"What?" Risst mocked, half believing his words.

"I choose not to come back," Ethan announced confidently, pulling out a dagger with his free hand from behind his back and lunging it directly into Risst's hip.

Risst fell backward, holding the dagger, pulling it out, and releasing a steady stream of blood. Ethan, who had just enough time to maneuver, grabbed his sword and lunged it directly into Risst's undefended chest. Risst squirmed for a moment before he stopped moving completely. His still face remained glaring into Ethan's eyes as he slowly slid off his blade.

"I told you," Ethan spat, as he looked down on Risst's dead body. He did not want to return. He had made his decision.

Nineteen

Ozwald struggled against the strong current of the river, his limbs aching from the effort he put into swimming upstream. He could feel the last dregs of oxygen slipping away from his lungs, a sense of panic setting in. He pushed himself to keep moving, despite the overwhelming urge to give in and let the water take him.

As he neared the surface, he saw a glimmer of hope. He reached out with one hand, straining to feel the cool night air. But just as he was about to break through, a large floating log collided with his hand, sending a jolt of pain through his body. He saw the water turn red with his own blood, but he did not let it slow him down.

With renewed determination, Ozwald broke the surface of the water and filled his lungs with fresh air. He was alive, but he knew he was far from safe. He looked around frantically for his brother, but all he saw were the dark trees lining the riverbanks.

"Marcus!" he shouted, his voice hoarse from the cold and the strain of swimming. He spotted a large branch floating nearby and swam towards it, using it as a makeshift raft to carry him downstream.

As he drifted, he called out for his brother again and again, but there was no response. He could feel his teeth chattering from the cold, and he knew he needed to get to shore as soon as possible. The white moon provided just enough light to see the shoreline, but the forest beyond was shrouded in darkness.

"Marcus!" he shouted once more, paddling with his hands to guide the branch towards the shore. The sound of the rushing river was deafening, and the smell of damp earth filled his nostrils.

As the branch finally ground to a halt on the shore, Ozwald jumped off and began to run along the riverbank, calling for his brother. He did not care about the cold or the pain in his body. All that mattered was finding Marcus.

But as he searched, he stumbled upon a body lying on the ground, a man he did not recognize. He checked for a pulse, but there was none. He had no time to dwell on it, and pushed on, his heart racing as he spotted another motionless figure in the distance.

As he came upon the second body, he saw the torn shirt and recognized the clothes. It was Marcus, his brother, lying on his back with his eyes and mouth open. Ozwald fell to his side, tears streaming down his face as he checked for a pulse, but there was nothing.

"Marcus, please, you need to wake up," he sobbed, cradling his brother's lifeless body in his arms. "You were telling me something before Kraegan showed up. You need to finish." But there was no response, and Ozwald knew that his brother was gone forever.

Ozwald crouched over his brother, Marcus, feeling the weight of danger heavy on his chest. Kraegan and his men would be upon him soon, and he needed to hide. He bunched Marcus's shirt in his hands, desperate to revive him, but the effort proved futile. Hot tears streamed down his face as he struggled to form words.

"We must keep moving," he muttered through gritted teeth, his voice choked with emotion. "I'm sorry. Let me fix you up." He noticed a cut on the side of Marcus's head, now drenched in blood, and a dagger stabbed into his lower neck from behind. The reality of the situation hit him like a punch to the gut, and he stared at his brother in shock, memories of their childhood flooding his mind.

With a heavy sigh, Ozwald sat back on his heels, resting his head on his knees, rocking back and forth. He gently wiped away spots of blood from Marcus's face, giving him a kiss on his forehead as he continued to weep.

"Oy!" A voice cried from behind. Ozwald glanced behind him slowly and saw a short, plump man peering at him with bloodshot eyes. "Oy, can't you speak?" The man cried. Ozwald remained motionless while staring at his brother's body. The man approached slowly as Ozwald watched him from the corner of his eye.

"I have no quarrel with you," he grunted.

"But I have one with you," the man said as Ozwald heard him draw a wooden axe.

Without warning or provocation, the man let out a war cry and attacked Ozwald with his axe held up high. With one motion, he swung his axe with great force and struck the ground just behind Ozwald, missing him only by a few hairs. Ozwald flinched at the vibration of the impact and turned to the man, perhaps more so out of his need to care for his brother's body than for fear of death itself. Ozwald arose and stared at the guardsman before him.

"Stop! I don't want to fight!" Ozwald stuttered, his hands held up. The man did not back down, and Ozwald knew that he needed to act fast.

"Blood payment is needed. That man killed my brother over there," the man uttered slowly as Ozwald took notice of the motionless body behind a bush. In that fraction of a second, the man swung his axe just in front of Ozwald's head, missing by a hair.

The duel had begun, and Ozwald understood quickly that it was one to the death. Although they did not train much, Merrick had always taught both him and Marcus to fight the opponent's weaknesses in a battle and never their strength. Ozwald knew that even if the man in front of him was stronger, he was slower. They dueled with back-and-forth jabs, the man swinging his axe while Ozwald swung with a large rock that he found on the ground. The man, however, drew first blood as he managed to stab Ozwald in his hip with a small dagger. Although blood gushed out, Ozwald knew he could manage a bit more as he pulled it out and fought with it along with the rock.

Between the slow lunges of the man and Ozwald's quick punches, he found his opportunity to strike. He kicked the axe out of the man's hand and buried the rock into his skull as it cracked upon impact. Blood oozed in all directions, and the man's eyes remained wide open as he fell to the ground. Ozwald panted heavily, staring at his bloody hands.

His brother always knew what to say when he had gone through something new. Now, he had killed his first man, and that guidance was suddenly gone, adrift in a place beyond return. He dropped to the side of his brother's dead body with tears spilling from his tired eyes. Even the physical trauma he had endured seemed to fade into irrelevance. All he wanted was to lay near his brother.

"How can I go on living without you," he whispered to his brother's dead body. He could not leave Marcus there in the dark and the mud. He had to take him away to lay him to rest. Ozwald stood over his body contemplating what to do just as he recalled how Marcus always said that he hated the idea of a grave.

"Why would I want to rest in one place for eternity? I'd rather be free. In life and in death."

With clarity in his thoughts, Ozwald knew what to do. He hoisted his brother onto his trembling shoulders. Every step felt like an eternity, each one heavier than the last, as he trudged towards the riverbank with a singular purpose. He found the tree branch still docked on the river shore and rested his brother on it before tying him down with thin branches. With a deep and aching heart and tears gushing down his face, Ozwald pushed Marcus out into the water and stood at the river's banks until his brother's body floated away out of sight.

"Goodbye, Marcus."

~

Ozwald stumbled through the dark woods for some while. When he was younger, he had always looked to Marcus for guidance, for a sense of direction in a world that often didn't make sense to him. And now, he was a killer. The shame and guilt and the deep sense of hollowness all pierced through his tired delirium. He needed Marcus to offer him words of comfort, to tell him that things would be alright and that they might go home and rest and that tomorrow the sun would rise, and they would take to the field together as they had always done. But Marcus was gone. Ozwald was adrift, alone in a sea of despair to bear the oppressive weight of what he had just endured, of the crime he had just committed.

He peered down at his hands. He had forgotten to wash away the blood. As he walked, the woods seemed to close in around him. The tall trees towered above him like sentinels. All the while, the forest sang alive the sounds of the night, the rumbling of the river as it grew ever fainter behind him, and the muffled chatter of the insects and frogs. But Ozwald was deaf to it all, consumed by the turning in his mind.

He kept on walking for hours. The night never seemed to end until all energy had depleted from his body just as he stumbled upon a clearing and lowered his tired body to the floor. Above him, the stars glistened in perfect order, vast and far removed. He had escaped his captors but remained trapped in his mind, a prisoner to his own bereavement. For now, as he laid his head down at last, he would remember and grieve alone in the darkness of the night.

He would stay here, he decided, alone as his wombs overcame him and until his last breath.

~

My love
My stars and sun
Your kisses I miss
Your touch I seek
You are my bliss

Come here for me to speak
Speak to you the language of love
For eternity and blessings from the above

Ozwald heard the gentle voice of a young woman in the distance as he lay on his back while beams of sunray flashed into his eyes through the leaves above. He shifted slightly, feeling aches across his body as he instinctively touched his wounds.

He tried to close his eyes again, but the continued sound of singing rang in his ears and in his head. Despite a sincere effort to resist, the louder her singing sounded, the more he felt the urge to rise and live.

He opened his eyes and saw the woman in the distance through the trees, her voice becoming even more enchanting as he took notice. She moved about full of life and hope as if suffering had no place with her. His vision lingered on her movements as his thoughts raced through what had transpired hours or days before. He could not tell.

He remembered Marcus's unfinished words. And as if clear as the sun rising in the sky every day, he knew what had to be done. He got up, through all the pain and fatigue rummaging through his body, and took his first step towards her.

Twenty

Cailda and Ozwald sat at the entrance of her modest abode, gazing into the impenetrable woods. Outside, the sonorous crackling of a slow-burning fire permeated through the air, accompanied by the rhythmic bubbling of porridge from their morning meal. The sun hung high in the sky, and the smell of moist green leaves filled Ozwald's nostrils. The river Ozwald had come from was no longer audible. Cailda had explained that the closest was at least a half day's walk away.

"I built this hut far away from everyone and everything," she told him. "No one can find me here."

Cailda was taller than Ozwald and was fit and strong. She was meticulous with her hands. Her eyes, concealed beneath her bushy eyebrows, held long-buried enigmas and clandestine secrets. Her blonde tresses flowed loosely and untidily past her shoulders, and she usually preferred donning dense, well-fitted work clothes with rolled-up sleeves that exposed her rough, calloused hands. Her garments barely fell right down to her mud-caked boots. Ozwald could discern a series of scars scattered across her skin. She spoke with a deep, raspy voice that was filled with wisdom and knowledge, and she always preferred to speak her mind before others could get a word in, a sort of strike-first mentality.

She had set up a makeshift bed for Ozwald to rest in as she attended to his wounds while he regained his energy. Cailda had built her hut with her own hands. The high arched ceiling was covered with charred black stains, and the only furnishings it held inside were a small, creaking table, two low chairs, and a bed in the corner that puffed out a cloud of dust upon every touch. She used a frail old box for her few clothes. The smell of burnt wood and dry dust lingered in the dark interior.

"Oren was the greatest city guard. That's what I always said. He always stood up for what was right. Stubborn, yes, but he did what mattered," Cailda explained as her pale stare roamed across the suffocating forest. Ozwald stuck his head out to catch a waft of cool air. "It's what attracted me to him and what got him killed," she added, Ozwald grimacing at the lime leaf stirring in his cup of lukewarm liquid.

"What is this called again?" Ozwald eyed his cup as he raised it.

"Utam. It keeps us warm up in Usall," Cailda snapped. "Asking the same thing twice means you're not listening," she added, annoyance clear on her face. Ozwald looked the other way, trying to decipher the rough etchings on the door frame.

"What exactly happened to Oren?" Ozwald coughed

before taking a short sip of his Utam. Cailda's facial expression did not match the tone of her voice.

"Back home in Djunall, one of Lady Teressa's cousins," she began. "Lord Rinko of house Haelin's wife,"

"Yes, you know your Lords," she commented as she snuck a glance at Ozwald. "One of her cousins, that is, Ulto, never shied away from manipulating others for his own gain. What's worse is that no one dared to stop him, as if he himself was an Ancient," she continued. "That is until two men opposed him, just verbally, in the center of town. He wouldn't have it, and he murdered both right then and there with two swings of his sword — as if it were *his* right. But it wasn't. It was the duty of house Haelin. He deserved execution," she growled, tightening her grip on the cup.

"Was Oren one of those men?" Ozwald asked, a ghostly look overtaking her face before she shook her head.

"Oren was on a normal city route with a new partner who'd joined just a month before, Zol. He was from some small town on the southern coast of Shekat. Zol saw what happened and told Oren, who, as expected, didn't take it easy. *Never on my watch*, he would always say."

"And Oren ran after him and got into a fight?" Ozwald interjected, breaking the silence. Cailda raised her hand in his face.

"You know, sometimes silence is ok in a conversation. Only a woman can teach you that," she mocked, gulping her entire Utam in one go. "Zol told him, and Oren ran to Ulto, who was still at the scene of the crime, joking with his armed men. Oren demanded that all three kneel for Zol and himself to tie them up," she added, clearing her throat. "And that's where both armed men fought him, pinned him down, and drove Jitaro down his throat. That ass, Zol, just stood watching as Oren suffocated and bled through his entire face," she spat as she rubbed her eyes.

"Then why not revenge?"

"Do I look like someone who would cry and blame fate? I caught that bastard and stabbed him good in his neck in the middle of the night," Cailda shot back. Ozwald saw her drool at the memory. "But then, this is revenge. I had to run away from everyone and everything I ever knew," she added.

"Do you regret it?"

"I don't know," she began. "But I sure don't fancy this life too much anymore. It's getting to me," she mumbled, slipping back into her resting gloom.

"I'm sorry for your loss," Ozwald sighed. Cailda glanced towards him before she broke out in a condescending laugh that rang through the hut and out into the trees as if it were a strong gust of wind.

"All my time here, I've been waiting for Ozwald Stonne to soothe me for my loss. What makes you so special that someone wants to kill you? From all you've told me, you're clumsy, ungrateful, and selfish," she barked, her face flushed red. Ozwald leaned forward and waited for her to finish. "You needed Marcus to stand up for you even after everything that had been handed down to you. People would die to have what you have, and it feels like you're squandering it. Why exactly again did you come here?" she added as Ozwald found his cue.

"My parents would never want me to waste my life away. They protected me for a reason, and I want to find out why, just maybe I'll find out what I'm meant to do," he said, conviction clear in his voice.

"And why is that important?" she shot back.

"I just do. I can't think of any other reason to explain what has transpired," Ozwald exhaled as Cailda got up and walked outside to continue with her work. Revelation suddenly became apparent on her face.

"You know you said that you came from the Haefe. I know the name of every city and town across all of Azra, and I've never come across your town. I even know, for a fact, that there's a huge forest, Legends Woodland, where the Haefe is supposed to be," she said, curiosity clear on her face. "The real question is, who are you?"

~

Cailda chopped wooden logs in half while Ozwald stood by staring, avoiding eye contact. She had rolled up her sleeves as sweat glistened across her reddened face and forehead.

"I would've assumed that a boy in a brothel could resist staring," she said, focusing on her task as Ozwald quickly looked away.

"Looking is not staring," he replied. "You've been quick to make assumptions about me over the last four days. I've proven you wrong each time," he continued.

Suddenly, Cailda turned and swung her axe with great force in Ozwald's direction. He flinched backward immediately as the axe landed directly into the spot where his foot had been. His face was quickly covered with confusion and fear as he glared at Cailda with shortness of breath.

"What's wrong with you?!" he choked as he pulled out the axe and threw it into the woods. Cailda laughed maliciously as Ozwald rested his hands on his hips, breathing heavily now. The sun had crossed its midpoint, and the forest was beginning to slowly cool and darken.

"No one is just able to flinch that way without special training, and you're hiding something that, honestly, I think you may not even know," she mocked.

"You could have chopped me in half with that. Who wouldn't flinch?"

"A normal person would not have done that."

"A normal person? So, it was either I die, or you prove a point. Are you insane?! I never asked for any of this. I never asked to be killed," Ozwald barked.

He stood for a moment as his breathing calmed down and sat nearby the crackling fire. Cailda sighed, her chin touching her chest as she walked inside her hut. She made a commotion ruffling through her cluttered abode before reappearing with her hands behind her back. She sat down opposite Ozwald and handed him a metal flask.

"Here, have a sip of this. It'll calm you down a bit."Ozwald looked up for a moment. "What is it?"

"Meillon, the best way to calm the nerves," she said. Without questioning, Ozwald took a few sips before handing the flask back to her. Cailda took a large chug as well and sighed.

"When I was a kid, my mother told me the story of the lost boy. Rason, that was his name. He came from a humble family, the son of a blacksmith with no real chance of building a better life for himself, according to him, of course. At a young age, his father taught him the trade. One day, he forged a sword his father had asked for, but it was not entirely to specs, and his father wasn't happy. Rason fought with his father and ran away with nothing but a sack of clothes on his back. He could not accept being ridiculed for a life he no longer wanted. He arrived in a new city at least a week's walk away from his hometown, full of hope and ambition. Its name was Nabay, and he had never heard of it. He didn't want others to know about his past, so he came up with a new story for himself. He told everyone that he was the youngest son of a Lord and had been taken out of the family's inheritance and that he was in search of a new life away from it all," Cailda said, staring coldly into the dense forest, taking a few more sips of meillon. "It worked, they treated him differently, and he loved it. He even changed his name to Nasor. After a while, though, he fell out of favor with his new friends. His lies could only get him so far, and he found it difficult to keep up appearances. The more they got to know him, the faster they discovered his lies. Eventually, he ran away from Nabay, embarrassed and shunned by everyone," she continued.

"Where are you going with this?" Ozwald grunted, Cailda smirking and staring at him through her devious eyes.

"Impatience will get you nowhere, just like Rason," she mocked, her eyes half-opened. "He traveled to another town and did the same thing and ended up getting kicked out as well. Depression overcame him when he realized that he could not live life the way he wanted. He saw no point in living alone and decided to return home to his father. It was the only thing that made sense to him — he almost died getting there as well. He knew that if his father wasn't a blacksmith, he would have never been able to return alive. What do you think happened?" she enquired, chugging more meillon. Ozwald glanced up at her, shaking his head.

"His father rejected him as well," he said loosely.

"Not really. The entire town accepted him back. They

treated him like a Lord, as if he had always deserved it. He did not understand everyone's reaction and naturally questioned it. They told him that they had no more blacksmith and that he had returned. Naturally, he questioned his father. Do you know what they told him?" she asked.

"He died?"

"No. His father had ventured off after him shortly after he fled. No one was sure what happened to him, though. What they knew was that the return of Rason brought joy to the town since no one knew the trade, and they desperately needed one. They needed his skills. And so, Rason returned to being a blacksmith. Many years later, his father returned to the town, an old man, unrecognizable to anyone. Even Rason didn't recognize him! His father asked him to forge a sword, which Rason produced swiftly according to the few specifications that his father provided. Rason handed the sword to his father, still not knowing who he was, for inspection. Upon checking it, tears fell from his father's eyes, and he proclaimed that he had perfected his craft and that he was proud of him. His father then pulled out the sword that Rason had forged before running away and told him that he had become better than even his father. Rason took the old sword and looked at it as tears fell from his eyes, embracing his father with all his heart," Cailda said, setting the flask aside and waiting for Ozwald to speak.

"I'm no blacksmith, and I don't have a father," Ozwald said, curiosity visible on his face.

"Sometimes, you have to leave to grow and discover your truth," Cailda exhaled. "I can see that you're an honest man. I've met a lot of people in my life, and I know you're special. Oren's childhood friend is in Aurom, and he would do anything for him. I'm sure he can help. His name is Jobra. Ask for him at the Old Legend's Tavern. You should find him there and mention my name," Cailda added as she got up and made her way to the side of the house. She reappeared shortly after and cleared her throat.

"This is for you. I'm never going to use it, and it'll bring you good fortune. I'm sure," she said, holding a long-sheathed sword in both hands. He got up and looked at it, his eyes glistening at the steel as she unsheathed it and held it in front of him.

"I couldn't. This was Oren's."

"I would never give you Oren's belongings. This is that bastard's, Ulto's," she said. Ozwald hesitated before taking the sword and holding it out in front of him. "I already wrapped the hilt so no one will know who it belonged to," she said as Ozwald began to swing it slowly.

"What will you call it?" She asked, taking a few steps back.

"Stonesaver," he replied, his voice deep and confident.

"Wish you could see me now, Marcus," he whispered to himself as he continued to swing his new weapon.

Crack. Crack.

Cailda flinched, staring erratically at the forest, searching for the source of the sound. She raised her hand while Ozwald began looking around as well.

"Over there," she whispered, pointing behind a high stack of wooden logs in the other direction.

"I'm not afraid," Ozwald resisted.

"I'm sure, but they'll ask less questions if it's just me. Trust me," she insisted. Ozwald took his place and searched for a peephole to look through as the clearance around the hut became dimmer with the setting sun. The smell of freshly chopped wood filled his nostrils.

"Stay still, stay quiet."

More cracking sounds came from ahead while Cailda stood there waiting. Then, two men emerged from the wall of trees. Cailda held her stance cautiously, her hand resting on a dagger hung on her waist.

"Hello, love," one of them said. Ozwald recognized the voice and fidgeted around for a better angle.

"I was good," Cailda said, indifference clear in her voice.

"That makes two of us," the other man growled.

Suddenly, another man spoke. "Calm down. I apologize for my ill-mannered partner, Grant. But if I may, we both could have sworn that there was another with you. We're looking for a dear friend of ours. He seems to have lost his way, and we're here to find him."

Ozwald, still holding his sword, grabbed its hilt tighter. He knew these men.

"Sorry to disappoint. your friend, Grant, must have weak eyes," Cailda snapped. "There's nothing for you here. Go now, or you might regret it," she added, both men breaking out in a low, menacing laugh. Grant made a dash toward Cailda and pinned her down. She fought back, but Grant got the upper hand and pressed a dagger to her neck to make her kneel. The other man walked to her without breaking eye contact.

"What is your name?" he asked as he lowered his head to her level.

"Cailda, and may it be the last name you ever hear," Cailda spat in his face.

"That name is familiar. No, it can't be. Are you her?"

Cailda growled, failing to overpower Grant, who held firm in his grip. "Yes, crazy Cailda, the lord killer who ran away."

"What are you doing down here in Adrovia? I always thought you ran to Cerzai or somewhere more east. More suiting for you and your type, I would say," he sneered. "There wasn't a tavern from here till Shekat that didn't talk about you. I heard you slept with the man and stabbed him in the heart just before the end. Cold killer you are."

"I would watch my tongue if I were you. Never call me that again," she fumed.

"I wouldn't do anything rash if I were you either. Cailda."

Suddenly, Ozwald leaped out from behind the pile of wooden logs, "I'm here, Harold, if you want me. Leave her alone, Grant," he demanded. Both men glanced at him just as Cailda managed to force her way out of Grant's hands. She jumped to the side wielding another dagger hidden in her high boots.

"I'm going to make sure that I'm the last woman you ever touch. I'm crazy, remember?" she spat, juggling the dagger between her hands.

"It was you all along! Kraegan has been looking for you," Harold smirked as he flicked a Lirkin to Grant. "Make this easy for all of us and come silently. No need for anyone to get hurt," he continued as Ozwald stood his ground, his eyes racing across the three. After a short while, he spat at Harold's feet and looked him in the eye, Harold continuing to smirk.

Without any warning, Grant immediately attacked Cailda after unsheathing his sword. Harold did the same and attacked Ozwald. Ozwald had never wielded a real sword with the intention to kill. Merrick's training had mainly been with wooden replicas. He knew that Harold was better trained and skilled and able to hit with more power. Ozwald, though could move and swing faster, knowing that he needed to use that to his advantage. After an exchange of a few swings, Ozwald managed to disarm him before he caught Harold's eyes, seeing only rage while he jumped from side to side, ready to attack with his bare hands.

"Kraegan won't let me kill you, but how much I would like that pleasure now," Harold hissed just as he attacked again. Ozwald managed to move quickly to the side and drive his sword deep into Harold's back. He let out a loud gasp as he took his last breath and fell to the ground, motionless.

Ozwald withdrew his sword and glanced back towards Cailda. He ran to her and held her in his arms. Blood dripped from her mouth as she coughed. He saw a dagger in her stomach. He then glanced at Grant, who lay on his back with a dagger stuck in his throat.

"I still got it in me," Cailda coughed, breathing heavily. Ozwald tried to attend to her wounds, but she stopped him. "I'm beyond fixing. This is my fate," she exhaled.

"But let me help. I'm sure I can help you get better," Ozwald said, a tear forming in his eye.

"Go before more come. Your captors are well trained and organized. Go to Aurom and find Jobra," she began, coughing heavily. "I know he can help." Ozwald held her in his arms while she took out the dagger jammed in her stomach and placed it in Ozwald's hand.

"Take this. It may just save your life. Now take me inside to my bed," she growled, mustering all the energy she had left. With great resistance, Ozwald nodded and brought her inside her hut, and set her down gently on the bed. He brought her food from the boiling pot and some water. He placed long rags beside her bed and stood at the entrance of the hut.

"You won't let me help you, fine. At least now, you can take care of yourself as you did for me for as long as you can breathe. I will see you soon, Cailda of the forest." Ozwald said, a small amount of optimism built up inside of him that she may just make it.

"Who knows what will happen. Go now!" she exhaled while Ozwald bowed his head and left the hut off to Aurom.

Twenty-One

than's muscles exploded with pain, and his back ached from the weight of his worries. His lungs screamed for comfort. He didn't dare look back. The only thing that mattered was moving forward. The trees around him became taller, thicker, and greener as the stench of dead corpses faded away completely.

His eyes continuously looked for a safe place to seek shelter. For almost a full day, he'd been unable to find anything, so he kept running. But to his surprise, he caught sight of a wagon moving in the distance. He looked up and saw the sky had already grown dark. The wagon drove along a road at the bottom of the valley just beneath him. He stopped in his place and frantically looked for a way down.

"Hello!" he shouted. He waited eagerly for the wagon to stop, but instead, it picked up speed as leaves flew behind it. He hesitated, scanning two possible rocky paths to the valley below. He blinked and went right. Breathing erratically, he ran down the rock and dirt path, holding on to overgrowth to stabilize his balance. He scathed his knee on a sharp rock, crying out in pain as he saw blood on his pants and felt a sharp pain. Determined, he shrugged it off and continued. He saw a ledge below and jumped to it just as the wagon passed.

Crouched on the ground, he glanced to the wagon ahead as dead leaves flew by. He ran, forgetting all the pain while trying to control his breathing.

"Wait!" he shouted, but the wagon did not stop. Still holding onto hope, he picked up his pace. He heard shouting from behind him and feared Dirk may have finally caught up to him.

"Stop!" he shouted again.

On the wagon, he made out two young girls in cloaks at the back and a man and woman sitting in the driver's seat.

"Father, there's a man running behind us," one of them cried. The mother glanced back at the sound of her daughter and quickly nudged her husband. The father finally looked back at Ethan and brought the wagon to a halt.

Twenty-Two

Ethan sat at the end of the wooden wagon, smiling with each glance at Roven and his family. They passed through a tree covered path with barely any sunlight peering in. The air was damp and heavy with moisture. He heard the sound of birds chirping in the distance, coupled with the buzzing of nearby grasshoppers.

He had never begged for anything before until he met Roven. Roven had accepted him on board on the condition that he would throw away his sword. Initially, he refused, but they both reached to an agreement that Roven would hold on to it until Ethan arrived at his destination. "What is your name, my Lord?" Roven asked, indignation apparent on his face. Ethan cleared his throat before ripping off his Aelgan tree emblem with a single tear.

"I found this cloak. I was cold and injured," he explained hesitantly. "Lords bring nothing but misery to this world," he continued as Roven chuckled at his words.

"I did not mean to intrude — just wanted to be respectful. It's common, you know." Ethan bowed his head, mad at himself for not being more careful. "Samor. My name is Samor"

Soren used the name Samor as an alias when visiting brothels in Horos. He once told Ethan, "it would bring shame to father if my name was mixed up with all of those whores," when Ethan caught him smuggling in women early in the morning.

"I'm Roven, and this is my wife, Trayma," Roven said, nodding his head in her direction. "Hemna and Khom are my daughters," he added.

"Nice to meet you all," Ethan smiled uneasily, trying to avoid looking cold.

"What is your story, then, if you're not a Lord?" Roven snapped. Ethan was visibly rattled and hesitated for a moment. "So?" Roven probed again.

Ethan cleared his throat. "I'm from Bograh. I was on a trading journey around Azra. I'm a sailor, you see. We were sailing around Azra to Valya. And our ship fell into a terrible storm," he added, slowing his words and pausing for a moment. "No one made it except me. I don't remember what happened. I just found myself on a beach with dead bodies and a broken ship all around me. I don't even know where I am," he exhaled, his breath short.

After a short while, Roven's tense face relaxed, and a smile shot across it. "Life is precious. To help another life is sacred. Welcome aboard. Although, we are sorry for those you've lost," he said, solemnly bowing his head.

"Thank you. Not many think like you," Ethan stuttered, not expecting his request to have been accepted so quickly.

"If it doesn't start with us, then where would it?"

Ethan took a breath of fresh air as the wagon began to move, nestling into his new journey. Roven's daughters began to sing in unison, their voices rising over the sound of the creaking wheels with a majestic song of their own.

Twenty-Three

Ethan had spent two days with Roven and his family. He'd learned that he had washed ashore in Usall. They stopped only twice a day. Ethan avoided talking too much to try to evade any questions about his past. He did, however, discover that Roven had a farm back in Usall. They lost everything from the drought and dying crops. The red blight, as they called it, claimed the entire northern part of the realm.

He spent his time off the wagon hunting for them, borrowing Roven's bow and arrow, and was able to catch rabbits rather quickly. On the second day, Roven grinned when he saw Ethan coming back with three rabbits only after half an hour of setting off for his hunt.

"The bow and arrow you carry. I see it answers you well. It is yours, Samor," he said, tilting his head, sincerity apparent on his face.

"No, Roven. That is not fair. I can't take this away

from you. How will you hunt?" Ethan hesitated, placing the bow and quiver back in the wagon. Roven stopped him as they made eye contact.

"That was my brother's. He's no longer alive, and therefore I have no use for it. Plus, I have a much better one of my own here," he said, showing off his set that had been hidden behind his daughters' seat.

"Your generosity knows no bounds," Ethan said, bowing his head.

Without any request on Ethan's part, Roven eventually handed him back his sword, "My father always taught me to never come in between three things of another man's. His woman, his meal, and his sword," Roven orated, pulling out the sword from beneath his seat and handing it to Ethan. Ethan had not expected Roven to be so kind nor accepting, an unusual attitude he had never experienced. Speechless, he took it without any complaints except for two words, "Thank you."

The wagon continued its journey south through Usall, passing by hills and large craters in the ground.

"Those are the old silver mines. At least ten thousand men, I heard, worked there at one point before it went dry," Roven said, pointing with his finger. "Most of the silver that is in circulation came from here at one point," he added.

Ethan nodded, seeing a large circular pit dug in the ground below with side roads spiraling down.

"Would need at least a whole minute just to hit bottom if you threw a rock," Roven estimated, measuring with one eye and whistling.

"I've never seen something so large," Ethan said, his eyebrows raised.

On the second day, Ethan remained silent at the back of the wagon, contemplating his family and their possible disappointment. He smiled at the thought that he had messed up their plans. They would find another way for an alliance, he was sure. However, why should he be the one? They did not treat him like their own for a long time, and therefore no reason for him to care.

"Stop," Ethan heard a subtle voice shout which only he noticed. Hemna and Khom's singing, coupled with the sound of the moving wagon, were in full force, rendering it hard to hear much from outside of the wagon. He glanced toward the source and saw a person off in the distance behind them, running through the forest. "Dirk," he whispered to himself, spikes rushing across his back. He did not want to go back.

He hesitated to look back before leaning forward on the wooden wagon, struggling to keep his balance as the sisters continued to sing, attempting to reach Roven.

"Roven, I think we need to go a bit faster," he stuttered before Roven glanced back quickly.

"Enjoy the scenery. No point in tiring the horses so fast," he said over his shoulder. Ethan, avoiding a scene, sat back, his face fluttering while glancing back and catching sight of Dirk still in pursuit.

Driven by an urge to try again and not accept defeat, Ethan leaned forward again on the wagon.

"Roven, there's something I didn't tell you," Ethan said, his voice just audible while Roven bent back and nodded.

"There are those that want to do me harm," he exhaled. Roven nodded, listening intently. "I think one of them is running behind us," Ethan continued. Roven, still focused on the horses in front of him and the reigns in his hand, did not look back as anger built up on his face. He whipped the reigns hard as the horses picked up pace.

"Thank you," Ethan sighed.

He returned to his place, looking back. This time though, Dirk was out of sight. Relief overwhelmed him, cracking a subtle smile across his face. Roven kept the pace up as the sisters stopped singing. The wooden wagon bounced more as it picked up speed. The road ahead curved as the trees to the side thickened while the sky became more visible. The sound of chirping birds was lost, and Ethan could only hear the moving wagon.

Suddenly, both horses slowed down and neighed as Roven pulled on the reigns. A cloaked and hooded figure stood in the distance ahead of them, blocking the road. Ethan's heart raced trying to decipher the cloaked figure in front of them.

"Dirk?" He whispered to himself.

"Wooh. Calm down," Roven shouted, trying to bring the horses back to order. The figure ahead of them began to run towards them.

"We're going down that way," Roven pointed to a forked road up ahead.

Ethan sat at the back, helpless, his hands clasped to the side of the wooden wagon and his heart throbbing in his neck. The sisters hugged each other, remaining silent.

"Stop," the figure ahead shouted, unsheathing a sword and raising it high. Roven lashed his reigns even harder, attempting to steer the wagon towards the empty forked road and away from danger.

Hemna and Khom began to squeal from the anarchical

speed and sway of the wagon.

"We're almost clear! Hold on!" Roven shouted over his shoulder, whipping the horses to go faster.

Ethan glanced ahead, trying to get a better look of the cloaked figure, who had reached their wagon and quickly caught hold of the horses just as Roven pulled back on the reigns. The wagon came to a rushed stop and was unable to move ahead. Ethan almost fell forward had he not held on tightly to the wagon railings. The cloaked figure unhooded himself, revealing a man with a bloodied face and blood-stained clothing. Ethan saw that he moved with ease as if the blood was not his.

"I mean no harm. I am just a farmer," the man said, his hands raised up high and breathing heavily. "I'm just looking for safe passage to Aurom. Can you help me?" He demanded, leaning forward on his knees. Roven cast an uneasy glance at his wife.

"What is your name?" Roven stuttered. The man in the street hesitated.

"Merrick," he sighed, taking deep breaths. Extreme fatigue was clear on his face. "What is yours, Sir?" He added. Roven hesitated for a moment, his face staring sternly at the man in front of him before answering.

"Roven."

"I apologize for startling you, Roven, and your family, but I would very much like to join you. I mean no harm. I am at your service. It would be very helpful if you could drop me off at the nearest point to Aurom," Merrick begged.

Roven thought for a moment, making eye contact with Trayma before exhaling.

"For starters, sheath that sword and put it away," Roven

commanded. Merrick quickly complied.

"Who and what are you running away from?" Roven questioned, scanning Merrick from head to toe. Merrick's face grimaced.

"Sir. Roven, apologies, but I mean no harm. I am at your service. I only ask for safe passage," Merrick exhaled, bowing his head. "I am running towards, and not from anything," he added.

Roven took a deep breath, his eyes still fixated on Merrick. He glanced back over his shoulder and gave out instructions.

"Make some room."

Twenty-Four

Like the river flows on and on
My love for you will not subside
I need you always next to me
No living has any purpose
Without your presence
Taste has no more meaning
I need you by my side always
Like the sun and the moon
We go hand in hand
I'll love you forever

Ozwald sat at the back of Roven's wagon alongside his family and Samor. Roven's two daughters, Hemna and Khom, and wife, Trayma, sang in unison to pass the time. Ozwald found their voices meditative and relaxing, reminding him of distant memories. He reminisced about the Haefe, especially its annual summer Sonvell festival, thrown on Lord Rorik's name day. Though he never attended, the festival always fascinated him. People celebrated over the course of three evenings. Singers and stage actors came to perform from cities all across Azra. Marcus and Ozwald would sneak to the back of the festival and lie down on any fresh patch of grass they could find. They would stare up into the sky and breathe in the cool summer night breeze listening and contemplating each lyric of the melodies.

Sonvell inspired Ozwald in its art and creativity, something he saw elsewhere in the Haefe. Ideas and stories from the outside fascinated him, and he knew from the first festival that he would leave, though exactly how he had no idea. Aurom had never been at the top of his list but became his only focus as he sat at the back of Roven's wagon. He was committed, trusting in Cailda's judgment.

Over the day and a half, Ozwald rode on the wagon, he saw subtle traces of red dust in the air and eventually the light stench of rotting flesh, a new normal he was not ready for, and neither were the others. He did not know what it was until Roven explained, "Red blight, where have you been living? It's eating up everything, slowly. Why do you think we're riding south?"

They passed more than a hundred traveling parties along their journey fleeing from the North, which Ozwald came to learn was most hit by the blight, especially Usall.

Samor and Ozwald sat together at the back and continuously bumped into each other as the wooden wagon made its way across the rough terrain. Ozwald, who introduced himself as Merrick, remained in conversation with Samor for the full duration of the journey. They debated ceaselessly, and at points, the volume of their voices spilled out from the wagon and into the woods and fields they rode through. Both always tightened their hoods when the group passed by other travelers. Most travelers, he saw, carried large sacks heading directly south.

Late in the afternoon of Ozwald's first day with Roven and the group, they passed by a burning wagon with two dead bodies lying nearby. Ozwald stared at the horrific scene in astonishment, as did everyone else but Samor, who noticeably avoided it entirely, preferring to look away disgusted.

"They should hang the wrongdoers," Samor spat, his voice heavy and audible only to Ozwald.

"Sometimes, no matter how hard you try, bad things end up happening," Ozwald sighed. Samor, rather than objecting, nodded his agreement while looking away.

The sisters began to sing songs from an older time that Ozwald had barely heard about, songs that he had never heard. And probably would not hear again for a long time.

> *Ancients be, Ancients see*
> *Beware the trouble you may conceive*
> *The Ancients shall return so soon*
> *Judgement they shall make*
> *Remorse they shall forsake*
> *For all with no appeal*

Ozwald listened intently, the music and lyrics dancing in his mind and mesmerizing his thoughts. He allowed himself to relax for a short while. On their journey, they would stop every few hours when they found a good space to eat and rest. Ozwald hated these stops. They allowed Kraegan and his men to catch up. He saw that Samor hated them as well. He tried convincing Roven to keep riding for longer, but he always refused.

"Let's rest over there for a bit, we haven't eaten all day, and we're low on water," Roven declared over his shoulder as they made their way out of the densely covered road and into a rather open area. Ozwald, still on the wagon, looked around and saw small hills near them. He also heard flowing water, "There's a river over there," he commented, pointing with his finger as Roven caught his gaze.

"Great. Fill these up," Roven responded as he handed him two sheepskin flasks. "And Samor, these as well," he added, handing over another two before he helped his daughters down to unload the cooking utensils. Ozwald and Samor quickly jumped out of the wagon and ventured in the direction of the water.

"We can't keep stopping like this," Samor sighed as he kicked the ground lightly.

"Why, what are you in a hurry for?" Ozwald shot back, adjusting the sheepskins on his shoulder.

"I could ask the same of you, Sir Hopeful," Samor scorned, continuing ahead.

"Having hope that I can build a new life for myself is not wrong. I'd rather have that than live on believing that we're doomed forever," Ozwald hissed from behind. Suddenly, Samor stopped and turned, grabbing Ozwald by his shirt.

"Didn't you see the burning wagon and the two dead people? Those will always be considered as no one, just another few deaths, and no real attention would ever be cast on them. Life has no meaning. Everyone is just a pawn in another person's game," Samor groaned as both boys studied each other's eyes, looking for answers.

"I could've stayed dead, but I chose to move on. At least I'm doing something about it. What are you doing?" Ozwald badgered, holding each other's gaze a short while longer until Samor let Ozwald go, panting.

Ozwald brushed his shirt and followed Samor into a thick patch of high bushes ahead. He lost sight of Samor but continued to move inside, expecting to find him eventually, while the sound of rushing water intensified.

"Samor! Where are you?" Ozwald called, hearing no response, picking up the pace and making his way deeper inside.

"Stop your whining. I'm over here, can't survive without me now?" Samor answered. Ozwald followed the voice walking through sharp thorns and small, dead bushes in the shade of the trees before finally finding Samor standing at a small stone cliff overseeing the river below.

"Why did you walk through all of that?" Ozwald badgered, brushing away dead leaves from his clothes, his voice barely audible over the rushing sound of the river.

"I didn't. My path was clear," Samor sneered. "Come over here," he continued, pointing below towards the river to ensure Ozwald heard him.

"It's more of a lake," Ozwald noted.

"Bigger and rockier than I thought it would be," Samor added, glancing back at the way they came in from. "Let's get down quick," he instructed. Ozwald nodded and began to descend from a nearby path he found.

Suddenly, a sharp cracking sound emanated from the rock below their feet. Ozwald glanced back towards Samor, who stood crouched in his place. Ozwald slowly began to take a few steps forward, his face washed with confusion and fear.

"Give me your hand, slowly," he gasped.

"Stay away. I can do this on my own. Any step closer and the both of us will drop," Samor shrieked, signaling Ozwald off with a subtle movement of his hand. Samor waited momentarily until he felt a balance he could trust before taking small steps. Ozwald quickly stepped back, making room for Samor to jump towards.

The cracking sound in the rock emanated again, this time deeper, as if the crack in the cliff was much deeper. Ozwald's heart raced faster at the sound of the cracking noise again. He caught Samor's gaze in a moment that felt like an eternity of silence. Then, all of a sudden, the cliff broke off completely, falling straight down into the flowing river. Ozwald saw Samor's face etched with fear and heard him shouting at the top of his lungs as he began to fall. Subconsciously and without hesitation, Ozwald dove forward, sticking out his hand. Samor saw him and stretched out his arm, while Ozwald was unsure if he caught him.

After a brief moment, Ozwald's body slammed into the ground on his stomach at the edge of the still-intact cliff while pain shot up through his arm. Just as he quickly peaked over the ridge downwards, a voice shot up.

"Lift me up now," Samor shouted from below, holding on tightly to Ozwald's arm.

"I can't hold on for too long!" Samor cried, his veins clearly visible across his arm.

"I've got you. Hold on,"

Once up, both boys laid down on their backs in exhaustion as they waited for the adrenaline to subside.

"I thought I was gone," Samor exhaled.

"It wouldn't be right. Everyone deserves a chance, right? Plus, you would've done the same for me," Ozwald panted, tapping Samor's chest, who gave a subtle nod.

"Let's find another way down. I don't think our Roven is keen on waiting for us for too long," Ozwald groaned, lifting himself up and dusting his clothes off before helping Samor to stand up.

"There," Ozwald pointed at a subtly visible path to the other side of the cliff, covered in low overgrowth. Samor, without a word, tapped him on his shoulder as both boys descended quickly from the cliff down to the river. After making their way, both boys washed up quickly.

"This river flows down from the Ancient Heights. It's quite cold," Ozwald uttered to a silent Samor. They both filled up their sheepskins to the rim and quickly made their way back to the wagon.

Just as they arrived, they saw everyone in their place on the wagon, ready to go. Roven looked ahead and acted oblivious to the boys. Without waiting another moment, the wagon began to move in a rush at the lash of Roven's reigns.

"They would've already been gone if we were a few minutes late," Samor grunted over his shoulder as they raced after the wagon.

"Let's make sure that we catch up with them first before we start analyzing," Ozwald said.

"We're back," Samor quickly said, holding his water-filled sheep skins up high for Roven to see. Roven quickly pulled on the reigns and glanced toward Samor. He gave an uneasy smile as both boys got into the wagon for the next leg of the journey.

"Are you all ready?" Roven asked from ahead.

"We gave him no reason to run away," Ozwald whispered his complaint to Samor.

"Welcome to the selfishness and greed of the world. Across the entire social hierarchy," Samor mocked, disappointment clear in his voice.

"Probably because of my sword," Ozwald said.

"You mean our swords," Samor replied, revealing a hilt of daggers and a sword in his bag.

Ozwald smirked as the wagon began to pick up speed. He looked up to the sky and knew they would not set up camp until another six hours, which would be his last night before making it to Aurom.

Twenty-Five

O zwald felt a strong nudge in his gut, adjusting his seating position after being lost in his thoughts during their long journey.

"Lower your hood," Samor whispered. Ozwald quickly complied after seeing two men ahead. They had entered a part of the road entirely covered by trees. The two men ahead had already unsheathed their swords. Their faces, though, were still not visible.

"Yours or mine?" Ozwald enquired. His hood covered his bowed head to the floor of the wagon. Samor shook his head.

"I can't recognize their uniforms," Samor relented.

"Uniformed men? You never told me that," Ozwald badgered, his eyebrows raised. Samor shrugged him off.

Roven snapped his finger at Hemna and Khom to stop singing. "Girls, put your hoods on," Trayma instructed. Ozwald saw them from the edge of his eye, putting on puffy cloaks as the wagon came to a stop.

"Hello, wonderful day to be riding outside," Roven opened to the silence of the armed men. No one responded.

"Apologies, but we have a long journey ahead. We would like to be on our way," Roven added with subtle hesitation in his voice.

"We're looking for a boy about this tall, likely covered in blood. Have you seen him?" One of the men questioned, spitting on the ground afterward. Ozwald recognized the voice as Patrick.

"Why, no sirs, this is just my family here, and we have a long journey down south," Roven trembled.

"South, aye? Off to where precisely?" Patrick said.

"Bograh."

"You've certainly done well for yourself and the family. A wagon and two horses. Rainbow and I were debating, but now I can see that he was right," Patrick mocked.

"We actually have a large farm up North near Baykel Bay. But it's all gone now, after the blight," Roven stuttered.

"Aye, something new is always scary, but honestly, I view it as the beginning of something nice for all of us," Patrick said.

Roven suddenly whipped the reigns of the wagon, motioning them to move, "I've heard of you lot," he snapped. Ozwald felt the wagon move at the sound of the lashing reigns. Quickly though, it came to a halt again.

"You seem to be in a hurry. What do you think, Rainbow? Good thing I was in front to catch hold of your fine beasts as they went out of control," Patrick sneered.

"Yeah, great thing," Rainbow hissed.

"And who are the pretty faces in the back? Come on,

let's have a look," Patrick instructed, tapping on the wooden rails of the wagon with the hilt of his sword. "Come on, wakey, wakey, let's see those beautiful faces of yours. The sun is out and bright," Patrick sneered, rocking the wagon. Ozwald saw the sisters uncover their faces from the corner of his eye.

"I'm Hemna, and this is my sister Khom. We —"

"Argh, alright, you can be seated. And you two, show me your faces, now!" Patrick growled, his diminishing patience audible. Ozwald heard Rainbow whisper in Patrick's ear, followed by the sound of their rapid movement around the wagon.

"I'll handle this," Samor whispered as Ozwald clenched the hilt of his sword.

"Oy, remove those cloaks now," Patrick commanded, moving to the other end of the wagon and pulling on Ozwald's and Samor's cloaks. Uncovered, Ozwald looked up to make eye contact with Patrick and Rainbow. Before he could take any action, Samor jumped out of the wagon, carrying a shining piece of metal in his hand. Ozwald unsheathed his sword and jumped out as well. He glanced towards the family, catching sight of their bewildered and pale faces, hopelessly gazing out of their wagon at the unfolding events.

Just then, he heard a commotion behind him. Rainbow had overpowered Samor and held him from behind, pressing a dagger to his throat. Patrick faced Ozwald, dagger in hand, ready to attack. Both Patrick's and Rainbow's eyes glistened at the sight of Ozwald, drooling like hungry dogs waiting to snatch a piece of meat.

"It's him! And look at that, he has a sword now,"

Rainbow sneered, glaring menacingly at Ozwald.

"Not really doing him much good," Patrick mocked, "And who is this supposed to be?"

"Doesn't matter. He'll die as well. They always do," Rainbow said.

"Why don't you drop the pretty sword then," Patrick shouted.

Ozwald's gaze raced among all three men in front of him, catching sight of the blood falling down Samor's neck. Patrick was well-balanced and able to handle his own. Rainbow was thin but visibly fit. A fight with either would prove difficult to overcome, no matter what advantage he could muster. Ozwald attempted to speak, to say something brave but couldn't manage to find the words. Both men broke out into malicious laughter.

"Can't stand up for yourself, aye?" Rainbow smirked. "I can't believe that we're going through all of this trouble for a piece of shit like this that can't even stand up for himself," he continued. "Are you sure Kraegan is right about this one?" He continued pressing his dagger tight to Samor's throat.

"I'll ask for your opinion when I need it," Patrick badgered. "Ozwald, oy, drop your sword so that we can get moving back to the keep. We have a long journey, and Kraegan is already furious," he continued.

Ozwald saw Roven and his family bewildered, their mouths gaping open. Memories of his deceased family and Cailda flashed through his mind. He could not lose another family, he did not want to be doomed to this fate. Looking for his next step, he saw Samor moving his hand slowly to his sleeve.

Samor suddenly managed to push off the dagger pressed

to his neck, catching Rainbow by surprise while pulling out a knife of his own and stabbing Rainbow straight in his neck. Ozwald could only observe as a spectator, anxiously waiting for his part to commence. Samor, though, had already acted fast, picking out his now bloodied dagger from Rainbow's throat before shoving it into Patrick's undefended back. Patrick, who had faced Ozwald the entire time, stood motionless, his eyes and mouth wide open, before quickly falling to the ground.

Samor began to drag Rainbow's motionless body while Hemna and Khom wept.

"Come here, girls," Trayma trembled, hugging both tightly and covering their eyes.

"Merrick, what are you doing? Come help me hide these bodies," Samor badgered. "Roven, get ready to move, and don't you try to run off like last time," Samor instructed, his voice commanding and authoritative. Ozwald rushed to Samor's aid, helping to hide both bodies within a thick stretch of bushes to the side of the road.

"That should be enough. No one will likely care after the bodies we've seen along this road," Ethan said, his voice melancholic.

"No one would notice, even if the bodies began to stink," Ozwald exhaled, clasping tightly to the hilt of his sword.

"That sword really helped you, I can see," Samor mocked, grabbing hold of Ozwald and nodding in the direction of the wagon. They moved quickly and jumped on the wagon before Roven lashed his reigns for the horses to begin galloping ahead. The road was clear in both directions as the wagon moved ahead.

Trayma embraced her two daughters tightly as they continued to sob while Samor looked beyond the wagon, his face pale. It was apparent that the killings had taken a toll on him. Ozwald did not push him and instead waited for him to speak on his own terms.

"Death never ends. It's inevitable. And all of us need to wield it just to stay alive one extra day," he began, speaking coldly for only Ozwald to hear. "Those were mercenaries. They were wearing these," he added, handing Ozwald two silver pins engraved with two circles overlapping at the center. "This is the sign of a secret order. Who are you really, Ozwald?" he asked.

Twenty-Six

Ozwald stood at the top of a hill overlooking Aurom. He watched Roven and his family, accompanied by Samor, continue eastwards towards Bograh along a dirt and grass road, disappearing into the horizon. Despite thanking them for their help, he had received overtly cold goodbyes. Ozwald and Samor did not speak much on the rest of their journey, and Roven and his family cast a constant cold stare from the moment of the killings on.

Ozwald didn't mind. His attention was consumed by the two silver pins Samor had given him. They became more intriguing after he discovered a common letter engraving at the back, *OD*, in the small fine print.

Roven had continuously looked for opportunities to escape, which was apparent to both Samor and Ozwald. Although he began to trust Samor, he was always cautious, never leaving the wagon for long. During their few stops, even in the middle of the night, he remained awake. Samor followed suit. An unspoken agreement had been built between them as each of them nudged the other to not fall out of line.

During their last evening, while seated around the fire, Hemna broke the silence and questioned why Samor had killed both men. He attempted to answer before Trayma barked at him to stop talking. "Don't you pollute my daughter's mind? She's a daughter of the Faith of the Children," she hissed, grabbing hold of her daughters to pull them away from him. Samor kept to himself and avoided any rebuke for the remainder of the night. Ozwald heard Samor later mockingly whisper to himself, "So, it's called the Faith of the Children now."

Standing at the head of the trail, Ozwald gazed out over Aurom, and the tribulations and obstacles of his journey rapidly faded into memory. The sun hung high in the sky, casting its radiant glow over the scene before him. His eyes scanned the entire cityscape from left to right, taking in the imposing stone walls that surrounded it, which towered higher than he had ever imagined. Behind the city, he saw a large strip of water, which he knew to be the Sayla River, one of the most crucial trading routes of Azra.

The splendor of Aurom mesmerized Ozwald's senses as he marveled at every detail of the city. Each part of it added a sparkle to his eyes. The distinct architecture of its buildings, which rose two stories high with pointed wooden rooftops, was almost otherworldly to him. The tightly packed structures added a sense of intimacy to the bustling streets below. The roads were adorned with an abundance of trees, carefully planted to create an enchanting atmosphere that made it difficult to distinguish anyone's presence. While gazing towards the northwest part of the city, his eyes caught sight of a grand courtyard that stretched far and wide, the emperor's residence, Ozwald knew.

As Ozwald drew closer to the city, he began to hear the gentle hum of its bustling activity. With the wind in his favor, he was able to catch a whiff of the tantalizing aromas that wafted from the city's many chimneys. The scent of burning wood and a symphony of exotic spices danced in the air, beckoning to his senses and making his mouth water.

Transfixed by the distant splendor of Aurom, Ozwald was abruptly jolted back to reality by the chaotic flurry of activity that erupted before him. The wagon he arrived on had vanished, and a stream of wagons rushed past him in a frenzied symphony of movement. The urgent cries of drivers rang out, jarring him from his thoughts.

"Out of the way!" One of them bellowed, causing Ozwald to quickly scurry to the safety of the roadside, lest he be trampled by the unyielding throngs. Some wagons carried livestock arriving for slaughter, while others brought in grains and fresh produce. Some wagons carried people, while others carried spices and other goods for the city. All the wagons coming out of the city, Ozwald could see, carried Lirkins, and crafted wares like furniture and weapons. He could not see more as many items had been covered. However, he had never seen such volumes of concentrated trade. Dirt and dust trailed each passing wagon as they rushed up and down the road. Everyone kept to themselves and only focused on business without paying interest on who or what passed by.

Ozwald's heart began racing as he anxiously awaited to enter and experience the city and its majesty firsthand. He saw all incoming and outgoing wagons and foot travelers passing through a single point at the draw bridge at the city's southern wall. Without wasting time, he checked what belongings he still had and made his way to the gates with a slight prance in his stride.

The closer he approached, the larger the city's towering walls loomed. His attention was drawn to the entrance, where he observed four guards stationed at the drawbridge. They donned gleaming armor, meticulously maintained and polished. Their faces were the only visible features beneath their long metal helmets, adorned with intricate gold engravings. The guards were arranged at the head of four lines, with one line, in particular, shorter than the others.

The draw bridge had been constructed of long metal beams overlayed with wooden planks to provide passage over a moat that circled the entire city. It was so wide that at least eight wagons could be placed side by side on it. The moat had been built, dug, and deep, Ozwald could see. Ahead of him, four well-dressed men stood as the guard interrogated each of them, one by one. The man at the head of the line carried dead rabbits and birds in his sack, an unfamiliar sight for Ozwald. In the Haefe, hunting was uncommon, and diets mainly centered on grain, vegetables, and fruits.

After a short while, all had passed save for one of the travelers in front of him. The traveler carried a sack. However, its contents were not visible to Ozwald. He overheard the traveler explaining that he was headed to the central trading square and that he had spices from Barma in Shekat. He then showed him a scroll with his invitation on it, which the guard took and went to read over before discarding it to the side of the road. The guard's face showed disappointment, his body language indicating he might deny the man entry. However, the traveler, visibly unphased, suddenly produced a small velvet pouch from his pocket. He dangled it freely in the air, which the guard caught sight of and approached while holding his shield and pike. He quickly put them down and took off his helmet to get a better view of the pouch's contents, a glow appearing in his eyes.

"What is this?" The guard enquired. His eyes sparkled as he dabbed a finger in the bag for a small taste.

"Salt from the Barma mines, and it has your name written all over it. That goes for at least thirty Lirkins on its own," the traveler beamed, the guard tasting more of the salt. After a short while, the traveler cleared his throat, pulling the guard out of his trance.

"I see everything in order here. You may pass sir," the guard uttered, a grin still visible on his face, pocketing the pouch and rushing to put his gear back on. The traveler bowed his head, adjusted his sack, and walked ahead across the bridge.

Ozwald began to shift lightly in his place. His turn was next, and he would enter Aurom at last. His priority would be to see the city, all of it, and then head to the tavern in search of Jobra. Cailda's words were still engrained in his head. As he stepped into the guard's vision, he cast a smile, his heart racing faster and faster. However, just before the guard could speak, he was called over to another line to inspect incoming wagons. He cursed under his breath before walking over, already upset. Ozwald impatiently looked behind him.

"Where you headed?" One of the guards asked another entrant.

"Good day. Sheep for slaughter for the butcher," the driver explained, handing the guard a small rolled-up piece of paper from his pocket. "And here's the order."

The guard opened it and quickly read it before putting it into his pocket.

"Tanio! It's for Zaenon," the guard's voice loud and clear for all to hear.

"How many sheep does Aurom need? Let him through Wlav," Tanio grunted, arriving at the wagon. "No need to call me for this next time. Otherwise, we'll be here all day," he went on. At Tanio's signal, the driver whipped his reigns for the horses to start moving. Hooves collided with wood across the draw bridge, emanating a clattering collage of clicking sounds.

"I can't keep teaching a new guard every week," Tanio cursed to himself, arriving back to Ozwald. Ozwald, becoming suddenly conscious of himself, began to adjust his ripped and bloody clothes.

"Yes, what is your business here, boy?" he demanded condescendingly as he stood tall and rigid, his pike rooted in the ground and shield at the ready.

"I'm here for a friend..." Ozwald began to stutter.

"Wlav, you insist on learning. Come over here, you runt," he growled over the sound of passer-byers. Wlav came running immediately.

"Yes, commander," Wlav said, standing straight and waiting for direction.

"This boy thinks he can enter from the fine trader's line. Where should he go if he's not a fine trader on foot?" Tanio demanded. Wlav looked up, searching for an answer in the sky.

"He should stand in that line over there, commander," he hesitated, pointing to the long line of people Ozwald had initially avoided. Ozwald saw at least a hundred people dressed in rags waiting to enter.

"But that line is barely moving. I see no reason to go there. I'm sure it's fine if you let me in, as I'm here to see a friend," Ozwald exhaled, waiting for Tanio to change his mind. Tanio, however, only smirked.

"Thanks, Wlav. You can go back to your post," he commanded before turning back to Ozwald. "Yes, I could let you in, but I have no reason to. See all those over there. They're just like you, eager to get a piece of whatever they think is inside, a few Lirkins for whatever piece of shit meal they can find just to fill their bellies. They are all waiting patiently. You should do the same. If you make it to Raemen today, he'll decide if you're allowed to enter," Tanio hissed, pointing to the guard at the head of the line. He then nudged Ozwald with his foot to leave and get out of his way. Ozwald took immediate offense at the touch. He took a step back and grabbed the hilt of Stonesaver. Tanio caught sight of the sword.

"What have you got there? Who did you steal that from?" He snickered, quickly grabbing hold of Ozwald and immobilizing him with his embrace. Ozwald could not help but shout while others stared and did nothing. No matter how much he strained, Ozwald could not break free, and Tanio eventually took hold of his sword and pushed Ozwald to the ground.

"You're lucky I found this. I'm confiscating it and will return it to its rightful owner. Now get out of here," he growled, panting while holding his pike to Ozwald's chest.

Ozwald seethed with anger as he stood stock-still, waiting for the guard to withdraw his pike. After the weapon was removed, Ozwald sulked and rose to his feet. His eyes caught sight of a discarded scroll on the ground, and he quickly snatched it up. He knew that he could not retaliate against Tanio. Tanio was better equipped, trained, and had the upper hand. Ozwald resigned himself to Tanio's demand and trudged to the end of the long line, his head bowed.

After an hour, the line had barely moved, and the sky turned a darker blue. Remembering the scroll, he pulled it out. His eyes could not break sight of it when he saw that there were no words but only scribbles. He checked each side multiple times and could not find any legible letters. He quickly pocketed it before he pulled out the silver pins and inspected them again, trying to link its two letters and symbol to anything he had read before.

Regardless, he continued to stare at them, waiting for the line to move forward.

"Interesting pins you've got there," a voice said from behind Ozwald. Ozwald quickly looked back and locked eyes with a boy who appeared to be at least two or three years his senior. The boy was of the same height as Ozwald and had a slender yet well-toned build. His hair was cropped short, almost to the point of being bald, and his eyes were a blend of sharp calculation and genuine warmth. He wore a reassuring smile as he patiently waited for Ozwald's response.

Ozwald pocketed them and cleared his throat.

"Yes, thanks," he uttered over his shoulder. He looked over the heads of the two women in front of him as the length of the line continued to make him anxious.

"Sorry, but how long have you been waiting here?"

Ozwald asked as both women turned quickly, fear apparent in their eyes. They were sisters, Ozwald saw. Both had curly hair and freckles on their faces and wore old rags covered with mud stains. Their shoes had holes, revealing their toes to anyone who stared. Their bodies were frail, as though they had not eaten in weeks.

"We've been here since before the sun came out," one of them sighed, their faces on high alert. Ozwald could only smile, attempting to console them.

"May I ask where you are from? You're sisters, right?"

"You have no right to talk with us here," she scowled."Mind your own business," she added as both turned around without another word. Ozwald, not expecting their reaction, took a step back, not wishing to bother them further.

"Everyone comes to this city to run away from something and build a new life. The city of opportunity and misery, depending on which way you look at it," the voice spoke from behind again. Ozwald chose to remain facing ahead. "Just like them, you're running away from something. I don't mean to intrude, but maybe we can help each other get in. Isn't that why you're here?" The voice spoke eloquently as if he knew Ozwald's deepest desires at that very moment. Ozwald resisted the urge to turn until his curiosity overwhelmed his ability to resist.

"How would you do it?" He blurted out.

The boy behind him smiled, his eyes glowing at the question. "My name is Yakenn. What's yours?" He offered, holding out his hand.

Ozwald held back for a short while before he slowly reciprocated. "Merrick," he hesitated, his senses on high alert and afraid to draw any attention to himself.

"Nice to meet you," Yakenn replied.

"So, how would you get in?" Ozwald asked again, glancing back to the line.

"Well, for that, why don't you come with me? No purpose in standing in this demoralizing line. We don't belong here," Yakenn grinned, signaling for him to walk up the hill that Ozwald had come down from earlier in the day. Yakenn took off, without waiting or looking back. Ozwald watched him go, weighing his options for a moment before getting out of line and following.

~

Ozwald sat with Yakenn in the forest the next morning. They struggled to open up to each other the prior evening until Ozwald explained that he came from the Haefe.

"Have you heard of it?" Ozwald asked, expecting a no.

"Have I? Best corn in all of Azra!" Yakenn grinned warmly. Ozwald broke out in a small laugh of relief. He had found someone to connect with, that understood him, he thought.

Later in the night, Ozwald disclosed his true name to Yakenn. Upon hearing this, Yakenn revealed, "I used to do the same thing, but then I came to the realization that I could never be my authentic self if I wasn't true to who I am." Ozwald embraced him shortly after, touched by his warm words.

Yakenn always had a topic to discuss. He filled the night with stories of his past and his adventures. His past, as Ozwald came to learn, was almost as tragic as his own. Before coming to Aurom, Yakenn's sister had been murdered in Ketida in Lazzos. One of the guards of King Edward of House Walda fancied her but she refused his advances. The guard then murdered her for insubordination. Despite Yakenn's demand for justice, the king would budge. And so, Yakenn decided to wield justice in his own hands. Although he avenged his sister, Yakenn's family disowned him for breaking the law, and he lived a life on the run ever since.

Ozwald opened up about his life as well. Even though the time was short, he managed to cover everything up to that very morning. It helped him remember the good memories of his past, not just the painful ones. Yakenn broke out in laughter when Ozwald detailed how he'd attempted to get into Aurom.

"This city is filled with workers, beggars, and the poor. They don't just let anyone in. They have enough already. See that line growing over there?" he said, pointing at the long line that Ozwald had stood in the day before. "They've lost everything. That's the evil of this place, in full view," Yakenn spat.

"Then why were you there in the line? Why come here?" Ozwald shot back. Yakenn, unphased, smiled back at him.

"It's a two-man job, honestly. I was looking for the perfect person to help me get in. I have friends inside, and we're putting something together. We want to put an end to the evil of these rulers. So, I thought that maybe I could find someone to help get me in and then possibly come join us," Yakenn beamed. "And honestly, you stood out from the rest. I saw what happened with you, I won't lie. So, I was naturally intrigued."

They sat staring at their dying fire as the sun began to

rise in the horizon. The morning fog hung low over parts of the city as houses began to light up under the sun.

"What's our plan, then?" Ozwald asked with excitement. Before Yakenn could start talking, Ozwald showed him the parchment.

"What is this?" Yakenn asked.

"This just shows that the guards can't read," he beamed.

"They will remember me, though, unless you have a wagon hidden somewhere," Ozwald exhaled.

"You leave that to me. We need to focus on getting you cleaned up first, though. You look like shit. Those clothes need to go into there," Yakenn joked, patting Ozwald's back and pointing to the fire.

Yakenn led Ozwald to a nearby stream and had him bathe. He even handed him new clothes from the small sack that he'd been carrying. While Ozwald bathed, Yakenn disappeared for almost an hour, returning back with two large bags of potatoes. By that time, Ozwald had dressed up in Yakenn's white shirt, long vest, and tight trousers. It made him feel new.

"We'll fool them with these. We'll tell them that we're potato traders," he said, his smile stretched across his face.

"Also, here's a parchment, a feather, and some ink for you," Yakenn said. "Better be safe and write down two bags of potatoes, I'd say."

"Time to go," Yakenn signaled, getting up from his crouched position and picking up one of the sacks of potatoes. "I hope today will teach you how bending a few of our own values can go a long way," he said, stomping out the remaining ambers and taking a moment to scan Aurom one last time. Ozwald did the same.

"Mine says, G.W.. Where did you get these again?"

"Like I told you. They were thrown to the side of the road. The same one you traveled on yesterday," Yakenn explained.

"A bit of injustice shouldn't be a problem," Ozwald said to himself. He looked through his sack again and saw it filled entirely to the rim.

"I hope these weren't stolen," Ozwald sighed, holding a potato out.

"Of course not. You know me."

They made their way out of the forest and down the road leading to the gates. Yakenn knew the area well, as their spot in the trees was well hidden. The volume of the traffic immediately caught Ozwald's attention. The lines were even longer than the previous day. Yakenn nudged Ozwald in that direction. "I'll do all the talking," he panted as they picked up the pace. Suddenly it began raining.

"As if we needed more problems," Ozwald sighed.

"Cheer up. This is to our benefit," Yakenn quickly shot back, tapping Ozwald's chest. The two circumnavigated the mud and puddles with ease. Wagons and foot travelers did not bother with them as they made their way to the shorter line. Just as they began to walk across the last portion of the road, Ozwald caught sight of the guards. He could not recognize their faces under their helmets.

"Head down," Yakenn whispered, stepping into line with only two other travelers ahead of them. The smell of mud, grass, and gravel filled his nostrils as they waited in line. It helped relieve his tension further as he recalled forest adventures with his brother when it rained in the Haefe. The woods always looked and felt different. Even though they would get mud all over their clothes, it gave them a feeling of purity and cleanliness that they loved.

Their turn finally arrived, and Ozwald's nerves tensed up even more. He bowed his head and pulled his hat lower, avoiding eye contact with any of the guards.

"State your business," a voice commanded.

"Hello, dear commanders of the gate. How are you? We're traders headed for the local market. Potatoes, you see," Yakenn told them. He pulled a few small potatoes from his sack for the guard to see. "All the way from Lazzos — the best in Azra," he said, his voice warm and friendly. Ozwald heard the guard sniff them.

"Checks out with me. Here," the guard exhaled, Ozwald caught sight of Yakenn's shuffling feet.

"In Lazzos, it is customary that anything presented or gifted is retained by that person," Yakenn uttered.

"Get going," the guard commanded, prompting them to move ahead.

"Of course," Yakenn replied, nudging Ozwald to follow him. Ozwald's heart raced, taming himself to put off celebrating until after they'd crossed the bridge. They stopped momentarily at the beginning of the bridge to gaze upon its grandiose design. The drawbridge was a magnificent sight to behold and was split into two sections. The first part, a solid stone bridge, provided a sturdy foundation upon which the second half, a moving drawbridge, was built to control access and entry. The initial section of the bridge, massive in build, boasted a width spacious enough to accommodate at least a hundred people walking side by side. Ozwald marveled at the sheer size of the wall at the end of the bridge, which stood taller than anything he'd ever seen built by man. The meticulous design was nothing short of awe-inspiring. It consisted of carefully crafted statues and stone etchings intricately embedded within its structure.

Their walk across the draw bridge felt like an eternity to Ozwald. Despite holding himself well in front of the guard, Ozwald saw Yakenn's hand shaking nervously.

Then, both boys froze in their place.

"Oy, you with the hood, come back here," the guard called back. Ozwald looked up to Yakenn and saw, for the first time, confusion across his face. He quickly nudged Ozwald to turn.

"Turn! Or he'll know something is wrong. It's just routine," Yakenn whispered uneasily. Ozwald quickly turned and faced the guard.

He caught his eyesight and saw that it was neither of the guards from the prior day.

"Yes, at your service," Ozwald declared as the rainfall became heavier.

"I needed to see your face," the guard began. His face was stern and filled with skepticism. "Where is your invitation?" he continued as Ozwald began to search his pockets.

"Here." Ozwald handed it to him under the pouring rain, his hand shaking.

"Where are you from again?" the guard asked.

"It's written on the parchment. Va... Lazzos, sir," Ozwald stuttered, gritting his teeth while the guard scanned him from top to bottom.

"Lazzos, you say," he sneered. "Fine, carry on. These potatoes better taste good, though," the guard said as he waved Ozwald off. Ozwald nodded with a smile and turned.

His back towards the guard, Ozwald began to rush into Aurom. He did not even stop at Yakenn, who waited for him in the middle of the bridge. Yakenn raced after Ozwald, his footsteps pounding the bridge's floor, clinging tightly to his sack of potatoes. After what felt like an eternity, they finally reached the end of the bridge, and the rain began to subside. Ozwald, drenched all over, hardly took notice.

He was filled with a sense of relief and gratitude that he could not quite put into words. Taking a moment to catch his breath, Yakenn clasped his shoulder, a broad smile spread across his face. The sound and scent of the city began to waft toward him, filling Ozwald with a deep sense of anticipation and excitement. He had desperately hoped to set foot in this bustling metropolis, and now, as he stood at the threshold, he could feel his heart racing with excitement. He knew that the journey ahead would be challenging, but he also knew that he was ready to face whatever lay ahead. With the promise of adventure and discovery just beyond the gate, he felt as though that nothing could stand in his way.

Twenty-Seven

Ethan pulled his arrow out of a dead rabbit, assessing its quantity of meat. He squeezed its thighs before stuffing it in a leather satchel Roven had given him. He looked up to the sky for the sun to catch his bearings before walking back quickly to meet the rest. Over the last two days, Roven and his family had barely spoken with him. Trayma would hold her daughters whenever she saw Ethan look at or approach them. An unspoken truce had been reached between him and the family. Ethan provided food during their long journey together while they allowed him to continue on as a passenger. Harvesting from the land proved insufficient and futile. Meat was their only option. As long as Ethan provided, he hoped they would not leave him behind. Regardless, he avoided testing the limits of their patience.

He took off his cloak and tied it around his hips as they rode into the warmer temperatures of South Adrovia along the southern shore of the realm. He learned that Felix Bay was a day's journey west and Bograh two days east. The path through the hills proved difficult for anyone who did not know the area well. The weather became humid south of Aurom, and the sun lingered longer in the sky. Ethan used every moment he could find to wash from the odious odor his body secreted, a situation he had minimal experience with, having lived his life in the cooler climate of Horos.

In the midst of the forest, the distant but distinct sound of gushing waves drifted up from the southern shores. The peaceful chirping of birds engulfed them, accompanied by a constant simmer of grasshoppers. Nearby, Ethan found a water spring that housed many thousands of loud, ribbiting frogs and filled up his sheepskins.

Usually, Ethan heard Roven's loud chattering from a distance on his way back to their campsites, which always faded away as the family took notice of his return. On this occasion, however, he heard nothing. Could they have left without him? He paused for a moment, but then, without waiting too long, he ran, holding on tightly to his rabbit and water-filled sheepskins.

In the distance, he saw the clearing where they set up camp but saw no movement. He frantically scanned the area. "They're gone," he whispered to himself, continuing to run.

Suddenly, he froze as he caught sight of the wagon. Its constituents were dumped out onto the ground. The horses were tied to a nearby tree. He ran to the sight, eagerly searching for Roven and his family.

"Roven!" he shouted. "Trayma!" No response came back. After a short while, his eyes landed on four tied-up bodies near the horses. He ran to them and slid into a kneeling position. He immediately began to untie the ropes around their hands and feet.

"I'm here. Who did this to you?" he questioned, pulling out his dagger to cut the ties. There were gags in their mouths, and he began to untie those as well.

"Roven, we need to move. Let's go." He urged. "Trayma, the girls need to get into the wagon fast." His face went pale. He nudged each of them again, but they did not move. Their skin was devoid of all color. They would never move again.

"Don't move much when they're dead," Dirk chimed in from behind him. Ethan hesitated for a moment. Before he turned, squinting his eyes and standing up.

"They were good people, Dirk," Ethan growled, his face flushed red with anger. He slowly walked towards the wagon as Dirk stood alongside three of his men.

"My twenty-five men, including Risst, were good people. They all died for you."

"You killed Risst!" Jander, one of Dirk's men, complained as he took a step forward. Dirk held him off with his hand and waved for him to get back in line.

"My prince, what has been done is done. We cannot change the past. We have a mission to complete. We still have time despite..." He took a deep breath and licked his lips. " ... despite your mutiny. But we must hurry. Nothing matters more than the mission. And you are our mission," Dirk said confidently. The other men stared at Ethan angrily. Ethan gritted his teeth, glancing at the wagon and then at Dirk and his men.

"Stop acting like a child," Dirk spat.

Ethan stuttered in his place. "This isn't right," Ethan

said.

"These people are nobody. No one will ever remember them. You are what matters. Remember what is important. We are important, not the masses," Dirk interjected.

Suddenly, Ethan jolted into the wagon, prompting Dirk and his men to laugh.

"Stop your games," Jander mocked as Ethan took a defensive position.

"Perfect time to take a shit, aye Ethan?" another man mocked. They stopped laughing as he unsheathed his sword. Ethan faced Dirk and his men, who chuckled again mockingly at the sight.

"You think all that training with wooden sticks is enough to beat us all?" Jander badgered. Ethan adjusted his attacking position.

"Cut it out, Ethan, and put it away. We have no time for your games," Dirk exhaled, signaling with his hand. Ethan was unperturbed, his demeanor focused and determined. "I would think wisely before doing anything rash," Dirk snapped as he and the rest of the men unsheathed their swords.

"I should have done this a long time ago. I just needed the right motivation," Ethan smirked, raising his sword high.

"Motivation? What are you talking about? We are brothers. You're heir to the Raynel throne," Dirk spat just as Ethan attacked and threw his first blow. Dirk dodged him and pushed him to the side as the other men got into position. They counterattacked him. Ethan had already anticipated them and dodged away, cutting one of the men's arms. He landed on the ground, pressing his arm tightly.

"I'm alright! Focus on him," the man cried.

"Master Boshol, isn't that his name? He's taught you well, I can see. All those training years sure are coming in handy," Dirk mocked.

"My family has forgotten me. They never wanted me. I was always going to die here. I can see it," Ethan raged, clutching his sword tightly in his hands. Dirk sneered as he attacked, his sword swinging from a high position. Ethan learned the fighting techniques of every city in Eurst from Master Boshol. He dodged Dirk's swings.

"It took you this long to figure it out?" Dirk spat. "You were always destined to be a decoy," he continued. Ethan attacked again, catching one of the men off guard and slicing his neck. Blood squirted on the man next to him, who flinched just as Ethan pulled out his sword and cut him down.

Ethan's bloodshot eyes glistened at the sight of blood, and every muscle on his reddened face tensed up. Vengeance spewed from his heart and his entire body. He wanted blood for Roven and his family. Even more, he wanted blood to soothe the pain of his family's betrayal. Dirk's face went pale, and he waved for Jander to come to his side. Jander stood in front of Dirk, his sword held from his waist, shaking. Ethan smiled at the sight.

"What do you mean, 'decoy?'" Ethan demanded as the confusion took hold of him. Dirk stammered in his place, looking at the two dead men on the ground.

"The end does define the means for you, I can see," Dirk said. But before he could elaborate any further, Jander attacked Ethan and kicked him to the ground. Ethan quickly dragged himself backward, evading further blows. He rolled to his side and got up, immediately engaging in a duel with

Jander, who poured heavy blow after heavy blow on him. Ethan managed to kick his knee, knocking him off balance before driving his sword into his chest. He squirmed, his eyes bulging from pain as he took his last breath.

"My family underestimates what I can do, and so you pay the price," Ethan spat, shoving the sword deeper into Jander's chest, all the while focused on Dirk. "You don't seem phased by the death of your men as you claimed to have been." Ethan sneered.

"Who said I was? Death is death. They were not strong enough to survive." Dirk tossed his sword between his hands before lunging to strike at Ethan, who just nearly dodged the swing. Ethan rolled on the ground and knelt defensively. He pressed his arm wound, glaring at Dirk with rage.

"You don't care about this mission. You've wanted me dead before we set foot on this land," Ethan snapped, breathing heavily.

"Isn't it obvious?" he sneered. "You are the mission. An attack is imminent, and Eurst's allies here will answer the call," he added. "Whatever you do is futile. You're just changing the timing, which I think we can accommodate now," he growled.

Ethan's heart swelled with anger as years of doubt were answered in a single sentence. The sorrow that he had expected to feel was replaced by a fiery rage that tightened every muscle in his body, causing his grip on the hilt of his sword to grow even fiercer. Suddenly, Dirk attacked, catching Ethan off guard. Though Ethan managed to avoid certain death on multiple occasions, he knew that he was still no match for Dirk's strength and speed. The end was near. With each blow that he fended off, Ethan's feeling of hopelessness intensified until, finally, Dirk landed a powerful kick in the center of his chest, sending him crashing to the ground. As Ethan quickly struggled to regain his footing while gasping for air, Master Boshol's teachings flooded back into his mind. The master had always stressed the importance of remaining calm and composed in battle, and Ethan knew that he needed to find his leverage before he could mount a successful counterattack. Taking a deep breath, he steadied himself and remembered the phrase that his mentor had engrained in his mind. "It is not rage that wins a fight, but the soundness of your cause," and Ethan knew he was justified in his cause. With a renewed sense of purpose, Ethan attacked once more, focusing his sword on Dirk's chest. Though Dirk was able to block Ethan's onslaught, he was caught off guard by Ethan's sudden change in demeanor. With each passing second, Ethan grew calmer and more focused until, finally, he found his opening and struck a fatal blow, driving his sword deep into Dirk's chest.

"Die!" Ethan cried out as he pushed his sword even deeper, finally finding the vindication that he had been seeking for so many years.

Dirk squirmed as he looked down at the sword in his chest, half expecting Ethan to have the last say.

"You'll never be one of them," he said, spitting blood in Ethan's face.

"Who said I cared anymore? For all I care, they can fuck off," Ethan hissed as Dirk took his final breath and fell to the ground motionless.

Twenty-Eight

Aurom, the bustling capital of the realm of Azra, was a city unlike any Ozwald had ever seen. As he stepped through the gates, he was immediately enveloped by the noise and commotion of the streets. The city was alive with the sounds of vendors hawking their wares, the clatter of hooves on cobblestone, and the chatter of people from all walks of life. The city was a labyrinth of winding streets, each one leading to a new discovery. Ozwald could not help but gawk at the impressive buildings that loomed over him, their grandiose architecture seeming to reach for the sky. It was a symphony of stone, and each building vied for attention like a choir of voices contesting for the lead.

But amidst the grandeur of the city lied pockets of poverty, and Ozwald felt a deep sense of discomfort as he passed through the slums where the destitute huddled together in cramped alleys. The disparity between the opulence of the noble mansions and the squalor of the streets was jarring, like a beautiful painting marred by a single smudge.

As he delved deeper into the city, the diversity of its inhabitants became clearer. People of all ages and from all parts of the realm bustled about, their garb and mannerisms reflecting their origins. He saw merchants in fine silks, warriors in gleaming armor, and beggars in tattered rags, all existing side by side. But with the bustle of activity came a seedier side to the city. He could ignore the furtive glances and hushed whispers that accompanied the exchange of coin in dark alleys. Criminal activity was rampant, lurking in the shadows like a predator waiting to pounce.

The smells of the city were just as varied as the sights. Ozwald was assailed by the pungent aroma of spices from the markets, the mouth-watering scent of roasting meat and chicken, and the sickly-sweet stench of sewage. Each scent added to the complexity and charm of the many winding streets.

Aurom was, for better or worse, a city bigger than Ozwald could have ever dreamed, a pulsing organism that was both beautiful and grotesque. In fact, it was a place where the grand and the grotesque coexisted in perfect harmony, a place where one could find both wonder and despair. It was a city that would stay with Ozwald forever, etched in his memory like a scar.

Ozwald had entered the city earlier in the day with Yakenn carrying their sack of potatoes. He took Ozwald around, showing him different places and retelling his stories and experiences from each quarter. It was past noon, and both stood near the main food market in the center of the city.

"Fresh bread! Fresh bread!" A baker shouted. Ozwald stood in an arched side alley away from the commotion while the bustling city center breathed in its own way.

"Ten potatoes for two Lirkins," one seller declared.

"We can probably sell our potatoes there," Yakenn said from behind Ozwald.

"Sure, you can take my pack. I'm not going there. That guard Tanio may be around. I'm going to make my way over from there and see more of the city," Ozwald said, scanning the area around him and pointing to a quiet, narrow path away from the commotion.

"As I said, we could use a man like you," Yakenn said, his eyes full of yearning as he grabbed Ozwald's bag of potatoes. "How about this? Let me go sell these, and I'll meet you over there by the fountain at the end of the road at sunset. If you change your mind, then great. If not, then that's fine as well," he added. Ozwald scratched his nose and looked out towards the bustling market.

"I'm already indebted to you," Ozwald said. "I'll make my own way, and besides, I need to find Jobra," he explained.

"On the contrary, I'm indebted to you. Where did Cai... Cailda, am I right? Where did she say he was?" he asked, shifting in his stance.

"Old Legend's Tavern."

"Well, follow that road up and then go east. When you pass by the grand temple, you can ask around," he explained, appearing deep in thought. "Don't forget, I'll be at the fountain," he insisted, pointing again. Ozwald bowed his head and tightened his hat before bidding him farewell.

Ozwald navigated his way through the dense crowd

ahead of him, opting for the least congested route. Finally, he arrived at the cobblestone road that Yakenn told him about and set off toward the tavern. As he walked, he marveled at the houses in this part of the city, with their ornate glass windows adorned with newly refurbished wooden shutters. The sheer amount of glass on these buildings was a sight to behold, and Ozwald found himself repeatedly awestruck by the myriad of colors and shapes he saw reflected in the glass, as well as the textures of wood and stone that framed them. The air around him was heavy with distinct dampness. Despite the moisture, Ozwald was entranced by the stunning architecture and continued his walk toward the tavern, taking in the sights and sounds of the bustling city around him.

As the sun emerged from behind the clouds, the cobblestone was illuminated with a magnificent radiance, exuding the grandeur and age of the area. The gleaming tiles seemed to whisper tales of countless travelers who had journeyed upon their surface, leaving behind imprints and memories. In every available crevice, majestic evergreen trees had taken root, their trunks wide and sturdy, proudly reaching toward the sky. The ground surrounding these towering behemoths was rough and uneven, bearing the scars of their age-old presence. The knobby roots snaked beneath the earth, delving deep into the soil beneath the road to claim their territory with quiet strength. Together, these elements created an atmosphere of timeless elegance, a reminder of the history and legacy that had been forged on these very grounds.

Ozwald continued his journey uphill for nearly an hour before he finally saw the grand temple. It was a structure like

landing on the ground in front of Ozwald, its metal clattering on the ground. Ozwald picked it up instinctively and stared at it before he tried to hand it back. The man shook his head, "you probably can't afford anything."

After a short while, Ozwald pocketed the Lirkin and followed their directions. He found it hard to keep his head up as he had never been mocked in his life. In the Haefe, respect was the norm, despite intense disputes being very common between its inhabitants. He continued to walk while the sun began to drop in the sky. In the distance, he saw a crowd of people gathered around a small red stone building. It was nestled between high trees suffocating all sunlight. It had been built away from the other buildings of the area as if it were an unwanted child discarded by its family. The crowd, Ozwald saw, gathered around a table and silently observed an inconspicuous object.

Ozwald approached them slowly, trying to peek at the reason for the crowd. He reached to clench Stonesaver before remembering that Tanio had taken it. Suddenly, he saw guards approaching from the other end of the road. Ozwald quickly put his hat back on, lowering his gaze in an attempt to blend into the background.

"Move away!" The guard commanded. The crowd made a path for them to enter. "What happened here?" the guard interrogated. Ozwald caught a glimpse of someone lying, face flat, on the table in the center of the people. His eyes fixated on the body as it lay motionless on the table, but he saw no blood. No one in the crowd spoke for a while until an old man came forward.

"That man, I know him. He comes every afternoon. He was drinking beer with someone else outside. In all my time here, he's never entertained anyone, especially out here. Then he just fainted, and here we are," he explained, his voice frail and melancholic. "These streets, this tavern, has never known such tragedy," the old man continued.

"Where's the guest that he was with?" The guard quickly demanded, but his question was met by silence. "What's this man's name, at least?" He badgered. No one spoke as though they were collectively hiding a shameful secret.

"Jobra Kull," one of them said.

At the sight of Jobra's motionless body, Ozwald's hope drained away like water breaking through a broken dam. He began to take small steps backward, moving slowly while keeping his head down. After a few steps, he quickly turned and bumped into an old lady walking with a cane, almost toppling her to the ground.

"My sincere apologies," he blurted, frantically looking at the floor and avoiding eye contact. The old lady grimaced at Ozwald.

"You headless chicken," she raged as a few eyes turned his way. He lowered his hood and hat once again, attempting to shield his face. The old lady smirked at him. "Now I know your secret," Ozwald stepped back quickly and began to run. He ran as if his life depended on it, his heart pounding through his chest. Fear had taken hold of him, leaving him petrified and desperate to escape whatever lay behind him.

"Guards! Over there!" The old lady screeched.

Ozwald's heart pounded in his chest as the sound of men in his pursuit exploded behind him. The clattering of bodies and the shouts of guards echoed through the narrow streets of Aurom, driving him to run faster and faster. He darted through alleys and side streets, desperately trying to retrace his steps as he remembered the hiding places Yakenn had shown him. But, as the clouds obscured the sun, he lost his sense of direction, and panic set in. He heard the guards' voices growing louder and closer, urging him to stop, but he dared not look back. Instead, he took whatever path came up in front of him, his breaths turning to ragged gasps. As he ran, the sky began to darken, and he found himself in a residential area of the city that he did not recognize. The architecture was unfamiliar, and he had to guess which way to turn. He spotted a set of stairs and ran up them, passing by a series of courtyards, each filled with strange and exotic plants emanating different fragrances. At the top of the stairs, he found himself in a bustling square filled with young men and women dressed in fine, flowing garments. Their carefree attitudes and exotic clothing were unlike anything he had ever seen, even at the brothel where he had spent so much time. But he did not have time to linger as they all stared at him in bewilderment. As he caught his breath, he glimpsed a sign set up next to the tree, but he only had time to read a few words.

From before time began...

The sound of the city died down behind him, and he could barely hear the guards anymore. Avoiding leaving anything to chance, he found a secluded place that he knew he could hide in for a while until it was safe to go out again. He did not know where he would stay for the night or how he could leave his hidden area.

From his hidden perch, Ozwald scanned his surroundings, taking in the view below him. A winding pathway snaked its way through the area, bordered on one side by a magnificent courtyard. Lush green grass covered the ground, and a riot of flowers bloomed in every color of the rainbow. Granite stones were scattered here and there, adding to the natural beauty of the space. As he gazed more closely, Ozwald noticed a round table in the center of the courtyard, surrounded by elegant chairs. The empty cups neatly arranged on the table suggested that someone had been enjoying a drink there recently. He could not fathom why anyone would want to drink outside when the houses were so grandiose and luxurious.

"Out now!" Ozwald heard a voice thunder out of nowhere. He looked intently at the courtyard and saw a heavy-set man dressed in gold and red striped linens staring in his direction. Ozwald, perplexed, could not understand how the man saw him through the wall he hid behind. The man had round cheeks and tied-back black hair in addition to a round belly that was so wide, Ozwald thought his clothes might burst.

"Where are you? Come out now!" he continued. Ozwald froze, and a sense of defeat overcame him. His hiding spot had failed him, and he would now have to pay the price of his decisions.

Just before he could do or say something, though, a young child came out quickly and ran to the man's side, embracing him. Shortly after, a group of three men and four women came out and stood in a line slowly. They had their heads bowed. Ozwald relaxed for a moment. The round man focused his rage on others.

"You, come here! Kneel here!" The man shrieked as one of the women walked out and knelt. "My son is all I care about. When he is happy, so am I. If he is not, then there is nothing and nobody that would ever stand in my way," the man sneered, his face going red while his eyes blazed at the kneeling woman. He produced a leather whip while Ozwald gritted his teeth at the sight, anticipating what would transpire.

"Never refuse my son's request," the man spat, raising his whip while shoving his son to the side. He ripped off the woman's robe with one tear revealing her naked body. The others remained silent with their heads bowed. "Why aren't they attacking?" Ozwald whispered to himself, gritting his teeth. He saw two armed guards standing on the other end of the courtyard. The woman sobbed as she knelt. Ozwald could see that she had already prepared herself for punishment as if she had no other choice. The man drew the whip back and lashed her back.

Slash. Slash. The woman sobbed, heaving and moaning from the pain. Ozwald turned his gaze away and heard five four more lashes.

"You see?" A voice whispered into Ozwald's ear. He jolted backward, heart racing. He thought the guards had found him. Instead, Yakenn stared directly into his eyes.

"You startled me," Ozwald said, holding his heart. It was already vacated. "Why would someone do that? They didn't deserve any of that!" Ozwald growled, his face flushed red at what he had witnessed.

"You're angry. I am too. I'll give you purpose and the means Ozwald Stonne. That I assure you, to stop things like that from ever happening again," Yakenn said, pointing to the courtyard. Ozwald's mind was a whirlwind of thoughts as he contemplated his next move. He tried to imagine what fate awaited him. The uncertainty of it all made his heart race and his palms sweat. The idea of Yakenn both scared and excited Ozwald. On the one hand, he knew Yakenn and trusted him to a certain extent. But on the other hand, he did not really know him at all. *Would it be worth the risk?*

Yakenn stuck out his hand, his eyes yearning for Ozwald's approval.

"Let's do it," Ozwald said as Yakenn smiled and embraced him again, nudging him to get going while helping him to tighten his hat on his head again.

"It's you again!" Ozwald turned around to see Tanio.

"The gallows for you, boy, and your friend..." Ozwald saw him swiftly unsheathe Stonesaver while he glared at it through his wide eyes.

"He's here," Tanio growled over his shoulder. Ozwald looked around for something to fight back with but couldn't find anything

Tanio began to speak again. "He's..." But just then, Yakenn turned around, produced a dagger, and stabbed it deep into Tanio's throat. Tanio's tongue made an awkward angle out of his mouth as he stopped moving and fell instantly to the ground. With Tanio dead on the floor, both boys stood still for a moment to hear if anyone was coming. In the meantime, Yakenn removed his dagger from Tanio's throat and wiped it with his shirt before picking up the sword lying innocently on the floor.

"I believe this is Stonesaver," Yakenn beamed, handing it to a happy Ozwald.

"Trust me more?" Yakenn interrogated. Ozwald could only nod back as he stepped over Tanio's body and pointed his sword at his motionless face.

"Never steal from others," he spat.

Twenty-Nine

"What is it that you want the most?" Yakenn asked Ozwald. Both of them stood atop a house in the east of Aurom late at night. Yakenn, Ozwald found out, had many friends in Aurom, and they all stayed together in a secret house. He had not met them yet as they were still off completing an errand. Ozwald scanned the silent city, pondering a response to Yakenn's question. The rain had stopped, and unusually chilly gusts of wind blew throughout the city.

"For Kraegan to pay. This is all his doing. I can't see it any other way. Somehow, they found out about Jobra. He is killing everything and everyone that I interact with," Ozwald said as Yakenn nodded along. "I have nothing else. I thought Jobra would help with something, but alas, that never was to be," Ozwald sighed, handing Yakenn the pins for the first time since they met in the line for the gate.

"I still don't know who these are," Yakenn said, shaking

his head.

"No one knows me in Aurom, and I've already been targeted. This is just where it begins," Ozwald went on, casting an icy stare over the city. Yakenn adjusted his stance, facing Ozwald.

"We'll prepare you for Kraegan, then," Yakenn fired back.

"Why me?" Ozwald asked.

"Why not? Is the right question to ask. I can see already that you're skilled if you made it here alive. All short-term, of course. We don't want to stop you from your affairs," Yakenn hesitated.

"Are you going to tell me about this house, at least?" Ozwald postured.

"The ends define the means. That's all you need to know," Yakenn boasted, folding his hands. "Come with me," he commanded as he began walking down the stairs. Ozwald hesitated, his narrowed eyes focused on Yakenn.

Yakenn and his friends resided on the eastern outskirts of Aurom, a relatively less densely populated portion of the city. From the roof, Ozwald perched higher than the adjacent buildings, able to see to his heart's content. To the west, he could see the emperor's majestic palace. The palace walls rose high and were only beaten by its towers that were high enough to graze the clouds. Every window, Ozwald could see was lit as if hosting a banquet.

"It has never been this lit during the night. They're probably busy with something," Yakenn explained when Ozwald enquired. The palace had been shaped as if it were one block of stone with spikes for towers. The structure cast a foreboding aura, causing even the bravest of onlookers to feel uneasy in its presence. To the north, he saw the calmly flowing Sayla River and the city's main trading port. The Sayla River flowed freely, its glistening surface reflecting the starry night sky. The riverbanks on both sides were teeming with a plethora of warehouses and stalls, brimming with an array of exotic grains, aromatic spices, and other materials ready for trade. The port, however, appeared curiously vacant, with only a handful of ships docked. Despite the lack of activity, the river was dotted with numerous fishing boats, their crews diligently working to secure a fresh catch for the upcoming fish market sale the next day.

"Are you coming?" Yakenn asked from below, as Ozwald broke away from his daze and began to descend the steep stone steps. He went down two stories and then took another stairway to a level below ground. At first glance, the underground level seemed bigger than the floors above. Candles lit up across the wall, revealing elaborately painted walls. The walls were the canvas, depicting battle scenes of land and naval combat with dead bodies scattered across the ground. He could not help but stare and revel at its melancholic portrayal of war. Suddenly, Ozwald heard a soft cough from behind, which snapped him out of his trance-like stare to refocus his gaze on the others in the room waiting to meet him. Ozwald saw a young man and two young ladies standing in the middle with their hands folded behind their backs. They stood side by side in a line. He glanced at them shortly before Yakenn spoke.

"Everyone, meet Ozwald. He'll be joining us for now," Yakenn said, walking around the room to the others. Ozwald broke an uneasy smile while giving a frail wave with his hand. The others did not react and glared neutrally and unamused.

Suddenly, all three stomped on the ground at once.

"My name is Rybae," the young man announced. Ozwald saw his wide-open eyes and noticed his excessive lip licking. He had a well-formed chest and messy hair.

"I'm Anella," the first young woman snapped. She had a wide jaw and tightly tied-back blonde hair.

"I'm Byrene," the final young woman said, her long brown loose hair falling to one side. Her forehead was long and hung well in place over her sparkling eyes. Ozwald, taken aback by the overwhelming introduction, gulped. His eyes raced between all of them, and he was lost for words.

"Hello, so..." Ozwald began.

"The four of us come from similar, let's say, upbringings. We've all met each other along the way, and now, we're here. We fight for justice. Isn't that why you're here?" Yakenn asked, his nose lifted high.

"Well, yes," Ozwald hesitated, the reality of his decision beginning to hit him.

"Then, we all share the same cause. All of us here trained each other when we joined, so you will be going through that as well," Yakenn instructed, walking back around the room to Ozwald.

"I'll train him. It won't take me long. He has the form, so I'll focus on his precision," Byrene said, excitement clear. "I'll make sure that Ozy —Can I call you Ozy? —becomes a combat master," she added without pause.

"You're all set up then. Tomorrow is a big day," Yakenn said.

"Wait, hold on. What exactly am I to be trained for, and why is tomorrow big?" Ozwald shot back, speaking over his shoulder as Yakenn laughed.

"See? I was right. He'll fit in just nicely. Of course, Ozy, this will prepare you for Kraegan. Isn't that what you really want?" Yakenn said, his words sharp, to the point, and what Ozwald wanted to hear.

"How do you expect to overcome him if you don't prepare," Anella added.

"Preparing yourself means having the right focus and a willingness to do what's necessary. And proper training is necessary," Rybae continued. Ozwald nodded in agreement.

"Because, always, the end defines the means," Byrene added with a gentle smile.

"And the end is that which we seek. The end that you are eager for is truth. Always truth," Yakenn added, the conviction in his voice.

"And how do you know who and what is truthful?"

The others kept silent but failed to hide their smirking. Yakenn walked behind them and gave them a tight hug while smiling as his thin mustache and beard twirled.

"Easy. Whoever shows they want it the most," he exclaimed. "Trust me, this world does not at all deserve our help, but we do it nonetheless. It gives us purpose, and that's why we're all here."

Ozwald contemplated Yakenn's words. They excited him. They showed him the possibility of a purpose regardless of what their truth was. His heart raced, and he yearned to belong to the group after seeing their passion and desire. Without saying a word, Ozwald nodded.

"Welcome to the Defenders," Yakenn boasted.

Thirty

Aelav sat idly at her desk, a feather in her hand and staring out of the high tower window facing north. Her pale face glanced to the thousand-page ledger while holding her head in her hand. She had gone through the entire ledger in the past two weeks twice on orders of Sir Walrick. Silence hung in the air except for the scratching sound of her feather to the parchment.

Suddenly, she heard footsteps outside and a commotion unraveling. She sat up and pushed her hair back, exhaling. The door opened quickly while a plump looking man walked in, his face red and round. His crossed eyes caught Aelav's.

"Ahh. Found you. I was wondering where you were," the man said, a warm smile struck across his face. Aelav shook her head slightly.

"Where else am I going to go, Sir Walrick. I've been busy with your *most important task for ages*," she sighed.

"Indeed. And what have you found? I'm sure that in

two weeks, something should have come up," he posed, picking up an apple from a nearby bowl before pulling out a chair opposite her. He took a big bite, staring momentarily out of the window.

"This red dust is showing up everywhere," he said before letting Aelav respond. Subtle worry in his voice while taking deeper and quicker bites into the apple. Sir Walrick, a genius to many, was more of a young boy in an old man's body, Aelav found. His mind kept racing with ideas and thoughts, and he found it difficult to concentrate on discussions in the room. It was normal when his mind wandered somewhere else while something was completely out of subject. Aelav, though, had gotten used to him and always stuck to the initial line of thought, rarely accommodating his side topics.

"Why, again, do we have this? The real reason? I thought that grandfather's court would handle this back in Adrovia?" She quickly interjected. Sir Walrick, still lost in his thoughts, remained glaring out of the window until Aelav slammed the ledger closed with a big bang. He quickly glanced at her, his face washed with surprise and confusion. Aelav could only smirk subtly while Walrick cleared his throat.

"Ahh, yes. Valya. Well, that's the agreement that King Klaytos struck with the emperor. This is simply because Valya, more specifically, Lord Rorik's court, reviews the finances of the realm more as a second opinion than anything else. Let's say that it adds flavor to their conversations when they meet," Sir Walrick spoke mechanically as if reading each line.

Aelav rolled her eyes at the statement, "You said the

same thing last time. Why can't you be more honest?"

"Aelav, that is the reason, no other. No one is hiding anything. If you're not happy with the answer, then speak with Lord Rorik, he'll tell you the same," Sir Walrick snapped, a rare reaction on his part before calming himself down and smiling. "Now, will you please, explain what you have found," he demanded, his tone sharper and more business-driven. Aelav, not happy with the answer, exhaled as she opened the ledger to her marked pages.

"So, as you can see," she began, turning the ledger and pointing to different parts of it for Sir Walrick to see. "No realm has been staying afloat. Everyone doesn't have enough Lirkins to cover their spending. Even Adrovia and all its gold mines spend more. Usall's silver mines down in Djunall are dry, as I saw, for the last year and a half. And this is all recent," she exhaled, taking a sip of water while Walrick stared at her intently.

"I get it. And all in the last two years?" He asked in a rush. She nodded while he adjusted in his chair and exhaled.

"What does it mean, though?" She asked, confusion clear on her face. "I've just been following bits and pieces here and there. So, what if everyone is short of Lirkins. We'll survive. It'll work itself out in the end. That's what father always says. As long as the right leadership is in place, nothing can stop us," she added, looking out of the window, Warrick remaining silent and visibly concerned.

"What is it that I'm really doing here? The prince hasn't sailed in yet," she badgered.

"I follow Lord Rorik's orders just as you do," he squirmed.

Annoyance clear on his face, Walrick got up and walked

to the door just as Johnson appeared in his dark cloak and pointed nose. Walrick stood straight and serious at the door, facing Aelav.

"Aelav, let me know if you find something else," Walrick blurted. Just as he turned to leave, Johnson threw an arm around his shoulder as both exited the room.

"There is one thing," Aelav coughed, stopping both men in their exit. Walrick turned and grinned uncomfortably while Johnson stood in the back, tapping his foot rapidly. Aelav blinked for a moment.

"And?" Walrick nudged.

"All the realms have some form of discretionary spend. They have changed a lot over the years. Here in Fallgarde," she began, flipping through the ledger. "The same spend is repeated each year and for as long back as these books go. It's even called the same name. *The Hand*," Aelav said, squinting her eyes while pointing to the ledger on several pages that mentioned spend items. Silence hung in the air for a moment as Walrick fidgeted slightly.

"Lord Rorik, like his ancestors, doesn't change much. Probably some old name that he wasn't bothered to change. Meaningless," Johnson interrupted from behind, his face neutral while his glare burned into the back of Walrick's head.

"Ahh. Yes. I wouldn't read much into it," Walrick uttered, slightly pouting before turning away and quickly leaving the room. Still standing behind him at the door, Johnson embraced him immediately and began to speak privately before closing the door behind them with a slam.

Aelav, not wasting time, rushed to the door, pressing her hands softly on its ragged surface while creaking it open.

Both men walked down the dimly lit windowless corridor before taking the stairs at the end of it. She glanced back at her ledger, which sat idly on the desk and unmoving in time. She still had work to do, but she knew it was meaningless.

Clenching her fist, Aelav slid out of the room and into the windowless corridor. She heard them mumbling below and followed the sound, quickly descending the spiraled stairway.

Like her chambers on the fourth floor, the walls were bare and only made of plain white stone. "Only what is necessary. No reason to be lavish," Walrick always said whenever she questioned the dull architecture of the castle. Both men continued their descent while Aelav attempted to eavesdrop, cupping her ear.

Following Johnson and Walrick's voices, she descended to the lower floors beneath the ground level. As she emerged into the dimly lit area, Fallgarde's Grand Temple loomed to her right. While she allowed her eyes to adjust to the lower light level, she heard mumbling voices, quickly glimpsing a moving light up ahead. Dusting off her hands, she hurried down the wide corridor toward the source of the sound. The air was still and quiet, as if hidden in a subterranean cave. All the doors, including those in the castle, were shut tight. Since the council, the castle had gone almost vacant, with only a handful of staff remaining. In Lord Rorik's absence, the castle was often devoid of visitors or the bustle of people. And Lord Rorik, who was constantly traveling, was rarely ever seen. "No one ever finds Lord Rorik. He finds you," Walrick would always joke whenever she asked about his whereabouts.

At the end of the hallway, a small round wooden door

stood ajar, its engravings beckoning her closer. She pressed her hands against the smooth surface, tracing the etched figurines of wild animals and battle scenes with her fingertips. The wood exuded a pleasant, freshly cleaned aroma, and she noticed a finely crafted stone engraving of a sailing ship caught in the midst of a wave just above the door. As she surveyed the door, she realized that it was unlike the other illustrious doors in the castle – those were always locked, but this one was open.

She peered through the narrow opening in the door, feeling a cool draft emanating from the void beyond. The long room was dimly lit, with several candles casting flickering shadows across the windowless walls. It was as if the room was another hall hidden underneath Fallgarde castle. "This place is full of secrets," she whispered to herself. In the center of the space, a long, thick wooden table was surrounded by intricately designed chairs. At the far end, a fireplace blazed brightly, flanked by deep leather couches and a bookcase stocked with unrolled scrolls. A rich red carpet ran the length of the room, and the air was thick with the scent of fresh wine, as though dozens of people had been drinking and conversing there just moments before. Satisfied that the room was empty, Aelav stepped cautiously inside, her senses on high alert. Above the fireplace hung a striking portrait of three men standing side by side, drawing her gaze. She walked toward it slowly, her eyes scanning the room for any signs of danger.

Suddenly, a door at the back swung open. Aelav glanced around and dashed to the desk, crouching behind the wide chair. The door, she saw, had been opened; however, no one stepped in. She did, though catch sight of Johnson through its opening, conversing heatedly with Walrick. After a short while, Walrick nudged Johnson in. Walrick quickly took a seat in front of the fire while Johnson paced in front of him.

"Tomorrow, tomorrow, I'll tell her." Walrick hesitated. Johnson exhaled and puffed excessively his already lit pipe, concern washed across his face. He paced in complete silence, his puffing pipe and the crackling fire the only source of sound in the room. Eventually, he sat down on the deep leather couch, creaking sounds bursting from his weight.

"She'll know, then all the Torens will know. Which means we'll have another existential matter to deal with. Rorik is pushing this too much, and I'm afraid this won't settle well with either Eurst or Azra," Johnson sighed, Walrick taking a sip from a cup in his hand.

"She can't stay here. At least take her away from my privy. Since when has Rorik let just anyone in?" Walrick urged, a stutter clear in his voice.

"You scare too easily. If Rorik says it's fine, then it's fine. I have complete trust in him. As should you," Johnson said, blind confidence clear in his voice. Walrick continued to stare into the crackling fire, taking long sips of his cup, anxious to finish it.

Johnson took a few more deep inhales of his pipe before nodding his head as both men stood up. They stared at the portrait above the chimney for a moment.

"The trio that is no more," Walrick shook his head before both left the room abruptly.

"Keep her busy," Aelav heard Johnson say just as the door closed behind them, leaving a silent room behind devoid of any soul but hers.

Aelav waited a moment and then stood up, her heart

racing. She hesitated for a moment, glancing at the door and around the room. She cast one more curious gaze at the portrait over the chimney, attempting to recognize the men that it depicted.

Suddenly, she whispered to herself, "Lord Rorik and uncle," squinting her eyes on the third man. After a short while, it struck her that Walrick would be looking for her. Not wasting any time, she ran to the door, opening it just slightly to peer outside into the dimly lit corridor while tying back her hair.

Suddenly, the door at the back of the long room creaked open. The sound of heavy footsteps thudding against the carpet began to emanate from the far end. She sprinted out of the room and into the dimly lit corridor without pausing to look back. Johnson and Walrick had already disappeared from sight while Aelav ran as quickly as she could down the wide hallway, her heart pounding in her chest. After a short run, she reached the bottom of the stairwell, constantly looking out for the two men but seeing no one.

After a brief hesitation, she ran up, taking three steps at a time. "Cannot get caught," she continued to say to herself, heavily panting. On her way up, she passed by a window, quickly gazing outside and catching sight of the already dark sky.

After a short while of non-stop running, Aelav reached the fourth floor, running down the narrow corridor leading to her room. Her heart throbbed through her neck while barging in and abruptly closing the door behind her. She leaned on the smooth wooden door breathing rapidly as if the air in the room was not enough. She wiped the perspiration from her head and quickly caught sight of her ledger.

Walrick's words rang through her head. "What are they still hiding," she whispered to herself, quickly dashing to the table. She sat down and began to ferociously flip through its pages. Although she had gone through it twice, something still was in there that she had not found.

"Found anything new?" A piercing man's voice asked. Aelav turned abruptly. Walrick.

"Not yet," she stuttered, shifting her gaze away from Walrick's curious eyes. He sat still on a chair in the corner, studying Aelav's every move and expression. Aelav sensed a change in his mood. His once warm and aloof features turned into a shrewd demeanor, one she had never expected him to have in him. Her heart throbbed, unaware of what he knew or had in mind.

"You won't be on that for long. There are new developments that we found out. Something not according to plan has occurred," Walrick grumbled.

"The prince," he started. "He hasn't arrived. He may have perished on his journey in. However, we are not certain," he exhaled, burying his face in his hand.

"Who killed him?" She began to ask rapidly, Walrick immediately raising his hand.

"No one said he was killed or died. That is yet to be discovered, and this is information just for you. No one else. Lord Rorik in fact, as I was told, is personally looking for him as we speak. He has various search parties of men all over the place," Walrick continued.

"The emperor must," she began.

"No, he will not. Rorik knows when to speak with him. That's not our job," he blurted.

"Then why tell me?"

"Lord Rorik wanted you to know," he answered immediately, glaring directly into her eyes.

"We'll discuss your role here later. For now, continue what you're doing," he blurted, not letting her speak. He got up and dashed to the door, visibly unwilling to speak or share anymore information. "As always, though, enlighten us with anything worth mentioning," he spoke, barely audible to Aelav while exiting the door. The door slammed harshly behind him just as Aelav exhaled in relief. She sat back in her chair, digging her fingers into her now loose hair.

"What am I to do now," she thought to herself, looking into the dark night through the window.

Thirty-One

Nearly three weeks had passed since Ozwald first arrived at Yakenn and his friend's residence in Aurom. Despite the absence of the house's original owners, no one had bothered to explain to him how they had come into possession of such a spacious place. As promised, Yakenn and, more specifically, Byrene put Ozwald through a demanding regimen of combat and strategy training.

Ozwald threw himself into his training with an unwavering determination that left no room for rest or respite. Time became an afterthought as he pushed himself beyond his limits with an unrelenting fervor. His unwavering trust in Yakenn knew no bounds, and he blindly followed every instruction without question or hesitation. It was as if the weight of the world rested on his shoulders, and the only way to lift it was through ceaseless effort and dedication. With every passing moment, he burned with a fiery passion, determined to atone for his family's past and ready to face any injustice that crossed his path. His spirit was unbreakable, his will unyielding, as he poured his heart and soul into his training. Every fiber of his being was consumed by a single goal: to become the strongest, most capable version of himself possible. For him, there was no other way forward than through relentless effort and an unshakeable belief in himself and his cause.

"Nothing and no one will ever wait for you," Rybae continuously shouted in his face.

However, it became clear early on that Ozwald was more than capable of rushing through their program faster than even he had imagined.

"Why did they train you this much?" Byrne asked multiple times when he bested her in his first attempt at a dual.

"Turns out there's much more that I don't know about my parents," Ozwald said, his voice low. Yakenn had a different reaction, though. The question *why*, did not concern him. He wanted to know more about the, *how much*, and *when* did he start and, *what* did he train on. He even asked about Ozwald's whereabouts in the Haefe and who he spoke with. Ozwald did not give much thought to Yakenn's curiosity and answered all that he could.

After finally getting the chance to rest on his first night, he eagerly threw himself onto the bed headfirst. He could not recall the last time he had a proper night's sleep. An hour after going to bed, though, he suddenly woke up to Rybae's eerie laughter as he poured a bucket of water in his face.

"Training starts now," Rybae shouted, eyeing Ozwald aggressively. Ozwald nicknamed him "crazy eyes." To Ozwald, Rybae was someone who would not mind stabbing him if he had the chance.

As part of his training, Rybae and Anella brought him to a serene, grassy garden in a secluded, vacant house early one morning. The courtyard was well-equipped with wooden mannequins and a makeshift archery range, providing an ideal setting for him to practice. Despite his repeated inquiries, they never provided a satisfactory answer regarding their knowledge of these vacant houses in the overcrowded city of Aurom. Meanwhile, Yakenn insisted that he knew everyone's schedule.

Starting from the first day, no one shied away from inflicting pain on Ozwald. No matter how hard he fought or what tactics he used, they always found a way to better him, at least during the first week. Instead of trying to help him get better, they continued to find ways to inflict more physical pain.

"It's the only way to toughen up and learn," Rybae would say.

However, on the fourth day of training, his claim was put to the test when Rybae decided it to be a great idea to fight with their hands tied behind their backs. Ozwald knew Rybae would enjoy it, never considering the level of injury that might result.

"You'll end up bashing each other's heads, you damn maniac," Anella badgered, the sun setting in the sky. "That's it for today, we're out. Come with me, Ozwald. And you over there, you can remain here if you want and give head to yourself if that's what delights you," she sneered, clearly frustrated.

Ozwald, lying on the floor at that time, spat blood. "First week is almost done," he whispered to himself, getting up and dusting himself off subconsciously.

"Evil shows no mercy. He needs to be ready," Rybae retorted, fuming.

"He already beat your worthless ass. Your tactics can fuck off for the first week, you maniac," Anella growled, ending the debate.

Ozwald later discovered that Yakenn and the rest usually went on secret quests at night. Even after three weeks, Yakenn had refused to give him a chance to join. He kept repeating, "You're not ready," regardless of Ozwald's many demands. The quests, however, made no sense to him, and Yakenn and the team were silent about the objectives and locations. The only tangible part of these quests occurred when they returned with one or two leather sacs. They never spoke about them, and the sacs would vanish immediately the following day.

After one mission, Anella came back with a deep cut on her arm. Ozwald tried to help, but she refused, acting as though his help would do more harm than good.

"I can take care of myself, boy," she snapped in his face, the others focused on their own worries and concerns. He tried to understand what had happened, but they were all in a bad mood.

The next night, he stayed awake. Making sure that everyone had slept, he went down to inspect the bags on the lower floor, where they had been stored. The stone construction of the house made it easier to move around silently, unlike the crackling wooden floors back in the Haefe. He picked up a candle from the ground floor and lit it with a small torch before descending to the cellar. However, he quickly searched for the bags but couldn't find anything.

Suddenly, a creaking door sounded from above, setting Ozwald's senses on high alert. He quickly put out his light and rushed up the stairs before anyone could see him. He did not know the loud sound's source, nor did he want to wait to find out.

The return to his room took much less time than he had expected. He made sure to follow his footsteps, taking caution to avoid making any loud sounds. At the top of the steps near his room, however, he froze in his stride.

"Why are you awake?" Ozwald heard Byrene whisper.

"I couldn't sleep, so I walked around a bit," Ozwald blurted, avoiding direct eye contact. She hesitated for a moment, Ozwald anxiously waiting for her response.

"Whatever it is, go back to bed. Yakenn wouldn't like it that you're roaming around alone at night," she whispered before he nodded and made his way back to his room.

A few days later, Yakenn summoned Ozwald to a small chamber. Ozwald was no stranger to this room, and he often used it as a secluded space to meditate in the intervals between training sessions, as it afforded a picturesque view of the rear courtyard through its expansive glass windows, a feature that never failed to astound him. "Marcus wouldn't believe what I'm looking at," he whispered to himself continuously. This time though, Ozwald followed him in uneasily, half expecting what he wanted to say.

"You're ready, I can see your readiness, and more importantly, I know how much you want to be of use. All of Azra will be thankful that it has someone like you — someone who only wants what's good for others. Someone that will end injustice and evil by whatever means necessary," Yakenn confessed, his voice confident and motivational.

Ozwald took a moment to contemplate, studying Yakenn's face.

"What happens next?" He asked.

"We've learned that Sir Rejji from Bograh is in town for the next few weeks. Do you know him?" Yakenn interrogated.

"No. Not really. Who is he?"

"Bograh is famous for its tobacco plantations, and this man owns them all. He's made quite a fortune for himself," Yakenn explained.

"Good for him. Why is that our problem?" Ozwald badgered. Yakenn immediately clasped his shoulder before leading him to the large window.

"You see that outside there?" He began, pointing to various spots outside of the window. "Well, if you look beyond our courtyard walls, you'll see a bunch of houses. Do you know how many Lirkins you need to build all of that? Well, a lot. This Sir Rejji, let's just say that he is not the best of men. He manipulates others. He owns all the Tobacco farms and has more than five thousand workers on these plantations. That is huge, right?" Yakenn continued.

"So what? All large lands need a lot of people. I don't see anything wrong with that," Ozwald started before Yakenn intruded.

"Right you are, but what if I told you that he did not pay them? He did not give them enough food to eat and he did not mind killing any of them, just to set an example for the others. In short, he terrorizes those people and leverages his personal guards and the support of house Mason to help him keep order. And the justice we need to instill here demands us to hit him where it hurts the most."

"So, you're going to go free the five thousand workers?"

Ozwald hesitated. Yakenn's face remained stern and serious as he shook his head.

"You are too limited in your thinking," Yakenn mocked condescendingly, tightening his clasp of Ozwald's shoulder. "Never limit your thoughts to what's in front of you. Dare to be creative. Serena's murder taught me what it meant to survive, the importance of it," Yakenn snapped. Ozwald waited for Yakenn to elaborate on his plan. "He's here in Aurom. We're paying him a visit later tonight," Yakenn said, his voice shrewd.

Ozwald broke from Yakenn's embrace, walked across the room, and sat down while rubbing his eyes. "So, you want to kill him?" Ozwald heaved, trying to understand Yakenn's thought process as he glared at him in disbelief.

"We're not going to kill him. Oh no. That would be mercy. We're going to rob him of all his Lirkins," Yakenn quickly responded. "He's here to pay off a large debt with the monarchy bank. If he doesn't, then no one will forgive him, and he'll lose everything. Honestly, when we succeed, you'll see," Yakenn smirked, his voice confident as he maintained eye contact.

"So, we hit him where it hurts?" Ozwald said while looking up. Yakenn knew how to read Ozwald by now. He quickly collected himself and made his way out of the room.

"I'm ready when you are," Ozwald said, standing up, while Yakenn froze in his stride and turned, nodding, a subtle grin appearing across his face.

"Get ready, Ozwald Stonne."

Thirty-Two

"Did you get it all?" Yakenn whispered, meeting Ozwald and Byrene at the foot of a large stairwell. Ozwald nodded while Byrene grinned as they opened a large bag for him to look into. Yakenn immediately picked up a coin from inside, which shined with a soft yellow simmer in the moonlit room. Lirkins, lots of Lirkins.

Ozwald found himself standing in a spacious hall next to Yakenn and Byrene. The hall's magnificent, marbled floors shimmered beneath his feet as he admired his surroundings, beholding the towering walls adorned with slender, stately columns, each meticulously etched with striking elegance. Above him, a grand candle chandelier hung suspended from the ceiling, unlit this time of night. Though the night outside was dark, the moonlight cascading through the hall's tall glass windows lent an ethereal quality to the scene. These windows, far from being mere apertures for light, were themselves ornate works of art, intricate designs foreign to Ozwald's eyes. Overwhelmed by the majesty of the hall and the painstaking attention to detail that went into its construction, Ozwald could not help but marvel at every aspect of its grandeur.

"First time I see something like this," he said, his eyesight frantically jumping between each part of the hall as the rest stared inquisitively. "Probably more than three hundred candles on that," he whispered while pointing for Byrene to see.

"Hold yourself together," she grunted, pushing his hand down while casting a cold gaze.

"Makes the Haefe look like a piece of shit, aye?" Yakenn mocked, walking right below the unlit chandelier.

"You've done well." Yakenn patted Ozwald on the back, pulling him out of his trance while grinning. Both had spent the last few days scouting the premise, studying the schedules and routines of every staff member and guard inside and outside of the house.

"Five minutes until the next night passes," Ozwald whispered, signaling with his hand for them to get moving. Yakenn, visibly enjoying the moment, opened his hands and twirled in the center, his face speaking with satisfaction. The rest could not help but break a smile while he carelessly twirled and waved his hands. Ozwald, not sharing the joy of the rest, shifted uneasily, anxiously waiting for him to stop.

"We need to leave now. Ozwald, did you see Rybae?" Byrene whispered.

"No," he said as they exchanged uneasy glares.

"He'll meet us outside. He's on another side mission," Yakenn interjected.

"You can't keep us in the dark like that. You did it

before, and look what happened, Anella almost lost her arm. If we don't know what the others are doing, then there is no way to help," Byrene fumed.

"Ok, ok. He's meeting us outside," Yakenn sneered, consoling Byrene with an embrace. She shrugged him off, her cold gaze apparent to the rest.

"We need to go now," Ozwald stressed, cognizant of their wasted time.

"I think it's..." Yakenn began, clearing his throat.

Suddenly, everyone went on high alert, listening closely to the sound of shattering glass from above. They all looked up, frantically searching for anything out of the ordinary. But instead of seeing movement, they heard barking dogs.

All eyes turned and focused on Ozwald, waiting for his intel, but he only shook his head.

"They're loose," he sighed.

"This way then," Yakenn commanded, confidently signaling with his hands. The others quickly complied, following him down an adjacent corridor towards the side entrance of the house and through the kitchens.

Just before they were to reach the kitchens, though, Yakenn raised his fist alarmingly. Glass shattered from inside the kitchens, setting everyone's attention on high alert. Refusing to linger any further, Byrene dragged Yakenn and Ozwald back up the corridor they had come in from.

Arriving back at the entrance hall, two large and ferociously looking black dogs waited for them in anticipation. Everyone pulled out their dagger in anticipation as Ozwald stood behind them, his heart racing as he looked around erratically. "We're trapped," he whispered to himself as he observed shadows of men approaching and heard the sound of unsheathing swords.

"What do we do?" Byrene asked.

"I'm thinking," Yakenn retorted, doing his best not to show his nervousness. A short moment later, the sounds of the marching guards changed in speed and rhythm.

"They're inside," a voice shrieked, followed by a door that slammed open from above.

"Who's in my house?" a barking voice followed. Everyone looked up and caught sight of a shadow of a short, round man from the upper balcony overlooking the hall. "Catch those imposters now!" The man commanded, his voice shrewd. "No one breaks into my house and gets away with it!"

"Breaks," Ozwald whispered to himself, his eyes suddenly lightening up as he clasped tightly onto Stonesaver. "Follow me now!" he urged, pulling on them both towards the main entrance while the dogs chased after them.

"It's locked. We don't have the keys," Yakenn said from behind. Ozwald continued unphased. At the door, he signaled for the rest to wait for him while he dashed to grab a wooden chair from nearby. He held it high in the air to the inquisitive looks of the others as the dogs approached. Not wasting any time, he threw the chair through the tall window to the side of the entrance door, shattering it into a thousand little pieces. In the background, they heard the short round man cursing for all to hear at the sound of the breaking glass. Although still out of sight, the man's footsteps could be heard as he descended the marble staircase.

"Good enough for you?" Ozwald snapped, urging the others to exit. They immediately jumped through the window, avoiding the glass as they escaped just before the dogs reached them.

They ran across the vacant courtyard while the sky began to turn dark blue across the horizon. At the unusually high front courtyard wall, they worked as a team to jump over. Byrene went first, followed by Yakenn, and then Ozwald. The dogs treaded slowly across the broken glass but finally made it. At the top, Ozwald paused for a moment, taking a final glance at the awakened house, unable to hold back a smirk. "He'll get what he deserves soon enough," he whispered to himself just as he jumped over and out of sight of everyone inside. They had made it. No other guards could reach them now. Yakenn called for him to hurry as the sound of the barking dogs could be heard on the other end of the wall.

They wasted no more time, making a run for it up the still dark and vacant streets of Aurom. Ozwald, catching up with the rest, saw Byrene standing in the middle of the street ahead. Yakenn stopped near her.

"Wait," Byrene shuddered, glaring at Yakenn. "Where's Rybae?"

Yakenn bowed his head and exhaled. As if synchronized to Byrene's question, another of the house's glass windows shattered behind them.

"Over there!" one of the guards thundered from inside the house.

"Kill them all!" the short, round man raged, his voice ringing in the night air.

"That's your Sir Rejji in a nutshell, useless. He'll kill himself when he knows what happened. People like him would never want to take the blame, even after death. They would rather kill themselves than be killed. The ego,"

Yakenn spat.

Byrene smacked him across the chest. "We can't leave without Rybae, not after all that we've been through," Byrene fretted.

"Hold on. Who said we're leaving him? He'll be just fine. Just a slight hold-up. You'll see," Yakenn explained, his eyes glued to the unfolding events of Sir Rejji's estate.

"Just fine?" Byrene fumed. "Like that friend of yours from Cerzei who never came out of that burning house? What did you say the target did? Owned all the silver mines up in Usall?" Byrene hissed. Yakenn remained calm but clenched his fists slightly. "And nothing ever happened to that man. He's still alive and with all those slaves. That friend's life was for nothing, and I won't accept Rybae's life to be the same."

Sir Rejji's estate suddenly caught fire as Ozwald saw Byrene turn away, rubbing her eyes and sobbing. The entire estate went up in flames in less than a minute, as if it had been entirely drenched in oil. The eerie sound of screaming voices emanated from within as if they would be trapped forever. The fire was so intense that they felt the heat where they were standing.

"He'll be out, you'll see," Yakenn stuttered, unable to make eye contact with the rest. Ozwald embraced Byrene without saying a word as she continued to sob.

Just as Ozwald felt all hope escape him, Yakenn suddenly cried out, "There he is!"

Ozwald and Byrene followed his gaze. Rybae, Ozwald saw, ran across the front courtyard and jumped over the fence at the same place before running up towards them, carrying a large bag on his back. He quickly reached them, opening his arms up wide, his smile visible to all.

"Did you think I would keep you all waiting for long?" he snapped, just as Byrene smacked him across the chest and embraced him, her eyes still filled with tears.

"We thought you..." Byrene began before he silenced her with his hand.

"Of course not. I'm tougher than rock. Isn't that what Anella likes to say?" He smirked.

"Did you get it, though?" Yakenn interrogated impatiently while his eyes sparkled.

"Get what? Yakenn, no more. We need to know all your plans ahead of time," Byrene sighed.

"Here it is," Rybae smirked, opening his sack up to display its contents.

"Tobacco?" Byrene complained.

"How can we serve justice for the dirtiest and most corrupt tobacco farmer in not just Bograh but all of Azra, and not try a bit of it. At least we can try it. What do you think?" Yakenn grinned, the house continuing to blaze up in fire.

Ozwald glanced back to the house as more screams emanated from inside. This time though, the voices were muffled and lower than before.

"Apologies for breaking up the reunion, but we have to go," Ozwald quickly commanded.

"There he is, our savior," Yakenn beamed. "He kept us in form at all times." They all began to rush along the path ahead while doing their best to move in stealth.

"What's next?" Ozwald quickly questioned, catching up with Yakenn behind the rest.

"What do you mean?"

"I want more. I helped bring down an oppressor, but I know there's more. I know there's more that I can do," Ozwald exhaled.

"Well, you're with me. We'll have more of these when they come and whenever they come. I don't seem to understand what you mean," Yakenn explained, his voice curious as he slowed down to walk with Ozwald.

"I know you're part of something bigger. This isn't just you lot on your own," Ozwald said, Yakenn continuing his inquisitive gaze. "You want to be part of the order? What difference does it make?"

"I want to do this on my own. I want to lead a team of my own. The more, the better, right?"

"Are you sure? This is a bit early to ask for that," Yakenn exhaled. "I'll see what I can do, Ozwald Stonne of the Haefe." They shook hands and caught up with the rest. Ozwald looked over to Yakenn and saw a bizarre, eery expression come across his face, one that he would not soon forget.

Thirty-Three

In its busiest moments, Aurom's trading areas filled up with foreign and local traders shouting over one another. Passing through any trading area required thick skin and an ability to shield oneself from the many enticing wares. Without that, one would be pressured into buying something even if they could not afford it. Traders would line up along every space on the side of the road in accordance with the unspoken rule that one should never block another. The fragrance fluctuated from the type of spice that made one sneeze to the smell of incense and perfumes all the way from the shores of Shekat. Nestled in between these traders, one would find bakeries and butcher shops ready to serve at a moment's notice.

The streets in Aurom were pristine and orderly. They were lined with lush trees and paved with gleaming granite tiles, giving the entire neighborhood a fresh and well-maintained appearance. The buildings were immaculate, with hardly a scratch or blemish to be seen.

"What do you see?" Yakenn asked, taking a large bite from his apple. He stood next to Ozwald on a shaded, first-floor balcony overlooking the bustling center below. Yakenn explained to Ozwald, after much debate, that the owners would not be back for another month and that they would not mind if they stayed there for a bit.

"A large group of people shouting over each other?" Ozwald uttered, his cold gaze focused on the street.

"Yes, well, that's the obvious. What is the truth that you see?" Yakenn questioned.

Ozwald observed the traders with interest, noting their assertiveness in sticking to their designated areas and following the established regulations. "The traders are aggressive yet disciplined. They stick to the rules," he remarked, pausing as Yakenn took another bite of his apple and nodded in agreement. Ozwald then pointed loosely towards a group of beggars in the distance, acknowledging the less fortunate. He sighed, accepting the reality of the wealth disparity within the bustling marketplace. Yakenn smirked and placed a comforting hand on Ozwald's shoulder.

"The truth, my new friend Ozwald, is nothing but a set of ideas someone made up long ago and convinced everyone else to follow, and by the sword, I might add. It is through fear of death, nothing else," Yakenn started, looking to the crowd and signaling with his hand.

"If some other bastard had decided that stealing was good and healthy for society, then we would all be doing it. That would be our truth today," Yakenn commented maliciously, ducking his head away as two armed men passed by below.

"Who were those?" he asked. Yakenn shrugged.

"The truth that I tell you is that we have been deceived. We have been told that the emperor, kings, and lords are good. We have been told that what they decide is law, even if it contradicts something they said before. We have been told that our societal constructs are what stand. Look at you. You're a farmer's son. By the rules of this society, you can never be a ruler. You can never be more than a farmer yourself because that is what society, what their truth, the truth of the few, tells you," Yakenn began, his face flustered.

"But we all live happily, there's nothing wrong with being a farmer," Ozwald hesitated, not completely convinced. "I mean, I've wanted more, but it does not mean that others are the same. Everyone is happier than you can imagine, so I don't agree. The truth you talk about is everyone's truth to live. But everyone is allowed to build the truth that makes them happy," Ozwald said with conviction. "As long as they don't hurt others nor their livelihood, of course," Ozwald took a brief pause. "And I disagree. Right and wrong are engrained in our minds based on what hurts and doesn't hurt others. For example, your notion of stealing is flawed. Stealing hurts others as it robs them of future Lirkins. Therefore it can't be right," Ozwald added.

Yakenn smiled. "I'm not going to argue that stealing is right. The fact is that we have been told what is good and what is bad. We have been told what to follow, with no chance of change nor a chance of doing things differently. We have it engrained in our heads. Some of these are great ideals, which we must uphold, but other truths are not. Other truths in fact, limit us, limit our potential, limit our freedom, and this is wrong. You say people are happy with what they have and what they are," Yakenn said, taking a deep breath. "I can tell you with all modesty, you have the ability to rule. Who do you know that has more knowledge than yourself?" Yakenn said with conviction. Ozwald remained silent. "You have been blessed, mentally and physically, and with the knowledge that I'm sure surpasses many a Lord. Shouldn't someone like you deserve a shot? Why should it only be a Lord or one of those families?" He paused again. "Not out of the lust for power but for the right for a chance to help others. Why should your talent be hidden from the rest of us? Now this is just you, we haven't started talking about others and what they can do," Yakenn added.

Ozwald glared at Yakenn as he began to walk around the balcony. Having a better view of it now, he estimated that the balcony was just as big as one floor of his house in the Haefe. It had long, shaved wooden poles that interlocked over each other with smooth, non-blistering surfaces. The poles had been lodged into the stone floor, giving the feeling that the structure could never fall or break.

After a short while, he sat on a nearby bench all the while contemplating Yakenn's words. He swiped the bench with his finger, not finding a single speck of dust. "Who cleaned this?" he quickly thought to himself.

"Are you going to explain everything to me? Am I to assume that everything is just a coincidence? That its just a coincidence that a man that I happened to bump into while trying to sneak into Aurom just has access to all these magnificent houses, knowledge of the whereabouts of the wealthy, and has already assembled a master team? And that these empty houses seemed to have been cleaned a moment before we arrived?" Ozwald barked, gazing intensely at Yakenn as he held out his clean finger. "You promised answers after Sir Rejji, but nothing has come of that, and now we're here, and I'm still in the dark," he continued, his voice washed with annoyance.

Yakenn, who had lost his smile now, exhaled and carelessly tossed his finished apple over the balcony. An angered cry rose from below. Despite his reputation as an honest and sincere person, Yakenn's mysterious eyes often betrayed his carefree and playful side.

"Look, Ozwald, I never meant to hide anything. You deserve to know, but it isn't something I just tell people about." He paused, sitting next to Ozwald while making direct eye contact. "What I can say is that this is a secret society, one that is quite old. It unites peoples across all of Azra, even Eurst. It unites people that think the way I just explained. People that think like you and me," he added, speaking sincerely and pointing to the both of them.

"And how do we think, then?" Ozwald asked, unable to break his gaze from Yakenn.

"Why, Ozwald, we believe in truth. We believe that society can never tell anyone who and what they are. It is up to the individual to decide. We believe that everyone deserves this. And that society's purpose is to make this happen by *any* means necessary," Yakenn said, looking at Ozwald strictly but sincerely. "And for us to do that, we have these quests. Just like the one for Sir Rejji. We never act on our own. There are always clear instructions that come to us. We carry them out without question," Yakenn continued, pausing before adjusting his position.

"So, you don't have a say? What if you don't agree with the quests? I find it hard to believe that every quest is justified," Ozwald snapped.

"You may object, but when you think about each quest, it becomes clear. I have objected in the past, but I've been proven wrong every time. I don't see a point in doing so anymore, and that's the commitment that we all maintain to break the shackles of society's confinement. Our cause is just. It is right, and I will continue to support it till my dying breath."

Ozwald listened intently before getting up and walking around the balcony. "Who is in this society? Ozwald asked with curious excitement.

"It spans the entire societal hierarchy. There are Lords, and there are farmers; there are merchants, and there are traders. We all have the same conviction, and we are many," Yakenn uttered, brushing his hair to the side.

"And, saying that, I agree. How do I get more involved? Where do I start?"

"Well, if you really want to join, you'll need to prove yourself. You need to show everyone that you mean what you say. It won't be easy. It won't be nice. It will, however, be right. It will help our cause and bring justice and equality for us all. Imagine we're all equal, and there are no more barriers. Imagine how much better off we would all be with no societal restrictions," Yakenn said, determination apparent across his face.

"What if I don't do it? What if I fail?" Ozwald confessed, unsureness apparent in his voice.

"You won't. I can see the determination in your eyes," Yakenn grinned. "I'm not going to hide my excitement anymore," Yakenn gleamed. "What do you say, will you join us?"

Ozwald immediately stopped pacing the balcony as Yakenn's words pierced his thoughts.

"Join us..." Ozwald whispered to himself as a subtle grin grew across his face.

Thirty-Four

Ozwald and Yakenn stood silently outside the estate's front door, both donning black cloaks as they waited for the signal to move. In comparison to the grandeur of other estates in Aurom, this one was modest, with two long, narrow floors and expansive underground levels. The actual house was dwarfed by the sprawling courtyard and surrounding evergreen trees, which lent an air of secrecy and seclusion to the property. The façade, made of aged limestone, was pocked with small holes and adorned with a coat of moss. The roof, designed for utility rather than aesthetics, allowed guards to keep watch from above. The cool evening air was amplified by the thick foliage, making it tempting for anyone within the estate's perimeter to remain indoors.

"Are you sure this is what you want?" Yakenn enquired, his voice unusually tense.

"I don't want to be a stranger," Ozwald said, confident

in his statement.

"Follow me, then," Yakenn uttered, tightening his hood and making his way out into the late summer night. Ozwald quickly followed across the courtyard and through its small front gate, where Rybae waited to see them off.

"We'll wait back for you here," Rybae said. Yakenn patted him on the back as he passed by him. However, when Ozwald passed, Rybae's face lit up. "I'm proud of you," he said, followed by a tight embrace before he locked the door behind them.

Ozwald and his companion strode along the deserted streets of Aurom, their footsteps echoing off the smooth granite pavement. The silence was punctuated only by the faint glow emanating from a few sparsely lit houses, lending an eerie atmosphere to the surroundings. Ozwald, careful not to disturb the stillness, watched his every step, tiptoeing around any loose cobblestones or debris that might betray their presence with a telltale noise.

"A few more turns before we get there. Keep moving. I don't trust these streets at night," Yakenn grunted.

After a short while, Yakenn pressed suddenly onto Ozwald's chest at the sight of a man walking across the street in the distance. Ozwald tried to decipher the man's features but could see nothing more than a black shadow. The man wobbled and stumbled on the ground as though new to walking or drunk to his ears.

"Hello," the man waved from afar, getting up and steadying his footing.

"I'll handle this," Yakenn murmured, his irritated face visible in the moonlight.

"Well, look who it is. Trying to run things on your

own, aye?" he said, his voice filled with malice.

"I think I know this man," Ozwald murmured to Yakenn, shifting uneasily.

"Tighten your hood. Stay here. I'll take care of him," Yakenn instructed.

"No, I'll come with you," Ozwald replied. Yakenn quickly grabbed him by his shirt tightly and looked into his eyes lividly.

"Damn it! Listen to me on this one. Stay here!" He snapped before dashing off, leaving Ozwald bewildered.

Yakenn unsheathed his sword and ran to the man, holding it high and ready to attack at a moment's notice. The man did not flinch, even as Yakenn approached aggressively. Ozwald wanted to run after him for support; however, Yakenn kept glancing back and signaling with his hands for him to remain.

Yakenn finally reached the man, and Ozwald cupped his ear in their direction. Before he could properly hear anything, the man ran off on his own, his hands flailing up high as he stumbled again. Yakenn stood behind, closely monitoring the man's escape as he sheathed his sword. Without wasting time, Yakenn ran back to Ozwald.

"Fucking drunkard," he cursed. "This place is falling apart if men like him are allowed to roam at this hour unchecked."

"That looked like one of those men, the ones that I told you about from the Haefe," Ozwald said, his voice slow. Yakenn quickly shrugged him off, though.

"That was a drunk man, nothing more. He ran off the moment I threatened him. Let's keep moving. We're late," Yakenn exhaled, nudging Ozwald to move before he could ask another question.

Yakenn led them next through a side alley. Emerging, Ozwald was met with a monotonous display of architecture that offered little in terms of distinguishing landmarks. He eagerly scanned his surroundings, searching for any semblance of familiarity that might help him orient himself.

"We're still going northeast, right?" Ozwald enquired, but Yakenn did not answer. After another half hour of silent walking, Ozwald gave up trying to search for any familiar landmark and focused more on the city in front of him.

Aurom's summer was drawing to a close, bringing with it a damp and chilly air that fell over the city. Ozwald did not mind it. In fact, he reveled in it, and his senses were heightened by the sweet fragrance of jasmine emanating from every courtyard he passed. The households on the eastern side were tightly packed, almost like they were built wall-to-wall. The roads were lined with tall oak trees with long, sprawling branches that obstructed his view, making it difficult to catch a glimpse inside. Despite the obstacles, Ozwald's eyes were fixated on every new household he passed by. Suddenly, Yakenn rushed ahead, stopping in front of an estate. Ozwald quickly rushed behind him and looked through its ominous gate. His eyes glistened at the sight. The estate had been built with higher walls and taller trees than the others, and its dark stones contrasted with the white stones of the other estates. He could not see inside as the gate had been completely covered with thin metal sheets.

"We're here," Yakenn said, full of energy as Ozwald broke from his daze.

"Let's get in then. We don't want to keep them waiting for us," Ozwald replied, his face already lit up. Yakenn nodded, signaling with his hand for Ozwald to follow him in. The gate opened with a creaking sound, and Ozwald quickly glanced to Yakenn for reassurance. With every step, Ozwald remembered his entrance into Aurom, and the feeling of rejection lingered in his thoughts.

They walked through the courtyard, treading across a cobblestone path between densely packed bushes. The courtyard itself felt distant and obscure. Bushes and trees had grown throughout, limiting Ozwald's view.

The ominous house loomed before Ozwald, its aged walls covered in green vines that seemed to stretch toward the sky. The rustling of leaves in the cool breeze sent shivers down Ozwald's spine as though the very air was filled with secrets that begged to be uncovered. The windows were dark and foreboding, except for a few windows downstairs that emitted a dim glow. The wooden shutters were beaten and battered, clattering against the window frame as if the house had been abandoned for years. Ozwald could not shake off the feeling that something lurked within its walls, something ancient and hidden from the rest of Aurom and Azra.

As they approached the main entrance of the house, it creaked open slowly and eerily on its own. Yakenn remained unphased and stepped inside, while Ozwald hesitated before following suit. Once inside, he looked around but could not discern who or what had opened the door. Before he could ask any questions, though, his eyes caught sight of the dimly lit chandelier hung at the top of the hall.

"We're over there," Yakenn whispered, tapping him on the back as the doors closed with a slam. He gazed back again, still seeing no one, and Yakenn continued walking ahead aloof.

"Who's doing that?" Ozwald asked, his voice filled with curiosity and slight bewilderment.

"Come on, it's just an effect. You don't really..." Yakenn mocked. "I'll explain later."

Ozwald's body language, though, demanded an immediate answer, an answer that Yakenn appeared eager to share.

Smirking and proud of himself, Yakenn rushed back to the door, pulling a small lever to its side.

"Counterweights inside the wall, see?" he smirked.

"Must be new," Ozwald gasped, his eyes transfixed on a new piece of technology that he least expected in this house.

"New? No, this place has been around for generations. I haven't told you, but one of my ancestors built this place a long time ago," Yakenn explained, his face revealing his self-satisfaction.

Ozwald was not taken aback by Yakenn's statement. In fact, a big part of him had already suspected that Yakenn was more than he had portrayed himself to be. It was clear that Yakenn was not just an ordinary member of a secret order but had strong family ties to it. Ozwald had already sensed this and was prepared to learn more about Yakenn's background in due course, no matter what it was. However, Ozwald's primary focus was not on Yakenn's lineage but rather on the mission of the secret order.

"Why haven't I seen you come here before?" Ozwald asked.

"Let's say I'm not on good terms with the owners here. I just come when I need to," Yakenn sneered, his voice low and calm. "Ahh. This way," he pointed. Ozwald nodded.

"I'm going to wait here."

"Why?"

"That's usually preferred," Yakenn continued, pushing Ozwald through the door. "No need to knock. Just open it," Yakenn whispered.

Ozwald stood at the door for a moment, casting a final glance at Yakenn, who immediately signaled for him to go ahead with an uneasy smile. Ozwald took a deep breath and pushed the door open.

As he entered the room, he noticed a solitary figure seated at the far end of a long table. The man's bald head was accentuated by greasy hair combed back on either side. His features were plain, but his nose pointed slightly forward. Ozwald could not help but notice the small pin on the collar of his tight black cloak. He tried to focus on it but was distracted by the rest of the room. The room was plain and windowless. The chairs were many and appeared well cared for. The walls had been painted from top to bottom with a peculiar scene that looked vaguely familiar to him. It was as if he had seen it before, and he felt a strange, unexplainable attraction to it. The painting depicted a vast land mass that appeared to have been split in half by a bolt of lightning, dividing two distinct groups of people. At the top of the land mass, he observed a ship that was sailing off into the distance. This sight intrigued him and stirred his imagination, leaving him with an unquenchable desire to learn more about the painting's origins and meaning.

"The great chasm. A marvelous piece of art, dreadful times though, I would say," the man said, his voice sharp and unforgiving. He remained seated and signaled for Ozwald to take a seat near to him.

"It looks familiar," Ozwald hesitated, taking a seat

opposite the man at the table. The man looked up at the painting.

"Curious. This, to my knowledge at least, is the only complete visual representation of it of this size at least. Unless you were there, I don't see how," the man said, his voice still shrewd and intimidating.

"You're here at your own request, I've heard," he continued. "Do you know my name?"

"No."

"That's safer. For you, of course," he said, leaning back in his chair. Ozwald did not respond, waiting instead for him to lead the conversation.

"What do you know about this order?" The man asked, fixated on Ozwald as he spoke.

"I've only seen what you do. Regarding the order generally, nothing. Yakenn has been silent. I don't even know its name. I just know that it exists and what it does." The man adjusted in his seat for the first time, his eyes glaring into Ozwald's.

"You're a farmer, right?"

"Yes."

"If I had a sword to mend and horseshoes to replace, would I go to a blacksmith or a baker?"

"Why, a blacksmith, of course," Ozwald said confidently.

"Ahh, yes, a blacksmith. The baker would have no chance to succeed."

"That's right."

"Then why do we need a farmer in this secret order? We don't grow food here and we don't accept mutts off the street. If we did, then we wouldn't remain a secret anymore."

Ozwald hesitated for a moment. "I was under the impression that your order would want someone like me."

"Someone like you? You're not special, and Yakenn is a fool to even speak to you about all this," the man said, visibly angry. Ozwald had not expected their conversation to evolve in this direction, while taking his time to contemplate a response.

"Wait. You asked about the sword and the blacksmith, but your answer is not entirely correct. Qualification is a close second to commitment and the will to do the job," Ozwald began, the man listening intently.

"A few Lirkins is that man's motivation. I don't understand," he shot back, his impatience mounting.

"Well, yes, but what if there was no payment? Then, the one with the greatest commitment is who you should select," Ozwald said, closely studying the man's reaction.

"And what about qualification?"

"Maybe the baker's good friend was a blacksmith's son and taught him a few things. With the right commitment, he'll get the job done. I'm sure of it," Ozwald said, his voice confident as he stared into the man's eyes.

"I came to this city to start a new path when I was about to give up on life itself. Yakenn has shown me that, and I want to be of more use. I'm done running. I've seen this order in action, and actions speak louder than words," Ozwald went on.

The man smiled, folding his hands. "Your motivation, your commitment, it pleases me," he said. His voice was still sharp but had taken on a warmer demeanor. "When Yakenn was still a young boy, he would tag along with his father..."

"You knew his father?" Ozwald interjected.

"Indeed, he owns this place," the man replied. "Yakenn's hospitality is a reflection of our hospitality and, in turn, a reflection of his father's," he continued, clearing his throat. "As I was saying, as a young boy, he was very active, always curious, and always watching. His father, however, would never reveal anything. Yakenn would stay in the hall you just entered, trying to catch a whisper through that very door. With that curiosity, commitment, and willpower, he begged his father to join as soon as he was of age. That was only four summers back, as I can recall. And since then, he has done wonders for the order," the man confessed, taking a sip from his cup. "I see the same in you."

"What happens now? I don't want to keep training and waiting," Ozwald said. "I want to get involved immediately."

"Training. I thought we agreed on that," he began, glancing over the wall painting. Ozwald sat at the edge of his seat. "However..." the man continued, curling what hair he could catch with his finger. Ozwald's heart raced, anxious to hear the rest of his thoughts. "Yes, baby steps. Yes, there is something you can do, something to prove yourself."

"Anything," Ozwald shot back, his entire face lit up.

"There is a man —a Lord, actually, that is in Aurom for the next two weeks," he explained.

"Who?"

"Does it matter? You trust us, don't you?"

"Yes, I do."

"Good, you are to kill him," the man said, his voice becoming shrewd again.

"Why kill him?" Ozwald hesitated.

"Isn't this what you want? I understand You need a reason. That I can give. This Lord is influential but uses his power to steer his own ambitions and desires. He's creating conflict, which will lead to war, and the death of many. One man cannot have such power in the shadows."

Ozwald did not speak, and his thoughts raced at the man's reasoning. Eventually, his gaze lingered back to the mural once more, and again, he marveled at it, attempting to remember where he had seen it.

"The end defines the means," he whispered to himself, remembering Yakenn's words. Suddenly, it all made sense. Ozwald looked up, his eyes dead-focused on the man.

"I'll do it," he said, feeling a heavy weight suddenly lifted off his shoulders.

Thirty-Five

Aelav sat on the back bench at the end of the courtyard, sheltered from the rain by a roof near the wall. Every evening, she sat there, waiting patiently for a visitor who never showed up. And every evening, her eyes would frantically scan the courtyard while squeezing water from her cloak and hair, and the sound of falling rain filling her ears and the smell of wet grass lingering in the air.

A week had passed since she had followed Johnson and Walrick to the hidden room behind the round wooden door near Fallgarde's Grand Temple. Since then, she had barely seen anyone except for the servants who brought her food and maintained her living quarters. Walrick had disappeared as well, leaving her free to wander the castle at will.

Every day, she ventured to the lower quarter's floor, hoping to gain entry to the room behind the round wooden door. But it was always locked, like every other room in the castle. She even tried visiting at different times of day, hoping for a change, but was always met with disappointment.

Suddenly, the back door on the wall opened. She glanced frantically, searching for someone.

"A rather curious night to be out and at such a late hour," a voice spoke from behind the door. Aelav did not linger and got up immediately.

"I've been waiting for you all week. Here. Just as we had agreed. Where have you been?" She blurted, frustration clear in her voice, while approaching the door and walking through. She shut the door behind her, along with the loud sound of rain and wet scent. Dampness hung heavily in the air inside. Without further hesitation, she descended the dimly lit stairwell after lighting a torch she had brought with her from a nearby fire that was always lit, inside.

"Can we please stop playing games and just meet somewhere up there instead of deep inside," she raged, her voice ringing on the walls just as she reached the bottom of the stairs. A face immediately appeared. Kodren. Aelav's face lit up.

"What happened to you?" She quickly questioned, her face quickly washed with disgust. Kodren's face had been bruised with cuts across his eye filled with dry blood and puss. He waved her off with his hand.

"Training. The whole army is on high alert," he said, coughing.

"Army. Why?" She asked, her eyes crossed. Kodren began to chuckle eerily, his eyes focused on Aelav.

"Haven't you heard? Usall is almost entirely gone. Drought and dead land. The red blight is here," he growled, his face flustered while raising his voice. Aelav did not flinch. Her face remained neutral. "What is there to report other than the prince not sailing in yet," he added.

"That's news from last week. This week, I found out that they actually lost him. He's probably dead. Rorik's men are already searching for him," she said, her voice neutral and eyes half open. Aelav paused as she saw Kodren's face reddened with every passing instant. "And also, never raise your voice in a Toren's face, you bastard," she added, her voice exact and non-forgiving.

Kodren began to grin instead, a sly look washing across his face. He grabbed her by her arm and stared down at her.

"I don't care who you are. I'm in charge here. I can do as I please," he growled. Aelav paused for a moment, boiling on the inside, while her free hand shook impatiently. He quickly let go of her, both panting from the embrace.

"What else is there to report?" He asked, massaging his eyes while his voice remained calm as if recent events had never passed.

"Why am I still here? That should be the first topic to discuss," she grunted, staring directly at Kodren and not blinking. He rubbed his eyes and took a deep breath.

"The marriage was never going to happen anyways. If he's alive somewhere in Azra, then the plan doesn't change. He dies," he exhaled. "As for you. I need to know Rorik's secrets. This castle's secrets. You won't be taken anywhere else. Emperor's orders. He has always been suspicious of the bastard here and you have confirmed that," he added, shifting in his place. Aelav exhaled tying her hair back.

"There is one thing," she began as Kodren's eyes began to open. "There's a secret room near Fallgarde's Grand Temple. I saw Johnson and Walrick inside."

"A secret room. Well that's a discovery," Kodren

mocked, ready to leave. "This is a huge castle with many rooms. You definitely can do better than that," he added, Aelav's face fuming. "This has clearly been a waste of my time. I'll see you in two weeks maybe three weeks. Maybe by then you would have something new to share," he continued.

Aelav remained still and took deep breaths.

"What would you have me do then for the next three weeks," she asked. Kodren began to walk slowly but deep into the darkness of the corridor, no light visible from the other end.

"First, you won't get anywhere without getting your hands dirty. Second, stop acting like a child. Wolves dominate life, not sheep," he snapped, his voice and body disappearing into the darkness. "Three weeks," he added.

Aelav stood silently while her cheeks reddened, as Kodren completely disappeared into the darkness, no sound coming in from his direction. She looked back up the stairs she had come from and began to ascend. "Such a Child," she whispered to herself continuously. At the top, she pressed her hands on the door and creaked it open. A small gust of wind blew in bringing with it the smell of moisture and a strong stench of dead corpses. "It'll be here soon as well," she said to herself. The rain had stopped though, making it easier for her to hear anything across the courtyard.

No one in sight, Aelav ran along the outer perimeter of the courtyard and through the bushes. She saw no lit window from the tower above, keeping her head down and running ahead. Her breath quickened. At the end of the courtyard, she entered back into the castle through a small door and into an open space. She saw the stairwell and walked towards it. The space had locked doors lined up all around save for the kitchen door which always remained open. The smell of raw meat emanated from it as she passed by. While the entire space had been lit by two small candles hung on a nearby wall.

Aelav began to ascend the stairs, while catching sight of a flick of light from below. She peered over the handrail and saw light emanating from the underground floors. She gasped at the sight and stuttered for a moment before descending. She measured each footstep to avoid making any sound, while cupping her ear for any sound.

Suddenly, she heard a creaking sound while descending the last flight of stairs. She slowed her pace, scanning in detail the space ahead of her while taking cover in the shade that she could find.

At the bottom of the stairs, she caught sight of the wide corridor below, her eyes frantically jumping around. No one could be seen. She remained motionless attempting to find her next check point until she caught sight of Fallgarde's Grand Temple opposite to her. The door, she saw, had been cracked open. A dim light came out as she paused for a moment. Suddenly, the sound of light footsteps could be heard. Her eyes stopped blinking as her senses focused on the hall's opened door. She dashed to it and peaked through its opening.

Aelav immediately caught sight of a cloaked figure at the end of it. Near the Promise Well. She covered her head and tightened her hood, while taking a deep breath and walking in. The figure did not glance toward her as she approached. She remained in the shadows to the side of the hall, attempting to understand what was taking place before her eyes.

She gasped when she saw light emanating from the fountain. She stood in the darkness observing closely without taking any further steps forward. After a short while, the cloaked figure entered a back room behind the altar. Her focus, though, remained on the glowing Promise Well, which she approached rapidly, while watching out if anyone else came in.

Aelav ascended the altar and approached the well. Her eyes followed the white and colorful play of the water. It swirled consistently as if in a storm, emanating a subtle water gushing sound. Aelav was drawn to it, as if it had a language to speak from a forgotten land in a foreign tongue. She put out her hand, her eyes jumping feverously around the hall. She held her hand right above the water as she felt the air of the moving turbulence.

"Stop!" A voice suddenly said, surely and astutely. Aelav turned and saw the same figure from before. This time, she saw his eyes.

"I know you. Jeb. That's right," Aelav squealed, her heavy breath calming down. Jeb glared at her, his teeth visible and his back straight.

"Who permitted you here?" He badgered, his stern face still fixated on Aelav who began to approach him calmly.

"Come on, it's me! Last month, you slit a goat right over there," she said, pointing to the area.

"We are one with them, and you are not. Jeb may be my name, but you're not allowed here. Trespassing is immediate execution," he hissed, grabbing both her hands and shoving her to the ground. He then proceeded to kick her in the stomach, his bare feet leaving a mark on her black cloak, while she remained lying on the ground. He then dragged her by her hands towards the back of the altar. Aelav began to shout and scream, kicking and punching in the air.

"Let me go!" She cried.

"You have seen what others have not. The secret must die with you to save Azra. Otherwise, complete anarchy," he growled, as if reading directly from a scroll. Aelav caught a glance of where he aimed to take her and saw a stone pole.

Just as she passed it, she grabbed on to it with all her might, squirming sounds pouring out of her mouth as her hair flew everywhere and covered her eyes. Despite wrapping her arm around the stone pole tightly, Jeb continued to pull on her. Suddenly, he produced a wooden rod and began to beat her on her arms, while she screamed out from pain.

As she would not move, he took a swing at the back of her head.

"Let me go," she said, barely able to be audible, as blood dripped down her face, mixed with her hair and sweat. She felt loose as her arms lessened their embrace around the stone pillar. Just as she let go, something flashed from the corner of her half open eyes. The blow had taken its toll. She saw Jeb smirk as he dragged her away.

She squealed as breath barely escaped her mouth while Jeb continued to drag her. This time though, her voice was much louder, which caught his attention. He stopped and stared at her, while she signaled with her finger for him to come closer. He rolled his eyes but eventually complied, kneeling above her.

In an instant, Aelav's expression shifted to that of a fierce warrior as she locked eyes with Jeb. With a deafening cry, she seized the old iron cup that lay loosely by the promise well and struck Jeb's head with all her might, causing him to stumble backwards. She swiftly rose to her feet and kicked him to the ground, then delivered a crushing blow to his face with the cup. Blood gushed from the wound where flesh met iron, as Aelav fell to her knees, gripping the cup with one hand and relentlessly driving it further into Jeb's face with the other. With her heart racing, she surveyed Jeb's motionless body. She stood up, still panting heavily, holding her head. Aelav saw her hands full of blood and immediately let go of the cup as it clattered on the stone floor.

"Look what you've made me do," she hissed, spitting on Jeb's motionless body. "I was asked for something worth talking about. You just gave it to me," she added just as she heard steps from outside. She hesitated before finding a dark place to hide behind one of the pillars to the side of the hall. She crouched waiting for an opening to escape as two figures entered the hall.

They ran to the front not speaking a word and standing over Jeb's motionless body. Both catching sight of the glowing Promise Well before them. The well's magnificent colors captured their gaze and would not allow them to look anywhere else, as if singing a thousand songs. They stood for a few moments before one of them spoke.

"It has started. We leave first thing in the morning," a man said. Aelav recognized his voice to be Johnson's. Just as they arrived unannounced, both men departed immediately, leaving Jeb alone on the ground as the door closed right behind them.

Thirty-Six

"Lost," Ozwald heard a man speak through an open window as he hid inside a thick green bush. He had been hiding for the past three hours with his ear glued to the windowsill. Rybae and Ozwald had monitored every part of the house, just as Yakenn taught him to, over the last few days, including guard tour schedules and the daily routines of the target. The target was a man who spent every morning in his office before leaving the house, only to return for the greater part of his evening as well, alone. Yakenn gave him his instructions, and Rybae accompanied him throughout.

Ozwald did not recognize the target, nor was he told who he was. He even tried asking around, but everyone was clueless. Blind compliance with the instructions was always expected.

The house stood at the southwestern end of the city, not far from the emperor's palace. In this part of the city, houses were not built wall to wall as in its eastern quarters.

If Ozwald had any chance to complete his mission, he knew it would be at night. However, he had not planned for guests, which he overheard while hidden below the open study window.

"When?" A deep-voiced man said.

"I don't know, but not too long ago," the man replied, his voice irritated. Ozwald listened closer.

"And why is this reaching me only now?" The deep voice shrewdly enquired.

"My Lord, I've been busy with the girl. I only received word recently, and I came at once when I did. And there's a development that we need to discuss. My Lord, if I may point out, we would've known by now, maybe we should…"

"I know!" The deep voice man shot back, "Very well, send out the search parties. All of them, but quietly. Otherwise, someone will notice. And we don't want anyone sniffing our way with questions. There's enough trouble as it is. This time, you end it," he hissed.

Ozwald, still well hidden in the bushes, lifted his head and peaked through the window, catching only the shadows of the men as they exited the study. He dropped his head back down, taking deep breaths.

Suddenly, he pulled himself up, slipping into the study's open window and landing quietly on his feet in a crouched position. The room exuded an air of elegance and sophistication with its generously proportioned wooden furniture, strategically placed to create a sense of balance and harmony. It appeared as though the room had just undergone a major renovation. The furniture was meticulously arranged to showcase its beauty and grandeur. The plush texture of the thick rug provided a delightful sensation for anyone who treaded on it, cushioning each footfall with comfort. A table in the center of the room held a few scrolls, which were arranged haphazardly, as if their owner had just set them down for a moment. Beside the scrolls, a jar of ink and feather lay, waiting for the next opportunity to be put to use. The walls of the room were painted a vivid red, which seemed to radiate warmth and energy, creating a cozy and intimate atmosphere. The overall effect was a space that was both luxurious and functional, where one could immerse themselves in intellectual pursuits or simply relax and enjoy the surroundings.

In the distance and through the still ajar door, he caught site of the two men walking out. One man wore a black cloak, while the other wore a loose red shirt with folded sleeves. They continued to speak quietly with each other. Ozwald's gaze raced between the two, monitoring their every movement, debating with himself over which one to follow. Finally, he decided to follow the man wearing the loose red shirt who walked up the stairs to the area of the private chambers. No one would be upstairs in the evening. It would be his best chance, he knew.

After his target had been set, Ozwald knelt at the study door, examining the outside open space. He saw the light emanating from a candle holder moving up the stairs, mixed with white moonlight pouring into the space as well.

Shifting his gaze to the right, he could not help but hold his breath for a moment. Before him was a circular wall that overlooked the city, constructed entirely of glass from top to bottom. The sheer size of the glass window was enough to dwarf the height of his own house in the Haefe. Upon closer inspection, he noticed that the glass was composed of small tiles, each one carefully crafted and intricately designed. It was a unique style of architecture that he had never seen before, and he marveled at the craftsmanship that must have gone into its creation. The wall's circular shape allowed for a breathtaking panoramic view of the night city below. A sense of awe and wonder overcame him from its sheer beauty.

He saw a sheltered area just at the base of the stairs, which he dashed to quickly, moving with his back arched. He avoided heavy steps, doing his best to remain stealthy while moving swiftly, putting into practice Yakenn's teachings. At the base of the stairs, he wiped perspiration off his forehead while looking up the stairs frantically. The man had already disappeared, and he heard a door shut from the other end of the hall where the black-cloaked man had gone. Not wasting any more time, Ozwald rushed up, continuously glancing around. He clasped Stonesaver, which was tightly fastened to his waist, before quickly searching for the dagger Yakenn had given him.

At the top of the steps, light emanated from a loosely closed door at the end of the corridor. He paused for a moment, listening intently for anything before making his way to it. He saw an open and unlit nearby room and quickly slipped in to hide inside until the right moment. Crouching, he cupped his ear, trying to catch anything from inside. Nothing. But he had to be there, he knew.

After a short while, Ozwald grabbed his dagger, got up and made his way to the lit and loosely closed door. He pressed his hand to it and began to push it in slowly, his heart throbbing up to his neck. He immediately caught sight of an empty desk and chair. "Where is he?" he whispered to himself, frantically searching for movement and listening for any sounds.

"Hard to kill someone when you can't see them," a deep voice spoke. Ozwald turned around immediately, his vision racing across the dark room.

"Show yourself," Ozwald hissed. No response came back, and he held his dagger in front of him.

"Despite being at a disadvantage, you continue to move forward. Are you sure you want to continue with whatever you have planned?" The deep voice sneered.

"This won't end well," Ozwald snapped back.

"My, my, lightning reaction," the voice sneered from another location.

"Where are you?" Ozwald snapped again.

"I'm right here," the voice whispered in Ozwald's ear. He quickly stabbed in the voice's direction, landing on a soft surface to Ozwald's satisfaction. He attempted to pull his dagger back, but it would not budge. A malicious laugh rang out.

"Missed your mark completely," the voice whispered. Suddenly, Ozwald was kicked from behind and fell flat on his face. Hands grabbed his arms and dragged him into the lit room. Ozwald tried to look for the man's face but failed. He was forced to sit on a chair while his hands and feet were quickly tied up, halting all of his movement.

"You still hide from me, you coward," Ozwald growled, struggling in his bonds.

"Oh, shut up. Only a coward tries to kill a man in his sleep," the man growled.

"Why are you here?" the man demanded.

"My friends will be here any minute," Ozwald hissed.

"Well, I'll take my chances. At least they can't see inside here, so I don't expect your saviors to barge in anytime soon," the man sneered. "Who are you?"

"What does that matter to you?" Ozwald spat.

"Well, at least I should get the chance to know the name of my presumed assassin. The coward."

Ozwald did not speak, and pain throbbed from where he had been tied up tightly.

"With one swing. With one word. I can have you dead. It's a mercy that you're still alive. Just because I'm curious to learn the identity of my would-be assassin. My first ever assassin in Adrovia of all places. Actually, come to think of it, the first that has ever infiltrated my household. Times are getting desperate, I suppose, and this may not be the last time. So I ask again, who are you? But better, who sent you?" The man demanded.

"That's what you're good at. Getting what you want, whenever you want," Ozwald spat, his face flaring up red.

"What are you talking about?" The man demanded, now standing in front of Ozwald in full view. "Do you know who I am?" The man hissed again, his face washed with anger.

"A corrupt Lord using your power to further your own interests. You don't care about Azra," Ozwald sneered, spitting in his face. "You don't deserve life."

"My own interests? Corrupt? Do you know what you're saying?" The man badgered, his face fuming as well.

"That's not the way you address the Lord of Fallgarde!" A voice said from behind Ozwald calmly and confidently.

"Lord Rorik..." Ozwald exhaled, dropping his head

while Rorik took a deep breath and stared down at Ozwald.

"Yes. And who are you?" Lord Rorik demanded once more. Rorik's stare fixated on Ozwald. "Your face is familiar," he continued as tears began to drop from his eyes. "Ozwald…?"

"How do you know my…" Ozwald stuttered as Rorik began to cut all his ties. Ozwald rubbed his wrists and fixated on Rorik, speechless.

"Why are you here?" Rorik snapped. The other man in the room stepped up from behind him. It was the black-cloaked man, and Ozwald remembered him as if from a dream.

Suddenly, Ozwald jolted up, tipping his chair backward. "What is he doing here?" He hissed, stepping back towards the door.

"Ozwald, calm down. I can explain," Rorik consoled.

"It was you! You were there. I'll never forget your face. You were there just before it happened!" Ozwald growled, his anger building. He felt for Stonesaver. Ozwald unsheathed his sword, prompting the other two to do the same.

"Ozwald. Put your sword down now. I can explain. You can't win, anyways," Rorik grunted.

"Ozwald. This is not what you think," the cloaked man started before Ozwald raised his sword and attacked with a loud battle cry that surprised even himself.

Rorik dodged him while the black-cloaked man moved to the side, his face flushed red. He swung his sword in Ozwald's direction in retaliation.

"Johnson, no! Don't!" Rorik shrieked while Ozwald and Johnson exchanged sword swings, each time blocking the other. "Not too fast, Johnson," Ozwald spat before Johnson kicked him in his chest, knocking the breath out of him.

"Whatever they told you, it's a lie. You're important. You're the hope we need, the hope that we thought we lost," Rorik explained.

Ozwald got up and launched a fierce attack, directing his sword toward Rorik this time. Quick on his feet, Rorik managed to evade his strikes but, in the confusion, accidentally sent Ozwald stumbling toward Johnson. Ozwald's sword pierced Johnson's side in the commotion, eliciting a painful cry.

As blood splattered onto the floor and Ozwald's face, Johnson stopped fidgeting and slid off of Stonesaver with a loud thud, clutching his wound. Ozwald froze, bewildered by what had just occurred. In the blink of an eye, Johnson seized the opportunity and, summoning all his remaining strength, retaliated by stabbing Ozwald in his fighting arm with a dagger.

"That's so you never stab without reason," Johnson gasped, his voice low but confident as he fell to the ground. Ozwald's eyes raced between his sword and a now almost motionless man on the ground.

Rorik dived to Johnson and held his head up. "Stay with me, my old friend," he urged before looking back at Ozwald.

"Is this what you believe in?" Rorik badgered, his eyes drenched in a mixture of worry and anger. "I don't know what hope we have left," he continued. "Help! Help!" He began to shout, his voice ringing through the entire house and sucking the life out of Ozwald.

Suddenly, the entire house lit up as the sound of people running around ignited. Ozwald sheathed Stonesaver and pulled out the dagger from his arm, discarding it on the ground.

Before Rorik could say anything, Ozwald ran out of the room, blood still dripping from his arm. The outside corridor and stairs remained as before, dark with no light save for the moonlight beaming in through the tall windows. He knew, though, that soon enough, all the lights would be on, and there would be no place for him to hide in anymore.

He rushed down the stairs and could still hear Rorik shouting for help from above. Once in the study, he shut the doors behind him and remained leaning on them for a short while as he listened to the commotion outside. He rubbed his eyes and then stared at his bloody hands before he saw Stonesaver's hilt drenched in blood.

Ozwald shook his head as he caught sight of the window and made his way to it, his back arched to avoid making any noise. Through the window, he saw the dark night sky dotted with clouds visible from the shining moonlight. He searched for Rybae but could not find him.

"You! We have an unfinished discussion," a voice suddenly spoke from behind Ozwald at the door of the room. He turned and immediately saw Rorik. Without a second to waste, Ozwald jumped from the windowsill, lifting his first leg outside before being stopped and brought back in.

"Leave me alone! Otherwise, you'll meet Johnson's doom," Ozwald hissed. Rorik wrestled him to sit and stop moving, this time, though, untied.

"Johnson will live. He's seen worse, you idiot," Rorik exhaled. "How did you get here, and why are you here?" Rorik snapped.

"What is it to you?" Ozwald began.

"That is not how you speak to your uncle, boy," Rorik growled.

Ozwald gasped, letting Rorik's words sink in. Rorik fidgeted in his place while his face transformed into a warm glow. "I'm sorry," Rorik panted, Ozwald's eyes beginning to flare.

"You're the reason my family is dead!" Ozwald growled, grabbing Rorik by his neck, mustering a power he never knew existed. Rorik squirmed, and his face began to go red. Rorik grabbed onto Ozwald's hands and dislodged them, breathing heavily once free.

"On the contrary, you fool!" Rorik shot back. "I heard what happened. I would've stopped it if I had known that they had found you," Rorik yelled, still catching his breath.

"But you didn't," Ozwald fired back, his eyes beginning to tear up. "You're no uncle of mine. Nothing good can ever come from you. You manipulate others and do as you please. Did you let my real parents die too?" Ozwald badgered, backing up again towards the window.

"Ozwald, everything you just said is a lie. If you would allow me to explain," Rorik began.

"There's nothing to explain, you snake!" Ozwald screamed.

"Listen to me! For a while now, I've lost all hope for Azra. But you — seeing you here brings me hope. Together, I know that we can find a way," he continued, his eyes glowing.

"A way for what? The way I see it, only your end will bring me hope," Ozwald spat.

"The red blight, that's all that matters. Azra has less than three months," Rorik sighed. "No one wants to admit it. And yet, it approaches faster than anyone imagined. Once it's done with the land, then there'll be a never-ending war until there is no one to kill anymore," Rorik groaned. "It's the end. Do you know what that means?"

"I've had enough of your lies," Ozwald said, his voice less confident than before.

"By the Ancients, you couldn't have come at a better time," Rorik continued. "I know what I say does not make sense. But if you give me a chance, I can explain everything."

"I don't need an explanation. I know a liar when I see one," Ozwald sneered.

"Think of it, why out of all the Lords of Azra, they sent you after me? They've attacked no one else except me. The Order of Defiance will do anything to destroy Azra, and they are using you as a tool," Rorik began.

"O.D.," Ozwald whispered to himself.

"You're helping them destroy Azra and life as we know it," Rorik trembled.

Ozwald pondered Rorik's words for a moment, his mind racing with possibilities and ideas. Rorik, though, used this as an opportunity to reach out and console Ozwald, clasping his shoulder. However, Ozwald snapped out of his daze and brushed Rorik's hand away as he remembered where he was and what he had to do.

"This is not finished," Ozwald suddenly hissed, making his way to the window.

"Ozwald, wait! Wait!" Rorik shrieked from behind. Before he could reach him, Ozwald jumped out and did not look back.

"Ozwald Lygem, come back here!" Rorik shouted from behind, his voice dying out in the distance. Ozwald's heart was filled with rage and sadness.

Thirty-Seven

It had been almost a month since Ethan made it to Bograh. He had walked across the southern seashore at the base of the bordering bloodshed hills. Contrary to his expectations, the bloodshed hills, once the site of a bloody massacre, were now draped in thick forests that hugged the southern sandy shores. The land was teeming with fertility yet was abandoned. A painful history was etched into the soil, prompting an official decree banning any settlement on the site of the largest tragedy in Azra's history. More than twenty thousand people from Adrovia and Bograh had perished in a matter of days during a futile conflict, the details of which had long been forgotten. In an effort to prevent stirring the dead, it had become a tradition to not disturb the area. But the conflict had been senseless, fought only for power and resources, resulting in the annihilation of an entire generation. Instead of trying to learn from it, the rulers of Azra intentionally forgot about it.

Although travelers warned him not to tread alone, he made it to Moj unscathed. Moj, Bograh's largest western city, bordered Adrovia. He avoided interacting with anyone unless completely necessary and walked only during the night when the light was meager and his presence was hard to detect. He refused to use the main road and only walked through the forest. The thicker the forest, the better.

In Bograh, he dismantled the gold windings across the hilt of his sword and sold them for a thousand Lirkins in a small town on his path. He used a small part of it to book a room at a local inn in Moj for the next year. He wanted to forget his family and Eurst, no matter where that would take him. As he explored the city, he was struck by its melancholic atmosphere. The sky was often gray and cloudy or shrouded in fog. Rain was a frequent occurrence. The hot, damp weather made it difficult to move about during the day, so people typically ventured out in the cooler, windier evenings. The city center was characterized by houses that were spaced apart and connected by rough, dirt pathways. The buildings were simple structures made of thin wood.

During his first week, he frequented the local tavern at dusk. The city's laborers usually visited for a drink or two prior to supper and bed, a tradition he had never heard of before. He had changed his wardrobe to better assimilate with the rest and tried to meet whoever he could.

Everyone knew that Ethan was from out of town, as was common in Moj, which limited suspicion of his origins. He introduced himself as Samor to break cleanly from his past. At the end of his first week, he met Farhet, Moj's only bakery owner.

Farhet sold his bread to customers in the city. Once a

week, at night, he visited the nearby tobacco plantations. He distributed what bread remained to the farmers. He gave away, on average, thirty loaves of bread per visit. When Ethan enquired about his reasoning, Farhet replied, "No point in excess when others don't have enough. Helps me sleep better at night." Ethan did not question further. He saw something different in Farhet — a willingness and enjoyment for life and a belief that he could always do something to help. Ethan saw him three nights in a row and eventually made a proposition.

"I'm not here for long, but I'd like to come by tomorrow. I'd like to see how I can help." Farhet's face lit up, and he shook Ethan's hand without question.

The next morning, Ethan paid a visit to Farhet as promised, meeting two of his main helpers, Jones and Ursula, at the bakery.

"If it weren't for these two, we'd not be able to do what we do," he joked. Jones had a thin build with greasy black hair, and Ursula always wrapped her head with a black cloth and was round at her belly.

At night, Ethan accompanied Farhet to one of the tobacco plantations. The sky was unusually clear, and a full moon hung high in the sky, emanating enough light for Ethan to catch a proper glimpse of acres upon acres of tobacco plants. At first, he thought that no more than fifty farmers would appear, but he turned out to be wrong. At least triple that amount appeared as they gathered around Farhet as if only he could provide them with enough food to fill their bellies. No matter how hard Farhet, Jones, and Ursula tried to get them in line, the farmers would not listen.

Once all the bread had been given out, the farmers

complained and demanded more. Farhet assured them that next week, he would be back with more. Still, the farmers objected. Although Ethan was happy with the act, he questioned the farmer's disrespect. "Ungrateful lot," he whispered to himself.

"I'll be back next week, same time, with more bread. I promise you," Farhet shouted, standing on a wooden box as he spoke out to the sea of farmers. Their faces were still covered in dirt from the day's toil.

Ethan gazed upon them, and frustration washed across his face. He walked in between them, trying to listen to their concerns as they spoke with one another.

"I haven't eaten all day. Why can't this idiot get more bread?" One of the farmers said to another.

"There isn't enough food tonight for my kids!" Another farmer complained.

Ethan's frustration grew the more he heard the complaints of the farmers. After a short while, all the farmers left, while he remained back with Farhet, Jones, and Ursula as they prepared to leave.

"Ungrateful as always," Jones complained, shaking his head.

"No matter how hard we work for them, they're always going to want more. Never grateful," Farhet said, raising his hands in objection. "We're not changing our commitment, though. Whatever we have left over, we share. That's my promise," he added, glaring at the others as they fell silent.

Ethan watched as the farmers disappeared in the night. He followed Farhet and the rest into town.

"We should at least charge them from now on, not full price, of course," Ursula proposed, shattering the lingering silence during their walk.

"If we charge them a smaller fee, then everyone is going to demand that fee. This way is safer, and no one asks questions," Farhet exhaled, staring ahead.

"Ursula is right. We were barely able to pay Bekhter for our last barley and wheat purchase. Any amount of Lirkins would do us good," Jones chimed in, tying his greasy hair with a wrap.

Farhet shook his head and pushed away from the rest.

"You two keep repeating the same thing. There's more to life than worrying about a few Lirkins today," he growled, walking ahead alone.

~

The next day, Ethan headed directly to the bakery early in the morning. He could not hide a certain pounce in his stride. Even the weather synchronized with his mood. The sun shined high in the spotless blue sky above. He found Farhet already hard at work finishing the final batch of bread for the day's sales as customers began to flock in.

Farhet's bakery stood on its own in a rather small and rundown wooden hut. He had removed the walls to let in the air around the brick oven. The hut's chimney started releasing smoke before the sun came out. Farhet was not one for subtle pleasantries when busy with something, especially work. He waved, smiling at Ethan. He nodded to Jones and Ursula, who looked exhausted already from their work. Their gazes never left Ethan as he moved around.

"You're back," Farhet sneered, handing a loaf to a melancholic-looking woman.

"Say hi to your parents for me," he told the woman,

who only nodded and cast an aloof look back.

Farhet flipped his gaze directly to Ethan.

"What can I do for you, Samor? Liked what you saw last night?" Farhet began, quickly returning to his oven to check its contents. Ethan approached him, half interested in his baking method.

"I want to help with the farmers," he beamed, holding out a small leather pouch that jingled. Farhet looked at him, his expression unchanged. He pushed Ethan's hand away, and went back to baking.

From the corner of his eye, Ethan saw Jones and Ursula staring with gaping mouths at the leather pouch in his hand. Ethan quickly pocketed the bag and moved closer to Farhet.

"Take that away from me. I don't want any trouble here. I don't need help from anyone," he spat. Ethan moved to the side, waiting for the last customer to leave as he caught Jones and Ursula shaking their heads.

"There is no trouble. This is mine," Ethan began.

"If it is yours, what are you doing in this small hut in Moj — in Bograh, for that matter. You should be somewhere west, like in Felix Bay. Isn't that where all the wealthy go this time of year? I don't need your pity," Farhet growled as he continued his work.

"I'm not a rich man," Ethan began.

"Then you're a thief," Farhet shot back. Ethan shook his head. "Then you're a liar, Samor."

"I want to help. I want nothing in return from you. Why would you refuse that?" Ethan badgered.

"You know why I'm not like those slaves on the tobacco plantations?" He began, clearly frustrated with the situation. "Because I go to bed every night and owe no one anything.

You see these?" He continued, raising his open and flour-covered hands. "These are all I need to live. They were enough for my father, and they've kept me going all these years," he said. "And the minute I take something from anyone, they'll feel that I owe them something forever."

Ethan stepped outside, and as he did so, his gaze was drawn upwards towards the sky, where the clouds were gathering ominously. From the north, the sound of thunder echoed toward him, carried by a warm and humid gust of wind. It brought with it a curious mixture of scents, both fresh soil and the unmistakable stench of death. This was the first time he had encountered such a smell since his arrival in Moj, and it hung heavy in the air, hauntingly foreboding. It was as if the town was unwittingly awaiting its imminent demise. No one had a clue. Ethan did not know how much time Moj had left before the blight would arrive. He hoped it would have ended by now, but the stench told him he was wrong. His desire to help burned strong within him. He sensed his aid would be crucial, although he couldn't yet discern how.

He walked away quickly without looking back. Suddenly, a hand caught him, and he turned, catching sight of Jones's worried eyes staring back at him.

"I thought you didn't want my kind."

"Samor, he means well. He's just stubborn. He doesn't like change. If you give me a few days, I'm sure Ursula and I can change his mind. You are a good person, and those farmers could use your help," Jones said, casting a warm gaze to Ethan.

"At least he could have been thankful. I only wanted to help," Ethan said, turning abruptly and taking off, not interested in hearing more of what Jones had to say. "Ursula and I will always be thankful," Jones shouted from behind. Ethan paused for a moment without turning and continued ahead.

~

Since escaping from the shores of Usall, Ethan promised himself that he would not be like his family. He wanted to give, not take. Farhet had made it difficult for him, and he decided Moj was not the best place for him to stay.

Early one morning, Ethan made his way to the tobacco plantations, eager to take another look before departing. After scouting out a hidden spot atop a nearby hill, he gazed down upon the vast field below, which stretched over at least twenty acres. The sun beat down relentlessly, prompting him to remove his shirt while he observed below for more than an hour. From his vantage point, Ethan witnessed hundreds of men, women, and even children laboring in the sweltering heat and humidity. Mounted guards roamed the fields, wielding whips and punishing those who failed to work to their satisfaction. No one was given a chance to rest. Three men, Ethan saw, collapsed from exhaustion without any assistance from the guards, who instead punished those who tried to help. Ethan struggled against the urge to charge down and lend aid to the suffering workers. This was not his fight anymore, he knew. Ethan left the plantation with a heavy heart.

On his final day in Moj, Ethan heard an unusual commotion outside the tavern. Despite the clamor of moving chairs and wooden cups, he remained seated in his corner, calmly sipping his beer. While others rushed outside, he simply turned his ear towards the door, choosing not to follow the crowd.

"Keep away! Nothing here for you. Get back to your businesses," a loud, deep voice instructed the crowds while another kept shouting. Ethan cupped his ear for more clarity.

"I haven't committed any of those accusations. I'm innocent. I'm not a thief," Ethan heard another man cry out. He recognized the voice though.

As he rushed towards the door, he found it already crowded by others blocking his way. Standing on his tiptoes, he searched for an opening to glimpse at what was transpiring. Scanning the scene, he estimated at least two hundred people had gathered. They formed a circle between the tavern and the traders' market spot on the opposite side of the dirt road. Ethan even saw people climbing trees on the opposite end, attempting to get a better view of the commotion. Suddenly, rain began to fall, and the wind picked up, filling his nostrils with the scent of mud. "What a criminal," a voice said from among the onlookers.

"It's enough that the Masons and their friends want to cheat us. Why would one of ours do that as well?" A woman sighed. Ethan continued to search for an opening to get a better view of the commotion, finally climbing on top of a wooden platform near the tavern. From above, he gazed upon the crowd and caught sight of the guards below.

"What evidence do you have against me? I demand you to speak!" Ethan saw Farhet shout, dropping to his knees in front of one of the guards.

"You're charged with theft and bribery," the guard said, his voice sharp and unforgiving.

"Why would I do such a thing? I have no reason to

bribe anyone. I've been the baker in Moj for the last thirty years, and my father before that. Don't you recognize me?" Farhet cried, ripping open his shirt.

"He's been bribing Sir Rejji's farmers! He's been supporting the overthrow of the honest and benevolent Sir Rejji!" A voice shouted from the crowd. Another onlooker concurred as the rest of the crowd began to chant.

"Guilty, Guilty!"

Ethan, awe washed across his face, began to shout.

"Let him go! He's innocent!" But his voice was barely audible across the crowd. He got down from the platform and rushed to Farhet, squeezing his way in between people to catch a closer glimpse.

"Move!" he continued to nudge, ducking when necessary to get to the clearing.

"Hang him! Hang him!" the crowd began to chant in unison. He pushed forward, almost reaching the area where the guards held Farhet. However, he got squeezed in between two tall, shirtless men stuck between their sweat-drenched arms. Finally free, he ran ahead just as the crowd began to break apart. He looked around frantically, searching for Farhet.

"Where did they go?" he demanded from a nearby woman.

"I hope he never lives in peace," she spat, shrugging him off. Ethan left the woman, unwilling to waste more time with her. The sound of the crowd became louder at this point, making it hard for him to think straight. After a bit, though, Ethan finally saw Farhet and the guards, but they were already in the distance. He ran after them.

"Samor. You're still here!" A voice suddenly struck

from behind, holding Ethan up before he ran ahead. He glanced towards the voice and saw Jones standing on his own, his demeanor calm but his face filled with concern.

"What happened? Where are they taking him?" Ethan demanded, his eyes filled with worry. Jones, remaining calm, cupped his shoulders, gazing warmly.

"One of those damn farmers must have complained. Ursula is asking around," he said.

"Where are they taking him?"

"I'm not sure. I think the town jail," he stuttered. Ethan broke free of Jones and took off, impatient to hear the rest of what he had to say. "Ursula and I, we need to see you. We're thinking of a plan!" Jones said from behind, his voice loud enough for Ethan to hear. "Samor, nothing will work if we don't work together!" Jones continued. Ethan stopped and exhaled, looking back.

"What is your plan?"

"We want to break him out of jail."

"So do I. What do you have in mind?" Ethan badgered, beginning to walk back to Jones.

"We can always try to use force, but that will be ineffective as this is Moj. There are guards everywhere."

"So, if this is Moj, then what do we do?" Ethan snapped, Jones looking away. "Well?" Ethan continued.

"You already know the answer."

"If the price is right," Ethan exhaled. "Fine, where do we go after?"

"There's nothing meaningful east. Ursula and I plan to go north towards Cerzai. It's definitely better than here. No one knows us there. There's the Frayjen Pass, north of here. It's treacherous, but it's the quickest and least guarded path to Cerzai, and specifically Nav," Jones said.

"What makes you think that you can make enough to live and eat there?" Ethan badgered, anxious to get on with the plan. Jones looked away again.

"Well. We thought that together, we would be fine," Jones sighed. Ethan looked at him in bewilderment.

"Fine, you want me to feed you. As long as we get out of here," Ethan exhaled impatiently. "You and Ursula, get ready, and we'll make a run for it when I'm back," he commanded.

Ethan quickly turned and rushed through the light crowds of people returning to their businesses. Jones's words hung heavily on his mind. Ethan, panting from his short run, approached the town jail. It was located on the western side of the city, conveniently situated next to the city guard's lodgings. The jail was a small, wooden structure with a single floor and a slightly dilapidated appearance. Time had taken its toll on the building, as evidenced by the numerous holes and gaps in the wood that offered a glimpse inside for anyone passing by. Despite the responsibility of guarding the jail, several guards were idly milling about outside, smoking, totally indifferent to their duties.

"A friend of mine just came in. I want to see him," Ethan said to one of the guards standing at the entrance, his voice clearly impatient. The guard, busy in conversation with his friend, looked down on Ethan as he picked his teeth.

"Who are you?" The guard asked, grimacing. Ethan stuttered for a moment.

"I'm his friend, Samor," he hesitated, fidgeting in his place. The guard stared him down and began to shake his head.

"I don't know anyone by that name. Be gone," the guard badgered. Ethan hesitated for a moment more before reaching into his pocket and retrieving five Lirkins. He jingled the coins in his hand before offering them to the guard, who inspected them closely. The guard, unamused, gazed back at Ethan with a skeptical expression. Disappointed, Ethan let out a sigh and reluctantly retrieved another five Lirkins, extending them toward the guard. After shaking the coins in his hand, the guard stepped aside, allowing Ethan to pass through.

"Down there, and fourth cell to the left," he added, holding Ethan back and pointing ahead. "You have five minutes, my Lord," the guard added. Ethan bit his tongue as the guard grinned back. He was not going to correct him. He had got this far, and there was no point in disturbing his mood.

Ethan nodded and quickly made his way in. Each cell in the small jail had a unique story to tell. Wooden doors, with the top half consisting of large black bars, separated the inmates from the outside world. As Ethan passed by, the prisoners clung to the door bars, glaring at him with animosity. The pungent stench of sweat and iron permeated the air, suffocating him. As he walked down the short corridor, he counted a total of ten jail cells, each one adding to the oppressive atmosphere.

"Tell them they've got the wrong man!" One of the inmates said desperately, sticking their hand out.

"The keys. That guard has them!" Another inmate scowled, his eyes yearning for freedom. Ethan shrugged everyone off as he continued deeper into the dimly lit jail.

Suddenly he ran, catching sight of who he had been

searching for. "Farhet! You're ok! I'm here to get you out. Jones and I devised a plan to get you out," Ethan stuttered, his breath barely keeping up with his words. Farhet shifted his stance and leaned on the side of his cell, barely visible. He spat on the ground.

"They'll help with nothing. They've wanted my bakery for a while now. Didn't think they'd do it this way, though. The greedy bastards want everything," he hissed.

"You're wrong. They want to help. Jones and I spoke of running away to Cerzai," Ethan stuttered before Farhet broke out in laughter.

"Run away? Life would not continue if we gave up fighting for our home, for what is ours, and for what is right. I'm not that weak a man," Farhet mocked.

"But there's always freedom elsewhere."

"Who said you can't be free where you are? There's always a choice," Farhet sighed. "My Lord, right? You don't have to hide it, and I can call you that. I can tell your kind. You're so blind. Your presence and that pouch of Lirkins just pushed them to finally swing their blow, and alas, I'm in prison, and they've taken over the bakery," Farhet hissed, grabbing hold of the bars on the door and glaring directly into Farhet's eyes, his mood flipping completely in an instant. His eyes, Ethan saw, were bloodshot and lustful for vengeance, a sight he had not imagined seeing from Farhet.

"My advice to you, Samor, is to leave me alone. Leave me alone and never come back. You don't help. You destroy. Let me deal with my life while you go ruin your own with your stupid ideals," Farhet barked, beginning to bang on the bars. "Get out!"

Ethan looked at him and took a step back. From the

corner of his eye, he saw the guard standing at the entrance.

"Your time is up," the guard declared, unsheathing his sword. "Leave now."

Ethan looked back at Farhet for a moment and then the guard before he began to walk away. "You're wrong. We will get you out," he said loud enough for only Farhet to hear. Farhet spat on the ground.

"Useless," he growled.

As Ethan approached the guard, he lowered his gaze and refrained from engaging in conversation. Soon, a torrential downpour began, drenching everything in its path. In the midst of the storm, a bright bolt of lightning illuminated the sky, causing Ethan to glance upwards. As he wiped the water from his eyes, he broke into a sprint, seeking shelter from the relentless deluge. He knew where he needed to go. He had seen this before and could not let things unfold without him having a say in it.

The rain had transformed the usually-bustling streets of Moj into muddy and wet thoroughfares. Deep puddles littered the road, a testament to the storm's intensity. Despite the adverse conditions, Ethan pressed on with unwavering determination, his feet splashing through the puddles as he ran. Finally, after several minutes, he arrived at Farhet's bakery, where the chimney stack puffed away at full blast. Inside, Jones and Ursula worked the oven with ease, unphased by Farhet's absence.

"Jones!" Ethan barked, his voice ringing and clearly audible over the sound of pouring rain. Both turned towards Ethan, their worried faces lighting up at his sight. They quickly waved for him to hurry and take shelter under the wooden shed.

"Samor. Did you find Farhet? When do you think you can get him out?" Ursula started, Ethan's face flaring red.

"You lied to me."

"What do you mean?"

"You wanted him gone forever, and now you're here continuing your lives as if he never existed," Ethan said, his hands held at his waist and near his sword and daggers.

Suddenly, their worried faces flipped to smirks at Ethan's accusations.

"Give us your bag of coins, and we'll leave you alone," Jones hissed, his hair now tied back tight and his eyes glaring at Ethan menacingly. "One can do quite a lot with a thousand Lirkins. That's right. We know what you're carrying. You can make this easy or hard. That's up to you," he added.

"You'll get nothing," Ethan growled, tightening his grasp around his sword just as both Jones and Ursula broke out into menacing laughter.

Ursula's hair hung loosely at this point. "Yes, we will. You forget that this is our town. We know everyone, Prince Ethan," she said. "And anyway, we already have enough. I always thought that princes took better care of their treasures," she added, pulling out a large sack of Lirkins hidden behind the long wooden counter.

Ethan quickly unsheathed his sword as Jones and Ursula did the same.

"I just wanted to help."

"Well, you did, just not how you thought you would," Ursula sneered.

"You don't deserve anything. No one does," Ethan exhaled, swinging his sword toward Jones. He wanted the first blow. Jones blocked and kicked Ethan backward just as Ursula jumped over the counter. Both her daggers were in clear sight. Ethan quickly rolled away to avoid her onslaught. However, he was not quick enough, and she cut his arm. He pressed it as blood began to drip out before he stared back at Jones and Ursula, his eyes lusting for pain.

"You're fine to let an innocent man rot in prison just for a few Lirkins?" Ethan growled.

"He made us a lot of Lirkins indeed. But that's nothing compared to what the price on your head is now," Ursula spat, attacking again with her daggers held tightly in her hands.

Despite the cramped space, Ethan knew that they had the upper hand. He needed some advantage and fast. He could not afford to remain there any longer. Although he was done with Moj, he did not want to depart without settling things with these two individuals who deserved no mercy. Ethan was determined to ensure they got what was coming for them. Suddenly his face lit up. He knew what he needed to do.

"You will pay," he swore to them. With one quick dash over the counter, he hit a glass jug near the oven with his sword, spraying oil all over the fire. The fire immediately blazed out of the oven and spread to the rest of the hut, flames engulfing the entire area. Before Jones or Ursula could overpower him, he turned and buried his blade into Jones's chest. Jones dropped to the floor, shouting in pain as a pool of blood grew beneath him. Ethan's glance shifted back to Ursula, who fidgeted in her place on the other side of the hut, both daggers held tight in her hands. She cast a menacing look toward Ethan, who stared back coldly.

"You people seem to underestimate me," he mocked. Ethan jumped onto the wooden counter and swung his sword before she could react, just catching the skin of her neck. She fell to the ground as well, squirming for air through the blazing fire.

Ethan then turned around and caught sight of the bag of Lirkins they had stolen from his lodgings at the inn. He heard Ursula continuing to squirm for air behind him as he grabbed the bag.

"This is what you wanted?" He mocked, turning around. He opened it up and scattered a few coins across the bakery's counter. "For your troubles, you greedy bastards," he added, picking himself up and making his way out. He paid no attention to their cries nor their pleas for help as the bakery went up in flames behind him.

Thirty-Eight

Aurom at night was a city of contrasts, with living areas and quiet neighborhoods coexisting in harmony. As the day turned to night, traders would pack up their wares, and shops would close, but the taverns would come to life. Young and old would take to the streets, enjoying a few hours of revelry, while the rest of the city remained calm and peaceful. The sound of laughter and conversation gave the city a sense of vitality, providing a comforting reassurance to both its inhabitants and visitors that life was good there.

Ozwald ran for his life, his feet pounding the cobblestones as he made his way east through the city. Just as he had exited the house, Rybae caught up with him and aided his escape from the courtyard of Rorik's estate. They ran together and did not pay attention to the noise they were making or the disturbance they were causing to the residents. Ozwald's fighting arm was still drenched in blood.

As they approached the north-south axis of Aurom, both heard shouting voices in the distance. Usually, Ozwald would want to have a closer look. But tonight, his senses told him to remain out of sight. He knew that the faster he ran, the better the chance he had to remain unseen and untraced.

"Did you get him? Tell me!" Rybae shrieked. Ozwald held up his fist for him to remain silent as they passed through a dense residential area. "Tell me, I don't care who hears me! Tell me now!" Rybae badgered him, grabbing Ozwald by his arm before spinning him and throwing him to the ground. Ozwald howled in pain.

"What's wrong with you?" Ozwald said, his face flustered while gazing up. Rybae remained quiet and began to tap the hilt of his sword across the walls and doors that he saw around him. The sound of waking residents began to rise in the night.

"Who's out there?" Ozwald heard a voice bark from the upper floor of a nearby house.

"You're attracting attention. Stop it!" Ozwald insisted. "We need to keep moving. Otherwise, we'll be caught when the guards arrive."

"Who are you?" A young lady wearing a silky white gown began to shout, appearing from the upper balcony of the home they stood in front of.

"Don't think that you can run from me," Rybae barked, licking his lips rapidly. "You didn't kill him, I am sure of it. He got you instead. You don't deserve us." Rybae spat on the ground in front of Ozwald's feet, disgust washed across his face. Before Ozwald could make a run, Rybae grabbed him directly on his scathed arm. Although he could still move his hand, the cut made it difficult to maneuver. Suddenly, the sound of rushing soldiers rose from across the city's cobblestone roads.

"You don't get it! Nothing matters more than our cause. The life of others is secondary to everything we will ever do," Rybae hissed, slowly approaching Ozwald.

"I would never touch him. That was Lord Rorik, and he has done great things for Valya," Ozwald barked, not paying attention to the residents lining up on their balconies. A few disgruntled residents began to step out into the streets as well.

"This man is covered in blood," the man with scuffled hair standing near Ozwald complained. "These are murderers! You do not belong here. Never have I seen such a scene," the man continued. "Guards! Over here!"

Ozwald broke away from the group of residents that began to huddle up around him. He saw Rybae on the other side of the road, making eye contact.

"You're coming with me back to the house. Don't think you can run away from us. You made a commitment and broke it," Rybae said, running to him. Ozwald, though, looked the other way and dashed ahead, bumping into residents.

Rybae drew out his sword and raised it high. "I will strike you down if you don't stop," he shouted just as a resident stepped in front of him.

"Stop! Put that down! We don't have such..." The man started to shriek before Rybae swung his sword, making direct contact with his neck. Ozwald glanced back and saw the resident drop to the ground with blood oozing out just as he saw Rybae's blood-hungry and mischievous eyes.

"They don't matter. Nobody matters in the face of

truth," Rybae howled while a woman nearby began to scream at the sight of the dead resident.

Ozwald turned and continued to run again, frantically looking around. Everything was foreign to him, and he ran in the direction away from the awakening residents, taking any path and alleyway that he could find. The more he ran, the more the sound of Aurom's residents and travelers grew. He kept running in that direction as a plan began to develop in his mind. "No one would be that crazy," he whispered to himself.

"You can't hide from me. You can't hide from us Ozwald Stonne," Rybae barked from behind. Ozwald continued to press forward, his breath heavy. Suddenly, a hand grabbed Ozwald by his shoulder, pulled him back, and threw him to the ground. He looked up and caught Rybae's eyes, sighing. "Again," he whispered to himself. Behind him, Ozwald saw the moon in clear sight with no tree cover to block it.

"Don't mind them. Look at me. I told Yakenn all along that you were never our material. You are unreliable, and you just proved my point. You'll never have a place in our order," Rybae sneered. He picked up Ozwald and held him tightly by his arm. "You're not running away from me again." Ozwald grimaced as he pressed on his arm injuries. "Are these cuts still hurting you? I've had deeper cuts in my groin and still have been able to move and fight," Rybae mocked just as two men stepped out of a nearby house with swords in their hands.

"Leave him alone!" One of them shouted. Rybae smirked. He winked at Ozwald before he lunged at the two men, swinging his sword precisely. The sound of steel on steel clung through the streets as Rybae battled both men on his own. He dodged each of the men on either side, and neither was able to overpower the other. Ozwald observed the duel as if it were a dance they had rehearsed.

Ozwald's cue to flee came soon after Rybae kicked one of the men in the chest, then turned to stab the other in the heart. With the first assailant down, Rybae swiftly swung his sword in the opposite direction and caught the second attacker between his shoulder and neck, causing blood to spatter everywhere. Rybae immediately turned to face Ozwald and demanded that he stop running. However, Ozwald disregarded his plea and sprinted towards the bustling city center, leaving Rybae behind to deal with the aftermath of his kills. Rybae started to laugh maliciously from behind.

"Did I scare you? We own Azra. We can do what we want," Rybae cursed. Ozwald disregarded him once more and pushed ahead.

As Ozwald hurried along, his gaze fell upon a set of pristine white stairs ahead of him, which were flanked by two small fox statues resting atop columns. Though unfamiliar with this part of the city, he knew that he could use this vantage point to evade Rybae, either by finding a suitable hiding place or a quicker escape route. Without hesitation, he bounded up the stairs and emerged onto a long, stone bridge that spanned high above the surrounding houses. The bridge was constructed from massive monolithic blocks that served as both the floor and the side walls. With no apparent exits in sight, he saw that the bridge towered over nearby house roofs below, and he figured he should jump. With this new sense of purpose, he picked up the pace and ran along the bridge. Glancing back, Ozwald breathed a sigh of relief as he could not spot Rybae anywhere. Nevertheless, he knew he could not let his guard down, and he continued his fast pace, determined to jump off the bridge. As he ran along, he saw more fox statues and torches aligned on either side, as if beckoning him forward and guiding his way.

After a short while, Ozwald could see a structure at the end of the bridge. He knew it to be an estate and needed to find a place to jump off. The house would be a dead end and create more problems than solutions. Below him, he finally saw the entire commotion of the bustling city at night. Taverns lined up the road, and men and women lingered on the streets.

Suddenly, Ozwald heard a menacing laugh from behind, and his brief moment of relief disappeared.

"You can't keep running away from us. One way or another, we will be the end of you." Rybae shouted, his voice ringing in the air. Ozwald did not glance back nor slow down and continued ahead at full speed. At this point, he forgot about the cut in his arm. The pain was secondary, and all he wanted was to escape.

"These are the filth of Azra. They won't be singing and drinking for long. That I can assure you," Rybae continued. Shortly after, Ozwald saw a moving torch ahead of him in front of the estate's gate, but he couldn't make out who held it.

He glanced behind and saw that Rybae was far off, as though he was afraid to approach any closer. He anxiously looked for a roof to jump on while he continued approaching the moving torch ahead. As he approached, though, two people became visible. They did not move, and they stood as if waiting for Ozwald to approach them.

"Don't be shy. You made it to the right place," Rybae shouted from behind.

Ozwald halted, stepping onto the wide stone walls of the bridge in between the fire torches. From his new vantage point, he could see that the bridge was, in fact, a secluded road to the house ahead of him.

Standing on the edge, a light breeze blew by, bringing with it a subtle stench of death. "Already," he whispered as he stepped back and took a deep breath, preparing to run.

"Ozwald! Why don't you join us?" A familiar voice beamed as Ozwald glanced at the lit torch at the end of the bridge. "Don't jump. We've been waiting for you," the voice continued, Ozwald raising his eyebrows.

"Yakenn?" Ozwald exhaled, squinting his eyes to see better.

"In the flesh." In an instant, the cacophony of background noise faded away, leaving Ozwald in a deafening silence as he laid eyes upon Yakenn. "Why don't you come closer. I heard what happened, and I'm here to help," he continued.

"I don't want this anymore," Ozwald shrieked. "How did you get here?" he added.

"Ahh. You know how," Yakenn began, giving Ozwald room to come up with the answer on his own. He did not. "The end always defines the means. You have Rybae to thank for that, of course," he added.

"It was obvious from the beginning we both think alike, and this was and is your home. The home of truth," Yakenn hissed. "I have someone close to you, I heard. I think you'd want to reconnect with him."

"Your truth is destruction. You're blinded!" Ozwald barked, squinting his eyes at the second person in the shadows, eventually jumping down from the ledge.

Ozwald picked up a nearby torch. He began to move ahead cautiously toward Yakenn.

"Good, there's still a sense in you. You don't know how much joy you've brought to me. We all make mistakes, but it's important how we get back up," Yakenn said, his welcoming voice becoming louder with every step.

The gate that Yakenn stood in front of at the end of the bridge appeared larger than when he first saw it. The house loomed ominously. It had four pointed coned roofs, littered with broken tiles at each corner. Its stones, of deep black color, bore thin white lines as if clawed by unseen talons. The dense layer of trees obscured a direct view of the front, yet a sinister, dark yellow light flickered from within. An uneasy silence hung heavy in the air as if the very walls held secrets best left untold.

"Your truth had me almost kill an honest Lord of Valya. You're just like the rest of them," Ozwald growled, his head slightly tilted forward.

"I told you, this is not easy. We need to be prepared physically and mentally for anything and everything to see justice and fight the evil that we're drenched in," Yakenn sneered.

Ozwald did not reply and continued to squint his eyes as he tried to make out the person standing next to Yakenn.

"I have your unfinished business here," Yakenn mocked sinisterly as Ozwald caught sight of Rorik gagged and tied up, standing beside him.

"Let him go," Ozwald shrieked, quickly unsheathing

his sword.

"I'm here to help you, Ozwald. I want to see you succeed. They wouldn't be happy back there if they knew you failed," Yakenn smirked, nodding his head in the direction of the estate behind him. Ozwald stopped and stood in front of the two men, tightening his grip on the hilt of his sword.

"Leave him alone!" Ozwald shouted. "He does not deserve any of this."

"What truly amazes me is that sword of yours. You told me that it was for that man. What's his name? Ul... sorry, I forgot," Yakenn said, scratching his head. "Yes, that's right, Ulto. The cold-blooded murderer." Ozwald looked at the hilt, shifting uneasily in his place. "Ulto represents what we oppose, and yet you erase his memory just by covering the hilt with a bit of string. As if covering the hilt will help you forget," Yakenn mocked. "Blasphemy. You oppose the unjust, but you hold the sword of one of them. I fight the unjust and am willing to dirty these hands for what is right," Yakenn fumed.

Ozwald stuttered to an attacking position, unsure of his footing.

"Come on, tell him that there is no one in Azra who hasn't done bad deeds. Tell him about your dirty hands," Yakenn spat as he ungagged Rorik.

Ozwald waited for Rorik to speak, his face clearly covered in blood and visibly beaten.

"Ozwald..." Rorik groaned.

"Come on, enlighten us with your wisdom, oh great Lord Rorik," Yakenn scorned. "Did you tell our dear Ozwald about it all? Did you tell him about his legacy?" He shook

Rorik again, but he did not speak. "He took you from that traitor father of yours and hid you from us all in a made-up place called the Haefe. What a joke!" Yakenn spat. Ozwald drew his sword back and arched his back, his face flushed red as his anger.

"Is that true?" Ozwald demanded, his entire body raging.

"I did it all for you. That's what Rupert always wanted— how he wanted it," he murmured. Ozwald gasped, his eyes wide open. A gust of northern wind picked up, the torch flames dimming momentarily. A subtle stench of death still lingered in the air. "I lost all hope until I saw you earlier tonight…" Rorik continued before Yakenn interrupted him.

"Bla, bla, bla, the lies continue. I promise you that nothing can stop what's coming. It's here. You're too late. We can all smell it. Whatever you had in your mind won't work," Yakenn shouted in Rorik's face, pushing him to the ground. Rorik fell at Ozwald's feet, his face and body bloody, while grabbing hold of his feet. Ozwald did not move, and he kept his eyes down.

"I've never met you, you never visited the Haefe, and yet you lie at my feet, begging? I never knew Lords to beg for anything," Ozwald sobbed, sliding his foot back. Rorik looked up at him, his heavy eyes catching Ozwald's watery eyes.

"If it weren't for the Haefe, you wouldn't be alive," Rorik said, his voice clear and truthful. Ozwald gasped as he stared deep into Rorik's eyes. Tears fell as his breathing turned heavy. Suddenly, two clicking sounds sparked from the shadows from behind Yakenn and Rorik.

"You had your chance. You failed, son," a voice said.

Yakenn immediately dipped his head. Ozwald's eyes fixated on the open doorway. He recognized the figure emerging from the shadows all too well. Kraegan, clad in a long tight white shirt, strode towards him with purpose, his sleeves rolled up to reveal sinewy forearms. But it was not just Kraegan's appearance that sent shivers down Ozwald's spine. An ungodly aura seemed to emanate from the man, causing the very air around him to vibrate with malevolent energy. A sight he had never seen at Vareston's Keep.

"Whatever he says is a lie," Rorik whispered, standing up on his own.

"Ozwald, you'll make this much easier for all of us," Kraegan sneered, his gaze fixated on Ozwald. "He's your last chance. Finish him," Kraegan said as he nodded toward Rorik. Ozwald's eyes raced between the two, bewildered. He gasped, catching sight of Rorik's eyes again and tightening his hold of Stonesaver.

"He used you to catch me. I let my guard down and ran after you. That is my fault, but do not listen to him," Rorik murmured.

"No," Ozwald exhaled.

"He farmed you for slaughter! And you still protect him!" Kraegan mocked.

"House Haemel has broken the balance of peace. You will pay heavily for this!" Rorik shouted, lifting his chin while gazing at Kraegan. "Very well," Kraegan hissed, his blood-craving eyes focused entirely on Kraegan in front of him.

Kraegan suddenly shouted, "Fire!"

From the corner of his eye, Ozwald saw four men stand on the house's parapet. Before he could react, Rorik caught him by his shirt and pulled him up to the stone wall, his feet just keeping balance. Rorik nudged Ozwald as they both started running.

"When I signal, you jump," Rorik cried, running around the small fox statues and erect torches as sleek whistles flew through the air around them. Arrows hit the stone wall all around his feet, just missing their target.

"You cannot run away from what is to pass!" Kraegan sneered, his eerie voice ringing in the air.

"Jump!" Rorik commanded. Ozwald followed, stalling his anger for now, while his eyes erratically looked for the safest landing point. Ozwald, without a second thought, immediately jumped while Rorik followed suit. Ozwald's feet floated in the air as if he had been held by a hidden hand while arrows swooshed by him. After lingering in the air for a while, Ozwald finally hit the roof and rolled twice before coming to a halt. Rorik landed behind him with a roll. Ozwald immediately caught his hand and lifted him up.

"Take this. You need to get as far as possible from here. Now!" Rorik shouted as he pointed to a nearby roof and pressed a scroll into Ozwald's hand. Worry was heavy in his tone, and his eyes were wide and fixated on Ozwald. "If it is meant to be, we'll meet again. You can't be here. This is not your fight. Go!" Rorik continued, shoving Ozwald to run on.

He saw a nearby roof to run off on. However, he glanced back at Rorik, standing confidently and ready to engage the two men lined up before him. Ozwald clasped Stonesaver's hilt and hesitated.

"Take this at least," he sighed, unbuckling his sword and throwing it over to Rorik, who took it without question and turned, ready for combat.

"Now go!" he commanded, a subtle warmth clear in his ferocious cry, while Ozwald pocketed the parchment, turned, and jumped to the nearby roof, running away as fast as he could.

Thirty-Nine

For the past two days, Ethan had been heading North with his sword at his side, his quiver and bow strapped to his back. He kept to himself and avoided crowds. He did not trust others. Ethan thought that coming to Bograh would allow him to become someone different, someone, that could help somehow against the lingering unjustness and cruelty that he loathed. However, he was mistaken, and to the contrary, he became convinced that no one deserved his help or his energy.

He had just crossed the Frayjen Pass, receiving directions from a small town along the way. "The Frayjen Pass is your fastest way to the Peaking Highlands if you want to get into Cerzai in under a week," one of the villagers told him after Ethan handed him a few Lirkins to entice him. Although he initially wanted to go east, Jones's warning and the knowledge that Bograh's guards were pursuing him convinced him otherwise. He needed to escape the kingdom as quickly as possible.

Dread clung to every step Ethan took while entering the treacherous Frayjen Pass, the sole pathway to the Peaking Highlands, which led into Cerzai. The jagged mountains towered above him, menacing and unforgiving, and the path ahead was wrought with endless, winding, rocky terrain. The path twisted and turned, and narrow crossways perched high above the abyss, leaving no margin for error. Twisted trees grew in the most inhospitable locations, and their branches clawed out as if to snatch Ethan away. Each step he took was a gamble, every stumble a potential fall to his doom. The landscape itself was a trap, made up of sharp stone edges that seemed to grow ever sharper and more jagged with each passing mile. His throat was parched from the dry, suffocating air, and his stomach ached from hunger pains as he rationed his meager supplies. Ethan could feel himself growing weaker with each passing hour, every breath a struggle. Yet, the most harrowing aspect of the journey was the deafening silence, a reminder of just how isolated and alone he truly was. There was no sign of life, no sound of animals, no trace of civilization. There was no one to turn to for help and no one to hear his screams except for the monotonous, gusting winds. Ethan knew that every moment in the Frayjen Pass could be his last. But he pressed on, each step more perilous than the last, driven by the thought of reaching the safety of Cerzai. The only upside of his journey through the pass was that there was no one in sight to rob or harm him. But as the hours wore on, even that small comfort began to feel insignificant.

Clearing the Frayjen pass, he began his ascent into the Peaking Highlands. However, Ethan saw the land to be different than what he had anticipated. Instead of thick forests covering its Mountain Range, he found barren lands with dirt and red dust. The continuous, grotesque smell of death lingered in the air. Dead bodies became common, emanating an eerie presence. He saw the bodies of women and children killed, as if their lives were unimportant.

He wanted to care, but the more bodies he saw, the more he was convinced that the land was beyond salvation. Bograh taught him that lesson the hard way. "They're getting what they deserve," he continued to say to himself. At one point, he saw an entire family slaughtered on the side of the road, their bags looted, and their blood still freshly spilled on the ground. He did not mourn them, nor did he fear his own life. Ethan merely clasped hard to the hilt of his sword and continued, repeating the same phrase to himself while looking out for himself only.

The Peaking Highlands loomed over and around Ethan, its jagged peaks thrusting up into the sky like spears. Once, they had been cloaked in a lush forest, as he had learned, but now the landscape was barren, scarred by the ravages of the red blight. Large patches of dirt and red dust scattered across the mountain range and filled up Ethan's vision. He strained to conjure an image of the mountain range, but his thoughts were consumed by visions of the pervasive blight. The sun beat down relentlessly, and there was no respite from its strong beams. Only the coolness of the air, however, allowed Ethan to persevere. He had brought a meager supply of food and water from Moj, but his supplies were quickly dwindling, especially while crossing the Frayjen Pass, where he failed to find any game to hunt along the way.

On the afternoon of his fourth day, he had had enough.

Ethan no longer had any water. No greenery nor streams could be seen around him as he moved throughout the mountain range. He walked along a narrow path with never-ending turns throughout his ascent. Despite crossing the treacherous Frayjen Pass, the Peaking Highlands proved to be another challenge on their own.. His body ached all over, and his energy was almost depleted as he underestimated the effort it took to move across a mountain range without a horse. He saw the peak of the mountain ahead of him and began to run along the path that had now become barely visible. At the top, he would have a proper vantage point and charter a better path out of Bograh.

Throughout his ascent, he continuously stumbled, and his clothes eventually became drenched in dirt and red dust as if a permanent mark on him. His entire body cried for water and food, which he could not provide. He needed it as he did not want to lose his life here, in the middle of nowhere.

After another day of walking and climbing, though, he finally reached the top of the mountain range. Suddenly his tired and aching body no longer mattered, and his entire struggle was lost in oblivion at the sight he saw to the other side of the Peaking Highlands.

He gazed across what he knew to be Cerzai, just as he had read about it back in Eurst. It was a realm nestled within mountain ranges encircling it. Cerzai extended beyond the horizon, and from his vantage point, he could see the shielding mountains shadowing its still green forests. The kingdom itself and its inhabitants hid beneath and within the forest.

Ethan had already decided he would enjoy life by

himself in Cerzai and forget everyone else while hiding out of sight. He gazed again upon the green realm and then on the path ahead, searching for the quickest way down.

Immediately, his eyes began to glisten, catching sight of a water spring below that fed into a small stream. The terrain ahead of him was steep and covered with small trees and bushes. The sun felt friendlier to the terrain while cool breezes rose from the valley, providing a refreshing gust for him to inhale. He could hear birds chirping, and he could smell the fresh air as if, suddenly, the red blight had become a whisper of the past. Soil and dirt covered the ground, feeling moist under his feet as energy refilled his body.

After rashly identifying his path, Ethan rushed down, ignoring the risks of falling and injury, desperate for water. The dry and desolate terrain that he had come upon made him forget how to navigate through the overgrown bushes, causing him to stumble and scrape his hands and feet while tearing his clothes. His last struggle, though, would be short-lived as he picked up the pace and jumped across bending roads.

Finally, he arrived at the water spring, dropping to his knees and sticking his hands into the water. He aggressively washed his face and drank from the water spring as fast as his hands would allow him to. When he had drank to his heart's content, he quickly refilled his sheep skin to the rim before laying on the nearby soil, listening intently to the moving water, his thoughts racing and escaping him.

"By the laws of this realm and by order of Queen Petra of House Haemel, it is forbidden to drink directly from the Peaking water stream. Do you know that?" A voice suddenly broke through the serene sound of gushing water.

Ethan flinched, opening his eyes and calmly looking for the source of the voice.

"Well, I can't change the past. What is it going to cost me?" He snickered, rattling a few Lirkins in his pocket for effect while making eye contact with a chubby-looking man standing over him. The chubby man had a bald head, thick eyebrows, and a dubious expression. His wide, hairy hands were visible, and his clothes appeared symmetrical but tight on him. He carried a long sword and daggers on his belt. With heavy breathing and a stern gaze, he looked down at Ethan, his suspicion palpable as he contemplated a response.

"So direct. And why do you think that I only seek to enrich myself with your *hard-earned Lirkins*? Is that what I should care about?"

"I've learned that people like a bit of Lirkins to sweeten anything. All that I see now, though, is that it brings out the evil in others. I'd rather give it away fast and get what service I desire than be picky and look for someone in need. And from what I've seen, everyone is greedy. And so, I have no energy to deal with the ill intentions of others," Ethan exhaled, taking out a Lirkin and holding it up for the chubby man to take.

"What is your name? I can see you're not from around here," the chubby man sneered.

"Again, the suspicion," Ethan whispered to himself. "I'm Samor. What is yours?" He quickly exhaled.

"Emwalo, I'm the guardian of this part of the kingdom," he continued, gazing at Ethan. "I'm afraid your Lirkins are no good here. In fact, no one is allowed through this pass without an invitation. I can clearly see that you do not have one. In fact, I can't remember the last time someone passed from this exact location. I'm assuming you took the Frayjen Pass. You must be desperate or running away from something. All in all, though, I do commend you. You must be skilled to have crossed that road alone, but I'm going to have to take you down to Nav for judgment. I wouldn't be surprised if you end up in prison," Emwalo exhaled, approaching Ethan slowly to pick him up. Without another word, Ethan rolled his eyes and took out two more Lirkins. He stood up and placed them into Emwalo's hands. Suddenly, his stern face flipped completely, and a smile appeared in its place., He cleared his throat.

"Well, it seems here that you are on some trade mission of your own. I see nothing wrong," Emwalo uttered. His harsh voice completely vanished, and he rushed to help Ethan dust off his clothes.

"There he is, I knew there was a kind man underneath that stern face of yours. I'm sure those Lirkins will help you do great things for yourself," Ethan mocked, disgust washed over his face as he patted Emwalo's cheeks. "If you would be so kind, could you take me to the nearest inn?"

"The inn is about another day's journey from here. Not too sure I can be gone for that long," Emwalo said, turning and beginning to look through the thick trees ahead of them. Ethan rolled his eyes and without any objection, slipped another two coins into Emwalo's front pocket. "I'd say it's a little passed mid-day, and if we hurry, we can make it by evening time. And I know just the place for a person of your stature," Emwalo said, a spark of joy clear in his voice.

"Take me there, Emwalo. You have the lead," Ethan exhaled as Emwalo bowed his head and led him along the path ahead. Ethan took one last gulp of water from the spring and followed, unamused.

As Ethan made his way down the intricate and hazy path toward Nav, he sensed his body being rejuvenated with every step. The fatigue and exhaustion that had set in during his uphill journey dissipated. The horrific sight of the blight's devastation that he had witnessed earlier now seemed like a distant, surreal memory. The crisp, cool air and the sweet fragrance of the surrounding trees erased the stench of death that had been lingering in his nostrils. The chirping of birds echoed through the verdant canopy, filling the atmosphere with a sense of vitality and vigor. The playful antics of the birds, flitting from branch to branch, provided a cheerful accompaniment to Ethan's descent. The burbling of water, flowing steadily and relentlessly from all directions, further contributed to the vibrant ambiance of the place. As Ethan continued his descent, he felt his spirit being lifted by the abundance of life and energy around him.

Their descent progressed without much talk until Emwalo broke the silence, speaking over his shoulder to an unwilling Ethan.

"Why are you here? Surely there are better places to be at a time like this," Emwalo questioned. Ethan shook his head.

"Isn't this the land of fantasies, where all my desires would be served? There is no better place for a man to spend his time than in the embrace of a woman? For as long as it lasts, of course," Ethan exhaled.

"Aye, this blight is sad. The only reason no Lord or King is doing anything is that they're indecisive about the action. The moment they declare it as a blight, there will be war. But until then, we continue living as if everything is fine —the hypocrisy of Azra," Emwalo said, his voice melancholic and aloof at the same time, as if he was just an observer of events.

"Then why are you here? Don't you have a better place to go to?" Ethan snapped.

"Well, until they declare it, it's better to stock up as much as you can. That way, you can last when the blight comes," he said, a certain pride clear on his face. "These Lords and Kings are smart. They may seem ignorant to everyone, but anyone that is able to pacify an entire realm for so long with its harsh laws is someone to be afraid of. In my opinion, it's easier to work with them than to try to find a way to oppose them," he added, Emwalo picking up the pace. After that encounter, they did not speak much for the rest of their journey until they reached Nav.

Continuing ahead, the roads became flatter and wider while the trees became taller. The sun in the sky began to drop until it sank beneath the horizon while the sky turned black. No moon could be seen in the night sky, however, and Emwalo knew the road well enough, which was lit majestically underneath the tree cover above.

The city of Nav was shrouded in a veil of mystique and secrecy, its unique architecture and bustling atmosphere captivating the senses of anyone who entered. Some houses hung high up in the trees, while others were nestled beneath tree trunks as if they were a natural extension of the forest. The blend of organic and man-made elements was a sight to behold, a perfect union of the ethereal and the tangible. At night, the city came alive with a dazzling display of lights, illuminating the entire area like a hidden world beneath the earth's surface. Despite the late hour, the streets were teeming with people, their voices blending into a continuous hum that echoed through the city's alleys and pathways. Traders and merchants hawked their wares along the dusty roads while taverns and inns dotted every corner, beckoning weary travelers with promises of rest and refreshment. Ethan had never seen so many taverns in such a small space, each one boasting a unique charm and character that drew him in. He saw whores standing everywhere, waiting for a lucky customer to come and swoop them up. The fervor and happiness that filled the streets stood in stark contrast to the desolate wastelands beyond the Peaking Highlands, a testament to the city's mystique and aura. Massive trees, their trunks as wide as five people standing shoulder to shoulder, had been planted and lined up in perfect rows as if placed by a giant hand. The majesty of the trees and the city they sheltered left Ethan in awe, and he could not help but wonder what other secrets the mysterious place held.

"Over there, master, Samor. That's the Happiness Inn. Mention to Yahoy, the owner, that Emwalo sent you over. We go way back," Emwalo said, pointing with his finger. Ethan followed his direction and squinted his eyes in an attempt to locate what he was pointing at.

"It seems you've earned an honest five Lirkins. You have more to use for when the time ends," Ethan exhaled, continuing to squint his eyes.

"Let's hope that the end doesn't come too soon. Who knows?" Emwalo jolted with a certain happiness in his voice as it dimmed out.

"Where again did you say I should go? I just see a temple," Ethan asked, his eyes still racing to the open space that Emwalo had pointed to. Emwalo remained silent until

Ethan glanced toward him.

"Where did you go?" He quickly questioned, shrugging and gazing around frantically. His eyes quickly returned to the area he had pointed to earlier. Suddenly, Ethan's eyes lit up with wonder as he caught sight of a bright light emanating from the temple door. The light was so bright that it seemed as though the sun itself had been imprisoned within the temple, and the door had opened just enough to allow a small fraction of its luminosity to escape.

With a sense of enchantment, Ethan was irresistibly drawn towards the light as though it was beckoning him with promises of hidden pleasures and secrets. The bustling noises of Nav ceased to exist, and Ethan was left standing in utter silence, mesmerized by the ethereal light. The light was his salvation, his way out of the troubles and worries that had plagued him. And, without a moment's hesitation, he began to move towards it with a sense of urgency, his hand outstretched as if to capture the elusive light.

Forty

The sun had just set as the freezing cold air howled through the air, eerily declaring its onslaught. The sky's bright moon hung low, illuminating the rock and snow-covered mountain range that glowed to reveal ice everywhere. Ethan found himself on a snow-covered cliff that stood taller than the mountain cliffs around him. He looked down and saw clouds glowing in the moonlight while one mountain peak courageously pierced through it, drawing his attention. The snow reached Ethan's knees, but he felt no cold as if he were part of the mountain and its snow. The wind did not topple him, although it had the power to flatten any wooden house. Ethan felt at home at the top of the mountain, as if he belonged there and as if he was meant to gaze upon the mountain ranges while the wind howled in all its purity. He did not move, nor did he find any reason to move.

Suddenly, a tall man walked over to Ethan and stood

next to him, observing the night sky as well. The rugged man before Ethan sported a long, unkempt beard and hair that fell down on his shoulders in disarray. He donned a thick coat that seemed to add to his already bulky frame while his sturdy staff provided support for his stout figure. The man appeared fixated on the majestic mountain range ahead, his head resting atop his trusted staff as he stood in stoic silence, seemingly oblivious to Ethan's presence.

Suddenly, though, the lone mountain pea went up in flames. The fire was huge, a size Ethan had not seen before. The sense of impending danger instigated him to take action. He glanced toward the rugged man, trying to catch his eyesight to communicate with him. Ethan began to open his mouth but could only manage a gasp as the rugged man turned and rushed inside. He tried to follow, but his feet would not let him. They were sturdily fastened to the ground. The rugged man had already disappeared inside, and bright light emanated from inside where it was pitch-black just moments before.

As Ethan stole another glance at the solitary mountain peak below, his heart raced with eager anticipation for what was to come. Suddenly, a blazing projectile soared out from its depths, starting its journey with a deafening silence that only added to the mystique of the moment. The silence was short-lived, however, as a resounding explosion shattered the stillness, sending tremors through the very ground beneath Ethan's feet. But he remained unflinching, unmoving, as if resigned to his fate and what lay ahead. For he knew, with a deep sense of intuition, that this was the moment he had been waiting for - the moment when the truths he had sought for his entire life would finally be revealed. Though he could not recall the questions he had asked, he could feel them stirring within him, beckoning him forward with an unyielding pull. As the fiery projectile hurtled towards him, Ethan braced himself, his entire being consumed by an unbridled eagerness to hear what it would bring.

Just as the fiery projectile had appeared, it quickly dampened and shrunk into a small spark, transforming into a cloaked man and landing behind Ethan. He was immediately made to turn towards the figure, but he struggled to see behind as if his entire body had hardened into stiff stone.

He began to shout, but his voice was nothing more than whispers in the air. But this did not deter him, and he continued to try to scream, hoping he might catch the attention of the cloaked man. After a short-lived struggle, he felt a change, and his body began to untighten.

"We need to get inside now," a voice spoke from behind as hands grabbed onto him tightly, pulling him out of the snow. Dislodged from his post, a cold and freezing rush overcame him.

"You're going to freeze to death dressed like that. We need to get in fast," the voice continued as Ethan turned and saw the cloaked man pulling on him erratically. He followed without a word as his feet sunk into the snow with every step. The wind blew even harder as its howling rang through his entire body to the bones. Despite his freezing and now aching body, he persevered and followed the cloaked man.

Finally, he reached the end of the road where the snow ended in a straight line, as if an unspoken agreement between nature and the lit cave. A sudden warmth washed over his face while he frantically rubbed his body as best as he could. He looked at himself and found that he wore no clothes save for an undergarment covering his genitals. He searched for a fire but saw nothing but richly lit rock carved to create an opening. Hot air embraced him as if the sun was just around the corner. His naked body, which was only moments before cold and blackened, was now rapidly regaining its temperature and color.

He heard heavy breathing behind him and turned as his eyes caught sight of a familiar face he felt he had not seen in a long time.

"What are you doing here?" Ethan said, his voice finally audible and emanating from his mouth with purity and clarity he had not heard before.

"We've always been here. We don't have much time," the man said, removing his heavy fur coat as snowflakes fell off.

"Ozwald, but I haven't seen you..." Ethan began before he paused. He could not remember, though. He could not remember anything except Ozwald's face.

"Does it matter? We are here now," Ozwald quickly said, his voice filled with confidence as he pulled Ethan into the cave. Ethan followed before stopping in his path, standing in his place stubbornly.

"I need answers. You can't just pull me," he hissed.

"Why does it matter?" Ozwald spoke again, his voice louder and more confident. "If I don't, then all is lost," Ozwald continued, pulling on Ethan's unmoving arm.

"They don't deserve us. None of them do. You're making a mistake," Ethan growled, remaining fixed in his place, unwilling to move ahead.

"You're going to regret that decision," Ozwald said, his voice low and disappointed, while quickly letting go and continuing ahead.

Ozwald glanced, one last time, back at Ethan. His face filled with sadness and agony, but he was determined to continue. Something inside Ozwald told him that that was the last time he would ever see Ethan, but he was stubborn and had already made up his mind. Ozwald did not speak or pull on Ethan again and progressed alone. He took a left turn inside the brightly lit cave and disappeared. Ethan heard nothing but the howling wind behind him and the steps of Ozwald fading in the distance.

A sudden gloom overcame Ethan at the sight of snow creeping closer towards him from behind, breaking through the once definitive barrier he had thought was permanent. The howling wind now seemed to roar with even greater intensity as if it were a beast unleashed upon him. The warmth that had previously enveloped him now began to escape, leaving him feeling increasingly numb. Desperate to escape the encroaching snow, Ethan tried to move deeper into the cave but found his feet rooted to the spot as if they were embedded in the cold, unforgiving stone beneath him. As the snow continued to pile up around him. He struggled to call out for Ozwald but found that his voice had deserted him, leaving only a pitiful gasp, much like his previous attempts at the edge of the cliff. With each passing moment, Ethan's body began to grow increasingly rigid, as if it were slowly freezing from the inside out. Despite his best efforts to resist, he could feel himself succumbing to the bitter cold, returning to the mountain but now as a guardian of the dark and lifeless cave.

~

Ethan found himself totally unable to move. He could only see and hear. His hands had become hole-ridden columns of stone, and his body one big unmoving boulder as if it had been hand-chiseled out of the mountain. The wind continued to howl melodically outside, a soothing sound that made him feel at home, as if he had always belonged.

Suddenly, dim light from inside the cave emanated timidly. Ethan felt no warmth, saw no shadow, and heard no movement. The ground began to shake beneath him softly. He heard a deep rumbling sound emanating from outside the cave, from deep below at the base of the mountain.

Just as Ethan glanced towards the inside of the cave, he saw crimson red blood trickling on the ground and moving effortlessly. He could not see the source as the dim light faded as quickly as it had appeared.

The ground did not cease rumbling and shaking below Ethan until he felt himself being dislodged from the ground as if being plucked out like a flower out of the ground on a sunny summer's day. He could not see what or who pulled him out as he began to hover above the ground. After a short while, he was hurtled out of the cave and into the now daylight sky. He had almost forgotten his time at the edge of the cliff, seeing it still covered in snow and unchanging. Without him controlling anything, his body hurtled down and into the clouds. The deafening sound of wind in his face continuously blew while he watched the clouds quickly approaching. He could not remember when he had been here last, the land beneath the clouds felt like a lifetime ago.

The smell of the icy air quickly transformed into dry and hot air as he approached the clouds. He dived into them, thinking he would feel their fluffy texture and bounce right back up, but he did not, continuing to move ahead. Just after a short while, he broke through the clouds and saw the land below. A land that he had not seen in ages. He vaguely remembered its trees and greenery, its people, and its structures. But he did not see that. He saw something entirely different, something eerie.

As Ethan gazed upon the land below the clouds, his heart sank with despair. It was a wasteland unlike any he had ever imagined, a place that seemed to belong to nightmares. The barren land stretched out before him, pitch black and devoid of any sign of life. The only flashes of color were the scattered specks of red dust he vaguely remembered from a lifetime ago, as if the earth had bled out in its final moments. Gone were the trees and the houses, vanished without a trace. The water and rivers that once brought life and sustenance to the land were now but a distant memory. The earth had been drained of all its resources, and the sea had long since dried up, leaving behind a gaping chasm that seemed to swallow up the entire horizon. In the distance, Ethan saw flickering flames that danced on the horizon, casting an eerie glow across the land. Deep valleys that he knew had once been vast oceans now lay exposed, a grim reminder of the world that had been. The air was thick with the stench of death, and the acrid smell of rotting corpses clung to everything. As the winds picked up, great clouds of dust and debris swept across the desolate landscape, obscuring everything in a swirling haze. Ethan could not help but feel a gruesome end to life as he had remembered it, a place where hope and life had no place to exist and where only despair and sorrow reigned.

He did see, however, a few bands of people in the

distance. Ethan could not control the direction in which he hovered. However, he saw these bands of people quickly approaching him. He stopped right above them and saw them fighting among each other with swords and daggers. Their faces were covered in black and red dirt, and their clothes were old and ripped. Ethan tried to call to them, but his mouth was dry, and his throat parched. They did not even see him in the air above, although he hovered close to them while his limbs had already retransformed back to skin and bones.

Suddenly, the fighting ended as one swordsman remained standing alone while the others lay motionless on the ground. Ethan quickly hovered down, making eye contact with the last standing swordsman. He tried to touch the ground, but he could not. He could not move at all. No matter how hard he tried. His heart immediately filled with despair, recognizing the eyes of the swordsman, eyes he had not seen in a long time, eyes that had shunned him away in anger. He tried to speak to the man, but he could not, and nor could the man see him. He walked through Ethan as if he were just air.

Ethan desperately attempted to look back, but his neck was unresponsive. His body was forcibly lifted and propelled through the sky once more. He has torn away from the barren wasteland that needed his help. A sense of guilt weighed heavily on his heart and consciousness. "I did nothing," he said to himself.

His body was pulled back to the mountain peak, with no clouds in sight. There was only an unyielding aridness that pervaded everything. This time, there was no blanket of snow to be seen, and the blazing sun's heat assaulted his eyes with an unbearable intensity. As he finally reached the cliff, his feet touched the ground, but he had turned to stone. He struggled to speak and shout, only to be consumed by a wave of anger and frustration that threatened to swallow him whole. He knew that he was forever bound to his post, condemned to gaze down upon the lifeless expanse below. This was not what he wanted nor what he had asked for. A deep, unrelenting sense of despair settled upon him, slowly consuming what was left of his spirit.

Forty-One

Ozwald's heart thudded in his chest as he knelt on the smooth and uneven blocks of stone at the back of Nav's grand temple. The stones, Ozwald felt with his hand, had been worn smooth from the countless feet that had traversed them over the years. The flickering candles cast dancing shadows across the mosaic walls, depicting interactions with the Ancients. The mosaics first depicted, on the left wall, the dawn of civilization more than four thousand years ago during the first coming of the Ancients. It was then that they enlightened Eursazure with farming, industry, and language. The story continued on the right wall of the temple, depicting the time of prosperity and then the period known as the *straying from the path,* when the inhabitants of Eursazure revolted against the ways of the Ancients. The final depiction at the front of the temple depicted the chasm when Eursazure became two expanses of land, Azra and Eurst, as punishment for the peoples' deviances almost two thousand years ago. Ivy had taught him these stories vividly, and now the words translated into images before him.

However, Ozwald did not have much time to linger on the images as sweat dripped down his face, and he struggled to catch his breath. His mind raced, trying to recall how he had come to be in this place. As he gazed around the dimly lit room, his eyes fixed on the large trays suspended from long chains, swaying softly and emanating a pungent scent that filled the air. The aroma was so potent that it seemed to cling to the walls, mixing with it the musty scent of old stone to create an otherworldly ambiance. He saw mages at the front of the temple chanting in deep voices that vibrated the air melodically, while they moved in circles around a small stone structure. Despite his confusion and exhaustion, the tranquility of the space soothed him.

Gloom and despair overcame him as if a pending death were closely approaching. His thoughts raced as they began to recollect images he had seen but now forgotten, images he could only feel. He felt for his pockets and his belongings, trying to look for a totem of some sort to remind him of his past of how he had arrived at the temple and why he was filled with despair.

Suddenly, all became clear to him, his eyes landing on a familiar face seated next to him on the other end of the temple's open space, in the corner. He could recall every detail and feeling of his past and how he had arrived at the temple. Ozwald vividly remembered his recent vision and its devastating ending, an ending he desperately wanted to change. He saw Samor and quickly got up. His body ached in pain as if he had only been kneeling for a week and he ran to him as fast as he could.

He arrived with a slide and saw that he was unconscious but still kneeling upright. He shook him as hard as he could, not worrying if it hurt or not, trying to wake him up from his trance. Ozwald saw his eyes rolled behind his eyelids and perspiration dropping from his forehead continuously. Samor, all the while, released small and intermittent shrieks as if in a terrifying dream he could not wake up from.

"Samor, wake up!" Ozwald yelled until Samor opened his eyes slowly, petrified and bewildered at the sight of Ozwald. His breathing was fast, and his eyes raced while he began to feel his limbs and his chest again. To Ozwald, Samor looked exhausted, dirty, and injured compared to the last time he had seen him at the entrance to Aurom.

"You're here. I saw you," Samor panted, worry overflowing from his eyes.

"You didn't follow me," Ozwald sneered, anger clear in his voice, while glaring at Samor as images of his vision began to rush into his mind.

"I didn't want to at first. They didn't deserve it. But afterward, I only felt guilt, extreme guilt. And when I wanted to, I couldn't move anymore. Something kept holding me back, and then it took me away," Samor sighed, despair clear in his voice.

"Samor," Ozwald began.

"Stop calling me that. You were in my vision. We saw each other. There's a bond I have yet to understand. My real name is..." Ethan exhaled, staring into Ozwald's eyes.

"Prince Ethan Raynel, the one everyone is talking about. I knew it when they described you," Ozwald interjected. Ethan looked away, ashamed at his lie.

"Why are you here? Everything and everyone died in my vision. Why?" Ethan rushed before Ozwald handed him a scroll in his hand.

"We had a vision together. Rorik gave this to me," Ozwald stuttered, his movements visibly anxious.

"Rorik as in Lord Rorik? What is he to you, farmer boy?" Ethan sneered.

"My uncle," Ozwald gulped, the air between them going still as the chanting mages continued their ritual.

"And you didn't know?" Ethan asked. Ozwald could only shake his head. Ethan opened the scroll and read it a few times, trying to understand.

As the moment draws near, heed the call
of ancient seers,
Let your will and purpose synchronize,
overcome all your fears,
Reach out and unravel the mystery, let
your hands guide,
Witness the elusive sight materialize, as
secrets come alive.
But if fate turn its back, and leave you
stranded in the dark,
Venture forth a steadfast heart, leave
behind regretful marks,
For though the path seems uncertain, the
way ahead unclear,
Strength gained will guide you on, through
trials and tears.
So when the moment arrives, listen closely
for the cries,

*Of those gone before you, and the secrets
they've disguised,
Let your determination rise, and your
spirit be your guide,
For when you trust in your own power, the
universe will provide.*

Ethan read it out loud as both boys cast curious glares at each other, trying to decipher the message.

"I don't know what this means. Aren't you supposed to be the one with all the knowledge?" Ethan exhaled, trying to re-read the scroll. Ozwald gazed deeply into Ethan's eyes, studying every feature he caught sight of.

"How did he give this to you? And why?" Ethan badgered before Ozwald turned the scroll over, revealing Rorik's directions. He then began to recall the events that led him to Nav.

Ozwald,

There's no time. Your father, Lord Rupert, handed this to me before his death. Go to the grand temple of Nav.
You are the key to defeating the blight.

Rorik

Ethan thought about the message while Ozwald began to recall every event that had transpired before arriving at the temple, not withholding anything. He described every emotion and interaction he had, relieving himself in the process of the pain he had been carrying while his emotions were on front display. Ethan remained fixated on Ozwald throughout, listening to each word without displaying any emotions.

After Ozwald finished his recollections, he had to nudge Ethan to do the same, who did so with a surprising eagerness. Ethan recollected the events that brought him to the temple, describing Bograh and his encounter with Farhet and the demise of Ursula and Jones. He then recollected his days in Eurst and why he had come to Azra. Ozwald had never known what the life of a royal was like and reacted with curiosity to different parts of Ethan's descriptions.

Suddenly, Ozwald stood up, his entire body cracking while his eyes bulged at the mention of the Council Ceremony. He rushed ahead to where the mages chanted, trying to keep his head bowed and silent. He waved quickly back to Ethan to follow. He reluctantly obeyed the orders with pain apparent in his movements. Just as Ozwald caught sight of the stone structure, it began to open into a well that filled with water on its own. Both Ozwald and Ethan gasped at the sight.

The well glowed and emanated beams of light while the chanting mages increased in volume and kneeled ahead of it. Ozwald had never seen or heard such rituals in the temple back in the Haefe and looked upon them with attentiveness and curiosity. He quickly caught sight of Ethan, who squinted as well while staring at the glowing well.

"There isn't supposed to be a third one," Ethan sighed, approaching it carefully while making his way between the bowing mages.

"What is it for?" Ozwald asked.

"This is for the ritual ceremony after the council approves nobility for marriage. There's one in Horos and one in Fallgarde, and that's it," Ethan said, confusion clear in his face. The well began to glow even brighter in his presence.

"It isn't even supposed to glow this way," he added. Ethan glanced back at Ozwald, standing attentively but unaware of what to do next.

"Come," Ethan said, signaling for Ozwald to stand next to him. Without another word, Ethan grabbed his hand and placed his and Ozwald's into the water. The water suddenly began to glow deeper. The mages chanted louder as both boys waited for something to happen while tension built up in the air. Ozwald knew something was imminent, and he glanced around frantically.

Suddenly, a faint clicking sound echoed from the mosaic ahead of them, gradually growing louder and more intense. The mosaic that stood before them, depicted the final conference between men of Eursazure and the Ancients. The mosaic was a scene of grandeur and terror, gathering all Lords from every realm, adorned in gilded armor, their long hair billowing in the wind as they gathered. The towering figures of the Ancients depicted in the center wielded a grand staff that struck the ground with a menacing ferocity. Men and women below, depicted as smaller than everyone else, fled away from the bottom from the wrath and ferociousness of the Ancient's staff that sent tremors through the ground.

As the clicking sound continued to grow louder, a small stone drawer in the wall of the mosaic opened slowly from its center. Both boys rushed to it while the chanting ceased. They quickly looked inside. Ethan, catching sight of a shining object, immediately pulled out a three-pronged dagger that glowed in the dim light. It had a green ruby at its hilt, and he began to feel its texture.

"What do we do with this?" Ethan exhaled, holding it in the air for Ozwald to see. Ozwald looked at it closely, his eyes squinting before he grabbed it and held it on his own, comparing it with the mosaic in front of him.

"This is that," he shrieked, pointing to the staff of the Ancients. "It's the same hilt. You see. I've seen this painting before at one of Yakenn's houses in Aurom," he added. Ethan looked at it as well before he nodded, his eyes glistening and acknowledging their discovery.

"What do we do now?" he sighed.

Before Ethan could say any word, Ozwald jumped in his place. "I know where we need to go," he said with conviction and assuredness in his voice. The silent mages in the background began to chant again as if acknowledging his intuition. "This is not a coincidence. We will find out soon. Follow me," Ozwald chimed, pulling on Ethan's arm as both quickly left the grand temple of Nav.

Forty-Two

Ozwald and Ethan raced through dry and drought-covered lands that were once trees and farming fields. It stretched out north across Usall, a barren and bleak landscape unlike any they had ever witnessed. Everywhere they looked, the land was lifeless, consumed by a relentless drought that had drained the land of all vitality. The red blight was here and in full force. The once green terrain was now unrecognizable, swallowed up by a thick layer of black and red dust that clung to their skin and clothes, filling their lungs with a putrid stench that lingered in the air. The sky above was no longer the clear blue they had known but a foreboding shade of darkened blue and streaks of orange, a warning of the imminent danger that loomed ahead. The few patches of greenery that remained were swiftly disappearing, leaving behind a barren wasteland that was utterly devoid of life. As they pushed on, Ozwald led the way, his eyes fixed on the horizon as they followed the border between Adrovia and Usall along Azra's main trading route. Along the way, they passed by bands and groups of desperate families, making their way south from Usall. Their faces were etched with exhaustion and despair, their eyes haunted by the horrors they had witnessed. For these people, the journey was a perilous one, fraught with danger and uncertainty at every turn. Many had already fallen victim to theft and death. As Ozwald and Ethan passed by, the refugees looked up. Briefly, their heads bowed in melancholic resignation before trudging on, the weight of their burdens dragging them down.

"There's nothing left. Red dust just came in the night, and by the morning, all our crops were dead. We tried to take our stored grain, but they confiscated it, all of it. So, we made it out while we could," one of the travelers panted after Ethan approached them.

"Who?"

"House Haelin," the traveler sighed. Fear washed across her face, and she was unwilling to continue speaking.

"Have you heard anything of Adrovia?" Ozwald badgered just as the traveler took off. Neither he nor his group cared to answer, and dust followed their stride.

Neither Ozwald nor Ethan could hold back a sense of despair as they remained alone in the drought-filled lands.

"We were here just a month ago. No one ever predicted this back in Horos," Ethan sighed, his eyes filled with worry. Ozwald, though, remained driven. His body language protruded knowledge that he was confident of.

"We wouldn't have received this dagger for nothing, whatever it is for," Ozwald said, holding it out for both to see.

"Probably useless. You actually think no one ever

found it there or knew about its existence?" Ethan sneered, grabbing it and studying its hilt again.

Ozwald stared into the darkened sky while thoughts raced through his mind. His eyes glowed, and he took back the dagger swiftly.

"My father, my guardian, actually," Ozwald sighed.

"Merrick, he always taught me that if you want to hide something, always hide it in the open. It's the last place anyone would ever expect," he added, a sad smile crossing his face while looking down. "So, if we are the ones that found it, then it was always meant for us. We just need to find out why and what we should use it for. We didn't see each other in that vision for no reason," he ended, sheathing the dagger.

Without giving room for Ethan to speak, Ozwald dashed off along the trade route while Ethan shook his head behind him.

"Better not be too late," Ethan exhaled, quickly following.

~

Ozwald stood at the base of a tall mountain south of Valya after an almost ten-day journey. The two of them had followed Azra's main trade route, crossing mainly arid land. The dry land and ubiquitous red and black dust subsided and quickly disappeared once they entered the frosty hills that Ozwald knew to be in the north of Adrovia.

The frosty hills were known to be chilly during the day and freezing during the night, regardless of the season. They did not disappoint. However, Ozwald knew there had been a change.

"Somehow, that blight hasn't crossed over the hills. But I can feel that it will come soon. It feels warmer," Ozwald pointed out, climbing through the hills.

Their journey up the hills was punctuated by the erratic chirping of birds that flitted amidst the still-standing trees. The soft breeze that blew across the landscape was purer and more invigorating than what they had experienced during their journey through Nav. He wasted no time in taking deep breaths to refresh his lungs, relishing the pure, untainted air before the drought caught up with them. The grassy terrain they traversed was scattered with trees that grew just far enough apart to allow them to easily navigate. The undulating hills merged into one another in a graceful manner, forming a sequence of slight mounds that gradually ascended toward the colossal mountain that dominated the horizon. As they progressed, the temperature dropped perceptibly while they could see Valya's land relief to the west of the hills, as well as the adjoining mountain chain to the north. Valya remained unspoiled by the blight and remained a verdant oasis in the midst of the desolate landscape.

Ozwald suddenly rushed ahead to a cliff while Ethan followed slowly, panting. "Over there, the Haefe is just at the edge of the horizon," Ozwald shrieked, pointing with his finger as he took a moment for the sight to sink in.

"Your made-up town that they hid you in," Ethan exhaled, gazing across the horizon and then up the mountain. "And I have a feeling we're going to find out why soon," he added just as the howling wind blew strongly from the top of the mountain, bringing with it freezing air. They were too high up and too far away to see any movement below. However, it looked peaceful, calm, and ready for the storm to come. Behind them, to the east, the sky was dark blue with streaks of orange. Usall existed in a world of its own, desolate and unlike what Ozwald had heard about it before.

"I'm never going back. My purpose lies elsewhere, I know it," Ozwald said, taking a deep breath as Ethan nodded. Ozwald checked the sun and saw that it had not reached the middle of the sky yet. "This way," Ozwald instructed, nudging Ethan to follow along a narrow path he'd found. "The frosty hills are behind us, now comes the hard part to the top of the Ancient Heights," he added, confidence dwindling in his voice as the Ancient Heights loomed over them. "It's where we had our vision," he ended, pointing up.

"There was so much sadness and guilt in that vision. You didn't see all that I saw," Ethan said from behind. "Are you sure that was the Ancient Heights?"

"It's the tallest mountain in Azra. I don't see it being anywhere else," Ozwald said as he glanced back, his face uneasy. The higher they ascended, the fewer trees and overgrowth covered the land as the grass turned into moist soil before hardening in the cold weather. The path they followed took them across narrow ledges to the side of the mountain, fit for only one person. The ground remained surprisingly flat as if feet continuously walked up its path. They did not question and continued ahead, rushing to gain as much ground as they could before the sunset.

As the hours passed, the sun started to descend, causing the sky to transform into a dense, dark gray hue, and an impending storm could be seen rapidly advancing. With the intensifying gusts of wind piercing through their ears, snowflakes started to plummet from the sky. Soon, the chill of the snowflakes became unbearable, and they had to shield their faces to avoid the sting. Meanwhile, Ethan began to gather small branches during their climb, bundling them together in his arms.

"Those are useless here. They're only going to slow us down," Ozwald said, frustration clear in his voice.

"You clearly don't like to prepare. We're going to need it very soon. Otherwise, we'll freeze in the night," Ethan hissed, standing in a thin layer of snow.

"Anyways, we don't really have enough clothes. We have one shot in the morning, and that's it. Otherwise, we're going to freeze to death," he added. Ozwald knew he was right and ended up giving him a hand before starting to look for branches as well.

~

Ozwald and Ethan trudged through the relentless snow and wind, their bodies wracked with exhaustion and pain from their arduous journey. The steep climb and frigid temperatures exacerbated their discomfort. The trail had become nearly indiscernible, and the encroaching darkness only added to their struggle. Amidst the gloom, a faint moon emerged from behind the clouds, casting feeble rays of light upon them. Despite their bone-chilling shivers, they scoured the area for a suitable place to light a fire, but to no avail. The wind howled so fiercely that they could barely communicate. They could barely hear anything except for the distant cries of wolves that pierced through the tumult. They exchanged a brief, silent glance before forging ahead, their progress hindered by the snow that had now reached up to their knees. They carefully traversed a lengthy ledge on the side of the mountain, which twisted and turned like a serpentine path etched out by a colossal finger eons ago. As they ascended, they attempted to catch a glimpse of the realms below from their higher vantage point. However, they were too high. The clouds and darkness obscured their view.

The higher they got, the sharper the inclines became, especially at path bends. They wore all the clothes they had packed back in Nav, but they were still not enough to repel the cold. Icicles formed near their mouth and nostrils.

"We need to turn back," Ethan eventually exploded from the back, his voice shivering and barely audible to Ozwald, who immediately gazed at him. His eyebrows had been covered in white snow, and his cloak as well. His lips were blue, and his hands had been tucked under his jacket to keep them warm. "We don't have the right gear," Ethan cried, his face visibly flustered.

"We're almost there, we'll be there soon, and we can light a fire up in the cave. I know it," Ozwald barked, upset with the comment. Ethan was right. Ozwald stopped in his tracks for a moment, confusion etched on his face. The wind howled with a ferocity that made it hard to hear anything or think.

Abruptly, Ozwald jolted as a low growl emanated from beside him. He instinctively stepped back, brandishing his sword, his heart pounding with terror, while Ethan followed suit. The snow mounted around their feet as a pack of wolves emerged from behind a cluster of boulders, their fur matted with ice and snow. Undaunted, Ethan and Ozwald stood their ground, their swords glinting in the faint light, poised to confront their lethal adversaries. The upcoming incline loomed ahead of them, a perilous path that they could not hope to outrun the wolves on. Ozwald knew that they had no other option but to face the challenge head-on as the wolves' snarls grew increasingly louder by the moment. Ozwald frantically surveyed the terrain for any potential escape routes, but each one led to a dead end. The wolves closed in, their piercing eyes fixed on their prey, and their sharp white fangs gleamed in the moonlight. Ozwald and Ethan knew they were in grave peril.

Without warning, the pack of wolves lunged toward Ozwald, baring their sharp teeth. Despite the imminent danger, Ozwald stood firm and prepared for the onslaught, crouching in preparation. But just as the alpha wolf was about to pounce on him, Ethan immediately grabbed his arm and pulled him up the incline, away from harm's way.

"We need to fight," Ozwald snapped, looking back at the attacking wolfpack behind them.

"Never fight from the damn low ground, you idiot," Ethan growled, situating himself and Ozwald in the best location to deal with the onslaught. "And the path is narrower here," he added. Both boys waited for the attack, their swords raised high as the snow blew harder.

"When they jump, keep your sword straight and point it in their direction. They have no swords. One pierce will be enough," Ethan instructed, with his focus dead straight on the wolves. The cold no longer mattered to either of the boys.

In the blink of an eye, chaos erupted as the pack of wolves attacked. The first wolf lunged toward Ethan just as he pushed Ozwald out of harm. Ethan was ready, and with a swift movement, he plunged his sword deep into the wolf's side, causing it to emit a ferocious growl as it landed on top of Ethan. The weight of the wolf caused Ethan to fall backward, struggling to keep it at bay. Meanwhile, another one of the wolves caught Ozwald off guard, and despite his best efforts, he was unable to pierce its skin with his sword. Two other wolves stood aside, the narrow pathway hindering them from joining in on the fray, forcing them to remain at the boulders. As the two men continued to fight fiercely against the wolves, their growls echoed in the wind, easily audible over the sound of the blowing wind. Ozwald grappled with his wolf, straining to keep its teeth away while attempting to stab it with his sword. Despite Ozwald's efforts, he was in a stalemate, unable to land a mortal blow. Finally, though, Ozwald released his sword and pushed the wolf away with both hands, causing them to roll to the edge of the ledge. He managed to hold his ground, but just barely, as the wolf remained on top of him. As the struggle continued, the wolf suddenly backed up, ready to take a bite out of Ozwald's arm. But just as it was about to sink its teeth in, it was pushed away with great force as if kicked by a giant boot. Ozwald quickly moved to the side, panting and covered in sweat and blood, while Ethan stood over him, his sword stained with blood. The wolf he had killed lay motionless on the snow behind him. Both men were panting heavily while Ethan helped Ozwald up, his arms also covered in blood.

"Let's hope that was the alpha wolf. Otherwise, I'll have to do that again three more times," Ethan panted, trying to catch his breath. The wolves, however, remained growling below. Ethan, though, Ozwald could see, had a plan, pushing the motionless wolf's body as much as he could forward for the others to see. Once the dead wolf was closer, Ozwald and Ethan took a few steps back while the other three wolves hesitantly approached and smelled their fellow beast. One of them tried to pull the dead wolf away with their teeth but failed. Instead of trying to continue with their attack, all three wolves growled, staring viscously at Ethan and Ozwald while drool dripped from their teeth. Ethan raised his sword and took a few steps ahead, unleashing a war cry of his own. The wolves groaned and ran away down the mountain, leaving Ozwald and Ethan on their own, tired and covered in blood.

Ethan stood in the snow for a short while before dropping to his knees in the snow, clearly exhausted. Ozwald ran to him, despite the pain all over his body, and held him up on his shoulder.

"I'll help you up. The summit shouldn't be too far," Ozwald said, his voice strained from the effort he gave to lift Ethan up.

"No, I can't. We need to rest for the night," Ethan began, holding onto Ozwald tightly. "Behind those boulders, I think I saw a place we can rest," he said, pointing with his hand. Ozwald did not try to object. He knew he was right.

"Wait here then, and let me have a look," Ozwald said. Ethan grabbed his arm and pulled on it.

"You leave me here, and I'll freeze," Ethan sneered.

The deep snow posed a challenge for both of them, but they persevered nevertheless. Ozwald managed to reach the top of the boulder first before pulling Ethan up. As they looked ahead, they glimpsed a darkness that loomed ominously in front of them. The ceaseless howling of the wind resounded in their ears, echoing off the walls of the dark rock formation that lay ahead.

"It's either this or we freeze," Ethan said, his voice hesitant. He quickly looked into Ozwald's eyes for some sort of comfort and support. "Shall we?" he added, nudging him before both entered together.

Forty-Three

Ozwald sat by the blazing fire, which crackled and flickered deep within the cave. The distant sound of the wind howling served as a constant reminder of their precarious situation. Ozwald had helped Ethan tend to the wounds the wolf had inflicted while fashioning a makeshift bandage for Ethan's hip. Despite his weariness, Ozwald could not bring himself to sleep. Instead, he stared deep into the cave, straining his eyes to see as far as the flickering light allowed him to while the vision of the mountain kept repeating in his mind, causing him to question why he and Ethan had come there in the first place. He could not shake the feeling that they were in danger and needed to leave as soon as possible. Together they had gathered enough wood to build a roaring fire, even finding additional branches that someone had stored there long ago, which helped to keep the fire burning bright throughout the night.

"Whoever stored these has not been here in a while," Ethan had pointed out while Ozwald got the fire going. The light revealed the cave to be large and deep, with sketches and engravings on the wall that made no sense to any of them. The stone was black and ragged with many sharp edges. Dripping water could be heard from inside, adding to the wet feeling they had. Both boys remained silent, assuming the other had gone to sleep, until Ethan broke the silence.

"Can't sleep either?" Ethan said, his eyes closed.

"No," Ozwald sighed, opening his eyes and staring at the dancing shadows from their fire. Suddenly he got up and started to pace around where they sat before he grabbed an unlit piece of wood and lit it slowly in the flame. He held it up and began to walk into the cave, his eyes filled with curiosity.

"Where are you going?" Ethan grunted, his eyes still closed. Ozwald did not look back.

"To see what else is hidden in this cave. Care to join?" Ozwald said, the flame in his hand unraveling more of the cave.

"Let me know what you find," Ethan shrugged, turning to the other side of his makeshift bed.

Ozwald headed in, taking careful steps. As he made his way through the cave, he noticed that it twisted and turned in many directions. As he delved deeper into the cave, he could feel the air growing thicker and drier. The sound of the howling wind that had accompanied him thus far disappeared, but the intricate sketches on the cave walls remained a constant presence. Finally, he reached the end of the cave, where he found himself staring at a blank wall. Nothing visible was out of the ordinary while he stood there, surveying his surroundings. This part of the cave was at least as high as his house on the farm and wide enough to accommodate ten men standing side-by-side.

"What is that?" A voice spoke suddenly. Ozwald flinched, and his heart raced. He moved his flame and caught direct eyesight with Ethan. "Got a bit bored. And besides, my leg is fine," he added, making his way to an opening in the side wall. Ozwald shook his head while Ethan bent down and looked inside the small opening to the side.

"What can you see?" Ozwald badgered while Ethan began to move a heavy object from within. After a moment, he pulled out a small stone chest from within the crevice. Ozwald knelt beside him while both inspected it. The chest was small and wide, with a wooden emblem in the middle that bore a phoenix.

"The Lygem's sigil," Ozwald exhaled, his eyes anxiously waiting to find out about its contents.

"Rorik's house," Ethan concurred, quickly opening the chest and revealing two old but still intact scrolls. Ethan took the smaller one, and Ozwald took the larger and thicker scroll.

Ozwald quickly unrolled it and found a map. He studied it for a short while, rotating it a few times to make sense of it. After studying it for a few more minutes, it finally made sense to him.

"This is a map to the top. We were right to come here," Ozwald uttered, his voice only audible to himself and Ethan. "What does yours say?" He questioned eagerly. But no response came.

"Ethan?" Ozwald nudged Ethan, who was so engrossed in reading his scroll that he seemed to be examining each letter. After a moment, Ethan looked up and handed the scroll to Ozwald, his eyes fixed and unmoving. Ozwald looked at him curiously while taking the scroll and beginning to read it himself, absorbing every word.

Dear Reader,

I cannot send this with more urgency.

The red blight has started. How many years it would take to consume our world, I do not know.

Our fire post has been lit for a week. The North Guard Heights caught it.

But Fallgarde has not received the message yet.

If I don't make it, and you are reading this, then I have failed. The Order of Defiance has caught me. You must tell the Lord of Fallgarde.

His wife is pregnant with the twins that can save us from this plague. He must act fast.

Rommel

Ozwald's face was etched with concern and worry as he looked up at Ethan. The silence between them was deafening, and both boys were at a loss for words. Suddenly, Ethan crouched over and reached out for another item in the crevice, pulling out a rotten wooden box. Despite the noise it made, the box was still intact. With a loud clatter, Ethan opened the box. Ozwald was so focused on Ethan's actions that he could not process the letter he had just read. However, as Ethan pulled open the box, it immediately crumbled and released a pungent, rotting smell. However, it also revealed two thick fur cloaks. Ethan dusted them off and held them up for Ozwald to see.

"At least Rommel was kind enough to leave us cloaks.

They should do," Ethan gulped, handing one to Ozwald while avoiding eye contact.

"I think we better go, we've rested, and these cloaks will keep us warm. We can't waste time," Ozwald uttered, his eyes hesitating to look at Ethan. Ethan nodded and got up, pulling the scroll out of Ozwald's hand and putting on one of the fur cloaks.

"Is that map any good?" Ethan badgered, brushing his hair back and steering his ear towards him.

"This isn't really a map, but it'll do the trick. Maybe Rommel drew it to remember this place," Ozwald said, getting up as well. He walked ahead, leading the way with the light in his hand as Ethan followed.

"We need another three hours, and we should be up there. As long as that leg of yours can keep up, of course," Ozwald said.

"You can count on it..." Ethan stuttered.

Forty-Four

Ethan stood at the edge of the cliff overlooking the now lit sky. Chills ran down his spine as it matched his vision in terms of look, feel, and smell. The snow piled up to his knees, and he saw the clouds below blocking his view. The wind howled fiercely, making it challenging to breathe, but Ethan still inhaled deeply, taking in the crisp, icy air.

"Just like I saw it," Ethan exhaled, his voice barely audible but filled with bewilderment. Ozwald nodded before eyeing the opening to the cave at the other end of the cliff behind them, just like the vision. The opening loomed eerily behind them as if a dark omen.

They began their climb just before dawn and ascended along a treacherous path that took them across thin ledges and fallen boulders. They saw no trails of anyone that had been there recently, adding to the gloom of their journey. The map took them on impossible paths which they trusted blindly. Even when a path looked blocked and non-traversable, they would find a way to overcome it.

Ozwald tightened his fur cloak over his head, casting away the cold air and making his way toward the cave entrance. "No one is dying today," Ethan said before following.

Ozwald did not wait for Ethan, nor did he watch his step, crossing the shadow threshold of the cave immediately.

"Together, maybe we have a better chance this time," Ethan sneered from behind, stepping through the shadow threshold at the edge of the snow as well. Inside, Ethan paused for a moment while waiting for his eyes to adjust before moving ahead. He quickly found the spot where he had been attached to the ground, his memories igniting vividly. Contrary to his vision, there was just a flat stone ground this time. He then caught sight of Ozwald, who produced fire stones and began to ignite a piece of wood that remained in his sack.

Click. Click. Ethan heard Ozwald curse while trying to ignite his piece of wood. In the meantime, Ethan saw the bend ahead of him that he never got a chance to pass into. He knew his time would come just as a light emanated from between Ozwald's hands.

"Got it," Ozwald exhaled, holding up the light high and studying the entrance portion of the cave. Ozwald nodded to Ethan and took cautious steps ahead.

"This is where you left me," Ethan cautioned.

"And that's where my part of the vision ended. Nothing is ending today, though," Ozwald insisted, walking ahead in the cold and moist corridor. His light illuminated soft, smooth walls that were evenly cut as if molded like clay.

They glowed in the light as if carrying specs of light.

"Starmoon marble. The Ancients brought these during their first coming. All had been lost, I read," Ozwald said, his eyes glistening and reveled at the sight. He could not hold his excitement, rubbing his hand across its entire surface while it squeaked. "Not a speck of dust," he added.

"That's what Starmoon marble gives you, eternal cleanliness. Among other things, of course," Ethan echoed, his eyes glowing as well.

They continued deeper into the cave while a deafening silence drummed in their ears. Ethan took off his cloak as the Starmoon marble controlled the temperature inside as well.

Just as they progressed further, Ethan heard Ozwald step over a brittle substance ahead. He stopped and inspected it as Ethan approached from behind.

"Whoever was here is no more," Ozwald said.

"This corpse had time to decay and dry off on its own. We must be the first people here since him," Ethan grunted while Ozwald shed light across the area. Eventually, both found the cave to have a dedicated living quarter containing two bed chambers with small, rotten mattresses. The rest of the cave was one miniature temple that appeared unused for more than a decade. The candles were flat, and the incense pots were long finished. Ozwald, however, quickly searched each part of it in search of something. Eventually, the temple began to light up as Ozwald found unlit candles in every corner.

What Ethan initially thought to be a miniature temple turned out to be a large one.

"This place is bigger than the one in the Haefe. Although, it has the same construction," Ozwald commented, his eyes gazing at every detail. The temple had high pillars along the sides and an elevated altar at the opposite end. Incense trays were hung from the ceiling with long rusted chains. The walls, however, were much different. Detailed mosaics, made of small tiles smaller than a pinky finger, covered each part of the wall. The mosaics depicted the same stories as the grand temple in Nav, as if a twin to its existence. At the back behind the altar, Ethan gasped at the size and detail of a mosaic, this time of Eursazure at the time of the chasm.

"I saw the same image back in Adrovia," Ozwald shrieked as both he and Ethan stared at the same mosaic. "Only difference is that the ship wasn't so low. Plus, this has a lot of people depicted in it, but they're suffering. It's like it's telling that we should be in constant mourning," Ozwald uttered, his voice dropping in volume while remaining engulfed in its sight. Ethan shook his head, beginning to pace around the temple. The air, although no wind reached inside, was stale and old as he studied every part of the temple.

After a short while, Ozwald glanced at Ethan.

"What are you doing?" Ozwald asked, casting a curious glance. Ethan was studying a part of the mosaic in front of them.

"I'm trying to find out what it is that we're supposed to find in here. We wouldn't have had that vision alone," Ethan exhaled, moving to another part of the mosaic.

"Well, I don't think we need to wait much longer. The depiction has a rather odd relief. Look over here. There must be something hidden somewhere like before," Ozwald said, curiosity clear in his voice. He approached the wall where the mosaic had been fixed and began to feel the bottom part near the ship. Ozwald continued to feel out different parts of it without any real success. Finally, though, Ethan joined him in his search, following his lead. Both further inspected the wall for anything unusual but found nothing. Unwilling to give up, they took a step back to recollect their thoughts, studying the wall and the rest of the room in detail.

"All this effort, and we'll probably end up with another dagger that we wouldn't know what to do with," Ethan hesitated, grooving his fingers in his hair and taking deep breaths.

"Are you still thinking about that letter?" Ozwald muttered, Ethan quickly nodding while looking away. "It mentioned twins," he continued. "Is that why you've been dead silent since the cave?" Ozwald badgered. "A boy from Horos and a boy from the Haefe, both in one place," Ozwald ended with an exhale.

As soon as Ozwald spoke, Ethan's face ignited with enthusiasm as if his words were the spark that lit the fire within him. His eagerness was so overwhelming that he could not even contain it.

"Where is the Haefe in this image?" Ethan quickly blurted. Ozwald hesitated before approaching the mosaic and pointing with his finger. Ethan quickly unsheathed the dagger from Nav.

"Stick it with this," he instructed, throwing it to Ozwald. With a swift motion, he pierced the tree-covered portion of the painting with his dagger, causing a drawer to pop out above him. As the area of the ship in the image flipped, a stone tablet engraved with mysterious markings was revealed, catching their attention. Both Ozwald and Ethan studied the tablet intently, trying to decipher its meaning. When Ethan appeared defeated, he took charge and read the tablet aloud, determined to uncover its secrets.

Behold, it was foretold that one day, two halves of a single whole would come, two halves of the chosen king. What you have not foreseen, for you could not have known, is that this whole, this progeny, cannot stand combined. As they grow in strength, a darkness befalls the heather. One shall fall by the other's sword, their blood atonement to halt the encroachment of the nether.

"Riddles are pointless. They just cover up other people's stupidity," Ethan hissed, shaking his head. Ozwald handed the dagger back to Ethan with a casual gesture, his attention fully captured by the contents of the drawer. Inside lay a single scroll that had stood the test of time. Ozwald picked up the scroll and unwrapped it, all the while keeping a watchful eye on Ethan, who could not help but glance back at the tablet a few more times. Ozwald cleared his throat, waiting for Ethan to focus. Ethan nodded as Ozwald held the scroll out in front of him and began to read out loud.

My Children,

If you're reading this, then the red blight hasn't won yet. There is still hope. There is no excuse for what I have done to you and no forgiveness. My acts were only the acts of a loving father.

I could not stomach that neither of you would be allowed a chance to live. Others would have done the act when you were born, but I couldn't. You deserved to live first.

By now, you would have heard the hidden prophecy. Fallgarde, the Promise Well, is where you make your decision.

Although I may never see you again, you will always be

my sons, Ozwald and Ethan.

Rupert,

The tension in the air was palpable as the two boys stood facing each other in silence. Ethan's heart was pounding so hard he could hear it echoing in his ears, his whole body trembling with a mixture of fear and anticipation of what was to come. The weight of others descended upon them both, suffocating them without asking their permission first. Ozwald and Ethan's eyes met, but neither of them could hold their gaze for long. Unspoken words hung between them, each understanding the other without a single syllable being uttered. The truth was there, plain to see in the way they carried themselves and the emotions etched onto their faces. Ethan and Ozwald both felt it. The raw power of their intuition confirmed at that moment. It was a moment of profound understanding, a charged moment. They both knew that everything was about to change, that their lives were irrevocably linked. A decision, though, had to be made, a decision that could never be changed.

Ozwald cleared his throat, breaking the silence in the room, the sound echoing on the still walls of the temple while the candle lights flickered.

"This can't be true," Ethan barked, frustration clear in his voice.

"But it explains everything. Hasn't what we have seen been a testament of that?" Ozwald began gasping. "A testament of what our father said?" He added, the words not feeling natural in his mouth. Ethan knew he was right, but he could not fathom it. He walked to the tablet and read it again, his eyes studying each letter, while Ozwald stood behind anxiously waiting for his decision.

Ethan did not speak, and Ozwald could not wait.

"We must go to Fallgarde then. There isn't much time left, and we can't lie to ourselves. You heard him," Ozwald uttered, his voice filled with confidence and conviction. "Are you with me, brother?"

Forty-Five

In just two days, Ozwald and Ethan raced down the mountain, finally reaching a high cliff that overlooked Fallgarde in the distance. However, it would take them another day to descend and reach the city. As they traversed the western side of the Ancient Heights, the blight was nowhere to be seen, as if the mighty mountain range had protected the land from harm. But the stench of death grew stronger as they cleared the snow. Suddenly, they stumbled upon an unexpected sight: standing armies camped to the south and north of Fallgarde, their banners proudly waving in the wind. Despite the raised house sigils, there was no sign of any impending attack.

"Everything is collapsing, and they want to fight," Ethan sneered.

"Why wouldn't they? Fallgarde has food and resources. That gives them a chance to survive a bit longer," Ozwald glared, his voice pale at the sight.

"Useless, instead of trying to find a long-term solution together, they prioritize short-term fallacies. There was a time when you would have thought that they came to ask polite questions," Ethan snickered.

"We don't have much time left," Ozwald said, nudging Ethan to keep going.

Fallgarde was small in the distance after they first cleared the clouds, growing in size the lower they reached. Ozwald led the descent, convincing Ethan against resting for too long. Determination was clear in his demeanor, but Ethan was the opposite, lost in his thoughts and unwilling to talk much. The weight of the truth beat down on him, leaving him feeling betrayed.

"My father...the emperor, I mean. He knew all along. The lies," Ethan sneered. Ozwald tried to console him but struggled to find the right words to say, leaving him alone instead.

At the base of the mountain, Ethan stopped, panting hard and looking at Ozwald. "Let's rest. There's no blight here yet, and Azra can wait a little longer for its guests of honor. Those armies won't attack either. They'd do everything to avoid a siege war."

"We leave before dawn," Ozwald relented, settling down next to Ethan in the sheltered area. Observing the dark blue sky that indicated evening's arrival, he gazed upon Fallgarde as the sun began to set. Between the mountain base and Fallgarde lay a grassy plain dotted with scattered trees to the north and farmlands to the south. "It's just a two-hour walk, brother. We'll be there in no time," Ethan uttered, his gaze focused on the ground and his body frail. "You heard him, we may have lived apart, but at least we lived," Ozwald said, nudging him.

"You're not thinking beyond that letter. We are the reason for the blight. It should have never reached this point. He could have saved all those lives if he had done what was right," Ethan erupted.

"Our father killed for us to live. He killed King Erdun, the emperor's son, just when we were born," Ozwald said coldly, disinterested in Ethan's complaining. Ethan broke out into a sinister laugh, clearly fed up.

"Why does it matter? Who killed who? These Ancients were right to damn us with this blight. We're all selfish and greedy. And our father is a prime example. He probably never cared what his decision would lead to. He just cared about himself. He kept us alive, but he killed for us. Others died for us," Ethan growled. Ozwald contemplated his words.

"The end defines the means. That was his decision, and we must live with it," Ozwald exhaled. "What matters is our decision, not his," he added.

"Ozwald, the philosopher," Ethan mocked.

"We have a mission. I'm ready for it, and I know you are too. You wouldn't have come down with me if you weren't," Ozwald hissed, getting up and beginning to pace in the open space in front of them, his focus fixated on Fallgarde. Ethan on the other hand, looked to the ground and began to trace shapes with his finger, lost in his own thoughts.

~

As the sun slowly rose, Fallgarde remained in the shadow of the imposing Ancient Heights. The towering city walls appeared to grow in size and become more distinct the closer they approached. Unlike Aurom, Fallgarde lacked a moat or drawbridge, and the land surrounding the walls was barren, devoid of any trees. Guards patrolled the walls with archers at the ready, vigilant and prepared for any potential threats. "This city is on lockdown. They better not shoot us down before we reach them," Ethan sneered, frantically disrobing, leaving only his pants and boots on. Ethan's chest bore an old visible scar that ran from the top of his shoulder and down his back.

"What are you doing?" Ozwald demanded, confusion clear on his face.

"Do the same unless you want to get shot down by one of their arrows," Ethan snapped, continuing his measured walk ahead. Ozwald sighed, stopping in his walk for a few moments and quickly disrobing himself before rushing behind Ethan again.

"This better work," he hissed, reaching Ethan's side.

Ethan's lips curved into a smirk as he came to a halt, positioning himself directly in front of the menacing gate. Four guards, stalwart and resolute, loomed above him, their shields braced and ready for attack. A tall banner, emblazoned with the sigil of a phoenix, fluttered above their heads, imbuing the scene with an air of regal grandeur. From each corner of the gate, archers stood at the ready, bows taut and arrows nocked. Ozwald squinted his eyes, catching sight of the intricate design of their armor, a blend of dark hues with streaks of deep purple, exuding an aura of power. Despite the gentle breeze that carried the fluttering sound of the banner, the tension in the air was palpable, making every breath feel like an effort.

"Who goes there?" The lead guard orated from the top of the gate, his voice shattering the silence. Ethan looked at

Ozwald and nodded.

"We're here to see Lord Rorik. We're his guests," Ethan said, his voice loud and slow, while the sound of waking roosters began to crow from within the city walls.

"And what are your names?"

"Ozwald and Ethan," Ethan said. The guards began to speak among themselves.

"Of house Lygem," Ozwald added, catching the attention of the guards, who stopped talking.

"You both have ten seconds to run away; otherwise, these archers will carry out their target practice for the day. Do I make myself clear?" The guard hissed. Ethan did not break his gaze, standing confidently up to the guards. Ozwald did not flinch either, his newfound brother's confidence rubbing off on him.

"I struggle to see how you will be able to explain to Lord Rorik that you struck down the long-lost children of his brother Rupert for no reason, without losing your head —without your entire family not losing their heads," Ethan sneered, maliciousness clear in his voice.

"One," the guard began to count, the sound of the archers nocking their bows tighter emanating from above. Ozwald glanced at Ethan, who remained unshaken by the ultimatum, his chest protruding even farther out.

"Two," the guard continued.

"Maybe we say something? There are standing armies outside. They're not letting anyone in," Ozwald whispered, a slight stutter in his voice, the wind continuing to blow behind them. Suddenly a loud wind picked up from the top of the Ancient Heights behind them as if demanding the city gates to open as well. The counting continued while both boys remained unperturbed.

"Eight," the guard went on, a stutter clear in his voice, the rest of the guards visibly fidgeting in their place without any attempt to reason among themselves.

"There you are," a voice suddenly beamed from behind. Ethan flinched at the sound while the guard stopped counting and gazed at the person behind them. Ozwald turned slowly, catching sight of eyes, malicious eyes he never thought he would see again.

"So, it's true, there are two," Yakenn hissed, just audible for Ozwald and Ethan to hear. Yakenn looked unusually worn down, his clothes dirty and scathed. Behind him stood Rybae, Anella, and Byrene, not in their best moods.

"Sorry for the disturbance, we'll handle it from here. These are runaway prisoners of ours, you see, and we've been running after them for the last week now," Yakenn panted but smiled up to the guards and saluted them. Rays of sun began to appear through the shadows and shine on Fallgarde from the east.

"Whose prisoners are they?" The guard snapped, not entertained by the interruption. Ozwald saw the guards still standing at their posts while the archers were ready to fire.

Yakenn cleared his throat. "Why, house Haemel, Queen Petra to be exact." He approached both boys, his sword unsheathed while the others encircled them, disregarding the guards at the gate. "Let's avoid a scene and just come with us silently. This is not the place for you," Yakenn mumbled for only Ozwald and Ethan to hear. It was the first time that Ozwald heard a stutter in his voice. Ozwald gazed at their eyes, and instead of their aggressiveness, for the first time, he saw deep worry. Suddenly, it became clear to him what they wanted and why. "I can beat them. We can beat them," Ozwald whispered to himself.

Just as they took another step forward, Ozwald winked at Ethan privately before unsheathing his sword. Ethan did the same while Yakenn and the rest stopped their advance.

With conviction fueling his every move, Ozwald launched into an all-out attack, determined to take control of his own destiny. Ethan followed suit. The clashing of swords rang loudly through the air as an intense battle ensued. Though outnumbered, Ethan's expertise with a sword shone through as he deftly parried and blocked blows. But as Yakenn and the others gained the upper hand, Ethan began to push harder. With each strike, he forced his enemies to retreat, leaving Ozwald to face off against Yakenn alone. The two warriors were evenly matched, their steel blades clanging together as they traded blows. Despite sustaining wounds that drew blood from their torsos, neither combatant showed any signs of slowing down. Yakenn's raw power and brute strength were no match for Ozwald's speed and agility. The two circled each other, their eyes locked in a death stare as they waited for the perfect moment to strike. Then, Ozwald saw his opening and lunged forward, landing a devastating kick to Yakenn's chest. The wind was knocked out of Yakenn, and he crumpled to the ground. In a flash, Ozwald was on top of him, holding his sword to Yakenn's neck. Yakenn though began to laugh sinisterly while blood dripped from his mouth. Ozwald knew he had emerged victorious. He had proven to himself that he could overcome any oppressor.

"You see, Ozwald, we would do great things together. We can still rid this land of its evil," Yakenn hissed, spitting blood.

"You are its evil. You never were going to kill me. You can't. You just wanted me as your hostage until the end," Ozwald hissed, quickly glancing at Ethan, who stood with his sword at the ready. Ozwald's gaze returned to Yakenn's despair-filled eyes.

"He's beaten, brother," Ethan advised, his voice calm and full of wisdom.

"You've already lost. Go now," Ozwald sneered while Yakenn dragged himself to the others.

They waited for them to start moving before looking back to the guards at the gate. The guards were speechless at that point and unaware of how to react. Instead of the four guards though, only two remained.

"Will you send someone at least to ask for Lord Rorik's permission?" Ethan quickly instructed, unwilling to wait anymore.

As soon as Ozwald uttered his words, he sensed an impending danger approaching. He heard an unusual war cry and immediately turned around, brandishing his sword. In a flash, he caught Yakenn's gaze and heard a shrill noise. To his horror, he saw that his sword had pierced through Yakenn's stomach, causing him intense pain and leaving his eyes filled with shock.

"Why? You lost. You should have fled!" Ozwald snapped his voice, a mixture of anger and sadness.

"The end defines the means," Yakenn exhaled, his voice dying. Yakenn remained lodged for a short while before Ethan pushed him off Stonesaver, creating an eerie thud that all heard. Ozwald remained fixated on the motionless body at his feet before looking up at the remaining three.

"You lot, the head of the snake is gone. The next time I see you will be your last day," Ethan spat. The others did not waste time, taking off as fast as they could while carrying Rybae and leaving Yakenn behind.

"This isn't the...!" Rybae shrieked just before Byrene smacked him on his head to shut him up.

Ozwald immediately turned back to the gate, and at its head, he saw a familiar face. A face he was embarrassed to see.

"Lord Ozwald, finally. Welcome home," Johnson orated. His torso and hand were wrapped up. Suddenly a creaking sound emanated from ahead of them. Fallgarde's eastern gate finally welcomed them.

Forty-Six

With every step in Fallgarde, Ozwald could feel his heart racing in excitement within him. Even though he had never laid eyes on it before, the stories he had heard of its timeless and grandiose build had already left an indelible mark on his imagination. As he walked through the city streets, he could not help but feel a sense of awe at the sheer size and magnificence of what he witnessed. Every inch of Fallgarde spoke of a bygone era, a time when craftsmanship was revered, and every detail was given the utmost care and attention. The rigid stone that formed the city's buildings seemed to have been carved with a precision that could only have been achieved by the hands of the gods themselves. Every corner he turned revealed new wonders and secrets, each more enchanting than the last. The narrow and wide roads that crisscrossed the city's labyrinthine layout only added to its mystique, and the known and unknown tunnels that lay hidden beneath its surface only added to the sense of mystery that permeated the air. As he walked through the city, Ozwald could not help but feel as if he had been transported to another world, a world where long-lost histories and forgotten legends still held sway. Everything was built of rigid stone as if the city was an entire palace, a palace fit for the Ancients, as per what he had read. And yet, even amidst all this grandeur, there was a gentle beauty that could not be ignored. Long threads of roses and flowers hung from windows and bridges, their fragrant scents mingling with the cool, crisp air to create a sense of peace and tranquility that soothed the mind and soul. Wherever he gazed, Ozwald was met with a mixture of deep and long-lasting colors emanating comfort, knowledge, and wisdom.

However, as Ozwald wandered through Fallgarde's majestic streets, his heart sank as he found chaos and despair. Everywhere he looked, people were on high alert. Their faces were etched with worry, hysteria, and fear as if they were constantly on the brink of some unspeakable danger. Everywhere he looked, people were hurrying to and fro, gathering whatever they could to survive. The air was thick with the stench of desperation as families fought over the minimal supplies they could find. It was a heart-wrenching sight to behold. The once-vibrant city was now a mere shadow of its former self. The only thing keeping it from utter chaos was the strict order enforced by the guards, who stood watch over the city like stern, unyielding sentinels. As Ozwald walked through its streets, his eyes fell on a group of young boys, barely old enough to wield a sword, being fitted with helmets and weapons. He felt a pang of sadness in his chest at the thought of such young lives being thrust into a war machine they never asked for.

"You can smell war and death in the air," Ethan whispered to Ozwald, both following Johnson through the streets of Fallgarde. "They've already lost with this attitude," Ethan added. They had attempted to speak with Johnson, but he waved them off at every attempt.

"Lord Rorik, you only talk with him," he continued to repeat. "He's waiting for you in the war room."

Johnson had met them at the eastern gate of Fallgarde. Anxiousness washed across his face as if he had been waiting for them all along. He opened the gate and immediately instructed that they follow. Johnson did not care to stop and hear how they had reached nor to understand the state of their health. Lord Rorik was his sole priority.

Johnson already had horses ready for them and led the way for them to follow.

"We ride west to Lord Rorik's keep," he declared without waiting for any response. He tried to avoid congested roads. However, it proved difficult as the entire city was abuzz and preparing for combat. After a twenty-minute ride, Lord Rorik's keep finally became visible. Ozwald gazed in awe at the seemingly handcrafted keep nestled amidst a grove of eight wide and tall Aelgan trees. Their leafy evergreen canopy provided a natural shade and a sense of tranquility that seemed to envelop the entire structure. As he surveyed the surroundings, the keep felt somehow detached from the mundane reality yet intricately intertwined with everything that made Azra vibrant and alive. The allure of the keep was irresistible, alluring him to explore its secrets and immerse himself in its mystical charm.

As they approached the keep, the gates swung open

with smooth precision, beckoning them inside. As they crossed the threshold, Ozwald was immediately struck by the vibrant scene before him. The front courtyard was a mesmerizing oasis of colorful flowers, lush green grass, and gurgling fountains that seemed to mimic the soothing melody of a cascading waterfall. The keep itself was a formidable sight, with towering structures at each of its four corners, all built of large and intertwined cutout stones within its protective walls. Ozwald could see holes in the rock as if it stood the test of time. He was puzzled by the sheer magnitude of the place, wondering how such a colossal fortress could be concealed within the walls. All the houses of the Haefe could fit at least two times over, he knew, within the walls of the keep. Each part of the keep, though, the more he gazed upon it, had a different shade of grey, as if the keep had been constructed over the years and in different phases. The bustling activity of guards and other workers added to the sense of urgency and heightened his awareness of the gravity of the situation. He noticed a row of archers standing atop the inner walls, their bows at the ready, as if ready to fight off the people of the city. Despite the overwhelming spectacle, Ozwald struggled to fully appreciate the beauty and grandeur of the keep, as he felt a part of the commotion and accountable for what would transpire.

Johnson immediately led them to a stairwell through a door in the courtyard wall. A guard stood watch and opened it immediately, handing Johnson a torch which he lit from a nearby fire.

"Follow me," he spoke, his voice grimmer than before as if the proximity to the keep raised the alarm.

At the bottom of the dark stairwell, Johnson pushed open a thick door revealing a calm and wide corridor. The air was still, and the silence deafening as no echo could be heard. Lit torches had been hung across the walls ahead of him, and the ground was made of warn out and hole-ridden blocks of stones.

"Our father used to be Lord here…" Ozwald whispered to Ethan, still not used to the words.

"A man of secrets," Ethan continued, awestruck by the size of the entire keep.

Suddenly Johnson stopped at the door decorated with detailed engravings of deer, lions, foxes, mules, snakes, and phoenixes. They had been carved as if depicting an undecipherable story that only the artist understood. It emanated importance, making Ozwald uneasy about what lay behind it. Ozwald gazed at Ethan, his face all-knowing just as Johnson knocked and opened the door. They found Lord Rorik sitting alone at the end of a long and wide table, carefully decorated with artistic etchings. The floor had been covered by a mat made of colored wool and silk, unlike Ozwald had seen before. The walls were plain, with one large painting hung on each side depicting epic battles, unknown to Ozwald, as if from an age long ago.

Ozwald immediately made eye contact with Rorik as he puffed a long pipe with deep inhales. A blanket of smoke hung heavy in the air as Rorik added to it insistently. His face lit up though at the sight of Ozwald as he got up and embraced him tightly, almost suffocating him, before he cast a curious and hesitant stare at Ethan.

Suddenly, Johnson closed the door behind them as Rorik went back to his seat, and Johnson sat behind him.

He waved his hand for both boys to sit nearby. Ethan cast a hesitant gaze at Ozwald.

"We don't have time for this," Ethan whispered, his voice only audible to Ozwald.

"I'm sure whatever your friend said can wait. We have much to talk about," Rorik orated, taking a deep breath while his vision raced between them.

"You had me on edge. I thought you never found your way to the grand temple in Nav," Rorik sighed as both boys finally sat.

"Why did you send me there? You already knew what was there," Ozwald snapped.

"Who's this. This is a matter for the family, not for guests," he said, frustration clear in his voice. Ozwald glanced at Ethan and then back, unclear of the question.

"This is my twin brother, Uncle. You must have known that there were two of us," he uttered. Rorik gasped, his eyes unblinking. Ozwald held in front of him the dagger and Rupert's letter before he could say a word. Rorik picked up the dagger, studying it minutely as if he were whispering to it secretly.

"That's from Nav. Didn't you send me there to get it," Ozwald spoke, both him and Ethan standing up and moving to the door.

"Lord Rorik, uncle, we are wasting time here. We need to get to the Promise Well. We have an idea of how to stop this… Blight," Ethan sneered, fed up with the waiting, holding onto Ozwald's shoulder. Rorik's gaze immediately fixated on Ethan at the mention of the blight.

Not following their requests, he raised his hands for all to remain silent while he processed what he heard, rubbing his eyes. Johnson stood closely by unflinching, waiting for instructions.

"You found the hidden prophecy... It's true. That means then that King Erdun found out about you two before the rest," Rorik said to himself, audible for the rest to hear. "What is your name?" Rorik quickly asked Ethan, his gaze still fixated on him.

"Ethan. Prince Ethan of house Raynel... house Lygem now, I believe," Ethan said, his impatience growing as Rorik let his words sink in.

Suddenly, he rushed to the door of the room.

"Let's go, Johnson, hold the men. No one is fighting. Prepare emissaries, Adrovia's armies, and the army of that traitor, Berdol, need to know before they attack. I'll meet you in my study upstairs shortly. And block all access down here," Rorik said hurriedly although visibly in complete control, grabbing Ethan's and Ozwald's arms to follow him out of the room. Rorik pushed the door open with such speed and force that Ozwald felt it would fly off its hinges, screaming with urgency.

Ozwald heard Johnson rush out behind them and back up the stairwell while Rorik took them to another large door.

"The prophecy. We have the same in Horos," Ethan shrieked, pointing to a wide tablet on top of the door just as he began to read it out loud.

Two halves to one whole, two brothers torn asunder. A left hand and a right hand, though by one body separate, doth ebb and flow as they wander. Unto a great prince they shall emerge, though long after he departs should they meet, ones blood will soak the others cloak at the toes of destiny's feet.

A chill ran down Ozwald's spine. Rorik led them straight through the door.

"Fallgarde's famous grand temple," Rorik mumbled while Ozwald and Ethan gazed around the already lit hall. It was a similar build to the one in Nav. However, this one was larger in every way, Ozwald could see.

"This is where the ceremony happens after the council. I thought it was just for that. Turns out I was mistaken," Rorik continued, pointing to the end of the temple at the Promise Well. "There," he added. Ethan gazed at Ozwald as both boys ran to it while Rorik followed closely behind them, sealing off the temple doors first.

The air in the temple was still as if anxiously observing the events to come as well. Ozwald's pain and fatigue began to hit him as if he were entering his house back in the Haefe after a long day on the farm. However, he was determined, and the Promise Well occupied his entire focus. As they reached it, they saw the water glowing with different colors, just as it had in Nav. This well, however, was much larger, and the water in it flowed continuously. The water was cold to his touch as Ozwald looked at Ethan uneasily.

"It has been glowing for more than two weeks," Rorik commented from behind while both boys remained fixated on the colorful and glowing water in front of them.

"This better work," Ozwald muttered, holding out his hand and cutting a small slit in his palm. Ethan did the same as blood trickled, from both of their hands, into the water while both boys waited for something to happen, just as in Nav and in the Ancient Heights. Rorik stood by them, this time a spectator to all that transpired.

"I had a feeling," Ethan finally exhaled after no one

spoke for at least two minutes. Ozwald shot a quizzical glance while Ethan did not look up. "We are the prophecy's promise," he said, his voice eerily cold and all-knowing.

"You both are the continuation of the sacred bloodline," Rorik murmured, his face filled with bewilderment. "Father and Rupert hid from me all along," he spoke to himself but audible by all.

Suddenly, a sinister laugh emanated from behind the wall at the back of the altar they stood on. The sound rang on the walls and all the metal pots and trays that lay around. A clicking sound followed as if one were calling for a horse. Ozwald knew these sounds too well, nodding at Ethan. Both boys immediately took a few steps back, their swords ready, while Rorik gazed upon them, unsure how to react.

Kraegan stepped out into the open, this time on his own and carrying a sword in his hand. His eyes glistened, and his lips were wet, visibly enjoying the sight before him.

"The leader of the great Hand of the Ancients, the last hope for Eurst and Azra, was lied to. All along," Kraegan hissed, maliciously gazing at the group in front of him. Rorik quickly unsheathed his sword as well, after catching sight of the tall and bulky man. Kraegan, though, was not his usual self. His face looked tired and beaten, and his white shirt was ripped and covered in dirt all over.

"I dealt with you in Aurom. You and that henchman of yours. I'm sure he'll be extra useful without his head," Rorik growled. "How did you get in?" He continued. Kraegan spat on the floor, disgusted and visibly bothered by his presence, not able to break eye contact.

"The girl. Of course," Rorik uttered after a few moments, Kraegan's smirk returning to his face.

"Not in control of all the strings anymore. Your balance is in ruin. Your pretty nephew, I mean nephews, were never going to create any type of peace," he sneered. Ozwald could not understand the conversation, but gazing at Ethan, he saw him fuming. Ozwald held the hilt of his sword tighter as the tension in the room hung heavily in the air.

"And you, Ozwald, I was under the impression that we had the same goals. That we thought the same. But you disappoint me. You've disappointed me for a while. Whatever you think you're doing won't work. It's too late. The blight is here, it will clean everything, and there will be nothing left but freedom. The Ancients lied to us like they always do. Soon, we will no longer live by their curse, nor will we ever need them," Kraegan hissed, tightening his grip on his sword.

"No one will survive the blight, you fool," Rorik snapped.

"There's much you don't know and much you won't ever be able to comprehend. Enough talk," Kraegan spat. "You two need to come with me. If you don't, Adrovia's forces will see that Fallgarde is nothing but dust by tomorrow," he continued.

Suddenly, Rorik attacked and swung his sword at Kraegan, who had anticipated his move, taking a step back and blocking the incoming blow. They fought near both boys, who stood on high alert, eagerly waiting for the right time to intervene while encircling both men.

"No! Leave him to me. Get back to the well," Rorik shrieked, defending blows from Kraegan, who was taller and bulkier than him. Rorik pushed Ethan away, who fell to the ground, while Ozwald took a few steps back and immediately helped him up. Kraegan was clearly winning the duel, able to overpower Rorik and block each one of his swings. Eventually, though, Kraegan managed to punch Rorik in the chest, flying and crashing into the well while spraying water all over the altar before falling to the ground. With Rorik immobilized and gasping for air, Kraegan turned to both boys, blood dripping from his arm and nose.

"You won't leave here alive," Ozwald hissed, attacking Kraegan in a frenzy, his eyes fuming and his war cry loud for all to hear. However, the battle did not last long until Kraegan managed to punch him in the face with the hilt of his sword. Ozwald fell to the ground holding his nose and going unconscious, Stonesaver flying out of his hand and away from him. Kraegan smirked at his conquest, picking up Ozwald's leg and dragging him towards the back of the alter, disregarding Ethan.

"Ethan. You understand what's happening and what's at risk. I can see it in your eyes. Aren't you coming? You know I'm right, and you've seen it time after time. No one deserves your concern, or you for that matter," Kraegan exhaled, speaking over his shoulder. Ethan held on to the hilt of his sword tighter, his face fuming while wrestling his conflicting thoughts. His vision raced between Rorik and Ozwald, both on the ground, immobilized.

"Nothing will ever get better. Men will always be doomed to their greed, cruelty, and lust for power at any cost," Ethan snapped, his eyes now unblinking on Kraegan while loosening his grip on his sword.

"So, we're in agreement," Kraegan smirked, visibly enjoying listening to Ethan's confession. Ethan nodded, sheathing his sword and making his way to Kraegan, who stopped in his place and let go of Ozwald, who looked up to his brother in bewilderment.

"What are you doing? He's a liar," Ozwald shrieked, using all the energy in his lungs. Ethan did not listen and walked up to a content Kraegan. He looked up to him while a calmness set over him at that moment as he recollected events leading up to Fallgarde. Ethan took a deep breath, his gaze piercing Kraegan's while the entire surroundings went calm and silent.

"But there's always hope to fight for," Ethan suddenly cried out at the top of his lungs, dashing to his brother and lifting him up.

Ozwald's senses immediately went on high alert as Ethan picked him up. It was his cue. He abruptly stood between Kraegan and his brother and quickly led both away from Kraegan's reach while grabbing for his dagger on his waist. His nose was gushing blood but no longer bothered him as he stood in an attacking position, his dagger tight in his hand.

"I've had enough of you," Ozwald hissed, attacking with his dagger and catching Kraegan off guard. He would not let others fight for him anymore. He would protect them and face the fire on his own. Kraegan was larger, more capable, and better trained than Ozwald. However, despite his efforts, Ozwald deftly blocked every move, anticipating his actions and putting to use his training with Yakenn. Kraegan gritted his teeth as he battled Ozwald, his muscles straining with each attempted strike as his tiredness began to kick in. Kraegan ferociously searched for an opening but hesitated for a short moment as Ozwald seized the opportunity, plunging his dagger deep into Kraegan's arm and leg. Kraegan cried out in pain but refused to give up. With a fierce determination, he swung his own weapon and sent Ozwald's dagger clattering to the ground. Then, in a blur of motion, Kraegan struck Ozwald with a mighty blow that left him crumpled on the floor next to Stonesaver. Ozwald, still completely conscious, firmly reached for his sword, which he picked up and plunged deep into Kraegan's stomach. Ozwald could feel the resistance of flesh and bone as he pressed with all his might, watching Kraegan's eyes bulge and his tongue loll out in agony.

Kraegan fell to the floor as he slid off Ozwald's sword, who stood panting and trying to catch his breath. Euphoria overwhelmed him for a moment before Rorik's squirms behind him brought him back to reality. The mission was not done yet, he knew as he looked for Ethan, who already stood over the well, arched forward and looking into its glowing and colorful water.

"No!" Rorik shrieked out, his face full of agony as he lay on the floor looking up at Ethan. Ozwald sensed danger as he dashed to the well and saw that his brother was shivering over it. Ethan had stabbed himself in the stomach, as his blood dripped into the well. Nothing, though, changed. The Promise Well remained as it had before. Ozwald's face was washed with fear. This was not in their plan, and it took him a moment to decipher what he saw.

"You fool," Ozwald snapped the first words that came to his mouth. Ethan struggled to remain standing as Ozwald caught him before he fell to the floor.

"No, keep me standing. This is how it'll work," Ethan growled, his voice full of anger and agony at the same time.

"What did you do?" Ozwald badgered him. "I can heal

this. We just need to find help. I'm sure there is everything that we need here," Ozwald stuttered.

"Listen to me," Ethan began as Ozwald kept rambling on. "Listen to me," he shouted again. This time though, his voice rang throughout the temple walls as Ozwald stopped his mumbling and looked into Ethan's eyes.

"I wish we grew up together. I wish we could talk endlessly. So much to share and so much to learn. But I knew it from the moment that I read the hidden prophecy. Rupert knew it as well. He could never bear to choose between us. I understand now," Ethan began as Ozwald's tears began to fall. Ozwald held onto him tightly over the well, his thoughts clouded as the prophecy made sense to him as well.

"I'm sure there's another way. This can't end now. Not like this. I've barely got to know you," Ozwald said as the Promise Well began to flash white light, changing just as Ethan's breath began to slow down. Ozwald glanced to Rorik, looking for answers but found him standing in the background watching over the boys, his shoulders slumped forward and head down.

"See, I was right. It's working," Ethan smiled as he began to cough heavily. "I don't believe that man has hope, but I believe there is still hope to fight for," he added, his face lightening up as if he had no more worries on his mind. Shortly after, Ethan slipped while Ozwald held onto him tightly, making eye contact with his brother's last smiling face as he began to take his last breath.

Forty-Seven

Ozwald stood next to Rorik, gazing at the southern and northern armies camped outside their walls. They observed emissaries riding out in each direction bearing a white flag and a flag with a Phoenix emblem. The wind blew strong in the late afternoon as no sun was visible in the grey cloud-filled sky. Ozwald took a deep breath of fresh air, a certain weight lifted off his chest, only to be replaced by extreme sadness he had never known existed. The red blight had ended, and he knew it. Although it would take time to recover, the sadness of the loss of his family and now his real brother weighed in on him. Rorik glanced at him and then back to the emissaries.

"I can't begin to imagine what you're going through," Rorik stuttered, unclear how to react to Ozwald. "I barely know you. I can tell you, though, that no one will be forgotten for their sacrifice. To respect that sacrifice, we need to see to it that the balance of peace remains. The balance that the Ancients entrusted us with that you and I are responsible for now," Rorik added, still gazing at the horizon. Ozwald listened carefully, his face cold and unemotional.

"Trade one destiny for another. Who said I wanted that," Ozwald mumbled.

Rorik did not flinch as if he had anticipated his response.

"A destiny is a blessing. It gives direction. At the same time, it's a curse that we bear. If we didn't, then there's no knowing where we would be," Rorik exhaled. "Without this curse that you and I have, then those armies would have come years before. There is peace to maintain, and these men can't do it on their own. They need control. They need influence, no matter its form. So, if you don't want it, then there will be nothing for you to return to. It would have been better if you had let the blight do its damage," Rorik said, his voice strict and not willing to negotiate.

"So, I will never be free," Ozwald said, his voice filled with emotion. Rorik rubbed his eyes before he spoke.

"Freedom. Yes, freedom. Everyone deserves it, but it has not always boded well," Rorik exhaled. "In time, you'll understand," he added.

Suddenly Johnson appeared from the stairwell on the other end of the tower. "My Lord, your presence is required below," Johnson declared. Rorik did not question but immediately left Ozwald on his own at the top of the tower and descended with Johnson. Ozwald did not look back nor bid him farewell, remaining at the top of the tower, caught in his thoughts.

After a while, Ozwald saw the emissaries begin to return from the advancing armies. It was not clear what message they would come back with. The sky was darker as the sun began to disappear in the horizon. The top of the tower felt safe to Ozwald at this moment, soothing to his wombs and mind. He planted his hands on the edge of the wall taking in as much of the sight as he could while his thoughts raced.

Just as he looked up to the sky, a young lady appeared from the stairwell. She walked to Ozwald and stood next to him, gazing at the camped army to the south. Ozwald had never seen her and did not know her purpose.

"I know what you did. I saw it. That Rorik has been hiding so much for all this time. Peace is no longer an option. My grandfather will see to it," she suddenly hissed on her own, gazing at Ozwald through her peering eyes.

"Who are you?" He questioned.

"The future," she hissed as she walked away, not waiting for Ozwald to respond. Ozwald thought about following her but had enough for the moment, returning his gaze back to the horizon.

"For a later time," he whispered to himself.

The End